CIRCLE OF INNOCENTS

It Must Remain Unbroken...

STEPHEN D. CURTIS

Copyright © STEPHEN D. CURTIS 2023
This book is sold subject to the condition that it shall not, by way of trade or otherwise, be lent, resold, hired out, or otherwise circulated without the publisher's prior consent in any form of binding or cover other than that in which it is published and without a similar condition including this condition being imposed on the subsequent publisher.
The moral right of STEPHEN D. CURTIS has been asserted.

This is a work of fiction. Names, characters, businesses, organisations, places, events and incidents either are the product of the author's imagination or are used fictitiously. Any resemblance to actual persons, living or dead, events, or locales is entirely coincidental.

In loving memory of Harley.

CONTENTS

ACKNOWLEDGEMENTS i
CHAPTER 1 1
CHAPTER 2 9
CHAPTER 3 18
CHAPTER 4 27
CHAPTER 5 35
CHAPTER 6 42
CHAPTER 7 50
CHAPTER 8 60
CHAPTER 9 68
CHAPTER 10 77
CHAPTER 11 84
CHAPTER 12 93
CHAPTER 13 102
CHAPTER 14 112
CHAPTER 15 118
CHAPTER 16 127
CHAPTER 17 134
CHAPTER 18 143
CHAPTER 19 150
CHAPTER 20 163
CHAPTER 21 174
CHAPTER 22 184
CHAPTER 23 190
CHAPTER 24 199
CHAPTER 25 206
CHAPTER 26 212
CHAPTER 27 220
CHAPTER 28 229
CHAPTER 29 236
CHAPTER 30 246
CHAPTER 31 258
CHAPTER 32 265
CHAPTER 33 276

CHAPTER 34 285
CHAPTER 35 291
CHAPTER 36 301
ABOUT THE AUTHOR 307

ACKNOWLEDGEMENTS

Very special thanks to Eva, Ashley and Emily, and all those who believed I could do this when I didn't believe it myself!

Additional thanks to Wendy Jennings of Wendy Jennings Creative for her invaluable advice, and Andrea, Belle, Sue and the rest of the amazing team at Jubilee Social Container Café, Letchworth, for all the coffee and lunches that kept me going when I was in need of inspiration!

And finally, my heartfelt thanks to my late friend, Annie Counsel. How I wish you were still here to see what your encouragement inspired in me.

CHAPTER 1

Monique was speaking in French again, little utterances of pleasure escaping from her lips and venturing through the slowly widening gap in the doorway. In his mind's eye, Wayne Terry was once again pushing that door open, remembering the French girl's writhing ecstasy all too clearly. Thirteen years had passed since he had caught them together, and yet he was still trapped in that moment – a fifteen-year-old-boy looking on helplessly, watching Monique, the only girl he had ever loved, being pleasured by his own mother.

Thinking back to his mid-teens often caused Wayne to punish himself for not seeing the truth prior to that night, and yet his lack of sight could only have been down to the naivety of his years. Perhaps his father leaving inexplicably should have been a signal, especially when Monique moved in only a few short weeks later. However, Wayne's mother's claims that the twenty-six-year-old drama student was good company and would help them cope better with the family breakdown had been entirely plausible, so could Wayne, at such a tender age, ever have imagined or suspected that she was going to be anything other than just 'a lodger'?

Over time, Monique lived up to Wayne's mother's expectations, becoming a huge comfort to Wayne when he became the target of bullying at school, yet the irony, tragic as it was, was that he was only drawing comfort from the root cause of his suffering. The schoolyard seemed to know the reality of Wayne's homelife, when those who claimed to love him the most, including the father he adored, only kept it from him.

Wayne could not have known that the solace he was finding with Monique would eventually lead to the loss of his innocence and worse. His and Monique's 'Little Secret' was all Wayne had to treasure in his abusive world, and in this latest torturous recollection of his eventual heartbreak, the *real* truth, the one that had been so callously hidden from him, was about to cruelly reveal itself once more. Through Wayne's mental portal of the slowly opening bedroom door, Monique was turning her head, her beautiful green eyes were about to see him standing in the doorway, and she was going to laugh at him.

Wayne could feel the anger and revulsion rising inside him, but this time the laughter never came. Instead, confused and muzzy-headed, he came to his senses on a park bench in a green, open space near a large pond. A rather heavy-set man acknowledged him with a brief nod as he jogged past, but Wayne didn't respond. The fingers of his right hand were wrapped tightly around a rolled-up magazine that he couldn't remember buying, and his body was barely protected against the chill of the early morning by a polo shirt and jogging shorts in which he had no recollection of dressing.

Having liberated the magazine from his grasp, Wayne ruffled his unkempt brown hair and pressed his fingertips against his temples. As his mind began to clear, he realised that he was on Hampstead Heath and not that far from home, but the comfort drawn from those familiar surroundings was tempered by the knowledge that this latest episode was just one of a number he'd been experiencing lately. None of the others, however, had been anywhere near as intense; the occasional bouts of depression Wayne suffered from he could easily cope with, but the personality disorders he'd once endured were altogether different.

Please God, it wasn't a return to that!

Wayne glanced down at the magazine he'd discovered in his possession, intent on trying to relax. The glossy publication was face down, but when he turned it over, he was dismayed to find that it was pornographic and certainly not a subject matter he would consciously have selected. Feverishly, he began to thumb through the pages, turning them faster and faster, tearing some of them as his anxiety and desperation grew. Page after page of filth and degradation presented themselves to him. But where had he bought this? And *when*? Despairingly, Wayne slammed the magazine back down on the bench.

With no memory of anything he'd done or anywhere he'd been, it felt like somebody else had got out of bed that morning instead of *him*. Wayne leaned forwards and gazed at the surface of the pond, seeing the flickering chaos of the wavelets before him as a fair reflection of his life. He'd been certain his mental issues were a thing of the past, but maybe he'd just been in denial. Recent occurrences, the duration of that morning's episode, and the magazine were irrefutable evidence that he was really slipping. Maybe the shock of receiving a letter from his mother, and the realisation that she'd finally managed to track him down after so many years could well have set him back.

She was the last person Wayne wanted to have anything to do with. It was all *her* fault he was like this, her and that manipulative girlfriend of hers. If he had the courage, he would go and see the Wet Hole that dared to call itself his 'mother' and let her into his and Monique's 'Little Secret' just to see the devastation it would cause. Yet all he really wanted was to have nothing to do with either of them, for the demons to leave him alone, or better, to forget that he had ever existed.

It seemed that despite all Wayne's best efforts to cover his tracks, including living and working under an alias, his hiding place had been discovered, but he was determined to never again cower in the shadow of their hellish wings. Wayne had lived in fear of them finding him for too long, and he would go where they could never follow. The waters of the pond had become as dark as the depths of his sudden and abject despair, yet in that darkness, there shone an unexpected beacon of hope, of salvation. Wayne began to wonder how deep the water might be, and if it could be deep enough and cold enough to free him from his torture should he offer himself to the mercy of its curiously inviting blackness. The weight of his personal hell would surely be enough to send him straight to the bottom.

*

Joanne Middleton was finding her morning run on Hampstead Heath with her daughter, Samantha, and their dog, Harley, a bit of a struggle.

'Can't we slow down a bit?' she asked.

'No chance, Mum,' Samantha replied. 'We're in a hurry! Push yourself!'

'But I've got a bloody stitch, Sammy!'

'Well, it serves you right for sneaking breakfast before we came out. You've been doing this long enough and you should have known better.'

Joanne put her hands on her hips and slowed to walking pace.

'Well, it wasn't my fault that the milk had gone off and that I had to go out and get a fresh carton,' she said. 'And besides, you little cow, I always eat breakfast, it's just that I had to eat it later than usual. Now stop being so full of your damned self!'

Joanne tried a few deep breaths to ease her discomfort, but the little daggers in her side merely twisted themselves with even more venom. A nearby bench suddenly became very inviting, and she flopped down onto it.

'Wimp,' Samantha muttered.

'Oh, *do* shut up ...'

Totally unmoved by her mother's hostility, Samantha unclipped Harley's lead. 'Okay then, Boudicca,' she goaded. 'You rest those old bones of yours. Me and Harley will just have to amuse ourselves for a while. Come on then, boy!'

Boudicca thought Joanne, removing her hair band to adjust her unruly locks. *I'll give her bloody Boudicca.*

Regardless of Joanne's objections, Samantha's nickname for her mother was rather apt. Not only was Joanne a redhead, who, just like the notorious queen of the Iceni stood the best part of six feet tall, she also had ambition and an occasional fierceness. An oval face and smooth jawline were framed by a mane of thick, auburn hair, and a naturally alluring expression made her a photographer's dream. But the majority of those who encountered Joanne were drawn by her strikingly beautiful, clear blue eyes.

With the exception of being a brunette and standing a fraction shorter than her mother, Samantha was otherwise her mother's clone, but the similarities didn't stop there. Although only nineteen, she was already a vibrant, confident young woman who oozed spirit and determination, a doughty blend of get-up-and-go underpinned by a razor-sharp wit. Joanne was immensely proud at not having raised a shrinking violet, but Samantha had grown up so quickly and become so independent, it was surely only a matter of time before she would be looking to make a life of her own.

Joanne smiled as she watched Samantha charging around with Harley, a beautiful black, long-coated German Shepherd, but slowly her smile began to fade. For the past five years, it had been just the two of them, and those years had simply flown by. What would she do when Samantha finally flew the nest? Life for Joanne revolved around being a driving force for her business *and* being a mother, and the thought of one day playing second fiddle to Samantha's independence and having to come home to an empty house was extremely unsettling.

Samantha had a tendency to be rather outspoken when it came to her mother's work load because although Joanne was effectively married to her company, it was also true that she hadn't always been quite so driven. Heartbreak had created the monster she'd allowed herself to become, for if *The Bastard* (Joanne's pet name for her ex-husband, James) had kept his tool in his trousers and hadn't thrust it so firmly into his secretary, she might never have become such a hard-nosed businesswoman.

Around the time of the affair, Joanne had been planning to fulfil a dream to own her own fashion and design label, but the consequential break-up of her marriage and *The Bastard's* insistence that she could never be successful on her own, made her even more determined to make that dream a reality. At first it had been solely to prove *The Bastard* wrong because a far as *The Bastard* had been concerned, Joanne was only ever going to be 'an ex-fashion model.' Using the cruel jibes as a motivational springboard, Joanne, with grit and purpose, garnered a great team, and it wasn't long before the business was providing security for her and her daughter. The problem was that it had become almost impossible for Joanne to see beyond anything else.

'HARLEY, NO!'

Samantha's sudden and sharp tone abruptly shook Joanne from her thoughts.

'HARLEY! Come back here, NOW!'

But Harley wasn't listening. He was far more interested in a seemingly unsuspecting grey squirrel, which promptly vaulted straight up the nearest tree at the sight of his full-tilt approach. Unable to stop on the twigs and loose soil under his paws, Harley careered unceremoniously into the trunk in a cloud of dust. It was all too much for Joanne and Samantha, who both exploded into giggling fits.

'Oh my God!' said Samantha. 'Did you see that? He looked so stupid!'

*

The sound of laughter swept across the pond to a brooding Wayne Terry. Inside his head, Monique was laughing again, too.

'He looked so stupid …'

Wayne stared, hate-filled, in the direction of the commotion.

*

Head down in canine embarrassment, Harley padded back to his owners, and Samantha noticed that there was some blood on his snout.

'Oh Harley! Look at your nose!' she said, bending over to take a closer look. 'Ah, no probs, Baby Boy, it's only a little scratch.' She kissed Harley's head and then reattached his lead before turning her attention back to her mother.

'Come on, Boudicca, we need to get you back home. You've got stuff to do today, remember?'

Joanne groaned inwardly. It was a beautiful morning: birdsong filled the air, the sun's rays sparkled upon the surface of the pond in front of her, and on a deserted bench just across the water, the pages of a discarded magazine were flapping lazily in the breeze. It was going to take a supreme effort for Joanne to tear herself away from such a tranquil scene, but as Samantha had reminded, there was other business to attend to.

*

'He looked so stupid …'

Wayne peered out at the two women from the security of a small group of trees, having stealthily moved away from the edge of the pond. He was going to have to show these two bitches his need. They wouldn't think he was so fucking stupid then, would they?

*

At a more sedate pace than the day had begun, Joanne and Samantha made their way home via a familiar pathway that led to the boundary of the Heath. Most of it was in open space, but a narrow section wound its way through some fairly dense woodland. An odd silence had descended upon matters as they strolled through the trees, but that was due to Joanne being totally wrapped up in her thoughts about her new venture into sports fashion and swimwear. She was so preoccupied about that morning's promotional photo shoot that she walked right into Harley, stumbling as he stopped abruptly in front of her. A muttered expletive was cut short when she realised he was growling and staring straight ahead.

*

A scowl was slowly making its way across Wayne Terry's face as he waited in the scrub. *Why had they stopped?* He had something to show them. This wasn't how it was supposed to be. *He* was the one in control here. Having stalked the two women all the way from the pond, he didn't want to have to wait any longer than he had to. They'd been in his head and seen his past. That's why they'd been laughing back there, wasn't it? They'd seen him sitting on that bench and they knew everything. That's why they'd come out in all that tight jogging shit; it was obviously just to prance about and toy with him.

Fucking little slappers!

If it hadn't had been him, no doubt they'd have been parading around in front of somebody else. Well, he had to show them who he was, who they'd messed with, and that they shouldn't be messing around with his need.

But *why* had they *stopped?* They were so close!

Wayne couldn't tell if they were mother and daughter, or sisters, but he'd suddenly become completely taken with the younger-looking one, and now it was as if nothing, and nobody else, existed. Despite all her bitch-faults, he considered she was worthy of him. Her body was toned and athletic, her dark brown hair caressed her shoulders, and her pert, beautifully formed breasts were crying out for attention from inside her fitted tank-top. She would be pleasured by him first.

Wayne slipped off his polo shirt, put his hand inside his shorts, and began to masturbate. The chill of the air on his exposed flesh served to heighten his arousal, and imagining himself entering the warm, lubricated softness of the young woman's innermost sanctum hardened him further. He was going to show her his need and she would undoubtedly succumb. Yeah, that's what he was going to do … show her his need and then take her with every last inch of its throbbing magnificence. Knowing that the supreme hunter was almost ready to strike, Wayne edged himself forwards. He was so hard it was painful, his need so strong, it felt like he was about to explode.

*

The low rumble in Harley's throat had given way to a full-blown snarl.

'What the bloody hell is up with this dog?' asked Joanne, trying unsuccessfully to push him forwards.

Samantha gave Harley's lead a slight tug but his gaze remained set dead ahead. 'God knows,' she replied. 'He won't budge. He seems …'

Joanne shrieked as a topless man suddenly leapt out from among the bushes almost right in front of them, a pair of dark blue shorts pulled down to his knees. He was lean and slightly built, his almost feminine facial features contorted with anger beneath a mop of messy brown hair. He was holding his erect penis, Samantha the sole focus of his alarmingly empty blue eyes.

'Look what I've got for you, you bitch!' he crowed. 'I bet you'd love to have a piece of this fucker!' He took a step towards her, and Samantha found herself being dragged forwards by Harley as he reared up on his hind legs, straining upon his lead. Joanne could see every tooth in Harley's slavering mouth as his savage barking reverberated among the trees. Instinctively, she grabbed his collar, and, despite her panic, looked directly at their attacker.

'GET AWAY FROM US, YOU DISGUSTING BASTARD!' she shouted. 'GET AWAY FROM US BEFORE I SET THE BLOODY DOG ON YOU!'

God above! What was all that noise? Wayne came to, polo shirt in one hand, penis in the other, confronted by two women and eye-to-eye with a huge and enraged hairy black dog. Horrified and disoriented, Wayne instantly recoiled.

'Oh Christ...!' he gasped, struggling in vain to pull up his shorts. 'I'm so ... so sorry ... I don't ... I don't know ... I'm not like this ... I'M NOT LIKE THIS!'

All that came out was nonsensical drivel. Wayne gave up trying to explain himself, and fled as best he could with his shorts still halfway down his thighs.

The whole incident had lasted only a few seconds, yet once their assailant had bolted and Harley's barking had subsided, the silence that followed seemed interminable. Joanne felt sure Samantha would have been very upset by the experience, only to find her daughter laughing uncontrollably instead.

'It was his bum!' Samantha said. 'His little white bum, flying through the trees and ... and he was still trying to pull his shorts up when he legged it! Oh my God, *what* a prat!'

Samantha started giggling again.

Was it shock? Surely, she didn't really think it was funny, did she? Joanne was as equally bemused by her daughter's attitude as she was disgusted by the flasher. But this was no time for discussion. All Joanne wanted to do was to get off the Heath.

*

Wayne carried on running until his legs felt like they were going to give way beneath him. Sweating, breathless and terrified, he did his best to hide himself, peering fearfully through the flimsy branches of a clump of bushes. He felt sure that the two women must have released the dog, and that at any moment the huge animal would come crashing through the undergrowth and start tearing into him.

But as the seconds and then minutes ticked by, Wayne's fear of being run down began to subside. His mind was a complete blank as he put his top back on, but that was probably a blessing in disguise considering what he'd found himself doing when he'd come to. The shame, the fear, the desperation, knowing that he really wasn't in control of himself any longer suddenly became too much. A failed, pathetic shadow of the man he wanted to be, Wayne curled himself up in a ball, and wept.

CHAPTER 2

Joanne and Samantha Middleton only lived a few minutes' walk from Hampstead Heath, and went running there regularly. Harley didn't normally go with them when they ran, but because they'd gone out later than usual and there was a risk that he might miss out on his morning walk, they'd decided to take him along. It was something that Joanne considered a stroke of luck, bearing in mind what had happened to them, although Samantha had thought it something of an overreaction on her mother's part when she spoke about reporting the incident to the police the moment they got back.

But it wasn't until Samantha heard her mother speaking on the phone that she realised how shaken she'd been, and to make matters worse, any attempt at conversation had ceased once Joanne had hung up.

'How long did the police say they'd be, Mum?' Samantha asked when the silence finally became too much.

Joanne took a cloth out of a nearby sideboard and began to wipe away energetically at something only *she* could see on the pristine surface of the dining room table.

'The woman I spoke to said they had a couple of officers nearby,' she replied without looking up. 'So pretty soon, hopefully, seeing as I've got so much going on today.'

'Well, I must admit I *did* wonder why you chose to call them right now; I mean, you could have left it until later.'

'Well, I'd more than likely have been so brain-fried by this evening that I might've had to put it off until tomorrow, and then something else would probably have cropped up and I would've ended up forgetting to report it at all.'

The duster was cast back into its rightful place, the drawer shut with aplomb, and this time Joanne *did* make eye contact with Samantha.

'Don't worry,' she said. 'I can forgive the fact that you think I'm going over the top, but no right-minded person does something like that. He could have been capable of anything for all we know.'

'Mum, I'm not saying you shouldn't have called the police, it's just that the guy was obviously a complete loser, and he didn't exactly do anything to us, did he?'

'Harley didn't give him the chance!'

'He just flashed us, and I just wondered … well, perhaps you've now put a bit more pressure on yourself, you know? Maybe you could have reported it at a more convenient time?'

As adult and responsible as Samantha could doubtlessly be, she was also typical of somebody in their late teens. Joanne wished that *she* could still see life that way, but the extra couple of decades she had on her daughter had somewhat eroded the feeling of invincibility that came with youth.

'Sammy, it's lovely that you're worried about me and all the stuff I've got to do today,' she sighed. 'But believe me, you can't just let people get away with things like that.' Joanne paused momentarily as the image of their masturbating assailant came back into her mind. '*Especially* that. Maybe I *am* overprotective sometimes and, God forbid, even occasionally matriarchal, but at the same time I can't help it if I find somebody playing with their cock in front of me when I'm least expecting it rather upsetting!'

'Well, I was rather flattered …'

'What …?'

'Well, it isn't every day that a man with a stiffy throws himself at me like that, you know.'

'How can you be so bloody dismissive and disrespectful? This is serious!'

Harley had begun to pace around in the entrance hall, the sound of his claws clicking on the floorboards distracting Joanne for a split second, and Samantha seized the chance to recover the situation.

'Mum, I'm really sorry,' she said. 'I'm not making fun of you; I'm just trying to lighten the mood. I *know* reporting this was the right thing to do.'

Joanne raised her eyebrows, clearly unconvinced by her daughter's sudden sincerity.

'It's just that you've been *so* on edge lately,' Samantha continued. 'Really uptight and you really needed all this crap like a hole in the head! God knows I know you don't need this today and I admire you for doing something about it when I'd have probably just let it slide completely, never *mind* leaving it until later. The thing is, you need to get ready … and *now*! Why don't I bring a cup of tea or coffee up to you while you're in the shower? I'll deal with the police if they arrive while you're upstairs, and I can even fill them in with what I saw while we're all waiting for you to make yourself look even more beautiful and stuff. I'm going to go and stick the kettle on right now!'

Any indignance Joanne felt about the questioning of her judgement immediately disappeared. Samantha had the ability to defuse pretty much any emotionally charged situation, a gift Joanne not only envied, but occasionally found herself relying upon. Nobody could cheer her up after a fraught, stressful day quite like Samantha – or a fraught, stressful morning, for that matter.

'Oh. My. God!' said Joanne. 'My PA organises my life at the office, and now my daughter does exactly the same thing at home. But a coffee would be great, you absolute shining little star! If I am truly incapable of making decisions on my own any longer, then having you was surely the best one I ever made when I was of sound mind! Where *would* I be without you?'

'An asylum …?'

'Don't push it! And while you're out there putting the kettle on, you'd better open the back door. Harley seems restless and I think he might want to go out … And don't even *think* about calling me bloody *Boudicca* again!'

Samantha giggled to herself as she crossed the entrance hall towards the kitchen and then opened the back door to the garden as instructed. Harley would usually have come trotting through straight away, but surprisingly he stayed put, and then Samantha started to feel strangely uneasy. The hairs on her forearms had started to rise, goose pimples had appeared on her skin, and she had the oddest feeling that she wasn't the only one in the room. To add to her uneasiness, Harley had begun growling. He was staring into the kitchen, not directly at Samantha, but past her. Slowly, he began backing away, as though somebody was moving towards him.

Tentatively, Samantha moved towards the kitchen doorway, and saw that her mother was also watching Harley from the other side of the entrance hall. The low, guttural rumble in Harley's throat had become a half-bark as he moved deliberately across the floor towards the staircase, his eyes focused on the landing, and upon something that apparently only he could sense or see.

Harley's behaviour was alarmingly similar to earlier on the Heath. Was it possible that somebody could be in the house? Cautiously, Joanne crept towards him until he was close enough for her to reach out and touch, and then she glanced nervously upstairs, watching, and listening for any movement. She was just about to take another hesitant step when Harley unexpectedly turned and bolted towards Samantha. Samantha was forced to take evasive action as he launched himself over the threshold of the kitchen doorway, landing awkwardly on the other side, and skidding into a kitchen cupboard. The impact had enough force to bounce Harley off the cupboard's double doors and onto his back, but immediately he twisted onto his belly and tried to stand, snarling, fighting for all he was worth to get enough purchase on the slippery surface of the quarry-tiled floor.

Samantha wanted to go and calm him down, but feared she might get bitten by accident. She'd never known Harley behave so strangely; it was as if he were trying to protect her, but protect her from what? As Samantha asked herself these questions, Harley managed to get himself upright. It looked like he was about to charge outside, but then the door to the back garden suddenly, and inexplicably, slammed itself shut.

The resounding thump brought Samantha back to her senses. She gazed open-mouthed at her mother who was just as mystified and still standing at the foot of the stairs. It was a relief for both of them to see that Harley had calmed considerably, but Samantha could tell he was still agitated, agitated enough to keep sniffing around the kitchen and the area around the back door in particular.

Harley's claws on the quarry tiles as he flitted around the kitchen was the only sound to permeate an unnerving silence that had fallen upon the house. Joanne felt completely frazzled by everything that had happened to her that morning and had even started to get the feeling that she was being watched. Instinctively she looked up towards the panoramic window at the top of the staircase, where, regarding her coldly from a lofty vantage point in a tree outside, was possibly the biggest crow Joanne had ever seen. She couldn't remember it being there before, and, just as strange, was the spellbinding effect that the bird's unfaltering gaze was having upon her. This strange feeling persisted until the crow finally lost interest, and lazily took to the air. Joanne felt like she'd been released and mentally berated herself for being so stupid. She was obviously still on edge about the flasher on the Heath and it was reasonable to assume the same could be said for Harley. What other reason could there be for his irrational behaviour?

Joanne suggested it might be a good idea to find somewhere else to go running. She'd had her fill of the Heath. 'And now Harley's even starting to get spooked by stupid crows!' she said. 'But that's a discussion for another time. The police are going to be here any minute and I need to get ready.'

Samantha nodded but didn't say anything. She was paying more attention to Harley, watching closely in case there should be any further changes in his behaviour. He was still standing by the back door but was acting more like his usual self, and the inflow of fresh air from outside was very welcome when she opened it. The bright, open space of the back garden eased a creeping sense of claustrophobia, and she didn't feel quite so hemmed in by the bizarre events of moments earlier. A feeling of being watched in the kitchen could easily have been Samantha's imagination, but she had no explanation for the presence she had felt rushing past her just before Harley had; something tangible, a heaviness in the air and a dragging sensation, as though a part of whatever Harley had been chasing had passed clean through her. And then there was the back door. How and why had it slammed itself shut like that? The force had been enough to rattle a stack of plates in a nearby cupboard, and there was no wind to speak of that could have caused it to slam so violently.

Everything *felt* like it was back to normal, but Samantha's questions continued to nag away. She was usually very down-to-earth, but it was rather disquieting to know that she was going to be alone in the house once her mother had left. She switched on the kettle and tried her best to think about something else.

Upstairs, Joanne was in no mood to dwell upon such dramas. Having showered and at last begun to get ready, she could finally focus upon catching up with her publicity guru and great friend, Leonard Slater. Smiling at the thought of seeing him, Joanne towel-dried her hair, selected something special from her underwear drawer, and began checking herself over in a full-length mirror. *Not too bad,* she thought, turning herself sideways, *not too bad at all, actually*. Her stomach was still flat enough, and she was more than happy with her legs and bottom. It was a shame about her breasts, though. No amount of exercise or gym work was going to make them any bigger, for sure! Maybe she *would* have that boob job she kept promising herself, but then again, where was she ever going to find the time? Or the courage?

At forty-two, Joanne felt she shouldn't be leaving it too much longer if she wanted to make any such tweaks or enhancements. What would be the point of having an impressive, twenty-one-year-old rack if everything else on her looked fifty?

'I've put your coffee at the end of your bed, Mum.'

Joanne had been so engrossed in her self-examination that she hadn't noticed Samantha come in with a mug of coffee.

'Wow!' said Samantha when she saw her mother. 'You look incredible in that set!'

'You think so?'

'It looks new ... might you be wearing it for somebody special?'

Under normal circumstances, Samantha would have expected to be on the receiving end of a blunt rebuttal, but instead Joanne began to laugh.

'Oh God! Look at me!' she sighed, sitting down heavily on her bed. 'Why am I even *thinking* about wearing this stuff today? I mean, it's ridiculous!'

'Ridiculous? Why?'

'No, not ridiculous, I mean ironic ... it's so *bloody* ironic!'

'I'm not with you, Mum ...'

'How I feel about Leonard! You've only met him a couple of times, but I've known Leonard since my late teens, back when I first began on the catwalk. I know he's got a few years on me but he's *such* a gentleman. He's kind, understanding, entertaining, and you've even said yourself that he's a great looking guy. I love how he makes me feel when I'm around him and ... and he's bloody well gay! Only *I* could have an interest in a man who wouldn't be the least bit interested in *me*. I might just as well be wearing my sodding *period* knickers for all the effect this stuff would have on him if he saw me in it!'

Samantha resisted a sudden urge to laugh.

'But it *is* beautiful underwear,' she said. 'And judging by your poses when I walked in, don't start telling me it doesn't make you feel good.'

'Well, yes … I suppose I do feel good in it, actually.'

'Well in that case it isn't *ridiculous* to want to wear it then, is it? If it makes you feel good about yourself and you're meeting a man who doesn't see you purely as a sex object, then that's a win-win in my book!'

'Oh, but if only he did!'

The doorbell chose to ring at that precise moment, and the house was abruptly filled with the sound of Harley's huge bark. Samantha could scarcely believe that such bad timing was possible. Her mother had just begun to open up, and in a way that had been so completely unexpected. Damn that bloody doorbell!

'I guess that'll be the police then,' she said. 'How about men in uniform, Mum … any interest in them?'

Joanne shook her head.

'Not really. Not even firemen! I sometimes wish Harley could be a man, though; you know, all that strength, loyalty and protective instinct. Anyway, I've already told you way too much. I'll be down in a few minutes.'

*

Having safely returned to his flat, Wayne Terry had been adamant that he wasn't going to venture outside again that day. It was Friday, and he'd found out, to his consternation, that he was going to have to wait until Monday before he could go and see his old counsellor. In the top drawer of a storage unit in his lounge was an exercise book that he'd once used as a journal, containing a record of his thoughts. It had proved invaluable during his treatment when he was younger, a way to release his anxiety, and, more often, his rage. Wayne hoped that he might find a degree of solace hidden in those old scribbled notes, some previous inspiration to lead him out of his darkening world, but as he flicked anxiously through the journal's pages, it was disconcerting for him to discover that everything he started to read was just as relevant to who he was right now.

Wayne felt that if he were to stay in for the whole weekend, he could occupy himself enough to avoid slipping again or having another episode. But he still couldn't remember going to Hampstead Heath, so the tactic clearly hadn't worked for him that morning. And what if his mother decided to come and pay him an unwelcome visit? There was nothing to stop her now his whereabouts were known, and it was impossible to see the lesser of the two evils.

Wayne's flat suddenly felt anything *but* the fortress he'd once considered it to be, its walls as weak as his will to keep running. It really was useless. Why hadn't he been able to throw himself into the welcoming waters of the lake on the Heath when he'd had the chance? Hadn't the darkness there wanted him to bond with its beloved solitude? That was the one thing Wayne *could* recall, and how he resented the episode that had denied him his chance of a blessed embrace with oblivion. There was no place for people like him. Wayne knew that the lake had offered him a simple way out, that he was better off dead, and that death was easier than life.

Not for the first time that day, desperate tears welled up in his eyes. One ran down his face and dropped onto the open journal, splashing down upon a page that contained a smiling face with a speech bubble saying: 'I am at my best when things are at their worst.'

Never had a quote had such an immediate impact. Wayne dried his eyes and hurriedly composed himself. To hell with it! He was going to shower, get himself ready and head out into town. He *was* worth something, and he was going to beat this. He had beaten it before, and he would damn well beat it again!

When Wayne eventually *did* shower, it was to symbolically purge himself of the disgusting creature he'd become on Hampstead Heath. Each tiny droplet of water helped to galvanise him in that fight, and once dressed and emboldened, he fulfilled the promise he'd made to himself while getting ready about heading out to the West End. To most people, this trip would have been nothing more than a little jaunt further into the capital, but to Wayne it was the start of a whole new journey, the first step towards being somebody altogether different.

He emerged from the London Underground, blinking in the brilliance of a sunlit Leicester Square. The first objective was to find somewhere to eat which was easier said than done when his eyes were still struggling to adjust to the light after the dinginess of the Northern Line.

Having missed breakfast, Wayne's stomach felt like his throat had been cut, but thankfully it didn't take him long to find somewhere that appealed to his tastes.

The manageress of his chosen eatery happily obliged his request for a secluded table, because wherever Wayne looked, he saw couples or groups of friends interacting. It made him feel uncomfortable to see how little he fitted in, lonely within a crowd, having to sit as far away as possible from everybody else, just like a mangy old dog that had been rejected by its pack mates. If only it could be different, but right then all Wayne could be was an unobtrusive observer of the happiness of others.

Before long, a beautiful young waitress named 'Gina' was asking to take Wayne's order. The leggy, grey-eyed dusty blonde was undoubtedly Eastern European judging by her accent, and wasting her time waiting tables, in Wayne's opinion, as he thought she would have made a fantastic model.

Despite his mental fragility, Wayne was very well positioned to make such a judgement. He was a professional figure photographer, a career he'd stumbled upon by accident having taking up photography as a means of coping with the mental issues of his late teens. Wayne had only just turned eighteen when he won his first photographic competition and his undoubted artistic talent had been duly noted. From there he was invited to take on a few supervised commissions before branching out into different fields, one of them being studies of the female form, and as it turned out it was an avenue that had paid the most dividends, for not only did it serve to curb Wayne's fear and hatred of women (a consequence of the heartbreak he'd suffered at the hands of his mother's lover, Monique), it was also a launch pad from where he would eventually start his own business.

But perhaps Wayne's stars had begun to align two or three years before that time. Unable to trust anybody on his mother's side of the family, the only other person Wayne could turn to when he ran away from home was the older sister of his late father.

Sylvia had always been Wayne's favourite aunt, and became a tower of strength during the early days of his estrangement from his mother, whom Sylvia openly detested. He was the son that Auntie Sylvia had never had, so when Wayne's talent for photography first became apparent, she saw to it that a maturing trust fund, originally set up for him by his father, would be suitably invested in that budding photographic future.

Having the talent was one thing, but Wayne knew that his success was nearly all down to the encouragement and guidance of his aunt. He took Sylvia's advice seriously, especially when it came to ways of staying hidden from his mother.

Under the pseudonym 'Joshua Gains', Wayne had been able to quietly establish himself in the art world, and enjoyed giving opportunities to people who had difficulty seeing their own potential. Many of Wayne's models were waitresses and barmaids, and some had even gone on to become full-time models. He was always up front about who he was and what he did. All photo shoots could be chaperoned, his subjects were welcome to bring whomever they wished if it meant they would feel happier, and he would never push them any further than they were prepared to go. In Wayne's creative eyes, all facets of the female form were art, however studied: the expression of the eyes, the grace of the hands, the sensuality of the mouth, the flowing curves accentuated by shadow as a silhouette. By capturing these qualities with his unique photographic ability, Wayne learned over time to respect and appreciate what he had once loathed and feared.

Gina was visibly flattered when Wayne told her she'd make a great model. They spoke some more once Wayne had finished his meal, and he gave her one of his cards. Then, he ordered an additional coffee, settled his bill and went outside to have a cigarette.

While he'd been inside and securely ensconced in a secluded corner, Wayne had been protected from the outside world, but now he felt completely exposed. After his smoke, he went back inside for his coffee. On a nearby table, two women were talking excitedly to each other … in French.

Wayne turned his head slowly in their direction, and his scalp began to tingle as the two friends shared a joke. *They knew, didn't they?* They'd been inside his head and now they knew fucking everything! *Little. Fucking. Bitches!* Listen to them … little bitches!

But the eyes that really *could* see into Wayne didn't belong to any of the flesh or blood seated around him at that moment. Unbeknown to him, Wayne really *was* being probed, but from a plane of existence far removed from his own. Cold and calculating, the entity continued to regard him with interest, for here was an unfortunate crying out for its assistance, a potentially useful tool in the quest to unhinge the *Great Plan*, a worm at a tipping point, and surely open to the right kind of persuasion. What made matters even more interesting was that the worm had also seen the girl. The entity grinned to itself. It could already see how easy this was going to be.

Just like the fucking rest of them! Wayne continued his mental rant.

All at it, in their skimpy little outfits, flouncing around in all their presupposed glory, flaunting their foulest femininity, looking for a heart to rip out, just like Monique and that fucking Wet Hole that dared to call itself his mother!

Wayne sprung up from his seat and strode purposefully out of the restaurant. Adrenalin was coursing through his body and he broke into a run. He knew where he was going and what he had to do. There was a new voice in his head and it didn't matter that it wasn't the voice of his own thoughts. It was making too much sense, promising that where his old world had been destroyed, and his innocence cruelly taken, the new world he was craving would begin.

Unseen and unknowable, the entity followed. It had found another puppet for the show. Another set of strings to pull.

CHAPTER 3

Detective Chief Inspector Chris Ryan stared glassily up at the ceiling of the corridor, polystyrene tiles blurring into a featureless grey as the paramedics rushed him towards the hospital's Trauma Unit. Strip light followed strip light, streaking along like shooting stars in the encroaching darkness of his failing vision. Everything was faded, distant and fleeting, but he wasn't afraid. There was nothing to fear anymore. There was no pain, only acceptance. All he wanted to do was reach out and embrace the calm that was cocooning him in those moments; moments that he already knew were going to be his last. If his final memories were to be chaos, the fear in a drug dealer's eyes and the roar from a hand-gun's muzzle, then so be it; he felt nothing – no anger, no malice.

'Christopher …?'

Although he was surrounded by sounds of desperate activity, a vaguely familiar word managed to find its way into his ear.

'Chris …? Can you hear me, Christopher?'

Christopher. That was his name, wasn't it? But it wasn't important anymore. It was time to let go.

'Single gunshot wound to the lower thorax. Significant blood loss.'

'No palpable radial pulse … check that airway …'

More voices … more distant now … Why wouldn't they let him sleep? All he wanted to do was go to sleep.

'B.P. eighty over forty …'

Sleep now …

'Christ, we're losing him! Come on, Chris … stay with us!'

Let me … sleep …

In the sudden darkness, there was light, white, blinding light. It was so bright that Chris couldn't see anything definitive like a floor, walls, or ceiling, and all was calm and peaceful.

'Hello …?' he called out in the silence. 'Hello …? Is anybody there …?'

No one answered and nobody came. Slightly agitated, Chris decided he was going to have a look around, but when he tried to move, he found that he couldn't.

'Hello, Christopher,' said a tall, solidly built man who had appeared as if from nowhere. His lustrous ebony skin was in shining contrast to the simple white shroud he was wearing, his voice rich and soothing, a spoken baritone befitting of his noble African features.

'I am Zambaya,' the man said.

'Zam ...?'

'Zam-by-ah ...'

'Oh, right! Well it's nice to meet you, Doctor Zambaya. I'm ...'

'You are Christopher John Edward Ryan, and it is good to meet you too. But I am not a doctor, I am your Overseer.'

'My ... what?'

'Your Overseer. I am a guide and you are my pupil, an 'Innocent', how we in The Truth look upon a first time incarnate. I am also the keeper of the door through which your soul entered your world, and through which you will return to us when it is time for you to come home.'

The African's tone had remained considered and knowledgeable, his kind and understanding brown eyes never straying from Chris, who'd suddenly become aware of a creeping apprehension swelling inside. It was a fear he instantly tried to dismiss.

'Yeah, whatever,' he scoffed. 'This isn't real, I must be hallucinating! It's the drugs they're giving me. I suppose the next thing you're going to tell me is that I'm dead, right?'

It was important for Zambaya to keep his subject calm. Chris was between worlds and still connected to his material being which meant he was still at the whim of his human emotions. The fear that Zambaya could sense might cause a severing of the fragile connection to his physical existence, and if that should happen, The Circle would be broken. Nevertheless, the connection had needed to be made, the risks involved deemed a necessity. Zambaya closed his eyes, and immediately Chris felt he was being embraced by comforting, invisible arms that held him until his fear subsided.

'Christ!' he said. 'I really *am* dead!'

'No,' Zambaya replied, with a slow and considered shake of his head. 'It is true that you stand at the doorway to another part of life, but it is not your time to pass through.' He cautiously extended a hand in Chris's direction, as one might reach out to comfort an animal in distress. 'Come with me,' he said. 'You must return until The Truth brings us together again.'

'The *what* brings us together?'

'The Truth, because it has chosen us.'

'Chosen us for *what?*'

'Patience, Christopher John Edward Ryan. Such things do not come easily to you. I will teach you how to look into the grey between the black and the white you only allow yourself to see. You will understand all in good time but until then, you must return.'

Considering his confusion, Chris felt complete trust in the stranger who had so dramatically entered his life, and when he *did* finally agree to take Zambaya's hand, it was with a great deal of reluctance. It seemed their meeting had only been an introduction and that far more was to come, but until then, everything was going to have to remain a complete mystery. In the strangest of ways, Chris felt like he was back at school, but unlike a school master deriding pupils for having the impertinence to question, Zambaya's enthralling manner commanded the utmost respect without his having to resort to using fear.

While Chris continued to wonder, he was carefully released by Zambaya like a responsible fisherman might gently return a catch into the water. The comforting surroundings in which Chris had been so lovingly cocooned suddenly began to break away and he felt like he was falling. Instinctively, he fought to stay connected to the safety of the light, but its brilliance was fading, moving further away until it resembled nothing more than a distant star in the darkest night.

And then, there was nothing.

*

Joanne arrived at Covent Garden Tube Station like a woman on a mission. She was late, nearly half-an-hour late, for the photo shoot and meeting organised by Leonard Slater, the most important man in her life.

If Joanne was the driving force behind her business, Leonard was surely her engine, and the man behind all the high-flying functions, client entertainment and photo sessions was being kept waiting. God, how she hoped the explanations she'd messaged to her personal assistant would help because the events of that morning had just caused everything to run riot. It wasn't Joanne's fault she'd been flashed at by a lunatic and had to report it to the police! And why were the lifts to the surface taking so bloody long?

It was only a short walk from the station to Joanne's offices, but she was in a bustling hurry, rushing out of the lift and into the street at the same time as a group of boisterous young people were sprinting past. Unable to get out of the way, Joanne was caught up in the mini stampede and dumped onto her backside. The boys whooped with laughter and carried on without so much as an apology.

An elderly couple that happened to be passing helped Joanne to her feet. 'Bloody yobs!' the gruff old man muttered. 'No bloody discipline! A bloody good stint in the army, that's what they bloody well need!'

'William Baines!' gasped his wife. 'You will mind your language!'

'It's fine, honestly,' said Joanne, dusting off the back of her jeans. 'I've heard much worse! And thank you so much for helping me.'

'It's a pleasure, dear,' said Mrs Baines. 'As long as you're okay.'

'Well the army never did me any harm … mind you, we had balls then …'

'Oh, do shut up, William!'

'It's all about delinquents and scroungers now!'

'William, that's ENOUGH!'

Mr Baines scowled and muttered something under his breath about bringing back National Service, but then he smiled disarmingly.

'Sorry, me duck,' he whispered to Joanne. 'I get a bit carried away sometimes. Wife gets pissed off, you know.'

'Oh my God, WILLIAM!'

Although probably well into his seventies, William Baines was still a tall, very upright gentleman. His salmon-pink scalp, sun-kissed by the early summer sunshine, was shining proudly through his thinning white hair. Sharp blue-grey eyes and a slightly hooked nose gave him a fierce, almost hawk-like appearance, and a large handlebar moustache completed the look of a brigadier. *Mrs* Baines, in complete contrast, was a short and petite woman of around the same age, still attractive and undoubtedly a real looker in her younger days. They seemed to be such a happy couple and had no doubt been head-over-heels in love forever.

The sound of a car's horn interrupted the brief encounter which was probably just as well because Joanne had once again lost all track of time. They said their goodbyes, but not before Mrs Baines had made sure that Joanne wasn't in need of a life-saving cup of tea or coffee, an invitation Joanne regretted having to pass up. How she would have loved to have spent some time with the wonderful old couple!

It was right then that Joanne had a very profound thought. Wasn't it amazing how some people had the power to enter one's life and have an immediate effect? Joanne knew that in all probability she would never see Mr and Mrs Baines again, but their brief encounter had shown her the true meaning of happiness.

The last thing Joanne really wanted to be was on her own. The self-sacrifices once perceived as necessary while bringing up her daughter were no longer that important. The break-up of her marriage was history, and if it were wise to remember how everything in life happened for a reason, then it would include her ex-husband's infidelity. Maybe life had something better in store. After all, if it hadn't had been his secretary, *The Bastard* would probably have ended up screwing somebody else anyway.

Yet, it wasn't as if the whole bitter experience with *The Bastard* had left Joanne feeling completely 'anti-man', either, as Samantha had once cuttingly claimed. There *had* been a couple of men during Joanne's sexual sabbatical, and she smiled to herself recalling the pleasures drawn from those short-term flings. She still had needs, and perhaps her feelings for Leonard proved that there were some windows and doors appearing in that once impenetrable wall behind which she'd so successfully managed to imprison herself. If it were truly the case, it certainly wouldn't be before time.

Joanne was looking at her wristwatch as she burst into her office. God, she was *so* late!

'I am *so* sorry, Leanne,' she said to her PA. 'Thanks for holding it all together. You wouldn't believe what it's been like for me today. Is Leonard okay?'

'Oh, *Leonard's* fine,' Leanne replied. 'Harvey's being a bit of a shit though.'

Joanne threw her arms out in frustration upon hearing the photographer's name. 'Oh no, God forbid! *Not* Harvey sodding Davies again! I just knew it would be him! That's all I need. Why *him* for heaven's sake? Why today?'

'Jo, come on, calm down. As long as Leonard's okay, that's all that matters, and he's been great, honestly. Don't worry.'

'Yeah, I'm sure he has, and thank you so much for keeping him sweet, but *Harvey* …? Why the hell can't Leonard hire another photographer?'

'Leonard likes Harvey …'

'Yes, and we both know why but he hasn't got a chance with him. Harvey's straight, for heaven's sake. I just wish Leonard would get it into his head!'

Leanne was well aware of the real problem between Harvey and Joanne, but now wasn't the time to discuss it.

'I'm sure that's not the only reason Leonard hires him,' she said. 'Harvey's a great photographer, Jo, *and* he really knows how to get the best out of his models.'

'Oh Christ, *don't* tell me you fancy him too!'

'No, I bloody well *don't*! I just think he's the best out there for this kind of shoot, that's all.'

'Yeah, yeah … okay, okay. I hear what you're saying. It's just a shame he has to be such a wanker though, isn't it?'

Bad language and Joanne didn't sit well together, but when she *did* come out with the odd expletive, it was always delivered with an uncanny (if unintentional) sense of comic timing.

'God, I'm *so* glad you're my personal assistant!' said Joanne as their laughter abated. 'Best go and face the music I suppose.'

Inwardly flustered, yet outwardly composed, Joanne strode brightly along the corridor towards another office that was used as a photographic studio. She paused outside its double doors, mentally preparing herself for one of

Leonard's greetings and Harvey's monumental attitude problem.

'Jo ... darling!' said Leonard, bounding enthusiastically towards her as she entered the room. *'Mmmwah ...!'*

Having kissed one side of her face, *'Mmmwah...!'* a slightly prolonged version was deposited on the other.

'Long time no see, lovey ... Let me look at you, let me look at you! Stunning ... no, no, make that absolutely *gorgeous*! You really were an outstanding model, you know! Still could be ...'

'Yes, maybe. But I became a mother and I wanted that more.'

'I know,' said Leonard. 'A Model Mum!'

Leonard, as ever, was as immaculately turned out as a thoroughbred racehorse. Not a single, pampered, greying hair was out of place, and the cultured, pale grey Italian jacket and open-necked burgundy shirt perfectly complemented the dark blue jeans he'd managed to pour himself into. His aftershave was pressing all of Joanne's buttons, and it disappointed her to think that Leonard's efforts were purely for Harvey's benefit.

'I'm so sorry I'm late, Leonard,' she said. 'I know how important this is.'

He waved a hand dismissively, but a terse voice from the far end of the spacious studio put an abrupt end to the pleasantries.

'Is there *any* chance we might get started today?' asked an impatient Harvey Davies. 'Now that we've got so *gloriously* reacquainted, perhaps I can do the job that I was hired for? I've been here well over an hour and time is money.'

Joanne didn't want Harvey to see that he was already getting to her, and was grateful for Leonard being on hand to discuss in more detail what he was looking to achieve from the shoot. After his briefing, Harvey went over to three stunning models who were sitting on a white leather sofa. They tittered as he whispered something obviously outrageous to them before they were instructed to follow Leonard and select the first outfits.

'Just give me a shout if you need any help back there getting into any of them!' Harvey said. 'I'm very good with my hands!'

The models tittered again.

Joanne thought she was going to be sick.

Which one of the impressionable and unsuspecting trio on Harvey's 'casting couch' had been earmarked to be his disposable bed warmer for the night? It was such an unwelcome thought that Joanne had to go and start making some coffee to distract herself.

Yet as much as Joanne hated to admit it, there *was* something about the photographer's dark, smoldering looks that she could see other women being attracted to, including (perish the thought!) herself. Harvey Davies was the polar opposite of Leonard's slick and stylish sophistication, possessing a Hard

Rock sleaziness that spoke volumes about the dubious character that lay beneath the thick, black, spiky hair, and various tattoos adorning his muscular arms. It was a typical bad-boy image and one that Harvey not only lived up to but clearly enjoyed because of the attention it gained him from the opposite sex.

Pretending she hadn't really just paid her nemesis a begrudging mental compliment, Joanne walked purposefully away with a confident, carefree strut that she'd once honed for the catwalk. On this occasion, however, it was an act of false bravado, knowing that Leonard was preoccupied with matters elsewhere and that she and Harvey were alone.

Joanne could feel Harvey's eyes undressing her as she went over to a small, secluded kitchen area. She felt like a rabbit trapped in a car's headlights, Harvey's headlights, just waiting for the inevitable as he swaggered over, the hollow sound of his boots on the wooden floor growing louder as he joined her in the kitchenette.

'Leonard's right,' he said. 'You look really good.'

'Thank you,' Joanne replied.

'How do you fancy going for a drink and grabbing something to eat later ... you know, make up for lost time?'

'I'm not sure that's a good idea, Harvey.'

'Well 'not sure' is better than 'no' I guess.'

'Okay, then, no!'

'Just because we had a bit of a misunderstanding?'

'I think it was far more than that!'

'A misunderstanding about you being the wrong sort of woman for me? I mean you've got everything I like, an *unbelievable* arse, fucking great legs ...'

'You can't see my legs, I'm wearing jeans ...'

'I know, just for me, and don't they just fit in all the right places? You know, whenever I watch you, I can almost feel it going in ...'

'Don't you *ever* give up, Harvey?'

The photographer raised a quizzical eyebrow.

'Not when I see someone that needs a sense of humour transplant as much as you do,' he said. 'I just *so* want to loosen you up.'

Joanne glared at him, nauseated by the predatory intent grinning back at her through his sculpted stubble and grateful for probably being the only woman Harvey knew apart from his mother who hadn't had the misfortune of feeling that stubble between her thighs.

'If only you knew what it does to me when you look at me like that,' Harvey sighed. 'Anyway, it's only a bit of banter, and stop pretending you're not interested.'

Much to Joanne's relief, Leonard ventured back into the studio with perfect timing, and Harvey shrugged his shoulders and sauntered away, having had his fun.

Joanne waited until Harvey was out of earshot. She was determined that he wasn't going to get away with it this time.

'Why do you *insist* on hiring that arrogant bastard, Leonard?' she whispered.

'He's the best.'

'He's a prat!'

'But Jo ...'

'I hear what you're saying Leonard, and I *agree* that he's damned good at what he does, but he's also very good at getting on my nerves, or offending me, or both, and I'm *pig* sick of it. I really don't need it, especially as I have to be here with him for every sodding shoot!'

'I'm sure he's only playing ...'

'Like hell he is! He's a sexual predator! I know I should have told you about this before, but I turned him down about a year ago and put a dent in his ego, and ever since then he's been nothing but a total shit to me!'

Leonard was astounded.

'But I just thought it was a clash of personalities!' he said. 'I thought it was Harvey just being abrasive that got to you, but we manage to work through it.'

Across the other side of the room, Harvey was busy making some final equipment checks and adjustments. Joanne felt it was safe to continue.

'No, Leonard, it's nothing like that,' she sighed. 'I mean it was stupid ... I was going through a bit of a vulnerable phase at the time and he was very complimentary about my work. He took me out, but I guess he was only being nice because he thought it might to lead to something else. I'm not averse to a little bit of fun, Leonard, but I'm not easy and God knows I knew about Harvey's reputation. I wasn't going to be used like that. I knocked him back and that's it, really. Pathetic, isn't it?'

'But why didn't you say anything? I could have sorted it out, and at least made things easier for you. I mean Harvey's not the only photographer I know, but for a new line like this and breaking into a new market, I guess it would still have had to be a case of 'better the devil you know' on this occasion. Jo, I've got every confidence Harvey will get this right, and then we can really capitalise on the interest we already have with this project. After that, we can hire somebody else for the next shoot before we go live with it. Once the buyers see this range on the catwalk, I know they'll want a piece of the action. When have I ever let you down?'

'You haven't,' Joanne replied, looking down at the floor.

'And neither has Harvey as a photographer, but you can be sure I'll be having a word with him about the other matter. He's been bloody unprofessional and I'm not prepared to see him upset you like this, especially when there *is* somebody else we could try; one guy in particular. He's a figure photographer, mind you, nude female studies mainly, but he's getting pretty big in the art world. I've also heard that a big lingerie label has approached him for their new advertising campaign, so he's obviously diverse.'

'It certainly sounds like it, although I'm not sure about the porn stuff if I'm honest, Leonard …'

'Erotic art.'

'Okay, erotic art, whatever … it's still tits and arse to me. Anyway, I suppose I'm more than open to suggestions because, like you say, this isn't the last shoot we're going to be doing with this line.'

'I was at an exhibition a few weeks ago and took a couple of the fellow's cards,' said Leonard, reaching into his jacket for his wallet. 'I remember the quality of his work, and he's certainly special. Aha … there you go, Joshua Gains, that's him! I'll get in touch with him for you, shall I?'

CHAPTER 4

Wayne stood staring at his mother's impressive white house. Properties in that part of Mill Hill went for millions, and to think that it was all hers was almost too much to contemplate. The only reason she lived in such affluence was due entirely to his late father's hard work, and Wayne could think of no one less deserving of such good fortune than an old whore who'd destroyed a decent man and then inherited his estate. As far as Wayne was concerned, the Wet Hole should have been rotting on the street.

The dwelling rose up commandingly from the top of a sloping, beautifully landscaped front garden. A herringbone brick driveway inclined upwards, curving through a green expanse of pampered lawn to a set of steps and a pair of imposing hardwood doors. The entrance was spectacularly framed by a mature, flowering wisteria, and the scent of its purple, chandelier-like blooms hung heavily in the air as Wayne drew closer.

'How fucking idyllic!' he muttered, but then a sudden movement and a fleeting glimpse of a face at one of the downstairs windows stopped him dead in his tracks.

Light-headed and a little dizzy, Wayne had to reach out and steady himself. He had one foot on the bottom of a set of brick steps and one hand resting upon the twisted stems of an established wisteria. An anxious glance back down the driveway revealed a street which, even in his muddled state, looked uncomfortably familiar.

Wayne covered his face with his hands in horror, hardly daring to peer at his worst nightmare between trembling fingers. The last thing he could remember was sitting outside a restaurant in Leicester Square, so what the hell was he suddenly doing there, outside his mother's?

As Wayne fought frantically to make sense of his predicament, the handle of one of the dark stained doors began to turn. He wanted to run but before he knew it, the door was opening. Heart pounding, he looked down at the floor. What would he say? What would he do? How would he …?

'Hello …?'

The accent was unmistakable and its soft, dusky vocal tone oddly soothing. Wayne lifted his gaze slowly and looked straight into the beautiful green eyes of Monique. At first, she was shocked, but then she began to smile, her entire face lighting up as she hurried down the steps towards him, excitedly.

'*Wayne?*' she gasped, embracing him warmly. 'Oh my God, I don't believe it!'

To Wayne's surprise, he began reciprocating her embrace. Monique's lustrous, thick red hair smelt clean and fresh, as did the fair skin of her graceful neck, her breath warm and welcoming upon his shoulder. For some reason it felt good to have Monique in his arms again, there was no hatred, and it was clear that the love he'd once felt for her was still there.

Wayne was so lost in his thoughts that he jumped a little when Monique spoke again.

'This is such a wonderful surprise to see you,' she said, pulling herself away from him slightly. 'You don't know what it means to me that you are standing here! It is such a shame that your mother is out. Please say that you will come in for a while?'

'Yeah, sure,' Wayne replied. 'Why not?'

With his mother out of the picture, what harm could there be in accepting Monique's hospitality?

He followed Monique inside, unable to keep his eyes off the sensual movement of her hips inside her flowing summer skirt. Monique's 'wiggle' had certainly appealed to him when he was a boy and it had lost none of its allure; evidently, she'd carried on with her dancing and Yoga.

'Your mother will be back about seven,' said Monique. 'Would you like something to eat?'

'No, it's fine,' he replied. 'I had something not long ago, thank you.'

'Okay, if you are sure. Now that you are here, I want us to spend some time together ... I cannot believe that you have hardly changed.'

'Neither have you.'

'That is very sweet of you to say so, thank you, Wayne. It looks like the years have been kind to me then! But maybe now I see that you are a bit taller, and yes, I think you might have filled out a little, but otherwise you look the same ... whatever you have been doing, you are looking well on it! Oh, listen to me carrying on ... chat, chat, chat. If you are not eating here, then perhaps I can get you a drink?'

'Maybe a glass of water.'

'Water? *Mon dieu*! At least have a tea or coffee. I have a choice of reds here if you would like a glass of wine. There is a fine Bordeaux that I opened at lunchtime, or maybe you might prefer a Merlot?'

Wayne had to smile at Monique doing her best to make him feel at home. About the only thing she hadn't done was roll out a red carpet, and eventually he caved in to trying a glass of Bordeaux.

'A fine choice, monsieur, if I may say so?' said Monique, passing him a generously filled glass and suggesting that they should go and sit in the lounge.

During the next hour, they spoke at length, filling in the missing years. Wayne was interested to hear that Monique had become a drama teacher at a nearby college, where she taught Monday to Thursday, and she in turn wanted to know more about his photography. It turned out that Wayne's profession had led his mother straight to him. Mrs Terry's interest in erotic art had grown over time and she had become keenly interested in the work of one 'Joshua Gains', and her research into the talented young man eventually revealed who Joshua really was.

As willing as he was to talk about his career, however, Monique had noticed how Wayne was loathe to talk about his mother, and, slowly but surely, passages of silence began to interrupt the previously steady flow of conversation. There was an awkwardness developing; Monique had become especially thoughtful, running a tentative finger around the rim of her wine glass, and Wayne sensed that it might be a good time for him to leave rather than face what might be about to come out.

But he was too late.

'I did not mean to hurt you, Wayne,' she said. 'God knows I would never have done that.'

Wayne knew he should have made his excuses and left long before Monique's frank admission. What *had* he been thinking? Why was he even *there*?

'I don't want to talk about it,' he said. 'Not now, not ever, and I don't want my mother to know I was here either ... I should go. I should never have come here!'

'Wayne, please! Don't go, not now ... I have wanted to talk to you for years ...'

'You laughed at me ...'

'Not at *you*, Wayne! I didn't know what to do ... I was embarrassed. Since then not a day has gone by when I have not thought about you ... about *us*.'

'*Us*?'

'Please, Wayne. I need you to know how much you meant ...!'

Monique's tone was laced with so much desperation that it stopped Wayne from getting out of his chair. Was it because he still had feelings for her, or was this moment going to be the closest thing to closure he was ever going to get? He sat back and looked across at Monique.

'Okay,' he sighed. 'Go on. But I meant what I said about not letting my mother know. But before you start, is it okay if I use your toilet?'

'Of course! But you will have to use the one upstairs. The downstairs toilet one is full of decorating stuff, and Wayne –? Thank you for giving me a chance.'

Monique could hear Wayne's footsteps echoing up the steep, wide staircase to the bathroom as she went into the kitchen for another bottle of wine. Perhaps it had been a mistake to bring up the past, but the wine had loosened her tongue and given her the courage to finally say what she'd always wanted to. Hopefully, another glass or two would also help Wayne to relax, and he would understand what she had to say.

It was difficult for Monique to decide where to start, but the beginning seemed as good a place as any, even if it did involve speaking about the affair that destroyed Wayne's family. Slowly, Monique withdrew another bottle of Bordeaux from the wine rack. She needed Wayne to know that moving into the family home so soon after his father had left had been a difficult decision for her to make. It didn't seem fair to blame Wayne's mother entirely, but she *had* metaphorically twisted Monique's arm, taking advantage of Monique's unhappiness with the questionable lodgings in which she'd been living at the time, a squalid house, shared with four other students who clearly disapproved of their developing relationship.

If Monique could just about justify her decision to move in so quickly, knowing she was the reason behind Wayne being so badly bullied at school had been something altogether different. That was when everything had changed. While Wayne's mother seemed content to bury her head in the sand, even more so after the sudden death of her estranged husband, Monique, in contrast, found herself becoming extremely protective of Wayne.

Being bisexual, Monique wasn't unaccustomed to finding the occasional man attractive, but finding herself being drawn to a fifteen-year-old boy was totally unexpected. Wayne just had a way about him. He was sensitive and vulnerable, with delicate features that made him almost too pretty to be a boy. He had the most beautiful clear blue eyes, and Monique would often catch him gazing at her. At first, she considered it nothing more than a teenage crush but, as time wore on, she found herself wondering if he was imagining her naked. Perhaps he was masturbating about her in his room at night, a thought that would become particularly arousing for her.

It had all seemed harmless enough to Monique, but curiosity had slowly been getting the better of her. She began privately flirting with Wayne to find out how he would react, and he loved the attention! Just seeing how she could make him happy was a pleasure in itself, feeding a growing desire to make him happier still.

Monique had been able to suppress her urges until one particular night when she and Wayne had got the house totally to themselves. Her hair was still wet, having just come out of the shower, and as she began getting dressed in her bedroom, she caught sight of Wayne reflected in her dressing table mirror, watching through a small gap in the doorway. At first Monique wondered how much Wayne had seen as she'd only just finished putting on her underwear, and yet strangely, she didn't make any attempt to cover herself up. Expecting him to be embarrassed at being caught out, she even made a joke about Peeping Toms, and glibly invited him into her room to get a better view! Instead of reacting coyly to being rumbled, however, Wayne came in and joined her. His eyes were full of wonder, he was smiling, wearing an amazed expression that was uniquely arousing and made her want to be his first woman.

Now, in the kitchen, Monique placed a hand on her breast, remembering how Wayne had so carefully reached out to her that night, how, when he touched her, there could be no turning back. The sensation of Wayne's gentle, exploring fingertips on her skin was innocence itself, and, in the moments that followed, that innocence would be so joyously and completely taken. From then on, Monique became teacher and Wayne became willing pupil. It was their 'Little Secret' and continued for months until the night Wayne caught her with his mother.

Remembering how good Wayne had felt that very first time was beautiful, but recalling his tearful gaze when he saw her and his mother together was anything but. Hurriedly, Monique went in search of a corkscrew, hoping the distraction would help to kill the pain of the heartbreaking memory.

In order to get to the upstairs bathroom, Wayne had to pass by what had once been Monique's bedroom. It then dawned upon him that Monique having her own room had been the only way that she and his mother could have kept their relationship hidden, and instantly he was fifteen again, walking along the landing, so desperate to be with Monique that he was prepared to risk their 'Little Secret'. Through the darkness he could hear sounds of female pleasure. Monique was speaking in French, just as she did when she used to masturbate in front of him. His body taut with excitement, Wayne turned the door handle and slowly opened the bedroom door, but instead of seeing Monique's fingers between her legs, it had been the face of his mother.

As he had countless times before, Wayne began to relive the appalling scene, but as Monique turned her head towards the door, her imminent laughter was replaced by a searing, shooting pain inside his head.

'Behold the scene of the crime, Wayne ...'

There was a strange voice speaking in Wayne's mind, smooth, persuasive, and terrifyingly devoid of emotion; it was unlike anything he'd heard before.

'I am the surgeon and you are the knife. Do you have what it takes to cut out the blight? Let me pull your strings ...'

The world began to spin. Wayne lost his balance and staggered into the bathroom. He'd never been consciously aware of any symptoms associated with the onset of his episodes; he just blacked out, but this was different, overwhelming.

'Let me pull your strings...'

Downstairs, Monique wandered back into an empty lounge, holding the unopened bottle of Bordeaux. There on the coffee table was the corkscrew she'd been looking for, but where was Wayne? Perhaps he'd left, but then again, she would surely have heard him?

Bordeaux in hand, Monique started to climb the staircase. She called out for Wayne as she approached the landing, but there was no reply, only the sound of whimpering coming from the bathroom. The door was slightly ajar, and when Monique carefully pushed it all the way open, she found Wayne, shaking and curled up in a tight ball with his hands over his ears. Tears streaked his sweat-soaked face as he looked up at her.

'L-leave me alone,' he whispered. 'You have to get away from me ...'

'Wayne? Oh my God, look at you ... what is wrong?'

'Monique ... please...You *have* to go ... get out!'

'No. I will not leave you, please let me ...'

And then to Monique's utter amazement, Wayne stood up and ran a sink full of cold water, bearing absolutely no resemblance to the gibbering wreck that had just been hunched up on the floor. Casually, he splashed a couple of handfuls of water on his face, and asked: 'What the fuck are you staring at?'

Uneasy, aghast at the sudden and dramatic change, Monique's mouth dropped open. Wayne looked and sounded the same, but that was where the similarities ended.

'Well?' he asked, drying himself off. 'I asked you a question didn't I, bitch? So, what the fuck are you staring at?'

There was nothing behind Wayne's once beautiful eyes. Shaking her head in disbelief, Monique backed away uncertainly before attempting to flee from the bathroom, but Wayne lunged after her, knocking her to the floor and sending the bottle of wine she'd intended as a further peace offering spinning from her hand onto the landing. Gripping her exposed throat, Wayne attempted to pin Monique down with one hand, while feverishly trying to unzip the fly of his jeans with the other. Instinctively, Monique rammed her knee as hard as she could in between his legs. Her desperate action bought her some time but not enough, and Wayne grabbed hold of one of her ankles as she scrambled to her feet, bringing her crashing down flat onto her stomach.

'I owe you this, you FUCKING BITCH!' he spat, grabbing a handful of her hair and slamming her face viciously against the unforgiving floorboards. Monique was stunned by the blow, blood streaming from her nose and into her mouth. She tried weakly to resist but Wayne was too determined. She could feel him struggling slightly with his belt buckle, but then he lifted her skirt, tore away the flimsy material of her underwear and began to force himself inside her.

Sobbing with terror and confusion, Monique hadn't even screamed. She was frightened that if she did, Wayne would hurt her even more. Perhaps if she let him do what he wanted she would be okay, but it felt like his erection was wrapped in broken glass as he penetrated her, each thrust more brutal and more painful than the last. Monique dug her fingernails into the floorboards and cried out in agony, and in spite of her indescribable fear, she knew that she had to fight back.

The bottle of wine lay just within reach of her left hand. Monique reached out, grasped it by the neck, turned as far as her position would allow, and then swung it towards Wayne's head.

Although the bottle didn't break, the impact upon his right eyebrow was enough to make him recoil with pain. Monique saw her chance and forced herself up onto her hands and knees. Rising unsteadily, she managed to stagger as far as the top of the stairs, but behind her Wayne had already recovered. This time Monique *did* scream and lashed out fiercely with the bottle as he came towards her, but the more meaningful impact she intended didn't materialise as, in her intense panic, she lost her footing, and crucially, her balance. Twisting, trying to grab anything to stop herself from falling, all Monique caught was a despairing handful of thin air. There was a resounding *thump* as the back of her shoulders clattered into the upper portion of the staircase, and a sickening *crack* when her momentum caused her to flip-flop violently backwards, the bottle of Bordeaux shattering in an explosion of red wine and glass as she tumbled over and over in a tangle of arms and legs into the entrance hall.

A spread-eagled, agonised mess, Monique was amazed that she was still conscious, but there was a terrible pain in her abdomen and a sharp stabbing sensation in her chest when she tried to breathe. She looked up and saw Wayne at the top of the staircase pulling up his jeans. If she were quick enough, maybe she could make it to the front door, but it was as if there was nothing beneath her waist when she tried to stand. In desperation, Monique turned onto her stomach and began to drag herself towards the door, legs trailing behind her like a child's pull-along toy.

Shaking, barely able to control his merriment, Wayne began to make his way down the stairs as Monique inched herself, pain-wracked, across the floor, her breath coming in tiny gasps and whimpers. Monique could hear Wayne's insane sniggering growing steadily louder as he came closer, the broken glass of the shattered wine bottle crunching horribly beneath his feet as he joined her in the hallway. It appeared that he was enjoying every second of her torture, but when she tried to cry for help, nothing came out. Any strength Monique had left was fading, ebbing away, a darkness forming at the periphery of her vision, and finally, she gave up her desperate fight and succumbed to its merciful embrace.

Wayne stood over Monique's unconscious form. Her breathing was shallow and rapid; she seemed to be dying, but he was still going to make sure these would be the last breaths she would ever take. He removed his belt, wrapped it around Monique's neck, and then with one foot pressed between her shoulder blades as an anchor, pulled on the makeshift noose with everything he had.

Only once he was sure that it was all over did he relinquish his grip, allowing Monique's head to fall cruelly to the floor. He smiled when he saw the purple bruising around her throat as he reclaimed his belt, testament to the force that he had applied, a mark of his strength. Then he strolled into the lounge and over to a large mirror that was hanging above the fireplace.

Wayne studied his face intently, half expecting his appearance to have changed in some way as a result of his victory. Instead, he was met by the same youthful and androgynous features that had always greeted him, large blue eyes staring guiltlessly back. Yet, regardless of the familiarity, the balance had been redressed, and now his mother would feel the unbearable pain of unimaginable loss. It would be *her* turn to grieve and to live in abject misery. How perfect that she'd been on the missing list, and that fate must surely have smiled.

A clock striking the half-hour out in the entrance hall cut through Wayne's blissful silence, and a glance at his watch told him it was five thirty. Without so much as a second glance, he stepped over Monique's lifeless, broken and defiled body, and walked out of the house into the late afternoon sunshine without a care in the world.

Striding back down the driveway towards the empty street, Wayne felt like a great weight had been lifted from his shoulders. The day seemed brighter than it had before and there was a renewed spring in his step. However, this was no time for celebration. He could do that in the safety of his Kentish Town flat …

Away from Mill Hill …

Away from everybody …

CHAPTER 5

Anne Ryan was gently stroking her son's hand and feeling totally useless. Having to wait hours for news of Chris's welfare had been bad enough, but the next forty-eight were going to feel like an eternity. Although surgeons had successfully removed the bullet from Chris's chest, the harsh surroundings of the Intensive Treatment Unit and its unfeeling technology filled her with dread, as did the ugly tube of the ventilator protruding from her son's mouth. His open, mischievous face was expressionless, not peaceful, his eyelids unflinching, and his usual smartly styled, dark-cum-greying hair was ruffled and unkempt. It was as though Anne was looking at somebody else, and how she wished that were the case! The thought of life without Chris was unthinkable. He was her only child, and apart from her grandson, Andy, the only thing she had left since losing her husband, Chris's father, to a heart attack three years earlier.

Anne was so proud of how hard Chris had worked to get where he was in the Met, and how dedicated he was to his role within it. It was like a second family to him, and she knew that were it not for the courage of that family getting him to hospital so quickly, the hard-working doctors and surgeons may not have been able to save him. Two of Chris's brave and quick-thinking colleagues had even stayed with Anne at the hospital during that long afternoon, trying to keep her positive and upbeat, giving her reasons to believe in his strength and fortitude.

'If anybody can pull through this,' they'd said, 'it's Chris.'

Tears began to well up in Anne's eyes. How could *anybody* have such a low regard for human life? Why would anybody feel the need to even have to carry a gun? At forty-four, Chris had so many great years ahead of him *and* he was a police officer, too! He'd only been doing his job, for God's sake, and knowing that the perpetrators were in custody was no consolation. Where would the justice be should the unimaginable happen, if Chris were to succumb to his injuries? As far as Anne was concerned, those responsible deserved far more than any punishment the British legal system had at its disposal.

'Nan,' said a masculine voice. 'The nurses say we have to go now.'

Anne looked up and smiled at the tall, muscular young man who had just joined her, almost grateful for the interruption of her silent vigil.

'My goodness, Andy!' she said. 'You look so much like your father.'

'Come on, Nan,' he said, smiling a little. 'It's been a long day so let's get you back to ours. I'm sure Dad won't mind. I know he's going to be okay; I can feel it.'

Anne gently kissed Chris's forehead. She didn't want to leave him, but she had no other choice.

But Chris was oblivious of his mother's anxiety as he lay in his sedative-induced coma. He was once again in Zambaya's presence, but the surroundings this time were markedly different. The Overseer smiled reassuringly before looking away, and Chris followed his thoughtful gaze into the distance.

They were sitting upon a rocky outcrop in a far different world to the one with which Chris was familiar. The sky of *this* world was a rich, twilight blue as though night was about to fall, but everywhere seemed to be bathed in sunlight. An expansive, fertile valley lay below, through which there coursed a wide meandering river with waters as deep a blue as the sky they reflected. Small groups of trees were scattered along its banks, and rich grasslands stretched, shimmering, in all directions to the far distant horizons.

'It is so incredibly beautiful,' said Zambaya. 'Do you not agree?'

Such simple words failed to do the breathtaking view enough justice. The vision was far beyond anything Chris could ever have imagined, proving without doubt that what he was witnessing could only be startling reality.

'Where am I?' he asked. 'Am I dead? Is this heaven?'

Zambaya slowly opened his arms, appearing to embrace the splendour surrounding him.

'You are very much alive, Christopher,' he said. 'But we need to make you strong again, which is why we have brought you here to this place of renewal, to The Truth. You may recall I spoke of it when we met before. It is here that all life force has its origins and where the energies and essences of all living things return when their time in your realm has ended. This is just one part of a Supreme Collective to which all are answerable, including ourselves as Overseers. We call it The Truth because everything that *is*, is a part of it, and in turn everything that *is* has a right to *be*. You have an inquiring mind, Christopher John Edward Ryan, and we will talk more in time, but there is much you need to know and learn from me *now*.'

To Zambaya, The Truth was a living, breathing edifice at the heart of all that existed, whereas to Chris, confused by the whole experience, it was more about finding answers, especially as Zambaya's tone had quickly changed from that of a friend to that of a teacher as he'd been speaking.

'The Truth wishes to send an envoy into your world in the form of a child,' said Zambaya. 'To many of your kind, they will be looked upon as a New Messiah. The child is to grow to adulthood whereupon it will unite your people, all humankind. Can you imagine your world free from hardship, cruelty and war?'

Chris could only respond by shaking his head in stunned silence. This was the last thing he'd expected.

'That is because humanity has become accustomed to witnessing such depravity,' said Zambaya. 'But I do not sit in judgement. I am a part of The Truth and speak as such. Your kind has its shortcomings, but humanity has not acted alone and it is important for you to know about its true enemy, for there is another collective, an adversary that endures as a completely different plane of existence from this one. We call its Brotherhood 'The Faithless', and its will and desire to manipulate humanity can explain much of the cruelty your species inflicts upon itself.'

Zambaya revealed that The Faithless had once coveted becoming a part of the Supreme Collective, but their methods and ideals had been questioned and their Brotherhood deemed unsuitable. Feeling rejected and scorned, The Brotherhood made a choice and removed itself from The Truth to exist in a dimension between *it* and 'The World of Men', upon the very shoulder of humanity itself, an account that to Chris bore an uncanny resemblance to some elements of *Paradise Lost*.

'The Faithless seek only to divide humanity as it is key to their objective for your kind,' said Zambaya, 'and their Brotherhood will not only be looking to prevent the envoy's birth, but it's very conception.'

'So how come this involves *me*?' asked Chris. 'It's only you and me here, so how come *I'm* so special all of a sudden … I don't understand.'

'The envoy of which I have spoken, Christopher, is no different to any other child in that it must be born to a mother, and the chosen mother will be in grave danger. *You* are going to protect her.'

'What?'

'You are a part of The Circle, the series of events by which the envoy will come to humanity. You would call it destiny because it has always been this way.'

'Like *that's* any kind of answer!'

'It *is*, because you *are* a part of The Circle …'

'So you keep saying!'

'And you too have been chosen.'

'You said that before, as well, but it still doesn't make any sense!'

'Christopher … You have made many decisions in your life and now you have arrived at this point. You chose your life pathway before you began to walk it. You are a first time incarnate and therefore an Innocent, the same as *all* those connected to The Circle. You were born for this and chosen as such, just as I was chosen to walk your pathway with you. *We* will be working together to protect the chosen mother; you will not be alone.'

Everything Chris heard made him feel like he was in a dream, yet everything around him remained constant, including Zambaya's captivating knowledge and otherworldly calmness. The African was both unfaltering with his explanations and his belief in what he stood for, and for all the enormity of the revelations and Chris's resistance, that steadfastness had remained throughout.

'This has got to be impossible,' sighed Chris. 'Absolutely impossible. What if I refuse; what then?'

'You cannot refuse. It is your pathway and The Truth has chosen you.'

'Then I have no say ... is that it?'

'You have already made your choice.'

'Like I can remember! And say I *don't* succeed, what then?'

'If *we* don't succeed, Christopher.'

'Alright ... if *we* don't succeed!'

'Greater hardship and suffering, and further divisions,' replied Zambaya. 'A perfect imbalance to fuel further hatred. New leaders will emerge to carry the flags of their nations, only to fall as humankind tears itself apart. The survivors of the slaughter will suffer under the New Order that will rise in the form of The Faithless. Only by unifying humanity against what seeks its demise can we prevent this. We have to succeed.'

As Zambaya continued to elaborate, it became clear that humanity's technological advances stood to be used against it. Rightly or wrongly, modern science was able to create life artificially. Genealogy and genetic engineering could be used to create the perfect human being, a new species.

'The Faithless do not accept evolution,' said Zambaya. 'They wish to exist as flesh and blood but believe only in perfection. None of their Brotherhood will bond with a physical body that is anything less than perfect.'

'Like a "pure race"?' asked Chris. 'I thought that was the Nazis' idea.'

'They were influenced,' Zambaya replied. 'Far more lay behind the Nazis and their experiments than you can imagine, and the facts are even darker than your historians will ever know. The Faithless saw an opportunity, but as advanced as Nazi scientists were, they possessed neither the tools nor the knowledge to achieve what The Faithless desired. Only by pure breeding could that objective be achieved, and the Nazis were defeated long before that. In your world today, however, your scientists have learned to create life outside of the womb and it is this advance that The Faithless will use to their advantage.'

Having grabbed Chris's attention by exposing a part of the horrifying past of The Faithless, Zambaya revealed more of what lay ahead. He explained that although The Faithless were looking for ways to break The Circle, they were unable to influence matters in the physical world without willing human accomplices.

'The Faithless enter your world through the portal of human subconscious rather like I am doing with you now,' he said. 'We use the human subconscious to teach and inspire, whereas The Faithless use it to tempt the unknowing in the form of dreams and visions, offering great rewards for the success of inhuman acts.'

A downward spiral of destruction. Man's inhumanity to man explained in the bleakest of terms. The greater the atrocity the greater the sense of injustice, and the more divided humanity became. According to Zambaya, one individual was responsible for it all.

'There is one among The Faithless who calls himself The Puppeteer. He is extremely powerful and heads The Brotherhood. He selects those he feels are best suited for them, preying on the most disaffected and vulnerable. Communication is more advanced in your world and manipulated individuals can assist him by manipulating many others. We must keep ahead of him, for he will be seeking the destroyer of the chosen woman.'

'But how can I protect somebody I've never met?' asked Chris. 'Have you stopped to think about that? And how will I go about even *finding* this woman? How do I get to her before *they* do? I mean, does *she* know anything about this?'

'You need not concern yourself with that; you will be guided,' Zambaya replied. 'The web of your life is woven in such a way that you are destined to encounter the chosen mother. She is not aware of her importance and she is safe for the time being, but we will hasten your healing as there is a need for us to work quickly.'

'So obviously this poor woman doesn't have any choice then, either, does she? Oh this is getting worse! And this … this *destroyer*. There could be hundreds; *thousands* of people that could be used! Surely this Puppeteer guy could gather an army if he wanted to. What chance do we stand against that?'

'Numbers will not win the day for The Puppeteer; he will use stealth. A lone wolf is easy to control. A pack, less so.'

'But what about what happened to me? Were The Faithless behind that? How do we know they weren't trying to break The Circle another way?'

'If they were, then they failed. And just as importantly, that event has given us the opportunity to get to know each other. You should learn to trust and not question so much, Christopher, for we can prepare you now. The Truth will make you stronger, you will become stronger than you can possibly imagine.'

But Chris could find no solace in Zambaya's words. Despite the Overseer's calming presence and powerful demeanor, he felt powerless, afraid and alone, standing on the edge of the proverbial abyss, staring into its inky blackness, and awaiting an unknown fate.

Zambaya stood up and placed a comforting hand on Chris's shoulder, sensing his pupil's intense anxiety. There was only so much that Zambaya had been permitted to share, yet nothing was more important than keeping the chosen mother safe until the envoy had been conceived. It had always been The Truth's intention to send a new envoy to humanity, and although The Faithless were no longer close to The Supreme Collective, they would have sensed the time had come due to their previous connections to that Higher Order.

An unexpected gathering of tiny blue, gold, and white lights briefly disturbed Zambaya from his considerations. He greeted them with a respectful nod, and then turned to Chris and said: 'The healers have come for you, Christopher. It is why you are here and I must leave you with them now.'

Chris looked up at the wondrous display forming in the air, a descending, twinkling cloud of tiny, iridescent orbs raining light so brightly that even Zambaya himself began to fade. It made Chris think about his family, the daunting task ahead, and how it was undoubtedly going to involve all of them. Next, he thought about The Truth and the trust being placed in him, but then the will of the healers finally engulfed him, and he could think no more.

*

Unlike Zambaya's constant and balanced spiritual realm, the physical world was hard and relentless, but in Joanne's Covent Garden photographic studio all the pressures had been worth it. The photo shoot had gone extremely well, Harvey Davies had once again excelled himself with the models, and Leonard Slater was going typically overboard about Joanne's new venture and the bold statement she was making.

Joanne had been very unsure about designing sports and leisurewear, but Samantha had pressed her mother into trying a new direction, and Leonard was convinced about the market being large enough to accommodate new lines, and that Joanne shouldn't underestimate herself.

Under Leonard's guidance, the *Middleton* label had gone from strength to strength. In fact, Joanne's company had grown to such an extent that it was difficult for her to believe how it had all begun so humbly in a tiny, rented office above a cake shop in Hampstead. Originally Joanne had only designed exclusive eveningwear, but she soon branched out to become widely recognised in the High Street for her affordable yet up-market casual ranges.

All things being equal, and despite Leonard's insistence that she didn't have anything to worry about, Joanne felt she was about due for a setback. What if things didn't work out with the new line? What if the potential buyers Leonard had spoken of ended up hating it?

Harvey noticed Joanne staring pensively into space.

'Are you alright Jo?' he asked, grinning as she jumped slightly at hearing his voice.

'Sorry Harvey, I was miles away ...'

'Sun-drenched beach? Poolside with a cocktail?'

'Neither, unfortunately!'

'Leonard's right, Jo. I can tell you're a bit worried but I think you've got something special here. I mentioned to him how *electric* the session was, and how the models really went for it. The girls just loved the whole range. You should have heard them back there!'

Joanne was flabbergasted. *Sincerity*? From *Harvey*?

'You're not still trying to get me into bed, are you, Harvey?' she asked.

Considering Joanne's earlier hostility, Leonard was pleased to see a more cordial exchange between his two charges.

'When do you think you'll be able to have the shots available, Harv?' he asked before the photographer could answer her.

'Well, I know how much you both want to move on this,' Harvey replied. 'I could easily upload the best images and email them to you tomorrow morning if you like; before, if I can.'

'That would be great!' said Joanne. 'I'd intended to be here at the office dealing with a couple of loose ends tomorrow morning, anyway, so I can take look at them while I'm here.'

'I'll get to work on them as soon as I get back. You'll be able to see them tomorrow morning for sure.'

Despite his many flaws, Harvey Davies was a very experienced fashion photographer, and praise from *him* was praise indeed. Joanne still couldn't believe his enthusiasm over the new range and was still in something of a daze once he'd packed up all of his equipment and left.

'Drink?' asked Leonard.

'I'd love one!' Joanne replied.

CHAPTER 6

The bright green display of an alarm clock glowed 8 p.m. in Wayne Terry's Kentish Town flat; an opened can of beer sat untouched on a bedside table, and a television was happily entertaining itself in the empty living room at the end of a short hallway.

Wayne had gone to sleep not long after he'd arrived home, but something had disturbed him, and he sensed he might not be alone. He sat up and listened intently, straining his ears for any sound that might be out of place, but, other than the background noise of the traffic outside and the TV in the next room, there was nothing unusual. Feeling a little foolish, he turned to lie back down, and then got the fright of his life as he saw his own body lying beside him on the bed, fast asleep!

Although it was still light outside, the room appeared to be getting darker, and Wayne got the impression that the shadows were spreading and hemming him in. *Shit*, he thought, *I'm dead!*

'No, you're not,' said a strange voice from behind him. 'I just wanted us to have a little talk.'

Wayne jumped out of his skin for a second time. The atmosphere in the room had suddenly become heavy and oppressive, to the point that he was afraid of who, or *what* he might see if he chose to look round, but unseen hands seemed intent on turning Wayne's head in the direction of his unexpected visitor anyway.

Although he had read about 'out of body experience', Wayne had never even begun to consider that the phenomenon was real, merely regarding those who'd claimed to have experienced it as nothing more than attention-seeking cranks. Yet, here he was, sitting on the end of his bed while his body slept, being addressed by a total stranger. It was bad enough in itself knowing that he wasn't in control of the situation, without the addition of the disturbingly large and imposing figure sitting in the armchair opposite. The man's long, black hair was swept back in a ponytail, exposing a high, sloping forehead. He was olive-skinned and his slightly pitted complexion gave him a rugged, near granite-like appearance. The broad face and square jaw framed a wide mouth with prominent lips, a mouth that was now set in an insane, almost surreal, grin that looked like it literally went from ear-to-ear. Wayne was drawn to that grin until his eyes met those of his guest's as they bore into him from underneath a heavy brow. Eyes black and impenetrable, like they had no irises, only large, fully dilated pupils. Eyes that stared, but didn't blink.

Wayne was terrified.

The man flared his nostrils, inhaled deeply, and grinned again.

'Relax!' he said. 'I'm just looking after my interests and I thought that it was about time we met.' He adjusted his position, appearing to make himself more comfortable. In his right hand, he sported a black cane with an ornate silver handle and as he laid it across his legs, Wayne could see that the handle was a figure of a reclining nude woman.

'I can see that we need to get properly acquainted,' the visitor said. 'So, Wayne Terry, allow me to introduce myself as The Puppeteer. It is a title which is of no consequence to you although I find it somewhat apt ... I actually have no need for a name; far too human.'

Wayne went to speak but found that he couldn't.

'What's wrong, boy, devil got your tongue?' asked The Puppeteer, his countenance changing again with the return of the lunatic grin. 'Anyway, you don't need to say anything yet, Wayne; I just need you to listen for the time being. I already know you, you see, because I've been in that exceptionally creative mind of yours for most of today. It's just such an interesting place to be you know, you should see it in there, it's *beautiful*, so much *expression*! I must confess I've been pretty impressed.'

Wayne managed an uncomfortable smile. The Puppeteer's demeanour was very threatening. It was obvious that there was a lot more to him than met the eye, and that under normal circumstances he would probably find it terribly difficult to be this approachable. Even so, his voice was strangely persuasive and hypnotic, smooth like melted chocolate, but at the same time dark, husky and inhuman. His accent sounded as if he was from everywhere at once, but there was, however, a subtle Central European lilt and an evident Texan drawl. The combination made him sound a little sarcastic, but also extremely sinister.

Abruptly, The Puppeteer stood up and began to pace the floor, quickly becoming an overpowering presence that seemed to almost glide as he put one foot in front of the other. Unexpectedly graceful and measured for one of such stature, he was a true giant, upright and barrel-chested, and well over six feet tall, maybe even seven. A full-length, luxurious trench coat was draped over his bulky shoulders, made of a material quite unlike any Wayne had ever seen. Black, with rich tones of burgundy, and highlights that appeared to shimmer in the dimness of the room, the coat was a perfect match for The Puppeteer's crimson, silky shirt, but such observations were of little interest to the wearer whose sole purpose was about making a completely different kind of impression.

'I see a lot of potential in you, Wayne,' he said. 'You are a rare talent, but those who feel that they don't fit in often are. Your kind are the ones who get a raw deal out of life, people who live in the shadows of others, abused, deprived people who need somebody to nurture them and bring their special gifts to the fore. I can do that for you, Wayne. Believe me, I know all about rejection, I know just how it feels to be discarded by my makers so we're one and the same, you and me. We can't help the way we are; we're just a little *misunderstood*, that's all. Well, how would you like to learn to bounce back just like me and kick sand in somebody else's face for a change? You know, get back at all those school bullies, for example, and make a name for yourself? I can bring it out of you, but only *you* can prove to me if I'm backing the right horse.'

Wayne's fear subsided a little with the anger generated by the memories of his school days, and he suddenly began to feel a little more at ease, more ready to listen to this man who seemed to know so much about him. The Puppeteer grinned again as he sensed the change.

'Do you like surprises, Wayne?' he asked. 'Do you like games? Do you have a sense of adventure about you? There are so many incredible things I could show you. Would you like me to show you what you're actually capable of?'

Wayne nodded.

'Good,' said The Puppeteer. 'Then let's *play*!'

Like obeying a command, the walls and ceiling of Wayne's bedroom began to fragment and fall away along with the floor until all that remained was the bed Wayne was sitting upon and his still sleeping body. At once Wayne's fear and apprehension returned at the sound of shifting and stirring all around him, an indistinct murmuring like a multitude of people about to take their seats in a theatre. Wayne could just make out indistinct figures that were nothing more than shadows *in* shadow as he peered anxiously into the gloom and realised that he was sitting in the middle of an arena being watched from the darkness by an audience without any discernable form.

The strange and abstract situation began to play on Wayne's mind, but the ordeal was only just beginning. Without warning, a shaft of eerie blue light from an ethereal spotlight struck him theatrically from the shadows, swiftly followed by another, illuminating The Puppeteer.

'Ladies and gentlemen!' The Puppeteer announced. 'Welcome to the show! It is my pleasure to introduce to you Mr Wayne Terry!'

A burst of canned applause broke out from the surrounding darkness as Wayne was introduced, and The Puppeteer began to circle him menacingly.

'We need to see how strong you are, Wayne', he said, 'because in this show there is no room for weakness. We need to see how you will measure up.'

Wayne wondered why it felt like several men had passed by even though he could see only one. The Puppeteer's presence seemed to be growing more powerful by the second, his intensity reaching out into the depths of Wayne's soul with cold, invisible fingers that made him feel he was being squeezed slowly inside.

'How far do you think I am able to take you?' The Puppeteer asked, leaning slowly towards Wayne until his lifeless, unblinking eyes were only inches away from those of his unwitting contestant. 'Granted, you have the potential, but talent is nothing without direction. Do you have what it takes to let me be your guide?'

Canned audience gasps and whispers broke the silence, but as hard as Wayne tried, he couldn't break away from the gaze that was cutting right into him and chilling him to the core of his being. The Puppeteer drew back, grinning, and Wayne was temporarily released.

'Of course', said The Puppeteer. 'You must understand that my kind assistance with the direction of your life carries a small price.'

Wayne went to speak but The Puppeteer cut him off before he could take so much as an intake of breath.

'You can have your say when I've finished, Wayne,' he said. 'But not before. It's the rules of the game, you see, me first and then you, but even though there *is* a price, there is also a great reward for success. I always believe in saving the best for my high achievers but don't fret, you *do* have a choice, although I genuinely believe that when I've finished, you'll be more than willing to make a deal.'

Ironic laughter from the 'audience' was followed by rapturous applause. Wayne was now even more firmly in the vice-like grip of fear, yet he couldn't help but be curious about what was going to happen next. He knew he couldn't run; he'd already accepted that he was completely helpless, and besides that, it was probably safer to go with the flow and take his chances with what he *could* see rather than what might lurk in the shadows around him.

Abruptly, flickering video screens appeared in those very shadows, and the odd sensation Wayne had had of being squeezed internally returned.

'Well, look at our little soldier,' said The Puppeteer as images from Wayne's childhood began flashing up in vivid, living colour. 'No clouds on the horizon then, were there? Ah ... but who's this I see? Oh yes, it's the mercurial, bi-curious lodger!'

Peels of hysterical laughter erupted from the formless gathering as Wayne's mind relived walking in on Monique and his mother. He clutched his head in his hands in a fruitless attempt to stop the flow of stolen recollections.

'SHUT UP!' he shouted. 'SHUT THE FUCK UP!'

To his amazement, the laughter stopped, but by then he was at his father's funeral, watching at the graveside as the coffin was lowered into the ground, watching the blank, expressionless face of his mother through stinging tears.

'Is this a little painful for you, Wayne?' asked The Puppeteer. 'I'll make no apology for the moment as it is the key to your unique gift, the key to the lock that I need to pick.'

'You said you were going to help,' Wayne whispered. 'What kind of man are you?'

'Oh, I'm more than just a *man*, Wayne ... I'm way beyond *anything* that you can ever begin to imagine, but I am also your friend. Keep watching and you'll find out what I've already been able to inspire in you.'

The Puppeteer's audience began to take even more interest, and expectant whispers echoed in the surrounding darkness along with the rustling of unseen bottoms on invisible seats.

'You see,' said The Puppeteer. 'Everything was all fine and dandy until that Monique came along and then it all went wrong for you, didn't it? If it hadn't been for *her*, you would have had a perfectly normal life and your father would possibly still be alive. She used you, rejected you, made a fool of you, and deep inside you longed for revenge, a chance to get even. What you *lacked* was the know-how, but luckily I was on hand to open your eyes and show you how to get in touch with your true *feelings*!'

Gasps of wonder filled the air as new pictures flashed up onto the screens, and Wayne stared in disbelief at the sight of Monique being pinned down and viciously raped. Then he realised with horror that *he* was the assailant.

'No!' he said. 'Please ... this ... this is *impossible* ... it *has* to be!'

'Oh no,' said The Puppeteer. 'I can assure you that was all your own work, well, that part of it anyway. Don't you just love it when they put up a fight? I mean, give her credit; she really had a go, didn't she? And then you finished things off nicely with that belt! What a creative masterstroke!'

Wayne was speechless as he watched the struggle and the cruelty that he alone had inflicted upon the only woman he'd ever loved. With the sound of the audience baying and celebrating Monique's violent and horrific end, it all became too much. Wayne put his head in his hands and wept.

'Grief?' asked The Puppeteer. 'I just don't understand you, Wayne! The Wicked Witch is dead, and you are under her spell no more. Now you can concentrate on your future without having to concern yourself with your past.'

'But I *couldn't* have done that ...!'

'Oh, but you *did*.'

'No! It's a lie! This is all bullshit!'

Wayne could feel anger building inside, rising like an uncontrollable surge of bile. The Puppeteer smirked as he sensed Wayne's rage.

'Why don't you just face it, Wayne?' he said. 'Your potential knows no bounds. You could be a real star!'

'But you've turned me into a fucking murderer!'

'*I'd* prefer to call you a Cleanser.'

'A what …?'

'A Cleanser. I don't want the *meek* to inherit the Earth; I want it for the strong and the worthy, for people like you and me. I have a vision of how things should be, and I happen to have a unique task set aside for you, which is to remove the things that stand in my way and conveniently dispose of them, especially *this* little matter.'

Suddenly Wayne was introduced to another missing memory. He was back on Hampstead Heath, peering through some bushes at a young woman and masturbating at the sight of her. Hysterical laughter erupted from the shadows once more, and Wayne was again stunned into silence, but The Puppeteer was about to up the ante yet again.

'Wayne, I'd like to share something I feel is important for you to know. I think I need to remind you that there is a problem with nature in that it is designed to be flawed. The females of any species get to make all the choices and humanity is no different. Women sit back and lap it all up, while men fight among themselves for prizes that might still reject them. As a Cleanser, you can change all that. Dominant males like *you* don't need to fight for females when they *themselves* should have the right to choose. This one even had the nerve to laugh at you after you had gone out of your way to show her your need, laugh at *you*, Wayne … remind you of anyone? She laughed at you after you'd tried to give her everything you had. You display your desires for her, and she mocks your good intentions … I don't think that's the way it's supposed to be! But that's the problem when you're a nail without a hammer though, isn't it, Wayne? People tend to ridicule you, but with me as your hammer *anything* is possible.'

The Puppeteer stepped back. The fuse had been lit. Wayne could feel a disturbance on the bed beside him as his hitherto sleeping self slowly began to sit up. Now he was two!

Enthusiastic applause and whoops of delight burst out, an eruption of joy at the awakening.

'Ladies and gentlemen!' said The Puppeteer. 'It is time for the final eliminator! We have two contestants but only *one* prize. Which one of them listened to me today? Which one of them is the Cleanser? The successful contestant will be justly rewarded. I took the liberty of choosing a little something for the victor's personal enjoyment, so consider it a little token of my appreciation for your time tonight, gentlemen. This little toy is the prize for the winner to play with whenever they like, but only if they choose to join me in my crusade. I think it is time I showed them what riches are available to the lucky winner. I think it is time I introduced them to our beautiful Naomi.'

A figure clad in a silken, hooded robe strode confidently into the centre of the arena, accompanied by a crescendo of yet more wonderous applause.

'Nature may be flawed but *we* are perfect,' said The Puppeteer, turning his attention to Wayne and his alter ego. 'There is no room for weakness among us. Let the eliminator begin and the choices be made. Tell me, gentlemen, is Naomi not perfect?'

As The Puppeteer asked the question, he theatrically removed the flimsy robe from the figure to reveal a strikingly beautiful, naked young woman. The woman took a few steps forward and stood before Wayne and his other self, her tempting mouth curving provocatively into a half grin.

Naomi's eyes were as piercingly black as The Puppeteer's, but nowhere near as dead. Long raven locks of curly, dark hair cascaded over her broad yet feminine shoulders, and there wasn't a blemish on the fair skin that hugged her flawless body. Wayne could only wonder at Naomi's perfectly proportioned curves, fixated by the subtle tensing and flexing of the muscles in her thighs and buttocks as she walked between him and his second side. Abruptly, Naomi turned and came back over to Wayne and pressed herself against him. He could feel the firmness of her breasts and the hardness of her nipples, and yet he was completely impotent in the face of her growing arousal.

Frustrated by the lack of response, Naomi turned her attention to Wayne's apparently far less inhibited other self.

'Naomi has made her choice!' said The Puppeteer. 'Now it's time for our winner to make his. Does he wish to seal the bond and make the contract?'

Wayne could only look on helplessly as the decision was made for him. His other personality lay back invitingly and Naomi slowly eased herself down onto his second side's erection. Before Wayne knew it, he was one with himself, staring up at Naomi's nubile form as she rode him, her gasps of pleasure bursting into his ears as she bore down on him, intensifying her efforts. There was a surge coming, impossible to fight, like an unstoppable tide, and as Naomi cried out in a moment of shuddering, all-consuming ecstasy, Wayne, too, climaxed, and sealed The Puppeteer's deal.

The Puppeteer allowed himself to be amused. Sometimes he even amazed himself at his ability to buy souls. The boy was totally smitten with Naomi, proving once again that there wasn't a human entity that didn't have its price. They were all so weak, and *this* little worm had been just as easy to turn. The Puppeteer detested worms; in his opinion they were nothing more than a complete waste of good, wholesome flesh, but it was a flesh for which he had a glorious ideal. Humanity was unfortunately necessary if he were to achieve his aim, and maybe the worm called Wayne would be different to the majority of his flawed and imperfect species. However, where would he, The Puppeteer, be, were it not for human weakness? Perhaps he *did* owe them something after all.

Wayne's usual timidity had been replaced by the confidence of his far more self-assured, second personality. He and Naomi were once again becoming passionately embroiled with each other upon the bed, but The Puppeteer decided that their playtime should be curtailed. The reward for the successful completion of the contract was made clear to Wayne, that his death, when it inevitably came, would unite him with Naomi for eternity. Naomi would also be there as an occasional treat for him to enjoy in the days to come, ensuring his hunger for the cleansing would be kept at its peak.

To Wayne, it was like a dream come true, but to The Puppeteer the symbolism was nothing more than a dog owner giving their pet a reward for good behaviour. Wayne had no idea that he was being sucked into a world that would accept nothing other than his absolute submission, as proved when his essence was sent back to the world of humankind with the ruthlessness of a disenchanted parent clearing away the toys of an untidy child.

The Puppeteer's new puppet had been safely put back in its box, leaving The Puppeteer free to focus upon other business that needed his attention. There was another light among the realm of Innocents to which he was being especially drawn, like a moth to an irresistible flame.

An extremely special and succulent light, indeed …

CHAPTER 7

The normal routine of London life continued into the night. Tourists anxious to take in its many attractions talked excitedly to each other in a multitude of exotic languages. Taxis hard-pressed to keep up with demand cut through the traffic any way they could and hooted their frustrations at any visitors lost in the metropolis. Lovers old and young walked hand-in-hand, altogether too wrapped up in each other to notice anybody else, while elsewhere, partygoers reveled in nightclubs, high on enjoyment and adrenalin.

On the outside it was just another ordinary night in a pulsating capital, but in another plane of existence, unseen by human eyes and unheard by human ears, the battle lines were being drawn.

As the sun had set and the night had thrown its shroud across the city, an unknown threat to humanity lay dormant, waiting to be unleashed. It wasn't a global plague or an irresistible army, nor was it a nuclear holocaust or some other cataclysmic disaster. It was an insignificant young man, a victim of his own misfortune, a manifestation born of humanity's cruelty to one of its own. Unaware of the magnitude of the deal he had struck with The Puppeteer, Wayne Terry slept peacefully in his bed.

Naomi was gazing longingly at him, yearning, waiting to satisfy his desires and her own lust. Soon the chosen woman would be hunted down. The death of a single individual would be all it would take to overcome The Truth's last throw of the dice, and how much easier could *that* be? Naomi smiled as she thought about living and breathing again, inhabiting a human shell, and experiencing the pleasures of the flesh that her unfortunate human condition had once denied her.

It was what The Puppeteer had promised when they'd first met. He'd explained everything and made it all so clear. She had carried out what had been required of her and he'd kept his word in making her a perfect woman.

Many of the people in Naomi's small Alabama town had either mocked or scorned her. There was no room for people like *her* in the Bible Belt of the United States. The local pastor said she was immoral, fit only for eternal damnation, but it had been her *parents'* fault she'd been born as a boy. Naomi felt no remorse for slaying them and the rest of the church's congregation when she'd sealed everybody inside and burned it to the ground. The agonised screams of the dying had been music to Naomi's ears, and watching them fighting to escape their blazing prison had brought with it the purest sense of victory and elation.

When her last moments came as a male, the agony of the flesh-searing flames had been worth every excruciating second, for it had brought a fitting release from the hell of living in that body. The intense heat had totally stripped it of flesh, and nothing about the charred remains would ever have resembled the body of a young man. The Puppeteer had welcomed her spirit into his Brotherhood, and the transformation had begun. What had once been a ruddy, uninteresting complexion became beauty, and perfect curves appeared in place of once straight and uninspiring shapelessness. The skin he gave her was soft and sensitive, her body, although taut and defined, subtly yielding.

'Norman' was gone, and Naomi had been released.

Naomi gazed at her reflection in Wayne's bedroom mirror and began to explore her flawless female form, imagining Wayne's hands squeezing her full and delightfully cupped breasts as she rode his magnificent erection. She had been created to enjoy the deepest and most fulfilling of pleasures, and one such desire needed to be satisfied right then. Unfortunately, Wayne was temporarily unavailable, so it was an itch that Naomi was just going to have to scratch for herself.

*

While Naomi fantasised, Zambaya watched over Chris, scrutinising the healing lights as they danced over his pupil's unconscious form. Zambaya knew that Christopher John Edward Ryan would have little recollection of their previous meetings once he came out of his coma, but a strong link had been established, the knowledge was in place, and the doorway to Chris's subconscious could now be opened at will. The rest was all about trust and his subject's willingness to accept.

But guarding Chris meant that Zambaya was part of the material plane, and therefore uncomfortably close to the realm of The Faithless. It was during his vigil that he had sensed a vibration in the core of that parallel world. Such a disturbance could only have been caused by the most powerful Dark Heart of them all crossing over into the physical dimension, a suspicion confirmed when Zambaya noticed the Innocent Lights circulating in the city reduce in number, by one.

As the solitary light vanished, The Faithless hoards had rejoiced, but such jubilation wasn't merely because another Innocent had succumbed to their influence, it was because The Puppeteer had selected the chosen mother's assassin.

Zambaya bowed his head, and began to pray.

*

In Winnington Road, Hampstead, Joanne Middleton was trying to find her front door key in the bowels of her handbag. *That bloody Slater bloke*, she thought. *He always manages to get me drunk and I always let him, the exploiting sod, taking advantage of me like that just because I've got a soft spot for him.*

Joanne laughed loudly, and then looked around nervously to make sure that there was nobody else around who might have heard her cackling to herself on her doorstep. Thankfully, she was quite alone, and she'd also managed to locate her door key.

Joanne's first attempt at finding the keyhole failed, and the next was equally as unsuccessful. She took a deep breath and paused for a second.

About that 'soft spot' ... Joanne really *did* fancy Leonard and cringed as she remembered asking him if he'd ever considered sleeping with a woman, preferably *her*. Leonard had nearly choked on his vodka and tonic, but unfortunately for Joanne it was an offer he was going to have to pass up as she had the 'wrong parts!'

'Oh my *God*, I can't *believe* I asked him that!' she whispered to herself, pressing her forehead despairingly against the irritatingly resistant front door. 'What the hell was I thinking?'

Eventually, the fatuous little key did its thing in the tormenting little slot, and the door opened invitingly, but Joanne found herself having to open it again to reclaim the bunch of keys she'd left dangling outside. *Come on, Jo*, she urged mentally, *sort yourself out, woman!*

Coffee ...

She needed coffee ...

No, she *had* to have coffee. To hell with it being so late!

Without turning on any lights, Joanne started to make her way tipsily across the entrance hall towards the kitchen, only to be unexpectedly felled, painfully onto her hands and knees, by something unseen in the darkness. The bunch of keys jangled on the floorboards as she tried to get to her feet, but the determined and enthusiastic shape came at her again.

'HARLEY!' groaned Joanne, trying unsuccessfully to push him away. 'What the hell's got into you? Get off ... go on! Back in your bed! *Bad* dog! *Bad* ... dog!'

Harley rolled over onto his back and whined pitifully at the sound of Joanne's displeasure. He'd only been saying 'hello' in his own way, and Joanne reassured him very quickly that she wasn't angry by hugging him and burying her face in the furry scruff of his neck.

'Oh I'm sorry, Baby Boy,' she said. 'I know you're only pleased to see me. Here, have some cuddles with Mama.'

While trying to get into her house, Joanne had been regretting her clumsy approach to one of the only *two* welcome male influences in her life. Now she was lying drunk in her entrance hall hugging the other.

'Dammit, Harley, why can't you be a man?' she sighed, slowly getting to her knees. 'Go on, then, you great lummox, cuddle's over … back in your bed!'

Harley gave Joanne an extra slobbery kiss for good measure before padding off obediently into the kitchen. He blinked slightly as she switched on the kitchen light and gazed lovingly at her, but he didn't seem to want to lie down. Joanne suspected he might want to go outside and opened the back door, but Harley stayed put. He seemed unsettled, and kept pacing around the kitchen; even his overzealous greeting had bordered more on relief than pleasure. Perhaps he was still on full alert having seen off the flasher that morning or felt the need to admonish her for staying out so late. Either way, Joanne decided not to dwell on it; her mind was once again full of the need for coffee, but her heart sank when she opened the fridge.

'No bloody milk *again*, then!' she said, throwing her arms out in frustration. 'That bloody daughter of mine … why can't she just go out and bloody buy some when it runs out?'

Harley tilted his head to one side, unsure about Joanne's outburst, so she tickled the top of his head and smiled at his confused expression.

'I know it's not your fault, boy,' she whispered. 'I just felt the need to tell somebody about it and you were the only one here. Thanks for listening!'

The idea of a coffee had suddenly lost its appeal. A combination of a one-sided conversation with Harley and the thought of having to have her coffee black appeared to have sobered Joanne up enough to pour herself a large glass of water instead, and she headed upstairs to her bedroom.

Joanne had seen Samantha's car in the driveway upon coming home, so the fact that it was so quiet in the house meant Samantha was obviously in bed. That was when it struck Joanne that this was what it was going to be like when her daughter finally left home. The thought of being all alone in such a big house made her feel strangely vulnerable all of a sudden, especially as it made her recall a local news report she'd stumbled across on her mobile while on the way home in the taxi. A woman had been found dead in a very select area of Mill Hill, and although the investigation was ongoing and few details had been released, the police were treating the death as 'suspicious'. In Joanne's experience of hearing such terms, the police were undoubtedly looking at a murder inquiry. The poor woman's body had been found in her own home, too! What kind of people *did* these things? Wasn't anywhere safe anymore?

The disquieting thought made Joanne unconsciously quicken her pace as she made her way upstairs to close a pair of heavy red curtains dressing the large panoramic window at the top of the staircase. Having swiftly negotiated the task with one hand, and determined to be separated from the outside world, she immediately set about attending to two other windows located at either end of the landing. During the day the area was bathed in bright, natural light, but at night the responsibility to illuminate the landing's considerable length fell upon two cut glass chandeliers. Having drawn the curtains at one end, Joanne had to march past five immaculately glossed white bedroom doors, a bathroom, and an airing cupboard, in order to repeat the exercise at the other. She was still deeply involved with her thoughts of Mill Hill as she approached the last window, but then she froze. Reflected in the glass and standing directly behind her was the leering figure of a most enormous man.

Consumed by panic, unable to scream or even breathe in the suddenly inexplicably heavy air, Joanne's terrified eyes stared helplessly into those of the towering reflection. Instantly, its craggy, macabre features broke into an ever widening, manic grin, an expression of evil and insanity being coldly mirrored against the backdrop of the night. The shock was enough to trigger Joanne's survival instincts, and her previously frozen lungs permitted her the luxury of a strangled shriek as she spun round to face the intruder ...

Incredibly, Joanne found that she was completely alone, her frantic breathing the only sound to break the near overpowering silence. There was a hollow *thump* as the tumbler of water she'd been holding fell from her hand, and all she could do was watch it roll serenely away across the carpet, through a spreading patch of glistening wetness.

Joanne didn't believe in ghosts, but there was no way that this had been her imagination. There had definitely been somebody, some*thing*, standing there behind her, its unearthly features clearly defined, staring back at her in the window. Just thinking about it made Joanne gag with renewed fear; her legs were threatening to give way beneath her and she had to use the windowsill for support.

And then she remembered something else ... Samantha!

Without risking another glance into the darkness outside, Joanne swept the curtains across the previously exposed windowpanes and hurried to her daughter's bedroom. She paused briefly and took a deep breath before opening the door, heaving a huge mental sigh of relief that everything on the other side appeared to be perfectly normal. Samantha was sleeping on top of her duvet, wearing a baggy T-shirt instead of her usual pyjamas. The air in the room was muggy, and obviously too warm for her underneath her duvet, but she still looked peaceful and far away, slightly parted lips wearing the faintest hint of a smile, her breathing making the softest of sounds. A few tresses of hair had dared to trespass onto the picture of serenity and Samantha stirred a little as her mother brushed them gently away from her face, the movements causing the makeshift nightshirt to ride up and expose her underwear. Joanne gently lowered it back down as though protecting her daughter's modesty from unseen prying eyes, and seeing as things were all as they should be, decided it was time to leave Samantha to the whim of her dreams.

Joanne checked left and right, up and down the passageway before closing Samantha's bedroom door quietly behind her, and then hurriedly completed the three steps it took to get to her own bedroom directly opposite. She cautiously turned the door handle and peered anxiously inside, watching the shadows flee from the encroaching shaft of light only to mockingly reestablish themselves in the furthermost recesses of the room. Unable to step into the darkness, Joanne fumbled for the light switch before she entered, but even though nothing appeared to be out of the ordinary it still took a significant amount of courage for her just to cross the threshold and shut herself in.

All she could think about was the reflection in the window. Perhaps it really *had* just been her imagination. Maybe it had been a strange kind of optical illusion. But however hard Joanne tried, she couldn't convince herself that it hadn't been something more sinister. Out of the corners of her eyes, once familiar objects began to assume forms fit to draw a suspicious gaze, and there was the most terrible feeling of being watched from another world. The clothes Joanne was wearing smelled of Leonard's favorite Italian restaurant, her hair felt lank and gritty, and yet any desire to freshen herself up in the bedroom's ensuite was tempered by unwelcome thoughts of the shower scene from *Psycho*. Not even the simple task of make-up removal was an option for fear of what might be lurking behind her in the mirror.

In Joanne's beleaguered mind, the dead eyes of the grinning vision were cutting into her again.

Across on the other side of the landing, Samantha could hear a strange sound in her bedroom. It sounded like breathing but it was ragged, impaired, like somebody trying to breathe through thick mucus. Samantha lay still in an oddly suffocating atmosphere, *very* still, listening intently. There it was again: breathing, laboured and heavy, except that it was closer now and there was a strange animal-like smell, musty, like damp wool.

A scrabbling sound made Samantha jump. It seemed to have come from right next to her, and at the same time the smell began to get stronger. Samantha could feel beads of perspiration beginning to tingle on her face. Did she see movement over by the TV in the corner? She strained her eyes, trying to see into the darkness, but nothing stirred until something bulky jumped onto her bed and sat heavily upon her shins. Samantha could see a large canine shape silhouetted against the window, and she was finally able to breathe a sigh of relief. *Harley*, she thought, *but what was he doing upstairs and how the heck had he got into her room?* She leaned over to her bedside table and switched on the light.

'Har–,' she began, but the name got stuck in her throat in horror at what was sitting there instead.

Two deep-set, crimson orbs stared balefully out at her from a cruelly deformed human face, a face set perversely on the heavy head of a wolf-like creature. Its broad, bony forehead was gnarled and ridged, and sloped down in a convex profile that ended at a huge, vicious muzzle. Samantha tried to scream, but her throat was so tight that all that came out was a strangled whisper. At the same time, a pair of nostrils located obscenely between the creature's eyes began opening and closing as it took in her scent, but by then, there was more movement in the room. Another beast was prowling. Although uniquely different from the one on her legs, it was equally as grotesque, having what appeared to be two faces until it became apparent that it was one, savagely cleaved in half.

'Hello, Samantha!' said a huge, husky-voiced man who had just appeared in the room. 'These little unfortunates are called Manforms, in case you were wondering. Perhaps you'd like me to call them off? They answer only to me and only I can protect you from them. Would you like me to save you?'

Samantha's heart was pounding so hard it felt like it wanted to burst out of her chest, and her panic-stricken legs wanted to explode into a run, but the monstrosity sitting on them was far too heavy.

'All you have to do is say 'yes' to me,' said the giant stranger. 'And then we can start talking about being friends.'

He sat down on the edge of Samantha's bed and began stroking one of her thighs. Samantha flinched at the unexpected touch but was completely powerless to do anything about it.

'Who … who are you?' she asked. 'And how do you know my name?'

'Oh, I know *every*body's name, my dear … I know because I am everywhere.'

At that moment the man looked up, and Samantha found herself staring into the most frightening eyes she had ever seen. She wanted to look away from the blackness reaching into her, but the unblinking gaze had enslaved her, and the blood in her veins felt like it was turning to ice. Grinning slowly, the man placed a large hand on his barrel-chest, and said: 'I, Samantha, am known simply as The Puppeteer. I actually have no use for a name because I can be anything to anybody, but I must say how pleasing it is for me to make your acquaintance.'

The smoothly spoken words had dripped with intent, but there had been no feeling in the sinister rasping tones that had delivered them. The Puppeteer was as hollow as his gaze, his vile grin and leering expression something straight out of bedlam, or hell. Samantha began to struggle grimly with the fear and desperation of her hopeless situation, but it was a battle she was always going to lose.

'Tears, Samantha?' asked The Puppeteer, cocking his head quizzically to one side. 'Are tears any way to greet a guest? I mean, I've come here just to be with *you* and see for myself the quality of the choice. I'm going to be your biggest fan, you know; this is just the *beginning* of our relationship, so why don't we try and entertain each other? How about we play a game? I like games. Would you like to play a game with me now and see how much we could do together?'

As much as Samantha couldn't make sense of what was being said, an inner voice was telling her she had to resist the offer at all costs. The Puppeteer, however, was quick to advise against any such bravado.

'My Manforms have your scent and I can come to you whenever I wish,' he said. 'Perhaps you might like to take that into consideration before you try and shut me out. Come on, Samantha, darling, just one tiny little game … for your honoured guest. What do you say? What have you got to lose? Wouldn't you like to see what you might be missing out on?'

'No … I wouldn't.'

'Oh well, then, I can only assume that if you don't want to play with *me*, you *must* want to play with my Manforms instead. My word, you *are* a spunky little thing! You see, my dear, a Manform is a failure getting a second chance to please me. Those who fall short of my high expectations are always very keen to impress me when they get another opportunity to prove themselves, and you can't *imagine* how these two could amuse themselves with a pretty little thing like *you*.'

The creature by Samantha's bed began to grin, its head splitting in half as it did so, and sticky saliva began to dribble like melting candle wax from the cavernous mouth of the other miscreation as it regarded her with sudden and renewed interest from its position on her shins.

Samantha went to scream, but The Puppeteer stopped her by thrusting two fingers of his right hand into her mouth.

'Come on, Samantha, let's play!' he said. 'Show me what you're made of …'

Without thinking, Samantha bit down as hard as she could, severing The Puppeteer's fingers which instantly began trying to crawl down her throat. She desperately tried pulling them out, but it was as if she were trying to grab a pair of slippery, squirming eels. Panic set in at the terrifying feeling of being choked and she began to retch violently, ejecting a foul-smelling, sticky black fluid that spattered onto her thighs.

'Perfect!' said The Puppeteer when he saw the mess. 'And now I will always have this part of you.' Grinning once more, he casually reclaimed his unattached digits that were writhing in the tar-like substance and took a small glass jar from inside his coat into which he scraped a small amount of Samantha's bile. Then he reattached his fingers.

'There,' he said, stretching and flexing them. 'No harm done.'

Samantha could only stare, mortified.

'No!' she whispered. 'No! NO! NOOOOO …!'

Joanne reacted immediately to the terrified shrieks coming from her daughter's bedroom, and burst in to find Samantha sitting bolt upright on her bed. She was staring straight ahead into thin air, but when Joanne tried to get close, Samantha began shouting hysterically and forced her away.

'GET AWAY FROM ME!' she screamed. 'GET AWAY FROM ME!'

'Samantha, it's me, it's Mum …!'

'NO! You're HIM! You're HIM and you're just PLAYING A GAME WITH ME!'

'No, Sammy, it's me, it really is … You must have had a bad dream or something, but it's over now …'

Samantha's face was streaming with sweat, her eyes red and tearful.

'I don't think it's over … I think it's just beginning …' she whispered. 'He told me. I don't ever want to go to sleep again, Mum, you won't believe what happened to me, what I saw …'

Once Samantha began to speak about her nightmare, it was as if she wanted to get it all off her chest at once so she would never have to speak of it again. 'The Puppeteer', 'Manforms' – Joanne was bombarded with the most bizarre titles and names. Given the normal strength of her daughter's character, it was difficult for Joanne to recall having ever seen her in such a state about *anything*. Fearing that Samantha was going to upset herself again, Joanne calmly argued that there was nothing to worry about and that it had just been a bad dream, but Samantha was having none of it.

'Whatever you say, it didn't *feel* like a dream. It wasn't *just* a nightmare. I know it sounds stupid, Mum, but this was something else, it was just too real! I could actually *smell* those bloody creatures and you can't smell in a dream. This man, who called himself The Puppeteer, was huge, massive, with really long black hair, and he was wearing this really weird looking long black coat type of thing. He had these terrible black eyes and this – this really *evil* grin. I remember him saying something about a choice, like I'd been chosen for something, but he didn't say what …'

Samantha noticed her mother had stopped paying attention and the colour had completely drained from her face. As implausible as it seemed, Samantha could only come to one conclusion.

'Have seen him too, then?' she asked.

'I don't know, Sam …'

'You have, haven't you?'

It had only been an account of a terrifyingly vivid bad dream up until Samantha's graphic description of her nightmare tormentor, but then everything had changed.

'I was hoping it was just my imagination,' said Joanne. 'Tonight … just a few minutes ago, out there on the landing, I saw something that sounds just like the man you saw in your dream. But that's impossible, surely …'

The sound of something approaching interrupted the discussion. Joanne's flesh instantly began to crawl at the thought of what might be coming along the passageway towards Samantha's bedroom. They both held their breath, but to their shared relief it was only Harley. Slowly he came creeping into the room, fearful, head down, ears back in submission. Downstairs in the kitchen was his place and he was normally very obedient, but it was clear he didn't want to be down there all on his own. Joanne reached out to give him some comfort and reassurance because she too sensed that the atmosphere in the house had changed. Suddenly, it felt dark and oppressive, tainted by something beyond comprehension, and she no longer felt like she wanted to be there. The property wasn't truly hers anyway; it was part of the divorce settlement, and even *that* had been nothing more than a hollow victory.

It had been almost a year since she and Samantha had last visited Greenoaks, the beautiful cottage they owned in a sleepy Hertfordshire village, and it suddenly occurred to Joanne that another visit was long overdue. Every part of her wanted to just pack up and leave but she'd had too much to drink and driving anywhere was totally out of the question.

Faced with no other choice but to wait until morning, Joanne, Samantha, and Harley would spend the rest of the night huddled together for comfort on Joanne's king-sized double bed.

CHAPTER 8

Samantha woke to the sound of her mother rattling through her large fitted wardrobe, and a fair collection of clothes, mainly jeans and casual tops, had already been placed in a suitcase at the end of the bed. Outside, another crystal-clear day had dawned, and shafts of early morning sunlight were breaking into the room through a small gap in the unopened curtains.

Joanne's purposeful activity had disturbed a myriad tiny dust particles that danced erratically in the rays, and when Samantha turned over, the trespassing beams caught her full in the face. The unexpected glare made her sit up, abruptly.

'Good morning, Sam', said Joanne, 'and how are we doing today?'

Samantha rubbed her eyes, and then squinted at her mother's alarm clock. 'Mum, it's Saturday. What are you doing? And why are you up so early? It's obscene!'

'I've been up for nearly an hour … I've charged around the garden with Harley, had breakfast and now I'm packing. I've done some of yours already.'

Thick-headed and groggy, Samantha felt like she had a hangover. Her mouth was dry, her throat scratchy, and her girl boxers felt like they were threatening to cut her in half.

'Packing?' she asked, attempting to deal with her rebellious underwear. 'What for?'

'Well, I think we're about due for a break so I thought that we could go out to the cottage for a while,' Joanne replied. 'I didn't say anything about it last night, but I think we could all do a lot worse than getting away from here for a while, wouldn't you agree?'

Samantha shuddered at the memory of her night terror. Having somehow managed to get back to sleep afterwards, she felt strangely uncomfortable with herself once fully awake, and there was a persistent sense of confusion, like a part of her had been changed in some way. Despite her best efforts to resist him, Samantha couldn't help feeling that The Puppeteer had managed to get some kind of hold over her, and the idea of a few days away in the country was very appealing. Perhaps he wouldn't be able to find her if she were somewhere else.

Puzzled by the lack of response, Joanne stopped what she was doing.

'Sammy?' she asked. 'Did you hear what I just said?'

'Oh yeah, sorry … yes, definitely, that sounds like a great idea.'

Samantha sounded flat, distant and preoccupied. Joanne supposed that it was only to be expected, and even her *own* bright and breezy, early riser act was nothing more than a façade for her daughter's benefit.

'Let's try not to dwell on anything,' she said. 'I'm sure all we need is a break to sort us both out. There's got to be a rational explanation for last night.'

'Last night was beyond *anything* rational.'

'Well, perhaps all the excitement of yesterday got to us more than we thought.'

'But it didn't have anything to *do* with what happened to us on the Heath, did it, Mum? And as for what *you* saw just happening to be exactly the same thing as me but in a totally different way? Try explaining *that*!'

Sometimes Joanne regretted having brought Samantha up to be so direct; trying to gloss over matters only insulted her daughter's intelligence and sounded hollow at best.

'I can't,' Joanne sighed. 'I can't explain it at all.'

'Like I said, then … beyond anything rational. Anyway, if we're heading off out, I'd better start getting myself ready.'

With all the upheaval of the night before, the plans Joanne had made about going into the office had all but slipped her mind, but there would be no need for any rushing around on Samantha's part.

'You're going into the office *today*?' asked Samantha.

'Only to check some emails and have a browse through some images from yesterday's shoot,' Joanne replied. 'I'll pick you up when I've finished and then we can go straight off. You've got all morning, so why don't you try and get some more sleep?'

'Well, how about me and Harley come with you?'

'You know we can't take Harley with us, Sam, because he's not allowed in the office building. We'd have to come back and get him after.'

'But if we take him to the office, we could go straight to the cottage from there. I know *I* don't want to stay here by myself and I don't think it's fair to leave Harley here on his own either!'

Joanne reiterated that it was the rules, but Samantha was adamant.

'Mum, it's Saturday!' she said. 'There won't be anybody else there! Who's going to know if Harley comes in with us?'

'Well, what about CCTV?'

'Jeez … Look, if it bothers you that much, I'll even stay in the car with him if it comes to it! We *can't* leave him here on his own after last night, we just can't.'

Harley was more than just their dog, he was a part of their family, and through her evident apprehension Samantha had made a very valid point. If *they* didn't want to stay in the house, why should *he* have to?

'Okay then,' sighed Joanne. 'Harley comes too. I was only thinking about the rules, but as long as you're happy to wait with him if needs be, I suppose it shouldn't be a problem. Anyway, another slight issue is that I'm ready for the off and you're still in your nightwear, so if we're all going to be leaving together, you'd better get a wriggle on!'

Two of the house's five bedrooms had ensuite showers, Joanne's being one and Samantha's the other, but Samantha found the thought of being alone in her own ensuite unsettling.

'It's fine, you can use mine,' said Joanne. 'I'll just go and grab you a couple of fresh towels. Do you want me to get any stuff together for you while you're in the shower?'

Samantha politely declined. Despite having reservations about her ensuite, she was happy enough to sort out her own clothes.

While her daughter showered, Joanne went to the airing cupboard for the towels and noticed that the landing curtains were still closed. It was as she made for the nearest window that she accidentally kicked something lying on the floor. It was the glass tumbler she'd dropped the previous night, and as she bent down to pick it up, her hands began to shake. Even though the cream walls of the landing were being kissed by a soft, pink hue from the brilliance of the daylight filtering through the red, unopened curtains, it was still a supreme effort for Joanne to part them.

The intense coldness.

The insane grin.

The penetrating stare of those empty, expressionless eyes.

It all came flooding back, the overwhelming fear, everything.

As the curtains swished open, Joanne heaved a huge sigh of relief that it was a familiar view of a neighbouring house that greeted her at the window, and not a vision fit for a nightmare.

The sooner they could all make their getaway, the better.

*

Switching off the TV and turning on the radio was just about the worst thing Wayne Terry could have done. The Saturday morning children's cartoons were far more welcoming than a regional news broadcast reporting on a brutal killing in the local area.

The name, Monique Dacourt of Mill Hill, had sprung out of the speaker and cut clean through Wayne's soul. He could remember being in Mill Hill, but nothing about how he'd got to his mother's house, or how he'd even managed to get home.

Wayne despairingly put his head in his hands but pulled them away instantly. Why was his right eyebrow so sore to the touch? And what was all that dirt under his nails, dirt that smelt like … like, floor polish? Why were his knuckles grazed? What the hell had happened? What the hell had he done?

Monique had been so pleased when she'd opened the door to him; she was still beautiful and had changed so little in all those years. In fact, it had been nice to see her again despite all the hurt. She'd been so friendly, exuberant, so full of life. What if *he* had taken that life from her? Although Wayne knew he would never have consciously intended to harm Monique, there *was* a side to his nature that was becoming increasingly unpredictable. The mind-numbing episodes were far more intense than he'd experienced before, their duration much longer, and the memory loss following them was nothing short of alarming.

There was a pleasant memory of sitting in his mother's lounge drinking wine, chatting, and how he and Monique had had a lot to catch up on. Then came the moment he'd gone to use the toilet, and a terrifying and overwhelming darkness had begun to envelop him, descending like a deathly black shroud. There had been a titanic battle of wills. Wayne remembered having to fight with everything he had against an impenetrable curtain of hatred that had threatened to consume him. But after that, it was all a blank. And it was clear that he *still* felt far from his usual self. Upon waking that morning, he had felt strangely detached, a sense of separation from himself that was growing, manifesting, leaving him feeling frightened and confused.

It was impossible. Wayne knew he couldn't go on like this. He had to make sense of something, *anything*. As terrified as he was of finding out what he might have done, he *had* to know the truth. He would go to the police; that's what he'd do, tell them that he had been at the house and had seen Monique yesterday afternoon. Maybe they could tell him what had happened, but then again, he was bound to be considered a suspect and they could even arrest him and question him relentlessly. They might even remand him in custody.

Wayne couldn't cope with the thought of being in prison. Losing his freedom was unthinkable, but wasn't he already a prisoner, peering through the bars of his own past? How could there be any future when his present was so endlessly dark and his entire life a lie? Even the art world in which he'd made so much headway only knew him by his alias: *Joshua Gains*. And Wayne himself had contributed to the veneer by choosing to hide behind the very same pretense. But there was an even greater twist to that irony. An inescapable tragedy. That pseudonym had reunited Wayne with the only woman he had ever loved, and now she was dead. Fate's unforgiving fingers had wrapped themselves around his heart and ripped it out once more.

No ... Fuck this!

Fuck everything!

Wayne may have been unable to drown himself the day before but he had a stack of pills in the bathroom cabinet, surely more than enough for a lethal cocktail. Perhaps that would be easier. He wouldn't be aware of anything. He'd just slip away rather than consciously have to fight his body's natural survival instincts. For the first time that morning, he was thinking clearly, sense and purpose present in beautiful, silent lucidity.

Frantically, he began to go through the variety of bottles on the shelves, until he was satisfied he had what he needed to do the job, but when it came to it, he discovered he was even more afraid to die as he was to live. Wayne headbutted the cabinet door shut, frustrated at his cowardice.

But how close had he come? How much further could he fall? With his head still pressed against the cabinet door, Wayne allowed his breathing to return to normal. Then, slowly, he moved away and regarded himself in the mirror.

'What did I ever do to deserve this?' he asked the face staring back at him. 'What did I *ever* fucking do?'

With shaking hands, he went to put the lids back on the pill bottles, but then he went rigid. Although *he* had moved, his reflection hadn't. Slowly, Wayne looked up and into its deathly eyes ... its *black* deathly eyes.

'You're dead already,' the reflection said. '*I'm* everything you are now.'

The pill bottles fell from Wayne's hands, scattering their contents noisily around the bathroom floor. Transfixed by his alien self in the mirror, he took an unsteady step backwards.

'Running away again, eh?' the image said. 'You never *were* one for facing up to shit, were you?'

'*She deserved it, Wayne.*'

Dizzy and nauseous, Wayne had to reach out to steady himself. This was *another* voice, but this one was inside his head.

'*She killed your father, she deserved to die.*'

'Who's that? Who's there?' he gasped.

'*Don't you remember what she did to you Wayne? She destroyed your life. Don't let her do it to you again.*'

'Who *is* that? Who the *hell are* you?'

'*You know I'm inside you, Wayne, can't you feel me pulling your strings? You like me pulling your strings, don't you?*'

Wayne staggered into the lounge, clutching his head in his hands. It felt like he had to hold it together to stop it from bursting apart.

'Why are you running, Wayne?'

The voice sounded even more surreal as it began to crackle, distorted and mechanical, now coming from the speaker of his radio.

'It is useless, I am everywhere,' it said.

'No, NO! Leave me alone! LEAVE ME ALONE!'

'Everywhere ...'

Wayne picked up the radio and hurled it against the wall in his desperation, intricate electronics strewn across the floor as the outer casing shattered from the impact.

'Everywhere ...'

The voice was incessant, leaving the splintered radio to take up residence inside his head once more. Wayne felt like a fish on a hook, and that no matter how hard he tried or whatever he did, he just couldn't escape.

'This isn't the Wayne I was dealing with last night,' the voice taunted. *'I much preferred that one. I know he's in here somewhere.'*

'What other fucking Wayne? Why don't you just FUCK OFF AND LEAVE ME ALONE!'

A strange hissing and popping sound cut Wayne dead, and he turned around to find a collection of large church candles on the dining table behind him beginning to melt and morph, becoming one. Unable to speak, almost unable to breathe, he shook his head in horror as a face slowly began to form in the dripping mass, its emerging features triggering a spark of recognition in a far-flung corner of his tortured mind. Holes appearing in the centres of the eyes began to draw him in, and the waxwork began to grin.

'Ah, *there* you are,' it said. 'Now, let's go over this again.'

*

Joanne could become rather obsessive when it came to security, and Samantha had lost count of how many times her mother had checked (and rechecked) that things were either locked or switched off before she was happy enough for them to leave Winnington Road. It was while waiting impatiently in her mother's Range Rover that things had come to a head, and Samantha's gaze had strayed back to the house. The brightness of the day had made the rooms behind the windows appear much darker than usual, giving the house an uncharacteristically menacing look, and Samantha had been filled with an overwhelming sense of dread that she was being watched from its shadowy interior. By the time Joanne had finally reappeared, Samantha was like a coiled spring, and neither she nor her mother felt inclined to make conversation as they left Hampstead.

The awkward atmosphere prevailed until they were approaching Covent

Garden, when Harley became sufficiently interested in his new surroundings to start whining excitedly in the back of the Range Rover. The welcome distraction lifted the mood, and with just a few more turns of Joanne's steering wheel, they were parking up at the rear of her offices. Samantha got out and opened the rear door, whispering soothing words of praise as Harley waited obediently for his lead to be attached to his collar.

'We'd better walk around here for a bit in case he needs to go,' said Joanne. 'I'm not saying he would, but I don't want to risk him having an accident in the office.'

Samantha giggled as Harley looked up, almost as though he'd been offended.

'Oh, look at him, you've hurt his feelings now!' she said. 'Don't listen to her boyzy-woyzy … *Nasty*, horrible mummy. Come and give me a great big kissy-wissy.'

Joanne rolled her eyes up to the heavens in disgust as Harley did exactly as commanded. Dog and daughter were as thick as thieves.

'Just see if you can get him to squeeze anything out, Sam,' she said. 'Okay?'

A good ten minutes and only one cocked leg later, Harley made his way out of the yard in tandem with his owners. It was just before eight-thirty, but the streets were already a hive of activity. Street entertainers toiled like worker bees setting up for their respective performances, some too busy to notice two women and a big black dog, but others smiled and nodded as Joanne, Samantha and their noble-looking sidekick passed them by.

Buoyed up by the buzz of Covent Garden and the compliments afforded to her trusty hound, Joanne mounted a short flight of steps up to the entrance of her office complex and punched a security code into a small silver keypad on the doorframe. All she needed to do was check out an email (or a few!), and then they could head for Greenoaks Cottage, and the welcoming, open spaces of the Hertfordshire countryside.

*

Joanne Middleton wasn't the only one feeling more positive about things. Wayne Terry's mobile ringing brought him slowly back to his senses, but he chose not to answer it. He was far too at ease to be concerning himself with trivialities now he'd been handed the gift of a fresh start.

After a few rings, his mobile gave up and then beeped as a message was left. The owner of the deep but slightly camp voice was called Leonard Slater, and he said he might have some work for Joshua Gains if he wanted it. Smiling, Wayne wrote down the contact number that Slater had provided. He felt so much stronger, elated; a new destiny awaited, and he knew exactly what was expected of him, yet at the same time it was very important to remain grounded and not stand out too much. Wayne knew it was going to be difficult keeping his gift hidden from the ordinary person, and even harder not to be condescending to others less fortunate than himself when he considered the depth of the scum with which he shared his planet. Not everybody was as blessed with a talent as unique as his, and not everyone had what it took to be a Cleanser.

Detaching another sheet of paper from his message pad, Wayne drew the outline of a heart upon the page and wrote a name inside it.

The name was Naomi.

CHAPTER 9

Anne Ryan had spent a sleepless night on a sofa in Chris's living room, having refused to leave the vicinity of the house phone as she waited for news of her son. Andy Ryan, who lived with his father in the same three-bedroomed semi in Edgware, had tried his best to get his grandmother to sleep in the guest room, but Anne had insisted that the sofa was where she was going to stay. A proud, slim, and attractive woman, Anne's looks belied her age of sixty-eight, and although her surprisingly authoritative sounding voice hid a very soft centre, Andy knew that when she got an idea in her head there was no shifting it, and that it was best not to argue.

Andy hadn't had the best of nights himself, and it appeared that the endless hours of waiting for any developments was taking its toll on them both. All he could keep saying was that no news was better than bad, but he was becoming more aware of the acuteness of his grandmother's pain as time passed without there being any positive updates. He had always been sensitive to atmospheres, and he could feel her anxiety as sharply as if it were his own.

It had been mooted that Andy possessed a psychic gift. Anne believed that it could be passed through the generations and that he'd probably inherited it from his great-grandmother.

'She always *was* a strange one, that mother of mine,' Anne had once said. 'She told me I was pregnant with your father before I even knew it myself!'

As much as Andy had never really considered the claim be true, he could point to numerous instances in his life that he couldn't explain. Seeing a mental image of his mathematics teacher at school in a soldier's uniform, only to discover at a later date that the same man had once served in the Falklands Campaign, was one such occurrence. Recognising when people were unwell without there being any outward signs of ill-health, and being able to identify a past associated with an object if he were to hold it were amongst several others. Andy very rarely disclosed what he had seen or sensed, but on the odd occasions that he had, whatever he'd revealed had been uncannily accurate. However, he was no fortune teller, and despite his persisting inner feeling that all was going to be well, the immediate future regarding his father's wellbeing remained frustratingly unclear.

There was nothing to talk about and nothing to do other than wait. Andy was just about to go and make yet another cup of tea when the piercing ring of the house phone in the hallway reverberated through the uncertainty. He and Anne looked at each other for a split second as though each was waiting for the other to go and answer it, but then Anne sprung from the sofa and raced into the entrance hall.

'Hello …? This is Mrs Ryan, Anne Ryan … no, I'm Mr Ryan's mother.'

For a few moments, Andy was almost too afraid to listen, but then he heard his grandmother exclaim: 'Oh, thank God! Thank God! Can we see him? Oh, right … yes, of course… A couple of hours you say? Wonderful! You've been just wonderful! Thank you *so much* … Yes, yes, we will … Goodbye.' There was a strange silence as Anne replaced the receiver, expectant yet disbelieving.

'Your dad's regained consciousness,' she said. 'They said they're going to move him to a surgical ward.'

'Wow, that's amazing!' replied Andy. 'But I thought he was going to be sedated for at least forty-eight hours! That's what they said to us yesterday.'

'Well, I don't care what they said yesterday because he's awake and talking now! They've asked us to give them a little while to make him comfortable and then we can go in and see him. Isn't it wonderful?' Anne stopped to wipe her eyes as tears of relief began to flow. 'I'm afraid you're going to have to excuse me,' she added. 'I'm very sorry, but I'm going to have to have a few minutes to myself. I said a lot of prayers last night, and I think I have some thanking to do …'

*

Unaware of his family's impending visit, Chris lay in a side room in Intensive Care, watching a pretty young nurse in a pale blue uniform removing some technical gadgetry. At the same time, an older, dark-haired man wearing a crisp white shirt and dark grey trousers, whom Chris estimated to be in his mid-fifties, was mulling over some notes on a clipboard at the end of the bed. After a few moments, the busy nurse left the room, and the man closed the door behind her.

'Please forgive the intrusion, Mr Ryan,' the man said, sounding every bit as professional as his appearance. 'I'm Doctor Paige. I'm a consultant here in Intensive Care. We met yesterday, but under much different circumstances, although I doubt that you'll remember much, if anything.'

'You're right,' Chris replied. 'I don't. All I know is what I've been told …'

'That you'd been shot?'

'Pretty much.'

'Yes, a single gunshot wound to the thorax, lower chest; very nasty.'

'Sounds like it.'

'You were brought in just before midday yesterday. You had to be resuscitated and stabilised before going into surgery. They were working on you for the best part of four hours in all. There'd been major trauma …' The consultant paused unexpectedly, and when he spoke again, his previously straightforward manner had noticeably slipped. 'Maybe the people here that are calling you The Miracle Man are right, do you know that?'

'No?' Chris replied, frowning.

'Well, Mr Ryan, let's just say that were it not for the fact that I'm now sitting here looking at you with my own eyes, I would doubtlessly have considered news of the speed of your recovery as something of an implausibility. I had to see it for myself.'

'I'm not following …'

'You don't think it's a little strange that you should be sitting up in bed like this, after going through all I've just told you only yesterday, then?'

'Doctor Paige, with all due respect, I'm a detective, not a surgeon!'

'My apologies, Mr Ryan. I admit that while I wanted to come and see you personally, it was never my intention to probe, it's just that every now and then something happens to rewrite the rulebook; I suppose one should always be prepared to expect the unexpected, but not, in my experience, where major trauma is concerned. Following surgery, you were placed in an induced coma – standard procedure – and you needed to be ventilated. However, at around six-thirty this morning you began breathing unaided and came out of sedation. In fact, you actually removed the ventilator tube yourself.'

'I don't remember doing that …'

'And that's not all, because there's this.' Doctor Paige pointed almost accusingly at a fresh dressing that had been administered to Chris's chest. 'The incision underneath looks like it's been healing for several days, but you were closed up only some fourteen hours ago. You haven't, as yet, complained of having any pain and there are no outward signs that you were all but a corpse shortly before lunchtime yesterday. Quite frankly, this should all be impossible … Or, maybe,' he added. 'We've stumbled upon somebody who really *is* actually superhuman.'

To Chris, the shock of waking up in a hospital had been disturbing enough, without having to contend with the bemusement of an otherwise unflappable consultant making him feel that he was in some way unnatural.

'But I'm *not* superhuman!' he replied. 'It was you and your team here that saved my life. Surely it's down to *them* that I'm still here, if, as you suggest, I *shouldn't* be.'

'Nobody is blaming you for being alive, Mr Ryan, least of all me, but you should understand that in the medical profession a recovery such as yours is nothing short of inexplicable. I will, of course, pass your gratitude on to all concerned with the greatest of pleasure. That'll be the easy bit. But after *that* I'm going to have to try and convince the Clinical Director that I haven't lost the plot when I report back to him.'

At last the consultant had come out with something to which Chris *could* relate. 'Superiors, eh?' he said, grateful for the opportunity to change the subject.

'Well, I'm not sure I'd call him *that*, but it'll keep him off the bloody golf course today, I suppose. Anyway, don't be surprised if he demands an audience with you himself. As for me, I really should be going, but I hope I'll be able to catch up with you again before you get discharged.'

After the doctor left, the young nurse came back into the room to carry on with her tasks.

'I've *never* seen Doctor Paige like this before!' she said. 'Meeting you has really changed him ... It's changed all of us.'

Chris smiled weakly, but news of his 'inexplicable' recovery was spreading fast. Increasing numbers of staff were passing by, and a steady mixture of amazed stares and surreptitious glances through the glass partition of the side room were beginning to make him feel like he was in a by-gone age, a caged attraction in a Victorian freak show. But however uncomfortable Chris was with suddenly being the centre of everybody's attention, it was obvious that there *had* been something distinctly bizarre about the events of the last twenty-four hours, and there was the strangest feeling in the pit of his stomach that he couldn't explain. How often in his line of work had reliance on a gut feeling been a necessity, and how often had that feeling turned out to be right? Right then, that all too familiar instinct was saying Chris's life was never going to be the same again.

*

'Oh, for f ... *sodding* computers!' Joanne threw herself back in her chair and grimaced at the ceiling, which didn't show a flicker of concern. 'Nothing's ever straight forward with them, is it?'

Samantha snorted as she tried to stop herself laughing.

'What have you done now? It's probably because you've asked it to do something that it doesn't understand.'

All too aware of her limitations when it came to modern technology, Joanne chose to ignore the swipe.

'If you want to cock up your life completely, get a computer!' she groaned.

A news bulletin on the radio in the background suddenly grabbed her attention, but before she could ask her daughter to turn it up, all the office telephones burst loudly into life.

'Who the hell's that calling on a Saturday?' she muttered, but then she thought it might be Harvey calling about the images he was due to email, and decided to answer. 'Hello, Middleton Designs, can I help you?'

'Yes, hopefully you can', said a polite and rather well-spoken male voice. 'Is it possible to speak to Joanne Middleton please?'

It wasn't Harvey.

'That would be me', said Joanne. *This had better not be a bloody sales call*, she thought.

'Oh right,' said the caller. 'Well, I'm sorry to call out of the blue, but I thought I'd take pot-luck and see if you were in. I'm Joshua Gains. Leonard Slater called me and asked me to get in touch with you? He said you might be looking for a photographer for some fashion shoots.'

'Ah, yes!' said Joanne. 'Leonard *has* told me about you. He said that you'd worked for some notable publications, so it sounds like you've got some pedigree.'

'You make me sound like a dog!'

'Hey, that's me all over – I always believe in putting a guy at his ease!'

There was laughter from the other end of the line, but Joanne was keenly interested to know more. Should this new photographer turn out to be as good as Leonard had suggested, it could rid her of the curse of Harvey Davies sooner rather than later.

'Do you have any material that you could email over to me, Joshua?' she asked. 'I'd like to see some examples of your work and then we can go from there, and maybe set up a meeting?'

'Well, I actually don't tend to email any of my images if I can help it, but I do have a portfolio that I can bring over to you on Monday if you like?'

'Oh, a traditionalist! A portfolio's just as good if you ask me! And how refreshing to see that not everyone believes in the digital age, and that the old ways haven't completely died!' Joanne stuck two fingers up at Samantha to reinforce her point. 'That'll be great' she added. 'Oh, damn, hang on …! No, I won't be here; I'm going away for a few days.'

'Don't worry about it … I can still come over Monday anyway and leave it at your office. Whereabouts are you by the way?'

Joanne gave her company details, but couldn't explain why she'd suddenly begun to feel uneasy. As the potential new photographer had relaxed and started to get into the conversation, his polished tones had slipped a little. It was like she'd heard his voice somewhere before, and no matter how hard she tried, the feeling wouldn't go away.

'Hello? Joanne? Are you still there?'

'Yep, I'm still here,' she replied, jumping a little. 'I'm sorry, I suddenly went away with the fairies, but as you spoke just then I couldn't help but wonder why you suddenly started to sound familiar. Have we ever met before?'

'No, not to my knowledge. I don't know how much Leonard told you about me, but I made my name in erotic art originally, so most of the women I tend to deal with are figure models. I hope that doesn't offend you.'

'Oh, it takes a little more than that! I'm sure we've spoken before, though.'

'One of those voices, I guess.'

'Maybe that's it.'

Joanne put the matter to the back of her mind, and advised that the portfolio should be left with her personal assistant.

'Leanne …' The name was repeated slowly, as though being written down at the same time. 'Consider it done, and have a nice break wherever you're going, but don't get sunburn!'

'I don't think there'll be much danger of that!' Joanne replied, laughing.

'Why? Aren't you one for the sun?'

'Oh no, I love the sun. It's just that I don't have time to go trotting off abroad much these days, so my daughter and I are just going to have to rough it in Hertfordshire.'

'Hertfordshire … Whereabouts? I've got some family out that way myself, an aunt and uncle in St. Albans.'

'Ah, I know it pretty well, but I'm a bit of country girl I suppose when it comes to getting away. I prefer the villages. I've got a cottage in a village not too much further on from there, actually, in Preston?'

Samantha exaggerated a yawn.

Joanne threw a stress ball at her and missed, but the caller wasn't aware of a place called Preston anywhere in Hertfordshire.

'I'm not surprised,' said Joanne. 'It's very rural, nothing but woods, hills, sheep and cows really, but it's a perfect retreat to get away from all the rushing around.'

'Sounds great to me, although I'm more of a coastal person myself. I love the sea; my parents used to like taking me to … Anyway, you don't want to hear about that now and I expect you're probably busy, especially as you're in on a Saturday and no doubt I'm stopping you getting on. Thanks for your time today, Joanne, I really appreciate it. Looking forward to speaking to you again soon!'

They said their goodbyes and Joanne was silent for a second or two. The conversation had ended suddenly to say the least.

'Who was that?' asked Samantha. 'It sounded all very friendly.'

'It was a photographer that Leonard's heard of. He thinks we should try him out on some of the sample shoots. Harvey can be such an arrogant pig sometimes, no, scratch that, *most* of the time, and I suppose I've had a gut-full of him really.'

'Maybe you'd get on better if you shagged him!'

'You really are *truly* unbelievable! I happen to be very proud of the fact that apart from to his mother, I'm probably the only woman Harvey knows that he hasn't laid, and there's *no way* that I'm going to be another notch on that slippery bugger's bed post, I can tell you!'

Mother and daughter giggled childishly at their little exchange.

'So is this new guy…' said Samantha. 'What was his name?'

'Joshua Gains.'

'Is he going to take Harvey's place then?'

'I don't know. I hope so, but Harvey's so good at what he does that he's going to be very difficult to replace.'

'Well at least *try* to think more positively! Maybe this Joshua guy will turn out to be better.'

The radio had begun playing music once more, and having turned it down while her mother had been talking on the telephone, Samantha turned it back up again.

'Was there anything about that awful thing in Mill Hill?' asked Joanne.

'Yes, there was,' Samantha replied. 'It's now been confirmed as a murder inquiry. They named the woman too, Monique something. I can't remember exactly, but it sounded like she might have been French.'

*

Andy Ryan pulled up near the hospital with his grandmother in full flow.

'I don't care what your father thinks!' she said. 'He's bloody well coming out to Whitwell to stay with me, *and* you too! I know village life may not exactly be the centre of the universe but Hertfordshire's hardly Outer Mongolia either, and it's an ideal opportunity to get him to put his feet up and rest.'

'Yes, Nan.'

'You *will* see to it that he comes to convalesce at mine, won't you Andy?'

An obliging driver vacated a space just ahead of them. Andy saw his chance and nipped into it.

'Of course I will,' he replied. 'Dad would be hell to live with at home anyway. You know what he's like when he gets bored. I can't see why he'd mind about being hell to live with at yours instead!'

Anne smiled.

'Good,' she said. 'Then that's settled. I'd better message ahead and warn the villagers that Mr Stroppy is coming to stay for a while! Now, what ward did they say he's on?'

As they walked through the main entrance of the hospital, Andy noticed a gypsy woman looking at him from the opposite side of the concourse. Middle-aged, maybe older, she was dressed in bright, traditional clothes, and as soon as their eyes met, she began to make her way gracefully towards him. Andy was surprised how nobody else seemed to be taking any notice of the colourfully attired lady, and was mildly shocked when, after what had only seemed to be the blink of an eye, she'd ended up standing directly in front of him as though having just appeared there.

'My, you're a tall lad!' the woman said, her friendly, dark brown eyes peering up at him with interest. 'You'll have to sit down, me boy, or I'll be getting a crick in me neck!'

There was a seat close by and Andy did as he was asked, his new position placing him conveniently below the gypsy's eyeline. He had no idea why he'd obeyed the lady's gentle command so completely without question, or why, suddenly, he should have turned to putty in the presence of a total stranger. Perhaps it was the understanding, wizened features of a true Romany, or the almost unnatural sheen of the concourse's lights upon her olive skin and ringlets of greying hair that fell freely over her shoulders from underneath her headscarf. Or, maybe, it had more to do with being transfixed by the warmest and kindest of smiles.

'My, my, you *are* a special one!' the woman said, gently taking his hands in hers. 'I sees it in ye! I knows a seer when I sees one and you're a seer if ever there was! I've got something very special for you, my lovely; something very special indeed. It'll see you right, so it will.' Then, with her hands slowly tightening around his, the gypsy closed her eyes and began saying a rhyme: 'With this touch of my hand, from The Truth I shall bless ye. From the Master of Puppets, with this kiss I protect thee.'

Softly, she pressed her lips against Andy's forehead, and immediately a strange pulling sensation began spreading between his eyes.

'Good luck, young seer,' she said, drawing slowly away from him. 'It is time to be brave. The Master of Puppets ... he *will* come for you.'

A sudden hubbub brought Andy sharply back to his senses. Numerous people were walking past, the sound of their footsteps and chattering voices harsh upon his ears. For an instant he felt mildly confused. He'd been so drawn in by the gypsy and what she'd had to say that he'd momentarily forgotten where he was. Even time itself had apparently stood still, but it wouldn't be the case much longer.

'Come on lad!' said Anne. 'You can sit down and make yourself comfortable in a minute ... I've found out which ward he's on.'

'Sorry, Nan, this lady was talking to me.'

'What lady?'

'The one just …'

But the gypsy was nowhere to be seen. Baffled, Andy cautiously touched his forehead with his fingertips. The strange feeling he'd experienced before was fading, but the warmth from the gypsy's kiss remained, tingling upon his skin.

'Well, whoever she was, she's gone,' said Anne. 'Come on, let's go and see your dad.'

CHAPTER 10

Andy had never been one to believe in miracles, and only the most unrealistic of dreamers could have imagined such a surreal recovery as that of his father. There was something different about him too; it was difficult to explain, but it was as though he had been altered in some way, reset, possessing an aura so dense that Andy felt like he could almost reach out and touch it.

Every now and then he would catch fleeting glimpses of tiny coloured flashes, diminutive pinpricks of light that danced erratically, forming glittering clouds in the air around them. The lights kept on showing themselves, tantalisingly, for the briefest of moments and then disappearing, only to reappear and continue their strange display. Mostly, they danced around him and his father.

As unnatural as it all seemed, Andy had suddenly developed a much greater understanding and awareness. Nobody had spoken to him of healing lights before, yet instinctively he knew that that was what he was seeing. It was clear that nobody else present could see them, only Andy himself, and there were no such illuminative displays going on anywhere else in the ward. What *was* becoming apparent, however, was that the lights had to have had something to do with the miraculous nature of his father's recovery, but Andy was clueless as to why the healing should happen to be so unique to his family.

Just who *was* the gypsy he'd encountered in the hospital reception? How come she'd seemed to have just vanished into thin air? Every time the lights reappeared, the 'pulling' sensation from the gypsy's kiss would return, and the old lady's words would leap back into Andy's mind as clearly as if she were speaking them to him again. *With the touch of my hand, from The Truth I shall bless ye. From the Master of Puppets, with this kiss I protect thee.*

A sleeper who had been well and truly awakened, all Andy could do was sit in silence wondering who or what the 'Master of Puppets' might be, and listen to an inner voice which said he might find out sooner rather than later.

*

Wayne had gone back to bed as soon as he'd finished his phone call to Joanne, and now he was dreaming about being involved in an on-location photo shoot. At least he *thought* he was dreaming, until he realised he could feel the heat from a flickering fire in an open fireplace. Flames dancing fitfully among a small stack of logs filled the room with a soft orange glow, and intimate studio lighting was focused upon a large four-poster bed covered with various furs and scatter cushions. The furs were luxurious to the touch and Wayne wondered if some more fun with Naomi was in the offing, but that didn't explain the empty camera tripod at the end of the bed.

'What do you think, Wayne?' asked a familiar voice. 'I don't think I've done a bad job setting things up, have I?' The Puppeteer emerged from the gloom beyond the atmospheric scene. 'Not bad for a first time, eh?'

'Not bad at all,' Wayne replied, feeling far less intimidated by The Puppeteer's presence on this occasion.

'Well, I'm glad you're feeling relaxed although you must obviously be wondering why you're here?'

'Well, yes, but I've learned not to question.'

'And how encouraging it is to hear you have learned that so soon.'

The Puppeteer's no-nonsense remark was reinforced with a penetrating stare, and Wayne felt himself wither under its weight.

'Anyway,' said The Puppeteer. 'That's enough of the pleasantries for now. I have something for your mind's eye, a connection, a bond, a little keepsake for your subconscious which is why you are here. Interested?' He gestured towards the empty tripod, adding: 'There will be no need for a camera, but of course we *will* be needing a subject.'

From an inside pocket of his lustrous coat, The Puppeteer produced a small, ornate glass jar containing a black, viscous substance which appeared to be stuck to the bottom.

'Take it,' he said, holding the jar out in Wayne's direction. 'And open it.'

A foul smell hit Wayne's nostrils as soon as the lid was removed, and he pulled his face away in disgust. 'It smells awful!' he said.

'Taste it,' said The Puppeteer.

'But what is it?'

'I thought you had learned not to question.'

Another searing look forced Wayne to dip a trembling finger into the jar's putrid contents and then stick it in his mouth, yet what he'd expected to be unspeakably vile tasted honey-sweet, strangely addictive, and he found himself wanting more instead. The Puppeteer grinned, and invited him to go on and finish it.

'Is there any more?' asked Wayne, once the jar was empty.

'Sadly not,' said The Puppeteer. 'That's all there was, but it will be sufficient.'

'What was it?'

'Fear, Wayne. The sweetest fear of an Innocent.'

All at once, Wayne was doubled up by the most excruciating stomach cramps that made him feel like he was being torn in half. Collapsing to his knees, he went to cry out, but the pain was so intense it had rendered him speechless.

'I think you should let her out,' said The Puppeteer.

'Her?'

Wayne began retching uncontrollably, projectile-vomiting the same sticky fluid that he'd just ingested. It was astonishing how the tiny amount in the jar had suddenly turned into gallons, but then another sheet of pain swept over him and he threw up violently again.

The Puppeteer looked at the bile thoughtfully.

'Once more should do it, Wayne,' he said.

And then, just as suddenly as Wayne's ordeal had begun, so it ended. Breathing heavily, the pain having subsided, he rose unsteadily to his feet, staring in disbelief as the bile began shifting across the floor of its own accord. With a mixture of repulsion and amazement, Wayne stared as the ooze began to snake its way up onto the bed, and the unmistakeable form of a woman started to emerge from the glistening mass.

'Time for the dog to see the rabbit,' said The Puppeteer. 'Not laughing at you now, is she?'

The bile had become the young woman Wayne had encountered on Hampstead Heath. Her beautiful face wore a dazed expression, and although she kept looking around the room, it was obvious she couldn't see anything.

'Shall I kill her now?' Wayne asked, instantly aroused by her vulnerability. 'I didn't think it was going to be this easy.'

'Oh, how refreshingly keen you are!' said The Puppeteer. 'But this is just a part of her essence; it is the physical body that must die.'

Wayne felt a little disappointed.

'What's her name?' he asked. 'It would probably help me find her quicker for you if I knew.'

'What is it with your kind and names, Wayne? Does the cheetah ask the impala? Or the lioness the zebra? This worm is nothing to you, selected only for cleansing. You have tasted her fear and now you have a scent with which to find her, but there will be no introductions. The day you look her in the eye will be the day you cleanse her.' The Puppeteer paused briefly, then added: 'I suppose you may as well have some fun with this little piece of her, though, but enjoy it while it lasts because this morsel won't be here for long.'

Wayne didn't need a second invitation.

*

The email Harvey Davies had promised duly arrived in Joanne's inbox, but she would be opening the attachments alone for the time being as Samantha had fallen sound asleep at her desk.

Slumped in a black leather high-backed chair, an open magazine in front of her patiently waiting to be read some more, Samantha was mumbling away to herself in the otherwise silent office. Joanne chuckled quietly and began to scroll through the first of Harvey's images, finding her daughter's incoherent murmurings amusing. What a great video opportunity, a stick of embarrassment with which to beat her later! Joanne was reaching for her phone when Samantha's words suddenly began to get clearer.

'No …' she mumbled. 'No …leave me alone …'

Frowning, Joanne noticed that Harley was also watching Samantha closely. She was flinching, but not in the normal way one might expect when watching somebody twitch in their sleep. It was more pronounced, jerky, as though something was physically causing the movements. Memories of her daughter's night terror instantly came back into Joanne's mind, and whatever was happening to her right then sounded as if it was building up to be equally as unpleasant.

'Why are you doing this …?' she heard Samantha ask. 'I don't want to …no …leave me alone …'

Samantha's tone suggested that she was resigned to something, despite her objections, unable to resist. It was far too disturbing to listen to and Joanne decided she should wake her. She was halfway across the office when Samantha's eyes opened abruptly, accompanied by a cry and a sharp intake of breath.

'Wow!' Joanne gasped. 'Talk about wake with a bang!'

But Samantha didn't answer. Clearly disoriented, she began gazing uncertainly around the office, unsure of her surroundings.

'Sammy?' Joanne asked. 'Sammy …? You fell asleep, darling.'

At last Samantha's eyes focused upon her mother and she finally sparked into life.

'Oh God!' she replied. 'Did I? I must have gone out like a light!'

'You certainly did … right off into a deep sleep.'

'How long for? God … I feel *really* weird … *Please* tell me I wasn't snoring!'

'Not really. Just a bit of mumbling if I'm being honest, just like a typical teenager!'

Yet in the back of Joanne's mind was the fear that whatever had terrified them back at the house might have followed them to the office. It was such a crazy, irrational thought that a change of subject was sorely needed, and the perfect opportunity was sitting upon her computer screen.

'Anyway,' she said. 'Now that you're back in the land of the living, how would like to see the shots from yesterday's photoshoot? I didn't want to say too much before because I had no idea how the shoot would pan out, but we used a number of your designs.'

Joanne remembered how excited she felt the first time she saw her own work being modelled and knew that Samantha would feel the same, but it was the models that grabbed her daughter's attention first.

'Oh my God!' said Samantha as her eyes fell upon the first of Harvey's jpegs. 'These girls are absolutely stunning! I'd love to model for Harvey if he could make me look like this!'

'Believe me, Sam, you have no idea what it's like having to work with somebody as arrogant and self-obsessed as Harvey.'

'But he's so professional! And look at the results he gets! How could you even be *thinking* about dumping him?'

As much as Joanne loathed Harvey Davies, she had to give him credit for knowing his stuff when it came to selecting the right models for the job in hand. However, Samantha was still new to the modelling profession, and the thought of her working with Harvey at *any* point was enough to make Joanne shudder.

'Because he's such a complete *arse*!' she replied. 'And he's got this knack of making me feel inadequate, and I'm the one bloody well *paying* him!'

'Well, I doubt he's the first person who's ever got under your skin, Mum.'

'Well of course he isn't! Oh, I don't know … I suppose it's my own fault that I let him get to me; I guess it's a bit like your father and me …'

'What …? Because *he* was a complete arse to you as well?'

'Don't talk about him like that, Sam!'

'Why? He's hardly a saint, is he, so why you do keep trying to portray him as one?'

Joanne knew there had been some issues between Samantha and her father that needed resolving. The problem had been there for a few months and it had become a matter of real concern for Joanne as she didn't want them to lose touch with each other.

'I don't portray him that way,' she said. 'I just said that he could be controlling, and that's hardly a saintly quality!'

Samantha marched back over to her desk in frustration.

'Jesus, Mum!' she snapped. '*Why* do you have to be so overprotective of me when it comes to Dad? He left you, *us*, and what I can't understand is why you always defend him because it can only be for *my* benefit.'

'But I'm not always defending him! You've always known that he left us, and it's never been a problem for you before, so what's changed between you and him?'

'Because I'm old enough to make up my own mind about Dad, and right now I think he's a first-rate dick! He even managed to forget my last birthday, or had you forgotten about that? I may not actually have said so at the time, but I was really pissed off, you know?'

'But I thought you'd got past all that! Sammy, I've never stopped you from forming your own opinions on *anything*, but I really *don't want* you to have such a low opinion of your dad and end up not seeing him at all. It's something that's very important to me after what happened when *I* was younger.'

Like Samantha, Joanne's parents had separated when Joanne was at an awkward age, old enough to understand, yet young enough to be very impressionable. It was something Joanne's mother used to her advantage by driving a wedge between Joanne and her father to such an extent that Joanne stopped having anything to do with him.

'And because of all that bitterness, somewhere out there is a grandfather you've never seen!' said Joanne. 'And what makes it even worse is that I ended up hating my own mother because of it too, so after all was said and done, I effectively lost *both* my parents … God knows your dad's got his faults, Sammy, but I loved my father, I really did, but because of my mother I've never had the chance to tell him. I just wish I knew how to find him; he may even be dead now, for all I know. Don't turn against *your* dad, please don't ever do that.'

An almost unbearable silence descended on the office. Joanne's head was bowed, and Samantha suddenly felt like a complete bitch.

'Mum,' she sighed. 'I know all about Gemma and the affair. *That's* why me and Dad fell out the last time I saw him. I found out by accident from an old Statement of Facts from the divorce case. It was in a chest of drawers in your bedroom. I was only looking for a pair of scissors when I saw it. Anyway, I thought I'd ask him about it outright.'

'Oh God, *tell* me you didn't!'

'Well, I'm not going to lie to you.'

'But you never said anything!'

'And what difference would it have made if I had, Mum? *Neither* of you had ever told me! Anyway, Dad was really embarrassed that I knew about Gemma and him and started to have a go at me about you, that you were just getting back at him even though you'd got so much out of him from the divorce, and how you must have left the documents *lying* around on purpose so that I would find them. As far as I was concerned, the only *lying* had been done by him and I bloody well told him that too! I wasn't going to let him talk about you like that, Mum, not after what he did.'

A huge weight felt like it had been lifted from Joanne's shoulders, and her eyes began to fill with unwelcome tears. The way Samantha had been prepared to speak up for her so fearlessly spoke volumes about the bond that existed between them. However, even though it was abundantly clear that Samantha needed no protection from the past, it was still Joanne's opinion that no amount of pride should be any reason for father and daughter to remain estranged from each other.

'Your dad was only defending himself,' she said, having managed to gather herself. 'I know he can lash out and he was wrong to have a go at you the way he did, but he was always going to blame me because that's how it works when people get divorced. They blame each *other*. Imagine how *you* would have felt in his position. Don't hold it against your father for reacting at being confronted by something like that, Sam; shock can do some pretty terrible things to people sometimes.'

Samantha assured her mother that she would try her best.

'But you're the only reason why,' she said. 'That and because I can see how much me seeing Dad means to you. Mind you, I don't exactly see *him* rushing to contact me either, do you? The ball's been in his court for quite a while, but I guess somebody has to make the first move, and that may as well be me.'

It was the kind of conversation that had been long overdue, and the lengthy embrace that followed was typical of the aftermath of such an emotive exchange. Neither Joanne nor Samantha was any more right or wrong than the other, and neither of them felt it was necessary to say anything else.

Right then was as good a time as any to wrap things up at the office and make good their intended escape to the country

CHAPTER 11

Wayne Terry had become a far more sinister proposition from the timid and vulnerable man that he'd once been. Dark and unknowable, driven by instincts far beyond the reaches of his former self, he now saw himself as a creature of the night, having sacrificed the light for the shadows without remorse or regret. He was special, a true Cleanser, reborn to fulfil a destiny and to create chaos, chaos which would eventually see in the New Order. The feeling of belonging, of being an important cog in a well-ordered machine was such that it filled Wayne with a renewed sense of wonder, of purpose, and that to The Puppeteer's downtrodden brethren he was going to be seen as nothing less than a god.

And what was just as interesting was seeing how much more power he had at his disposal in the physical realm, and over the subject matter for his other life as a photographer in particular. Wayne's search to that end had brought him to *Electrix!*, a strip club in Colindale where he'd unearthed a few would-be models in the past. In Wayne's experience, erotic dancers tended to have quite high opinions of themselves and didn't always make favourable models, but those that *had* worked for him had all danced to his tune eventually, captured on film, forever ensnared in a moment of time in which they'd succumbed to his wishes, like circus animals obeying the commands of their ringmaster.

The thought was enough to bring a grin to Wayne's face as he allowed his eyes to wander around his surroundings. Set in a small, run-down industrial estate, Wayne's chosen haunt had once been a transport café and bar, and apart from a gaudy neon sign above its entrance advertising its presence, it sat otherwise inconspicuously in a street lined with small industrial units and warehouses, half of which stood empty. Inside, however, the venue was surprisingly comfortable and intimate. Tables were strategically placed around a red carpeted floor meaning the clientele was never far from the dancers that sexualised the small and cosy stage, and the lighting, subdued and moody, cast subtle shadows in which those who didn't want to be seen could hide themselves away. Nevertheless, Wayne could still make out their dusky forms as they lusted and fantasised about the range of 'talent' on display. More obvious was a couple of rowdy stag parties that had been drunkenly fawning over the flesh parading in front of them throughout the evening. Wayne shuddered at the thought of what it must be like to be so basic, forgetting that his own recent past had been just as chequered, and looked at his watch. None of the previous routines had done that much for him and it was getting late, but then the opening bars of a raunchy heavy metal track came crunching loudly out of the speakers and made him lift his head unsuspectingly.

And then everything changed.

'Zoe French!' Wayne whispered to himself, astonished that one of the three dancers strutting confidently out onto the stage happened to be somebody from his schooldays. 'Zoe. Fucking. French!'

He leant forwards in his seat, interest rekindled, a smile slowly forming on his lips. No longer the geeky, brown-haired swat that he remembered, Zoe had morphed into a smoking-hot blonde. Her pixie-styled hair complimented her impish facial features perfectly, and her fair skin, subtly oiled for maximum effect, was glistening provocatively under the colourful stage lights.

Wayne shook his head as the former Little Miss Goody-Two-Shoes began grinding in her tiny red thong, wrapping herself around a metal pole like it was a shiny, chrome-plated lover. For a moment he was so taken with Zoe's tight body and erotic performance that he'd forgotten about the hard time she used to give him at school. Memories of her laughing at him along with the rest of the crowd that used to mercilessly hunt him down and taunt him came back into his mind, and his smile began to fade with all the hurt and deep-seated resentment generated by those recollections. Those feelings were only going to be compounded when Zoe inadvertently looked right at him, and then instantly looked away.

The bar seemed a very appealing place to be all of a sudden. Wayne had nothing else to do, so why *not* have another drink? One more, just for the road. Although more concerned with getting a refill than he was with applauding the end of Zoe's act, he was struck by a sudden wave of inspiration! What was the sole purpose of his mission in *Electrix!* that night? Didn't he have the world at his feet and wasn't Zoe just a low-life stripper? What better way to have Zoe French eating out of the palm of his hand than offer her a few scraps of modelling work? After all, he was a Cleanser, and as secret as his new position was, such superiority was bound to be recognised.

Fresh drink in hand, Wayne made his way towards a door he assumed led to the backstage area, but as he approached the rather tired looking entrance, a bald, burly doorman in a white, open-neck shirt and dark suit barred his way with a semi snarl.

'Wrong door, mate!' he growled. 'I think you'll find the Gents is that way.'

Wayne fixed the bouncer with a stare that made the man feel a little uncomfortable, despite the considerable differences in their statures.

'I know Zoe, one of the dancers,' said Wayne. 'I'd like to see her. I haven't seen her for years, not since we were at school together.'

The doorman drew himself up to his full height and tilted his head back slightly for added effect.

'Who shall I say wants her?'

'Wayne Terry.'

'An old school friend, you say?'

Wayne nodded.

'Wait here, I'll go and see if she's alright with it.'

A few people had seen Wayne talking to the bouncer and had begun to stare, making him feel a little conspicuous, so he sauntered back over to the bar so as not to arouse any further suspicions.

After a couple of minutes, the doorman returned. 'Zoe says she don't remember you, mate,' he said. 'But she'll see you anyway.'

The previously off-limits door was opened, and Wayne was shown into a narrow, brightly lit passageway where a pungent combination of various perfumes and body sprays permeated the air. The scents got stronger as he walked a few steps to the end of the corridor where two more passages led off left and right. By chance, another dancer appeared who was mildly surprised to see Wayne but seemed otherwise unperturbed.

'Can I help you?' she asked.

'Yes, maybe you can, I'm looking for Zoe, I'm ...'

'Oh, you must be Wayne! I wondered if that's who you were. It's nice to meet you! I'm Kirsty. I heard Danny the doorman talking to her about you, that you knew her from school or something?'

'Yeah, that's right.'

'Well, now you know what she looked like underneath her uniform!'

The quip made Wayne laugh.

'You'll find her chilling out in there,' Kirsty said, pointing towards a slightly open door at the end of the passage. 'Good luck!'

Wayne knocked politely, and a woman's voice that he assumed to be Zoe's invited him into a small, sparsely furnished room. Sure enough, Zoe French was alone and sitting at a dressing table in front of an old Hollywood mirror that like her bleach-stained, dark red shower robe had seen better days. Half of the bulbs surrounding the dull mirror didn't work, but Zoe didn't seem bothered by the lack of celebrity status as she wiped the back of her hand across her top lip and turned to face her visitor.

There was a fine, white powder on the surface of the dressing table.

'Fancy doing a line, Wayne?' Zoe asked, but he declined with a shake of his head, barely able to conceal his disgust.

'Oh, I remember you now,' said Zoe. 'You never *did* have much of a sense of adventure, did you?'

Wayne chose to let the barbed comment go over his head, feeling that the offer he was about to make would change her opinion and that he should be giving her another chance.

'People change, Zoe' he replied.

She laughed ironically.

'I know I have. I bet it was shock for you to see me doing this!'

'You can say that again! But I must admit that I was very impressed.'

'Thank you.'

'You're welcome. Listen, Zoe, the reason I wanted to see you is that I'm a photographer, and I was wondering if you'd be interested in doing some modelling for me? I know it's a bit random, but you've certainly got the potential to ...'

The pretty dancer wiped the tip of her index finger through the remnants of the powder on the table and placed it in her mouth, sucking it suggestively. The sight of her full red lips closing round the digit stopped Wayne in his tracks, and his reaction made Zoe smile.

'Do you want to fuck me?' she asked.

'What ...?'

'That's why you're *really* here isn't it? Because you want to fuck me?'

Zoe's alluring hazel eyes hadn't left Wayne's as she'd spoken, and he realised that things weren't going his way. Her challenging attitude was making him agitated. *He* should be the one in control.

'Everybody wants to fuck me, Wayne, join the queue. Why should you get to have a piece of me before anyone else?'

She began to open her shower robe, teasingly exposing her small, beautifully cupped breasts and a tiny strip of dark brown pubic hair which she began to stroke affectionately.

'Men go crazy for this,' she said, parting her thighs a little. 'I always take a pride in my fanny, Wayne, because I believe that first impressions are very important. Do you like her like this, or do you think she'd look better shaved?'

The ice Zoe was skating upon was getting thinner by the second as far as Wayne was concerned, but then another young woman came in and joined them. She smiled and apologised for the intrusion, but then stood behind Zoe and began massaging her shoulders.

'Do you want to share a cab, Zo-Zo?' the woman asked.

'Oh, you're a love, Emma. But no, it's okay ... I've got to stick around anyway. I asked Danny to call me one ... my phone's gone flat ...' Zoe closed her eyes in exaggerated ecstasy. 'Ahh ...!' she said. 'That's wonderful ... that's the spot ... just there! Ooh yeah ... Oh, this is Wayne by the way, we went to school together.'

Wayne's blood began to boil at the way he'd been introduced almost as an afterthought, like Zoe was trying to make him look and feel completely insignificant.

'Smitten with our Zo-Zo, are you?' asked Emma. 'Can't say I blame you, love. Isn't she just divine? Pure sex on a stick!'

Emma's fingers had turned their manipulating attention to Zoe's breasts, and Zoe smiled slyly at the perspiration appearing on Wayne's forehead.

'What's the matter, Wayne?' she asked. 'I'd have thought you of all people would be used to this sort of thing. Doesn't this remind you of anyone? Hmmm ... let me see ... your mother, perhaps?'

It was Wayne's considered opinion that humanity would be far better off were it not being afflicted by creatures like Zoe French, and the only thing helping him keep his temper was knowing that *he* was far superior to *her*. He'd given Zoe the chance to better herself and she'd thrown it back in his face. It didn't seem appropriate to look upon her as a person anymore, and it made him realise just how cheap and worthless she was.

Without saying a word, Wayne got up and went to leave.

'Leaving us so soon, Wayne?' Zoe asked. 'Why not stick around? The party's just getting started!'

An explosion of hysterical, girly laughter burst through the doorway, burning in Wayne's ears, boiling in his mind as he hurriedly closed the door behind him. He was a Cleanser, and now Zoe was going to have to pay the ultimate price for her disrespect.

As he strode back along the passage, Wayne happened to bump into the doorman, who rather obligingly escorted him back out into an almost deserted club.

'Goodnight, mate,' the doorman said.

'Yeah ... goodnight, Danny, and thanks for your help. I'll see myself out.'

The doorman smiled at the mention of his name, and nodded before taking a mobile phone out of an inside pocket of his jacket. Wayne watched as Danny put his finger on a business card on the wall and began pressing the numbers on his mobile's keypad.

'Yeah, hello, mate,' he heard Danny say. 'It's Danny here from *Electrix*. I need a cab for one of the girls ... Zoe French.'

Wayne listened intently as the cab was booked for half-past two. A plan had suddenly begun to form in his mind about how he might be able to get Zoe alone. It was just approaching a quarter to two in the morning, so it was worth a try because it wouldn't involve him having to wait around for too long. Zoe had mentioned that her mobile was flat, so all he needed to do was to cancel a cab in the next few minutes, and then hope that the rest of the pieces would fall into place. Wayne waited until Danny had gone, and then went over to store the taxi firm's number in his phone.

Back in her dressing room, Zoe had just completed her make up. By then, she, Danny and Kirsty were the only ones left in the club. The doorman and Kirsty were rather fond of each other, and Zoe didn't want to keep them waiting. Danny was on a promise that night, *that* much was very obvious.

Zoe smiled at her reflection in the mirror, wondering when her own prince charming would come along to save her from herself. The stripping wasn't the problem, it was her cocaine habit that meant she *had* to strip (among other things) that was the issue, and she needed to sort herself out.

Money, or the lack of it, was the reason why Zoe had chosen to stay behind. She owed people, one of them being her dealer, and he was running out of patience with her. The club's owner had promised he'd pay her that night, but he hadn't shown, caught up elsewhere apparently. *Pissed out of his skull, more like*, Zoe thought. It looked like she was just going to have to settle her debt another way. The mental image made her shudder, and she hurried out into the bar where Danny and Kirsty were deep in conversation.

'I'm so sorry to keep you guys waiting,' Zoe said. 'Looks like I've made you hang around for nothing.'

Kirsty smiled wanly. She was acutely aware of her friend's desperate situation.

'How's that cab doing, Danny?' asked Zoe, fearing she might burst into tears if she didn't ignore the concern on Kirsty's face.

The doorman checked his watch.

'Should be here anytime now, Zo-Zo, they're normally very reliable. We'll wait with you.'

But Zoe shook her head.

'No,' she said. 'Don't worry about it; I'll be okay.'

'Well, I don't like it. How about we give you a lift home instead? My car's only parked down the road outside Kirsty's place'

'Danny, it's fine … I'm a big girl now. What's the worst that can happen? You lock up and get Kirsty home before she gets too tired!'

Danny looked down at his feet and managed an embarrassed chuckle, then he and Kirsty made their way with Zoe to the main door.

*

Wayne was waiting in an alley between two empty warehouses. It was a little way down from the club and from his position he could clearly see its front door reflected in the window of a building opposite. He felt like he'd been waiting there for ever, and his entire body was as taut as his nerves. His skin felt prickly as if he were coming out in a rash, and his mouth was dry, not with fear, but with excitement and anticipation.

Then, at last, Wayne saw Zoe, Danny and what looked like the girl who'd called herself Kirsty emerge into the dimly lit street. Kirsty and Zoe embraced each other, and the doorman locked and secured the door.

Would the three of them wait together? Or would Zoe be left alone as Wayne had hoped?

There was a brief conversation, but then the doorman and Kirsty turned and walked down the street together, leaving Zoe alone and sticking out like a sore thumb in her high heels, tight top, and mini skirt, waiting for a cab that Wayne knew was never going to come.

Outside the club, Zoe watched her friends until they were out of sight, listening to the sound of their footsteps and laughter echoing into the distance as they made their way towards the housing estate where Kirsty lived. It was so eerily quiet once they'd left, and for a moment, Zoe wished that she'd accepted Kirsty's final offer of staying with them for the night. However, as much as Zoe suddenly wanted to run after her friends, she knew that Kirsty and Danny needed to be alone, and didn't want to impose on Danny's night of glory. The cab was bound to be along in a few minutes anyway, the company was probably just busy.

Zoe looked at her watch. Where *was* that fucking cab?

She peered nervously at the darkened windows of the building opposite, fearing for a moment, that she'd seen some movement reflected in them, but as hard as she strained her eyes to see, nothing stirred. This was no time for her mind to playing tricks on her and give her the willies!

Where *was* that *fucking* cab?

Being alone was one of Zoe's biggest fears, along with dying alone. The thought of that really terrified her, but why should she be thinking that way? Maybe the cocaine was making her paranoid. Bobbing up and down as if she were cold, walking on the spot, shifting from one foot to the other, Zoe was doing everything she could to relieve the apprehension building up inside her.

She took another look at her watch. Gone ten to fucking three, and she couldn't even phone for another cab! After rummaging around in her handbag, Zoe tried her hitherto unresponsive mobile, and discovered it was *still* unresponsive. Why the hell had she come out without charging her bloody phone or without a phone charger? She really was crap!

There was nothing else for it but to head to the taxi company's offices about ten minutes' walk away in the Edgware Road. It would mean having to walk through the dingy, poorly lit industrial estate in order to get to it, but at least she'd be able to get a cab there.

Wayne's knowledge of the local area meant that he already knew Zoe would have to pass right by where he was lying in wait to reach the taxi rank. He breathed heavily with anticipation as his plan began to come to fruition, adrenalin surging at the sound of Zoe's heels on the pavement growing steadily louder as she walked unsuspectingly in his direction. But then he had a horrible thought. The top predators always had an instinctive sense of self-preservation, and although he was ready to pounce, the element of surprise might not be advantageous enough on its own. Zoe would undoubtedly fight back and would need to be subdued, so he needed a weapon unless he wanted the opportunity to quite literally pass him by. Wayne frantically looked around and saw that there was a small skip just a few feet further back in the alley. A black refuse sack at the front of the over-filled bin had split open, showing its contents invitingly to him, a refuse sack that happened to contain some empty spirit bottles …

Click, clack, click, clack, click, clack.

The sound of Zoe's footsteps echoed along the deserted street. *Jesus!* she thought, *I couldn't make more noise if I tried!*

Click, clack, click, clack, click, clack.

Through the gloom, she could just make out the end of the street some distance ahead, and the lights of the Edgeware Road. *Almost there, girl!*

Click, clack, click, clack, BANG!

Zoe was sent sprawling onto her hands and knees by a bone-crunching blow to the back of her head. Her handbag fell from her grasp, scattering its contents onto the pavement in front of her. Sickened and confused, she felt herself being half lifted and half dragged before being thrown viciously against a wall. The world was spinning, the ground swaying like the deck of a ferry in a rough sea. Zoe tried desperately to get to her feet, but as she got to her knees, she was pinned face first against the brickwork. She tried to scream, but all that came out was a gasp as she felt what little she had on in the way of underwear being torn away, followed by an excruciating pain as her attacker brutally forced his erection into her.

'Bitch, bitch, bitch!' said a male voice, his words spitting hatefully into Zoe's ear in tandem with each one of his brutal thrusts.

'Bitch, bitch, bitch!'

The man grabbed a handful of her hair and pushed her face even harder against the wall.

'Bitch, bitch, bitch!'

His thrusts were getting faster and more violent. Zoe's whole body shook with the force of the appalling abuse, and tears of pain, humiliation and terror flowed from her eyes.

'Bitch, bitch, BITCH, B-ITCH!'

Zoe felt the man's body go rigid as he climaxed, and prayed that her ordeal was finally over, but before she could recover any semblance of her senses she was dragged to her feet and made to face her attacker.

It was Wayne!

Sneering, he took a step towards her, and she felt one, two, three severe blows to her stomach, each one followed by an indescribable sheet of pain as something sliced right into her. Screaming in panic, Zoe immediately clutched her hands to her punctured abdomen and tried to staunch the flow of lifeblood that was squeezing itself copiously through her desperate grasp.

Grinning at Zoe's plight and her terrified cries for help, Wayne stepped back to admire the result of his craft. Who could have thought that a broken bottle could be used to such devastating effect? He was truly gifted. The dark, glistening patch spreading across Zoe's top and down her mini skirt made him feel like a million dollars, the orange glow of a nearby sodium streetlight making her blood appear almost black as if exposing the darkness of her soul. The grin abruptly left his face at the thought of her intrinsic evil and he moved towards her again.

'Wayne ... no! Please Wayne, no more ... WAY–'

Zoe's pleas died in her throat as Wayne's improvised weapon sliced clean through it. The only sound then was a gurgling as she slid down the wall, trying to scream through the gaping wound.

Wayne made sure that he scent-marked his kill by relieving his bladder on Zoe as she died, and then cautiously approached the entrance of the alleyway. He checked up and down the street, but it was totally deserted. Nobody would have heard a thing, so his biggest problem then was how he was going to get home. It was too far to walk, there was a lot of blood on his hands, and some spatters on the white shirt he'd chosen to wear that night, but luckily it was less obvious on his dark grey jeans and black denim jacket. Wayne hastily buttoned up the jacket to cover his shirt, but needed to do something about his hands. It was when he noticed some wet wipes that had fallen out of Zoe's handbag when she'd fallen, and he used them to clean himself up as best he could.

Only once he was happy that he was no longer too conspicuous did Wayne choose to leave the scene of the slaughter, strolling casually away towards the taxi office at which Zoe had intended to find safety. He could sense, too, that Naomi was close, and found her approval of his actions pleasing.

Wayne's reward was waiting for him.

This was truly going to be a night to remember.

CHAPTER 12

Considering the length of time since Joanne's previous visit to Preston, she was pleased to see that it had remained completely unchanged. Hertfordshire was a very desirable county in which to live and properties were at a premium, but in the village the march of progress in the form of characterless new housing developments had been refreshingly averted.

Preston nestled comfortably and inconspicuously in the hills of the north of the county, surrounded by sprawling areas of woodland that gave it an almost Brigadoon-like feeling of seclusion, and the welcoming feel of Greenoaks Cottage when Joanne stepped over its threshold was almost like being reunited with a long-lost friend.

For all its charm and serenity, however, the one thing that Preston didn't possess was a village shop, and having consumed the hastily gathered supplies that she and Samantha had brought with them from London, some emergency restocking was urgently needed that Monday morning. A full shop could wait until later, however. Breakfast was more important, and although the nearest convenience store was only a few minutes' drive away in the next village, Joanne's mind began to wander, and she began to think about how selling up in London and moving out permanently to Preston might be a good idea.

It was a subject that Joanne had raised with her daughter in the past, but Samantha had previously been totally against the idea. Samantha's life had always revolved around her friends in London. How would she get to see them if she and her mother were to move away? But much had changed since then, including Samantha being in possession of a full driving license, and the unexplainable events back in Hampstead might be the perfect opportunity to revisit the matter. Just knowing that they were going to have to return at some point was making Joanne feel decidedly anxious, but why should she already be thinking about going back when they'd only just arrived?

As she pulled into the local store's tiny car park, Joanne decided that right then was as good a time as any to start thinking about something else.

*

Wayne had disposed of the shirt he'd been wearing on his return home from the strip club, carefully wrapping it in a couple of carrier bags and burying it deep inside a large communal wheelie bin outside the apartment block. He'd then placed his blood-spattered jeans straight into the washing machine, along with his denim jacket. On closer inspection, there had been more blood on him than he'd originally thought, and it was a stroke of luck that contactless card payments were widely available in taxis. The taxi driver himself didn't seem to have noticed the mess on Wayne's clothes. Perhaps he wasn't that observant, or maybe it was because Wayne had been able to make such a quick exit, eliminating any chance of suspicions being raised.

Another precaution Wayne had taken was asking to be dropped off a little way from his flat, and he'd even walked in the opposite direction until the taxi was out of sight. Feeling that his tracks were well and truly covered, and with the sound of the washing machine whirring gently in the background, Wayne had then settled down for what remained of the night, hoping to be reacquainted with his spiritual reward, and he'd not been disappointed. Naomi had been very accommodating, and he couldn't wait to continue his invaluable line of work to see what else she could do for him.

Such a hectic night meant that Wayne spent most of Sunday in bed in order to recharge his batteries and maintain his sharpness, but he rose early on Monday morning in readiness for other challenges that might be coming his way. He felt he was perhaps still being tested and that he still had to prove his worthiness, but even so, he felt alive and fulfilled, and far from the nobody he'd been before his salvation and rebirth. He had no memory of that previous life and didn't feel the merest flicker of remorse for the cleansing of Zoe French. She had succumbed to his mastery, assisting with honing necessary skills in preparation for Wayne's bigger prize, and he was grateful to her for the sacrifice she'd made to those ends.

As Wayne walked calmly towards the offices of Middleton Designs, he knew it was time for the utmost discretion. 'Joshua Gains' was no longer a pseudonym behind which to hide for fear of discovery by his mother; it had become a fortification guarding the secret of his burgeoning gift as he pretended to be an ordinary man, and, on this occasion, his expected presence demanded exactly that.

Leanne, for her part, had been made aware of his visit via a note left by Joanne on her PA's desk, along with an explanation about taking a few days off. The reception area was temporarily unattended by security, but Leanne duly buzzed her visitor up when he announced himself on the intercom. Most of the time, she was pretty good at getting a mental impression of what people looked like by the sound of their voices; it was a game she enjoyed playing, but on this occasion she'd got it completely wrong. The voice on the intercom had been quite precise, befitting of a man far better presented than the one who ended up standing in front of her in blue jeans, a round-necked T-shirt, trainers and a black leather bomber jacket. At about five feet eight (at a guess), he was also shorter than Leanne had imagined, but an intense demeanour made up for any perceived lack of height, his vivid blue eyes, set in a strangely delicate face, nothing more than chips of blue glass focused disturbingly upon her from underneath a mop of messy, light brown hair.

'You must be Leanne,' the visitor said, his empty eyes warming a little as he spoke. 'Joanne told me I should leave this with you? It's my portfolio.'

Leanne reached out and took the portfolio from his outstretched hand.

'Thank you, Mr Gains,' she said.

'Joshua ... please ... or even better, Josh.'

'Thank you ... *Josh.*'

Wayne smiled. Leanne seemed to be pleasant and well-mannered, appearing obedient and submissive, the way he knew a woman *should* be. Her politeness was beginning to turn him on a little because she'd obviously recognised his dominance, but he still had to continue the charade of being an ordinary person.

The office phones began to ring as Leanne looked for a place on her desk that was free of piled-up paperwork.

'Oh God, I'm sorry, Josh!' she said. 'I can't seem to find my desk right now and I'm on my own at the moment. Would you mind putting it over there on that one in the corner for me?'

She gestured towards one of three unattended desks, one that was bigger and more impressive than the others. Wayne guessed that it had to be Joanne Middleton's, and he smiled as he took the portfolio back.

'Good morning, Middleton Designs ...' he heard Leanne say, but her efficient tones faded into the background as his heart missed a beat, for staring out at him from a photograph on that very same desk was the girl from Hampstead Heath! Next to the picture was another photograph of her, but this time she was with an older woman who was equally as familiar.

So *that* was Joanne, was it?

Wayne was temporarily at a loss, having stumbled so unexpectedly upon a huge marker towards his quarry, but his surprise turned to something much darker as Leanne began to giggle on the telephone across the other side of the office: an intense rage, triggered by the sound of her laughter.

They really *were* all the fucking same, *weren't* they?

On Joanne's desk was an open box of business cards, and an impressive-looking letter knife with an invitingly heavy blade. Wayne glanced over his shoulder. Leanne had her back to him and was rummaging around in the bottom drawer of a filing cabinet, still being entertained by the ongoing conversation with her caller.

With a barely disguised scowl, Wayne helped himself to a couple of business cards and slipped the letter knife inside his jacket. Leanne's merriment was turning up the heat beneath his mental fury, and slowly, he turned and moved towards her.

*

Joanne had been pleasantly surprised by the variety of groceries on sale in the well-stocked village store. The woman who ran the little shop was extremely grateful for Joanne's custom, and the pair of them had struck up quite a conversation which had flowed seamlessly until Joanne's mobile interrupted matters.

Making her apologies, Joanne liberated the device from the confines of her handbag, only to cancel the call from the 'withheld number' with a dismissive swipe of her finger. The unwelcome intrusion sparked a new topic of discussion about nuisance sales calls, but then Joanne realised that she ought to check in with Leanne and make sure that all was well at the office. Her decision to make a bolt for the country had been sudden to say the least, and a grovelling apology by way of a hurriedly written note might not have cut it with her PA.

Joanne loaded her purchases into her Range Rover, and plucked up the necessary courage to ring in. She tried several times but couldn't get a reply, which was most unlike Leanne, and Leanne's mobile was just as unresponsive. Perhaps she was ill. As a last resort, Joanne attempted Leanne's home number, but after six or seven rings a recorded message cut in stating that the 'lady of the house' was unable to come to the phone because she was 'in bed with Brad Pitt'. Joanne laughed out loud despite her growing concern, opting not to leave a message as she wasn't great at talking to machines, but no sooner had she rung off, than her own phone rang again. Just as before in the village shop, the number was withheld, but this time Joanne decided to answer. Whoever was calling would only keep trying if it were a sales call, and despite her irritation, the best thing to do was probably just pick up and get rid of them.

'Hello,' she answered. 'Who is this?' but her question was greeted by an eerie silence. *Just as I suspected*, Joanne thought, *a bloody call centre*. She sighed impatiently, but then came the sound of road traffic in the background at the other end of the line.

It *wasn't* a call centre, and there was the unmistakeable sound of breathing in her ear.

'Listen!' she snapped, raising her voice. 'I'm very busy. Now, who are you and what do you want?'

There was anxiety as well as irritation in Joanne's voice, the mix causing the heavy breathing to become interspersed with sniggering, the kind of sniggering a child would make when trying to suppress laughter about something they shouldn't be doing; except, this wasn't a child. It was a *man*.

Joanne felt herself going cold, and then the line went dead, leaving her bemused, unnerved, and staring at a screen that would only tell her: *Call Ended*.

In a sunlit Covent Garden, Wayne placed his mobile back in his jacket pocket, uplifted by the power he'd been able to wield over Joanne in those few joyous seconds. He didn't have a clue where Preston was, apart from her saying that it was in Hertfordshire somewhere.

But it didn't matter. Everything was slotting beautifully into place, and he would know soon enough …

*

There was no jolly 'Hello!' from Joanne when she walked into Greenoaks; it was almost as if Samantha and Harley weren't even there.

'You're very quiet,' said Samantha, frowning. 'Is everything alright?'

Joanne set two brown paper carrier bags of shopping down on the kitchen table. 'I'm not sure,' she replied.

'Why? Did Leanne have the hump with you about coming out here so suddenly? I guessed you'd be calling her because you just can't leave it alone, can you?'

'Okay, I admit it, I did call her, but …'

'But you're the boss, you can do what you like!'

'No, Sam, it's nothing like that; nobody picked up. It's just that I've had a bit of a creepy phone call, that's all.'

The word *overreaction* was a favourite choice of Samantha's to describe her mother's responses to certain situations, but even *she* felt the hairs stand up on her arms when Joanne went into more detail.

'It was just really strange,' said Joanne. 'I cut a call from a withheld number before it happened, so maybe it was the same man. Oh God, maybe he's a stalker!'

'How can you be sure it was a man?'

'It was *definitely* a man.'

'Could it have been Harvey?'

'Well, of course it bloody well wasn't Harvey! His ego wouldn't allow him to withhold his number for one thing!'

'But only people you know really well, or business people, have got your mobile. Maybe it was just a pocket call or something like that. We've all called somebody by mistake before.'

'Pockets don't withhold numbers either, and they certainly don't snigger,

Sam. It was such an odd sound, too; almost insane, and I *know* it was directed at me!'

Both of them jumped as Joanne's mobile suddenly began ringing and vibrating on the dining table. For a moment, she appeared unwilling to see who was calling her, but then her demeanour changed dramatically, and she hurriedly picked up her phone.

'Oh, *there* you are!' she said, smiling at Samantha and mouthing Leanne's name. 'And there was me thinking you'd been lost at sea or something!'

Samantha would normally have been dismayed at her mother's insistence about staying in touch with the office, but she'd seen her looking so vulnerable in the lead up to Leanne's call, and then there were the reasons why they'd both come out to Greenoaks in the first place. Everything seemed to have changed since the encounter with the flasher on Hampstead Heath, the incident apparently a catalyst for a series of unexplained events, and Samantha had a growing sense of foreboding that her mother's mystery caller might just be another part of something unknown that was yet to unfold. To stop herself from overthinking, she focused her attention on an annoyingly overly secured pack of bacon, and started to make breakfast. As the packaging gave way with a rip, Harley's interested black snout appeared above the level of the worktop, hopefully sniffing the air. He, at least, seemed to be his normal self, even if nothing and nobody else did.

'So, it's been very eventful there this morning by the sound of things,' said Joanne, making herself comfortable in the living room while her daughter slaved away in the kitchen.

'Very,' Leanne replied. 'I'm so sorry I didn't get back to you earlier, Jo. Like I said, though, it was bedlam here for a while.'

Joanne joked that she held her PA fully responsible for the tube delays and staff sickness that had caused that morning's issues, and Leanne stated that she considered herself severely reprimanded. But then Leanne remembered something else.

'Oh shit, I nearly forgot!' she said. 'That photographer chap popped his portfolio in earlier, too. Oh my God, I can't believe I nearly forgot to tell you that!'

'I wouldn't worry too much,' Joanne replied. 'I was more worried about dropping you in the crap today! What was his name again? Joshua something, wasn't it?'

'Gains.'

'Yep, that was it … Joshua Gains! Well? What's the verdict, then? Have you had a chance to look at his portfolio yet?'

Bearing in mind the pressure that Leanne had been under that morning, it was probably a silly question, but the possibility of breaking the shackles of Harvey Davies was making Joanne curious as to her PA's opinion.

'Well, I *have* actually managed to have a quick glance at it,' replied Leanne to Joanne's pleasant surprise, 'and for starters it's very well presented. I've only had a quick flick through, and there's an awful lot more to see, but as first impressions go, I have to say that what I've seen so far is truly outstanding. It's already obvious to me that Joshua is an extremely talented photographer.'

'First base negotiated, then!' said Joanne. 'You know how much I trust your judgement on things like this, and it all sounds very encouraging so far.'

But then came a slightly ominous pause from the other end of the line, and Joanne feared her balloon of hope might be about to deflate.

'I don't have any doubts about Joshua's *work* from what I've seen so far,' said Leanne. 'I'm just not quite so sure about *him*.'

'Oh? Why's that? *Please* don't tell me there's another man on this planet as arrogant and pig-ignorant as Harvey Davies!'

'Oh God, no! Don't worry on that score; Joshua was nothing like Harvey! He just made me feel a bit uncomfortable for some reason. I couldn't read him at all, and the way he looked at me when he came in was … well, rather unnerving. He's got the most amazing eyes, by the way, but at first it felt like he was looking right into me. It was really strange, like I was being vetted. The only other person who's ever made me feel like that when they looked at me was my old maths teacher, and *he* ended up getting arrested for being a pervert!'

Both Joanne and Leanne instantly erupted into a fit of hysterics.

'But he had *amazing eyes*, though,' said Joanne when she'd eventually calmed down.

'I just felt he might be a bit weird,' said Leanne. 'But then again, these arty people often are. You know the type: intense, a tad eccentric, but that didn't stop him wanting to know more about the two women in the photos on your desk!'

'Interested in me, was he?'

'I think it was more Samantha!'

'Typical! The price of having a super-hot daughter! Anyway, if you think Joshua's weird, then I'm not interested, she's welcome to him … Are you *sure* you're going to be okay there being a couple of pairs of hands down, Leanne? I mean it *was* very short notice my going away and all that.'

As far as Leanne was concerned it was about time that Joanne took some time off; there was nothing for her to worry about and everything was under control.

'Well, apart from the fact I'm having to open today's post with my fingernails!' she added. 'I can't find that offensive weapon you call a *letter opener* anywhere. Anyway, I'm going to have to say cheerio now because some of us have got work to do!'

A smile stayed on Joanne's face after they'd finished. Maybe she *didn't* need to be in the office quite as often. Modern technology, despite her shortcomings over its use, meant that she could easily work remotely if need be, and while relaxing outside in Greenoaks' spacious back garden (having negotiated Samantha's delicious bacon sandwiches), thoughts of moving permanently into Greenoaks came back into Joanne's mind.

Not that those thoughts prevailed for any length of time, however, for the air was fresh and clean, and the sunshine warm and welcoming, a combination that caused Joanne to doze off on her lounger in the short time it took Samantha to load up the dishwasher and tidy up the kitchen.

Samantha smiled when she saw her mother asleep against a colourful backdrop of geraniums and delphiniums, but she resisted the urge to take a quick snap with which to embarrass her on Facebook. Harley's morning walk was long overdue, and although Joanne would have been more than happy to have accompanied them, disturbing her simply wasn't an option for Samantha who decided to wander off alone with Harley instead.

But behind the picture of serenity, all was not as it seemed as Joanne stared into the distance in her dream. There was something out there, indistinct shapes moving distantly in a formless haze, a pack of nightmare creatures Joanne knew would be totally unlike anything she'd ever encountered. They were coming for her, their awful cries echoing, primeval and animal-like across a remote, forbidding landscape.

Joanne was afraid; all her instincts were telling her to run, and yet she was being drawn towards a lone figure clad in simple, ancient robes, who was sitting calmly upon the trunk of a fallen tree a little way ahead. A hood, similar to that worn by a medieval monk, was pulled over their head, and they were surrounded by a multitude of tiny, brightly coloured lights. Whoever the person was, they were clearly undaunted by the malevolence closing in, but Joanne kept finding herself looking anxiously towards that same, arcane malice, watching as the creeping darkness spread around them like a black, oily shadow.

As fearful as she was, Joanne still felt drawn to the mysterious, cowled figure. One of the tiny lights was lovingly held in their cupped hands. It was different to the others, pulsating brightly, white, silver and gold. Slowly, the figure looked up, and Joanne heard herself gasp in astonishment when she saw the captivating violet eyes and exquisite beauty of the woman beneath the hood of the humble robes.

'Behold the Shepherdess,' whispered a distant voice that Joanne felt rather than heard, and the woman's serene face broke into the most radiant of smiles. The angelic expression immediately filled Joanne with a feeling of warmth and wonder, but then the Shepherdess looked back down at the flickering light in her hands.

'This one is very special,' she said, her voice soft and calming, and then, unexpectedly, she reached out and presented it to Joanne.

To begin with, Joanne was unsure what to do as the light was brought within her reach, but then she swallowed her uncertainty and allowed the fingertips of one trembling hand to reach out and touch the tiny orb. It was surprisingly cold at first, but then came a strange tingling sensation in Joanne's fingers which soon spread up her arms, her neck, and finally into every part of who she was. As the surrounding darkness exploded into the most perfect light, there was a sudden sense of liberation and a release from the confines of her physical body. The baying, anguished howls of the previously onrushing hoards faded instantly from Joanne's ears as if they had never existed, replaced by a freedom beyond anything that could be imagined. The answers to all her questions flashed fleetingly, temptingly, before her eyes, as if she were an empty vessel being filled with everything missing in her life, and then …

Joanne woke to find herself alone in the garden at Greenoaks. Her heart was racing, not with fear but with excitement. She felt elation beyond anything she'd ever known, and yet there were tears streaming down her face. Joanne wiped her eyes, trying desperately to hold on to the fading memory of the beautiful vision that had blessed her dream, while deep inside a faint yet mesmerising sensation of butterflies was slowly but surely beginning to subside.

Elation quickly turned to despair. While in the presence of the Shepherdess, Joanne had felt whole and protected, but back in the conscious world of cold, hard reality, all she felt was empty and alone.

Consumed by an overwhelming sense of regret, Joanne began sobbing uncontrollably. It seemed even her dreams ended up leaving her, and these profound feelings would go on to dishearteningly resurface, albeit secretly, throughout the rest of the day. As that day succumbed to the inevitable will of the night, Joanne would go on to have other dreams, and this time there would be no Shepherdess in them to protect her. This time the screaming pack she'd heard before would not be deterred. This time it would continue to pursue her, merciless and unrelenting. Joanne would find herself alone and searching for Samantha, desperately calling out her name to try and save her from an irresistible force that at times was close enough to smell. Every time Joanne closed her eyes, the pack would be waiting in the darkness, a darkness that hid its unspeakable horrors, but not its terrifying sense of inescapability.

Joanne didn't know it, but The Puppeteer's Manforms had found them …

CHAPTER 13

Daylight surged into the garage as its up-and-over door rose with a teeth-grating, metallic grinding. Wayne stood silhouetted against the brightness outside, motionless, as though temporarily transfixed by the lock-up's contents. Cars had never really held too much of a fascination for him, and he didn't often drive his BMW M3, but this time it was different. Stepping into the semi gloom, Wayne lovingly ran a finger along the M3's lustrous silver bonnet, appreciating the remarkable machine for everything it was, an engineered version of himself, perfection designed and built for a purpose.

Such was Wayne's desire to ready himself after his fated discovery of Samantha Middleton, everything else had faded into insignificance, including a photo shoot he'd had booked for later that day. Now once again in control of the situation, and having managed to successfully rearrange several other engagements on his planner, Wayne was clear for a few days, and his window of opportunity was large enough for him to relax and enjoy the thrill of the hunt.

A sweeping feeling of euphoria suddenly came over him, a stirring so intense that it made him shiver with excitement. Naomi's presence was unmistakeable, and she was gracing him with it once again. Wayne could feel her wanting him, desiring him, the strength of her lust a carnal motivation for him to both complete his duty and fulfil her insatiable needs.

Determined and empowered, Wayne slung his bags onto the back seat of the BMW, tossed his jacket onto the passenger seat, and started the engine.

*

Considering the disturbing dreams that Joanne had experienced the previous night, the last thing she wanted was to be away from her daughter, but Samantha was adamant that she wanted to venture into the nearby market town of Hitchin, and feeling rather tired and irritable due to her poor night's sleep, shopping wasn't on Joanne's agenda. Joanne had conceded defeat despite her reluctance because having to reveal the true reasons behind her objections would probably have made her sound stupid. Instead, she decided to take Harley out for a good long walk after dropping Samantha into town, hoping the fresh air would go some way to help clear the annoying fogginess in her head.

Joanne pulled up in a side street near the town centre, and Samantha got out of the Range Rover, completely oblivious to the attentions of two young men sitting in a nearby coffee shop window. Joanne glared at them, but they didn't notice.

'Now don't worry about me, Boudicca,' said Samantha. 'I won't talk to any strangers. I won't take sweeties from anybody and I won't accept lifts from any dodgy blokes or lorry drivers … I'm a big girl now, honest!'

The light-hearted insolence made Joanne laugh, but she still gave her daughter a telling look. 'I can see that, Sam,' she said. 'Dressed to impress as usual!'

'And by that I'm guessing you think this skirt is too short, then?' Samantha replied, checking her reflection in a nearby shopfront.

'I'm not sure there's enough of it to be called a 'skirt', really.'

'Sun's out, legs out! Is there something wrong with my legs, is that it?'

'Well, of course there isn't! You've got fabulous legs, and by the look of things I'm not the only one who thinks so.' Joanne gestured towards the young men in the coffee shop window. 'Their drinks will be going cold if they don't stop checking you out!'

Samantha noticed the admiring looks and smiled, but decided to change the subject rather than risk getting a lecture from her mother about being dressed for a nightclub when she was only going shopping.

'So, I'll meet you in the market car park in front of the church in a couple of hours or so, then,' she said.

'Will that be enough time?'

'Yeah, plenty. I only want to have a look around. You won't forget to pick me up now, will you? I know you only too well!'

Joanne pulled one of 'those' faces, but Samantha ignored it and tapped the screen of her phone with fake authority.

'One minute over and I'll be right on your case, Boudicca!' she said, and then turned to Harley who was vying for her attention from behind his dog grill in the rear. 'See you soon, Harley Farley Foo … you too, then, Mummy Bear!'

Harley protested a little when Joanne drove away, but his mild distress soon ended once they'd left town and found themselves in open country. Joanne was heading towards Hitch Wood, a large area of natural beauty only about a mile or so from Preston, but as it so often did, her mind soon began to wander, and she was revisiting her nightmares of the previous night, dreams so abstract, so removed from her normal routine as to be almost portentous. It was the helplessness, the feeling of being hunted and pursued by something unknown which had etched itself into Joanne's memory, and another peculiarity was how she could recall everything with such uncomfortable clarity. Nothing had made any sense, and yet the effect upon her had been profound.

By the time Joanne pulled up in a small, gravelled parking area on the edge of the wood, she was almost on autopilot, but all Harley wanted to do was get out among the squirrels and rabbits. His excited yelps were a welcome distraction, and Joanne happily released him from the confines of the Range Rover's storage area and walked slowly after him into the wood.

There had been no other cars in the car park, so Joanne and Harley looked like they had the entire woodland to themselves, and Joanne intended to take full advantage. Some of the trees were hundreds of years old, with thick gnarled and twisted trunks. Others were much younger but no less impressive, stretching directly upwards towards the sky. It all amounted to a feeling of calm seclusion; any light that made it through the canopy overhead was a cool green, almost as cool as the air in the wood itself, but here and there, shafts of sunlight managed to find their way through to the woodland floor as dancing patches of light, celebrating the completion of a demanding journey.

Although Mother Nature had welcomed Joanne with open arms, she needed to be mindful of where she and Harley were. Dogs were supposed to be kept on leads, and even though Harley was very well behaved, she didn't want him to go cavorting off too far. There were also a number of badger setts dotted around in the woodland, and although badgers were nocturnal, any unexpected confrontation with one of the powerful little animals could result in some serious damage being inflicted upon her dog. It was then that Joanne spotted Harley standing motionless by some scrub a short distance ahead. From his rigid pose, he obviously had his beady little eyes on something, so perhaps then was as good a time as any to attach his lead. But as Joanne got closer, she was shocked to find Harley trembling instead. Far from focusing on a potential wrongdoing, he was distracted, hackles raised, every turn of his head accompanied by low growls and semi-whimpers.

The entire wood had suddenly fallen silent. Totally transformed from the previously idyllic setting, it felt more like a tomb. Every single one of the birds had stopped singing, and even the whispering breeze had stopped playing in the leaves above. The strange feeling Joanne had experienced during her disturbing dreams the night before began to return. The dense canopy overhead that had been shading her so lovingly from the sun now made her feel like the woodland was closing in around her, sealing her in with a presence that was stalking her, hunting her down ...

*

Chris Ryan wasn't the greatest of passengers. As far as *he* was concerned, when it came to cars, *he* knew how to drive and nobody else did. That was especially true when the driver of the car he was in happened to be his mother.

Anne could sense her son's discomfort and began to smile. She gave a knowing look to Andy in the rear-view mirror, and he silently responded by rolling his eyes up to the heavens.

'You never *were* one for patience, Chris,' said Anne. 'I always remember you asking, *Are we nearly there yet?* whenever we went anywhere when you were little. Sometimes you'd even start asking as we'd turned out of our street. It used to drive your father crazy!'

Chris ignored the swipe. He was looking in his passenger side wing mirror.

'You've got a few cars behind you. Maybe you could go a little faster?'

'Oh, I'm sure they won't mind, dear, after all, the pace of life out here is a little different to what you're used to.'

'Yes, but you can do sixty along here and …'

'I'm going as fast as I want to go! Besides, this is *your* car and I'm not used to it. I'm just doing Andy a favour because he's been driving me everywhere lately. Anyway, you just remember what the doctors told you. Miraculous recovery you may have made. Miracle man you may happen to be, whatever, I don't care! You'll still have to rest and take things easy, and that *includes* putting up with me.'

Andy stifled his laughter.

'Come on, Dad,' he said. 'Leave Nan alone … I think she's a great driver.'

Anne smiled her appreciation.

Chris sighed and bit his lip.

*

In Hitch Wood, Joanne's mouth was going dry. As much as she wanted to run, she was rooted to the spot, but then she heard the sound of splintering branches and thundering hooves, and a herd of deer came stampeding through the trees and bushes in front of her. Unable to get out of the way, Joanne tried to make herself as small as possible by pressing herself up against a nearby tree trunk, while Harley did his best to protect her, barking and snapping at the leaping, bounding exodus. A magnificent stag appeared in the melee and stood firm before Harley's ferocity, only sprinting on after his herd once all of their number were safe. Not even an animal of *his* courage and fortitude, it seemed, was prepared to stand his ground against whatever was heading in their direction.

Already, forbidding shadows deepened further amongst the trees around them, as the oily blackness from Joanne's nightmares began to manifest itself as an oozing, terrifying reality. With the sound of the deer herd crashing through the undergrowth behind her, Joanne turned and ran with Harley as fast as she could in a stumbling, desperate fashion. There was a pressure on the back of her neck as though it were being squeezed by an unseen hand and the skin of her entire body was prickly from countless stimulated nerve endings, imaginary needles urging her to go faster. God, how she was praying not to fall!

With Harley bounding along ahead, Joanne ran like she'd never run before, hurdling fallen tree trunks, forcing her way through bushes, branches snagging in her hair and whipping the bare skin on her arms. The deer herd had already cleared the edge of the wood, stampeding into a nearby field. Through some gaps in the trees, Joanne could see their sprinting grey forms streaking across the pasture, until at last, the trees and bushes cleared for her too, and her Range Rover came into view.

Joanne flung herself gratefully at the car. She opened the driver's door and let Harley jump in while she herself turned and dared to look behind her.

For a moment she stared, breathless and confused, into the woodland. Joanne had expected to see something approaching, something the size of a train emerging from the gloom towards her, but all her eyes could make out was a normal scene of woodland tranquillity. Joanne shook her head disbelievingly. There was no way she had imagined all that. Still brimming with suspicion, she climbed into the Range Rover, gunned the engine, and sped out of the parking area. Once safely on the move, she began to breathe a little more easily, but then Harley started to whimper on the back seat. Instinctively, Joanne glanced in her rear-view mirror – straight into the eyes of The Puppeteer. At once, The Puppeteer began to grin, the malevolence spreading slowly across his face like an ever-widening tooth-filled maw. Joanne let out the most awful piercing scream, and Harley cried out too, but The Puppeteer's grin just widened further at the sound of their terror. He leant forwards, his nightmare countenance in the mirror looming large and horrifyingly clear, steadily drawing Joanne's terrified eyes into his.

*

'There you are,' said Anne. 'The road to Whitwell. You see, it didn't take long now, did it?'

She turned into the lane and accelerated slowly away.

Chris was still wishing the pedals were on *his* side of the car.

*

Joanne couldn't tear herself away from The Puppeteer's unblinking focus and, in her panic, involuntarily pressed her foot down even harder on the accelerator ...

'Jesus Christ, they're going way too fast!' said Chris, his eyes widening at the sight of a black Range Rover tearing down the hill towards them. 'They'll never make that bloody bend!'

And then Joanne duly realised her mistake. The Puppeteer's hideous reflection was still there, out of the corner of her eye, but that fear was now compounded by the sight of the onrushing bend in the road. Joanne hit the brakes but far too late, airbags exploding into life as she careered into the far bank of a ditch. The impact lifted the Range Rover into the air, propelling it through a thick hedge, causing it to come down heavily in a grassy field on the other side. Unable to grasp the steering wheel, Joanne's head was slammed painfully against her driver's side window as the vehicle lurched and veered uncontrollably, barely staying upright.

After what seemed like an eternity, the car finally rolled to a stop some distance from the road. Joanne managed to open her driver's door and staggered out into the field, dazed and nauseous. The world was spinning, her head was stinging like it had been on fire, and there was a searing pain in her right shoulder from the inertia of the seatbelt that had undoubtedly just saved her from more serious injury. As she stared glassily through the haze, it looked like some people were hurrying towards her. She took a few unsteady steps forward and then collapsed.

'Chris, come on, slow down!' said Anne. 'You're supposed to be taking it easy!'

'There are some foil blankets in the back of the car,' he replied, completely ignoring her. 'Can you go and grab them for me? And the First Aid kit ...'

'Should I call for an ambulance, Dad?' asked Andy as they came upon Joanne.

'No ... no, I'm fine ... really I am ...' she replied, trying her best to get up.

'Try not to move,' said Chris. 'Can you tell me your name?'

'Oh my God! Samantha! My daughter! I'm supposed to be picking her up! And Harley... he was in the back ...!'

A large black German Shepherd dog came running towards them and began licking at Joanne's face.

'Is this Harley?' asked Chris.

'Yes ... yes, it is ... oh thank God! Harley, baby, you're okay ... Has he gone, boy? Has he gone?'

Harley looked across at the Range Rover and whimpered, and Chris noticed a renewed expression of fear on Joanne's face.

'Why us?' he heard her whisper. 'What does he want with us?'

Chris hadn't seen any other vehicle, but what else could have made the woman drive so fast and erratically unless she'd been trying to get away from somebody? Before he could dwell anymore on anything, however, his mother arrived with the First Aid kit and foil blankets.

'Here you go,' said Anne, and then asked how Joanne was feeling.

'I can't stop shaking!' Joanne replied, and then she began to cry. 'Oh God

... and now I've started bloody well blubbing!'

'Well, that's very understandable after a frightful accident like this,' said Anne, placing one of the foil blankets gently around Joanne's shoulders. 'And I don't suppose these two have introduced themselves to you either, have they?'

'No ...'

'Well, in that case let me do the honours on their behalf! I'm Anne Ryan, and these two handsome men are my son, Chris, and grandson, Andy, and just so you know, we don't live very far from here so we can stay with you until we get something organised.'

'But I have to get my daughter!' Joanne sobbed. 'She's in town and she's expecting me! I need to get my phone ... it's in the car!'

Joanne went to stand up, but Anne stopped her.

'You stay right there; the boys can get it for you,' she said, looking up at Chris enquiringly. 'I think that might be a good idea, don't you? Along with anything else she might need from in there?'

Chris wondered at how easily his mother could make him look so completely idle, and went over to Joanne's car to fetch her belongings as instructed, with Andy in tow.

'My phone's in my handbag,' said Joanne. 'And I think that's all that's in there, apart from Harley's lead.'

Anne smiled reassuringly.

'Oh well,' she replied. 'It'll keep those two occupied for a few minutes anyway!'

'And it's Joanne ... my name, I mean ... Oh God, I'm in absolute bits at the moment. I'm really sorry, I'm not usually as bad-mannered as this.'

'I'm sure you're not!'

'And thank you so much for stopping and helping.'

'Don't worry. Just try and relax.'

'You're very good at this, Anne.'

'Well, that's probably because I used to be a headteacher. Honestly, Joanne? You'd be amazed at some of the stuff I've had to deal with!'

While Anne did her best to comfort Joanne, Chris went to search the driver's side of the Range Rover. Andy had already made his way to the other side, and it was as he walked towards the rear passenger door that a feeling of incredible nausea swept over him. The suddenness of its onset brought him to his knees, normal time ceased to exist, and everything around him stopped as though thrust into a state of suspended animation. It wasn't *unlike* what he'd experienced in the hospital after the gypsy's kiss, but this time it was far more pronounced, much stronger.

The nausea came again. Andy's eyes were being drawn towards the side of the car facing him, which had begun to ripple like the surface of a pond, the effect increasing in intensity, until a large, shapeless form began to emerge. The mass tore itself free, and once the hypnotic metamorphosis had run its course, Andy found himself staring up at the biggest man he had ever seen.

Slowly, the huge figure began to turn around.

The Puppeteer knew that seers still existed among humans, although the genuinely gifted were rare, but what he hadn't bargained for was having one so close to him at that precise moment. What was more, this boy was different, a 'Pure Channel', an Innocent seer, who knew little about his unique ability and it would be that very naivety that could make him strong. This young seer was no different from a child peering into a mysterious world full of fascination for the very first time.

Andy suddenly found himself the focus of the most unearthly stare as The Puppeteer glared down at him.

With the touch of my hand, from The Truth I shall bless ye
From the Master of Puppets, with this kiss I protect thee.

The gypsy's words came back into Andy's mind once again.

'The Puppeteer, *actually*,' said the apparition in a voice every bit as unnatural as its appearance. 'And how fitting that you should be on your knees in my presence.'

'We've prepared him for you!' said a woman's voice, unexpectedly.

The gypsy from the hospital had mysteriously appeared at Andy's side, but The Puppeteer appeared unmoved at the interruption.

'With just a kiss?' he asked. 'I think not … Let's see if there may be a place for him at my table, for instance. There are such wonders waiting for you there, young Andy. Do you have a sense of adventure about you? I think you do.'

Andy began to feel like he was being crushed by the air around him. Simply breathing was becoming difficult, and he began to panic at the sensation of his life being slowly squeezed out of him. The gypsy tried to stand firm and protect him, but she was no match for The Puppeteer, who started grinning at Andy's mounting distress.

'But I thought you might like to play, Andy! Am I playing a little too rough for you? I only want to see what you might be made of …'

A large African man clad in a white shroud appeared at Andy's other shoulder. He had appeared just as unexpectedly as the gypsy, but unlike the old lady, he was accompanied by an almost blinding light. Immediately, Andy found that he could breathe again, and began gratefully sucking in huge gulps of air.

'And then the erudite *Zambaya* makes a timely appearance,' said The Puppeteer. 'On overseeing duties, are we? And why is this when it should be so entirely beneath you? Have you fallen out of favour with the faceless graces of the Supreme Collective *as well*, my old friend? Is that the reason why you are showing your face here? Or might it be something else that calls you?'

Zambaya didn't respond, choosing to hold The Puppeteer's searing gaze in defiant silence, a silent rebuttal that drew a caustic response. 'Then it must be a sense of duty that brings you to The Circle,' said The Puppeteer. 'And so once again we will be drawing swords against each other. Do not attempt to insult my beautiful intelligence by not engaging with me, Zambaya; my abilities are worth far more than your contempt.'

The gypsy and Zambaya moved closer to Andy as The Puppeteer's deathly gaze fell upon him once more.

'But I must say, young Andy,' The Puppeteer said, grinning, 'that it has been a pleasure making your acquaintance, and how enthusiastic I am for our paths to cross again. Who knows where your inquisitiveness might lead us next time …?'

The Puppeteer's menacing comment was left hanging as he dissipated like cigar smoke into thin air. The gypsy looked up apologetically at Zambaya.

'He was too powerful,' she said. 'I tried, but too much hate there was in him.'

Zambaya nodded reassuringly, but it was all getting a little too exclusive, a little too cosy between the two of them as far as Andy was concerned. Regardless of how grateful he might have been for being saved from The Puppeteer, he didn't appreciate being left out after what he'd just had to endure.

'I remember you from the hospital,' he said to the gypsy. 'And I remember that rhyme you said to me. Who are you and *what* is going on?'

'My name is Oshina', the gypsy replied. 'And I am your Overseer.'

'Oshina walks with you … I walk with your father,' Zambaya added. 'We are watchers over you both.'

Up to that point, Zambaya had remained silent, yet his first words had been delivered with the utmost authority. His tone, smooth yet unequivocal, had taken Andy completely by surprise, confirmation that he was undoubtedly someone of great importance. But why was it so? Oshina seemed to be almost in awe of Zambaya, and even The Puppeteer had considered the 'erudite' African a worthy adversary. Andy hadn't meant to sound so sharp as he had before, and felt it might be wise to show a bit more respect.

'Like Guardian Angels?' he asked. 'But I thought it was all just made up!'

'To doubt such things is understandable,' said Zambaya. 'For in your realm such truths are all too often dismissed. We know ourselves as Overseers and we are many, but few of your kind are aware of us.'

'Which is why we needed to make *you* aware,' said Oshina. 'I came to you as I did to wake you from your slumber. We need your eyes.'

'Because of The Circle?' asked Andy. 'I heard The Puppeteer mention it, but what is it? I mean, that's what all this is about, isn't it?'

Zambaya explained that a group connected by a shared goal was known to Overseers as a Circle. 'And in this case, young Andrew Ryan,' he said, 'The Circle is a *cycle* of events of which you are a part. You have the eyes of The Circle, and it must be so if the others are blind.'

'The Circle needs a seer,' said Oshina. 'There is somebody that you will have to keep safe. Someone so special that the Master of Puppets seeks them out for his own ends. It is your *feelings* you must learn to trust, young Andrew, and not your thoughts.'

'So, Joanne must be a part of this too, then,' said Andy. 'Is this why this happened to her? Is it her who I need to protect?'

But Zambaya would only elaborate upon how The Puppeteer had used Joanne's car as a portal.

'He can use any object associated with an individual once he has established a connection with them,' he replied. 'The Puppeteer was crossing over from your world into his when you encountered him. You are in the flux between those worlds, so if you will excuse me, I will need to close that portal to make sure The Puppeteer cannot use it again.'

Andy had so many more questions, but they were going to have to remain unasked and unanswered. Zambaya closed the portal, and both he and Oshina began to fade.

Time restarted when Andy came back to his senses, with everything exactly as it was the moment he'd accidentally entered 'the flux'.

But *had* it been accidental? The Puppeteer had clearly been the cause of Joanne's crash, and it was just as obvious that Andy's family just happening to be in the right place at the right time was no coincidence, either.

Andy wondered how he was ever going to be able to 'trust his feelings' as Oshina had suggested, because he certainly didn't know what to 'think'.

CHAPTER 14

Anne Ryan didn't much care for dogs; in fact, she was rather frightened of them. It was a childhood thing, but Harley was very different from the average mutt. His unwavering devotion to Joanne was undeniable, and yet he hadn't showed any signs of aggression towards Anne or her family even though they were all complete strangers. Harley's profile was as noble as his expression was aloof, yet his chestnut-brown eyes had such a softness to them that Anne couldn't resist stroking him around his neck. She didn't even flinch when Harley gently licked her forearm to reciprocate her affection.

'Isn't he beautiful?' she said. 'Just look at those eyes! *What* a handsome boy!'

'He likes you,' said Joanne.

'Thank God for that, he's huge!'

'Oh, he's a gentle giant really, nothing but a big softy with a big bark.'

'Still, big softy or not, I don't think I'd like to get on the wrong side of him.'

Anne felt it was important to keep Joanne talking, especially as what little colour was left in her face had suddenly started to drain away. Anne was already reaching into her handbag for some tissues when Joanne obliged her foresight, and promptly threw up.

'Oh Christ!' she said, horrified. 'I'm so sorry!'

'Don't worry about it, Joanne. I can assure you you're not the first person who's ever done that in front of me! I'm sure it's just shock, that's all.'

It was then that Anne noticed some swelling over Joanne's right eye.

'You've got a rather tasty bump coming up there,' she said, gently moving Joanne's hair out of the way, which also revealed a congealing rivulet of blood on the side of her face. 'Quite a nasty little cut as well. I wouldn't be surprised at all if you've got concussion. I think we ought to take you to hospital and get you looked at.'

'Oh God, no! I hate hospitals! There's no need to …'

Joanne began retching again and threw up for a second time.

Chris and Andy were talking to a farmer who'd just arrived on the scene when Chris happened to look over and see the concern on his mother's face. Anne noticed him frowning and went over to join him.

'How's she doing?' Chris asked quietly.

'I'm not sure,' Anne replied. 'She's got some swelling over her eye and quite a nasty looking cut; she's had a real crack on the head by the look of it. She's been sick a couple of times, too, so I really think we should take her to hospital, but she seems very anti about it.'

Joanne watched Anne and Chris talking to each other, but she couldn't make out what they were saying. Her head was clearing a little, and it suddenly struck her what an attractive man Chris actually was. He was lean, yet solidly built and upright, probably around six feet tall. His dark hair, greying slightly around his temples, gave him something of a distinguished look; he had the same kind brown eyes as his mother, and exuded a similar air of calming assuredness. All things considered, Joanne felt interested enough to look for a wedding band on his finger. *Great*, she thought, when it became apparent that he wasn't wearing one. *No make-up, and probably puke in your hair. Fabulous, Jo ... how to create a lasting impression!*

In Hitchin town centre, Samantha's feet had begun to complain about such an irresponsible choice of shoes for a shopping trip, so she decided to take the weight of her tortured pedes, bought a magazine, and ordered a cappuccino at a nearby alfresco coffee outlet in the market square.

Subtly adjusting her skirt as she sat down, Samantha smiled to herself as she remembered her mother's reservations about its lack of length. Shopping wasn't quite the same alone, and it was most unlike her mother not to have wanted to come along. She'd seemed a little inattentive that morning, like her mind was somewhere else entirely, but Samantha hadn't felt it necessary to ask why. If there had been anything that needed to be shared, then something would undoubtedly have been said, so it was safe to assume that it was probably due to her mother being away from the office and her usual difficulty in switching off.

On the upside, however, it gave Samantha the opportunity to touch base with one or two other important people uninterrupted, and then, as if on cue, one of them beat her to the punch. Samantha grabbed her mobile out of her handbag to find Abigail, one of her closest friends from back in Hampstead, who was keen to know if she was interested in a night out with the girls, but Samantha had to decline.

'NO CAN DO, ABI – I'M AWAY WITH MA!' she messaged.

'DAMMIT, BESTIE! WHERE YOU AT THEN?' came Abi's reply.

'IN HITCHIN RIGHT NOW DRINKING COFFEE'

It was another bright and beautiful day, and the town centre was both vibrant and colourful. Samantha struck a pose and took a selfie with the market square and its period architecture proudly displayed behind her, and promptly sent it to Abi. At about the same time, a sudden and unexpected breeze got up and blew Samantha's magazine open. Written boldly in what looked like black marker pen across the exposed page were the words: *I HAVE FOUND YOU!*

Before Samantha could make any sense of anything, her phone pinged again with Abigail's response: 'NICE! IS IT HALLOWEEN THERE BY THE WAY? CHECK OUT THAT GUY BEHIND YOU. SCARY OR WHAT!'

Samantha automatically looked round, but all she could see were a couple of empty tables.

And then the random breeze blew up once more, causing more pages to flick themselves over as if turned by an unseen hand, stopping at a full-page advertisement over which was scrawled: *I HAVE FOUND YOU BOTH!*

Barely able to hold onto her phone, Samantha checked the selfie she'd sent to Abigail and immediately went rigid. Something was in the shot that *hadn't* been when Samantha had taken it – The Puppeteer.

Blind panic set in the moment she saw his gloating, sneering expression. People sitting and talking nearby were stunned into silence as Samantha grabbed her handbag and shot up from her seat all in one movement, the aluminium table at which she'd been sitting crashing to the granite cobbles of the market square like a clashing cymbal, along with her barely touched coffee.

But Samantha couldn't have cared less about what anybody else might have been thinking. All she wanted to do was to get out of town. She ran from the square as fast as her high-heeled shoes would allow, not stopping until she reached the carpark where she'd arranged to meet her mother. A few days earlier, Samantha had woken from a short but deep sleep in her mother's office, distantly aware that something had happened to her that she'd been powerless to stop. Perhaps it had been The Puppeteer toying with her then, too, and if he'd followed her to her mother's offices, he could easily have been able to track her to Greenoaks.

Frantically, Samantha began searching through her mobile for her mother's number.

*

'Joanne, maybe it's best that we get you to hospital to be on the safe side,' said Chris, but Joanne just seemed to stare at him as though his words had gone in one ear and straight out of the other. 'Joanne?' he asked again. 'Joanne …? I think we should …'

'Oh yes! Oh God, I'm sorry … I didn't mean to be rude. I'm just not quite with it right now.'

'Well, that's what's bothering me a bit. I really think we should get a doctor to look at you.'

Joanne thought for a moment.

'I suppose you're right,' she sighed. 'But I hate hospitals, and the thought of waiting for hours in casualty really doesn't do it for me.'

Having only just come out of hospital himself, the last thing Chris really wanted was to go back into another one so soon, but he still didn't want to take any chances.

'Well, you've had quite a bang on the head by the look of it,' he said, gently checking the swelling his mother had spoken about. 'They don't mess about when it comes to head injuries and that's quite a spectacular bump you've got there! I don't think you'll be hanging around too long before they take a look at you.'

'But I *can't* go to hospital – I have to get my daughter! She's going to be expecting me. And what about the car? I can't just leave it here and, oh my God …! Look what I've done to the farmer's bloody hedge!'

'Don't worry about all that now. There's nothing here that can't be dealt with later when things have calmed down a little. Why don't you call your daughter *now* and tell her what's happened, and then we could all go together and pick her up? And *then* we all go over to casualty because you really ought to be checked over by the hospital. What do you say?'

'But my car. The farmer …'

'But the farmer's fine about everything; he's just glad you're okay. He's talking about towing your car to his yard and keeping it safe until it can be collected.'

Slowly, Joanne began to calm down.

'You seem to have everything under control,' she said. 'God, it was lucky you guys were around. I would've been completely useless on my own. Thank you so very much again for stopping and helping.'

Although Chris was used to dealing with people in traumatic situations, he'd never actually felt himself blush at an expression of gratitude before, and the reddening of his face didn't go unnoticed. Joanne couldn't remember the last time she'd made *anybody* blush, let alone a man, and Chris's awkwardness made him all the more endearing.

'I'd better call Sam,' she said, and then gestured towards the handbag Chris was holding, having salvaged it from her car. 'I don't think it suits you, really …'

'Oh God! Yes … Of course, I'm so sorry!'

Chris blushed again, but thankfully for him, Joanne's mobile had started ringing just as he handed the handbag over. It was Samantha.

'Hi Mum,' she said, although she sounded unusually strained. 'Is there any chance you can come and pick me up now?'

For a while following the accident, Joanne had felt muddled and detached, but all at once the full impact of her predicament hit home.

'I would Sam,' she said. 'But I might be a little while yet.' She bit her lip. The tears were coming again, and there was nothing she could do to stop them. 'I've had a bit of an accident,' she sobbed. 'I'm so sorry ...'

Anne was first to react.

'Oh, you poor love,' she said as Joanne fell to pieces. 'Here, let me speak to her... Samantha, isn't it?'

Joanne nodded. She just couldn't compose herself enough to carry on the conversation, and reluctantly handed the phone over to Anne who calmly assured Samantha that everything was under control, and that her mum, although shocked and upset, was otherwise fine. After listening in for a few minutes, Joanne managed to gather herself sufficiently enough to give Samantha some added reassurance, and it was agreed that they should go and get her immediately since everything else had been sorted out, albeit temporarily.

But Samantha was in turmoil by the time the call had ended. News of her mother's accident and the reappearance of The Puppeteer had turned her into a fidgeting mess. Unable to work out whether to stay in one place or walk around until she saw the white Audi that had been described during the conversation with Anne, Samantha ended up sitting on a low wall, trying to take her mind off matters by immersing herself in some clothing websites on her phone, oblivious to everything else, including the eyes of a driver staring at her from a silver BMW.

Wayne Terry could scarcely believe his luck, but maybe it had been more than that, because for some reason it was as though something else had taken over as he had approached the town, and a strong, overriding sense of purpose had told him that he needed to be right where he was at that precise moment.

There was no doubt about it – just like a guided missile, Wayne had been delivered right to his target. The problem was that it was broad daylight, and although the Middleton whore was alone, it was hardly a secluded spot, and he didn't have the necessary tools about him with which to sort her out. It was going to be a case of having to think on his feet. The little bitch had just been talking to somebody on her mobile, so maybe it was best to wait and see what panned out; after all, hadn't his mother once told him when he was a child that all good things came to those who waited?

Wayne smiled when he realised the truth of his mother's words. It had taken him thirteen years to get even with the old lesbian whore, but when he had, boy, *hadn't* he!

From his opportune parking space, Wayne could survey his quarry, as engrossed in Samantha as *she* was in whatever she was looking at on her phone. Sitting with her right leg crossed over her left, Samantha's short skirt had ridden up, exposing the soft curve of the underside of her right thigh almost up to the buttock. Every now and again, she would flick away at a persistent tress of shoulder length, brunette hair that kept venturing onto her face, until, with an unintentional expression of innocence, she cocked her head to one side to stop it happening again.

Wayne felt himself hardening in his jeans. He loosened his belt, undid his fly to relieve some of the pressure, and began squeezing and manipulating his liberated erection. He was going to have the little tart's respect if it were the last thing he did, and succumbing to his need was going to be such a glorious way for her to go out!

A white Audi estate car pulling up in front interrupted Wayne's fantasy, and a dark-haired, rather athletic looking man got out. He said something to Samantha, and she rushed to the back of the car and embraced someone whom Wayne assumed was Joanne. With his throat burning from a surge of bile at the sight of their closeness, he started his engine and waited.

Harley was beside himself when he saw Samantha, and began to whine incessantly from the Audi estate's boot space, but the only thing on Samantha's mind was her mother.

'Oh my God, Mum! I'm so glad you're okay!' she said, but then she noticed the dried blood on Joanne's face, and frowned.

'Well, maybe not quite a hundred percent,' replied Joanne. 'Anyway, these wonderful people who stopped and helped have already talked me into going to A&E to be checked over.'

'Which is where we're going right now,' said a rather determined female voice from the driver's seat.

'So, you must be Anne, the lady I spoke to on the phone!' Samantha said. 'Lovely to meet you, and thank you so much for helping Mum!'

'It's lovely to meet you too, Samantha, and you're very welcome ... And just so we can all get off on the right foot, this handsome devil here is my son, Chris, and that equally handsome young chap in the back with you and your mum is my grandson, Andy.'

A simultaneous chorus of 'hello, Samantha' followed and she suddenly felt strangely shy. The eye contact she'd shared with Andy had lingered a little longer than she might have intended, and he added a smile when she happened to glance over in his direction again.

Anne pulled slowly away, unaware that a silver BMW was moving smoothly and stealthily out of a parking space behind her.

CHAPTER 15

Joanne could be extremely devious when it came to inventing ways of avoiding things that she found unfavourable, but her protestations that it was unfair to take Harley with them as she didn't know how long she would be stuck in A&E were entirely reasonable. Samantha, however, was adamant that they should go straight there rather than go via Preston to drop Harley off first. She feared there was a chance her mother might refuse going on to the hospital once they'd got to Greenoaks, and she wanted to prevent the situation from arising. She was also growing increasingly concerned about her mother's welfare. Joanne was not only in a great deal of pain with her neck and shoulder, but also pallid and occasionally vague from the head injury she'd sustained.

Eventually, Joanne relented. She could see that Samantha was desperate for her to be seen by a doctor, and not only that, Anne had said she was happy to go back to the cottage with Samantha and Harley once they knew how things were progressing.

Andy was tasked with looking after Harley upon their arrival at the A&E department, a request that, as a dog lover, he was happy to carry out. Harley was a pleasure, either laying peacefully at Andy's feet or sitting obediently by his side, and the dog's exemplary behaviour gave Andy the chance to reflect upon what had happened when he'd approached Joanne's Range Rover. The whole encounter had been so completely removed from reality that the word 'surreal' simply didn't cut it. Andy had already concluded that his father's incredible recovery had less to do with good fortune and more to do with design, just as he was certain that those very same forces had been responsible for bringing them all together in such incredible and dramatic circumstances. Perhaps that was the reason why he'd been able to accept Oshina's and Zambaya's words so easily, in spite of the numerous and as yet unanswered questions that remained.

Unanswered or unanswer*able* questions was another question in itself. Andy let out an audible sigh as he tried to establish which. His were to be 'the eyes' of The Circle, that was all he knew, but in amongst all the uncertainties there was one consequential and uncomfortable fact. *He* was going to have to endure the crushing presence of The Puppeteer again, and when that time came, it would be by The Puppeteer's ruthless design.

Andy shuddered to think what kind of torment The Puppeteer might consider appropriate for their next meeting, and suddenly felt rather exposed as he stood alone with only Harley for company, but little did he know that another person with connections to The Puppeteer was also there outside the hospital. Wayne Terry was getting irritated that the A&E doorway was being partly obscured by a waiting ambulance, its iridescent Battenberg markings causing him to squint as he peered into the contrasting shade under the unit's covered entrance.

The day was getting hotter by the minute, and in trying to find a parking space that offered him some protection from the sun, Wayne had had to sacrifice a clearer view. The shade provided by the sparse canopy of the immature maple tree under which he was parked was partial at best, and as the temperature in the car steadily began to increase, so did Wayne's exasperation.

The driver's side electric window disappeared into its door cavity with a steady hum, followed by the passenger's side. The through draft, although welcome, just wasn't enough, but Wayne didn't want to risk wasting precious fuel by switching on the engine and using the car's air-conditioning. He only had a quarter of a tank left and didn't know how much more driving he was going to have to do. To make matters worse, he was also nearly out of cigarettes, but he daren't drive to a filling station to resolve either issue in case he missed something important.

There was so much he wanted to know. Who was that guy standing there with the dog? A boyfriend or something? What were they all doing at the hospital? Who was the other bloke that had got out of the car in the car park in the town? So many questions and no fucking answers. Wayne hated that. He began drumming his fingers on the steering wheel, but the incessant beat eased as he began to fantasise about how close he was to his magical moment of destiny, and earning his deserved eternal reward.

Lost in his lurid thoughts, Wayne reached out towards the passenger seat beside him. He wasn't really paying attention as he fumbled around for the box containing his few remaining cigarettes, and was surprised to feel something hard to the touch. Instantly he looked down, and there, just visible above the inside pocket of the jacket he'd casually tossed onto the passenger seat that morning, was the top of the ornate letter opener that he'd stolen from Joanne Middleton's office. Wayne laughed openly to himself. He'd completely forgotten taking it. So, he *did* have a tool to do the job!

Wayne slipped the letter knife out of the pocket to take a closer look and wondered why somebody would want to use such a beautiful item in such an uninteresting way. He had a *much* better use for it. The decorative brass handle fitted snugly into the palm of his hand, now a little clammy with the excitement generated by the unexpected discovery. The heavy blade was silver, although probably plated, about five inches long and around an inch wide. Its edges were a little blunt as was the tip, but it was nothing that a good old-fashioned sharpening wouldn't put right, and a few practice wrist movements confirmed to Wayne that it was going to make a formidable weapon.

Considering the implement to be as perfectly balanced as himself, Wayne slipped the letter knife back into the pocket, and refocused his gaze upon the entrance of A&E.

While Wayne had been amusing himself with his new toy, the ambulance that had been obstructing his view had pulled away, and as soon as he turned his attention back to the hospital building the automatic doors swept open, and Samantha appeared. She was accompanied by an older woman and the older man who had got out of the car in the car park. The younger man with the dog approached them and they began talking. Wayne fastened his seatbelt, and waited.

'How's Joanne doing, now?' asked Andy.

'Still very shaken,' Anne replied, 'but otherwise she's okay. She's been registered, and they've dressed her headwound, but she's still waiting to be properly assessed. I think she'll be a little while yet so we'd better head back and drop Harley off as we said. Chris is going to wait here with Joanne while we're gone.'

Anne reached down to pet Harley, and he wagged his tail excitedly, then she suggested to Samantha that they should pack some overnight things for her mother. 'Because it wouldn't surprise me at all if they keep your mum in,' she said.

Chris glared at his mother. Why was it that she *always* had to be so direct?

'It's only standard procedure *if* they do, Sam,' he said. 'And only as a precaution because she's got a head injury. Your mum's going to be fine, honestly.'

'Wow!' said Samantha. 'Mum's never had to stay in hospital before, apart from having me of course. I never even thought about that happening.'

'Well, as Chris said, they might not even keep her in at all,' Anne replied, regretting her previously blunt assessment. 'And if they *do* ... well, we'll be prepared, won't we? Anyway, whichever way it goes, I think we ought to be getting a wiggle on, wouldn't you agree?'

Wayne craned his neck. His suddenly rekindled interest in the situation had quelled his urge for a smoke as it appeared that things were about to take another turn. His suspicions were confirmed when the meeting broke up, and Samantha, the young man and the older woman got into their car. Wayne started his M3's engine and made sure that he was ready to follow.

*

When Chris returned to the waiting area, he noticed that there were a few more empty seats. One or two people glanced up at him as he made his way past them to where Joanne was sitting, but otherwise his presence was barely acknowledged. Legs outstretched and crossed at the ankles, arms folded across her chest, Joanne looked every bit as sullen as everybody else when Chris sat down next to her on a tired blue chair.

'Lively in here, isn't it?' he whispered, making Joanne chuckle slightly. 'How are you feeling? Any better?'

'Not really,' she replied, tilting her head from side to side as if to relieve some discomfort in her neck. 'And God only knows how long all *this* is going to take. I wish I hadn't bothered coming.'

'I don't think you'll have to wait too much longer …'

'Oh God, listen to me … I'm so sorry, Chris; I'm being such a miserable bitch!'

'Joanne, it's fine, honestly.'

'No, it's not. You and your family have been so good to me … to us, and I should be a lot more civil. You've really put yourselves out, and please feel free to call me Jo. Was Samantha okay when she left?'

'She seemed fine.'

'It's just that I thought she looked a bit upset.'

'I just think she's worried about you. She's got a lot on her mind, probably just the same as you, so feel free to talk if it helps; I'm a good listener – it's what I do.'

Chris's inquiring eyes studied Joanne intently, almost expectantly.

'Well, I think you've done more than enough already,' Joanne replied, a slight smile playing on her lips. 'But what is it that you *do* exactly? After the cool, calm, and collected manner you went about things earlier, I'm rather interested.'

Chris laughed, and looked down at the floor.

'I'm a copper!' he said.

'Oh shit, no way! I promise you I don't usually drive like that!'

'I'm sure you don't … And don't worry, I'm not traffic, I'm plain clothes, and I'm going to be off duty for a while in any case, convalescing … at my mother's! She lives up the road in Whitwell which is where we were going when we came across you.'

'So, you're not local, then?'

'No, I live in London with Andy, in Edgware to be exact, and I'm a Detective Chief Inspector in the Met, based in Colindale.'

'Wow! That's a pretty high rank, isn't it?'

'Yeah, reasonably.'

There was nothing flash or over the top about Chris, which Joanne found very endearing. He was grounded and unpretentious, and even though she hadn't been at all 'with it' following her accident, his professionalism in organising everything to do with her car had been so evident that his occupation shouldn't have come as such a surprise to her.

'Well, I'm not local either,' she said. 'We're just out this way having a break ... or we were! Anyway, Samantha and I live in Hampstead. I've got my own business and I work in Covent Garden. I'm a fashion designer and professional workaholic.'

The conversation flowed, and while Chris didn't go into much detail about his own profession, he seemed keenly interested in what Joanne had to say about hers. He could more than just relate to the pressures of work, and before long, Joanne found herself talking about other elements of her life, including the cottage she owned in Preston, but that she and Samantha didn't go there as often as they'd like.

'Anyway,' said Joanne. 'That's quite enough about me. My line of work's boring compared to yours! So, what's all this about you convalescing? Have you had to have an operation? Or were you injured chasing a baddie or something exciting like that?'

There was a pause while Chris considered his answer.

'Not exactly chasing,' he said. 'More like cornered a few villains, and then I ended up getting shot.'

'Oh no! That's awful!' Joanne replied, putting her hand up to her mouth in horror. 'I'm so sorry for kidding around like that, I had no idea ... You mean, they just pulled out a gun?'

'Don't worry, how were you to know? But it wasn't quite what you think because it's not generally as exciting as TV! It was just a routine operation following a tip-off; at least it was *supposed* to be. I didn't even need to be there because as a DCI I don't go out on operations, but we had a new recruit on their first assignment and I wanted to supervise her. There were drugs involved so it was a shared operation with the Drugs Squad, a couple of our people were there because one of the names we were given was a dealer who we suspected might have been behind a recent murder, but there was no question of any firearms being involved. Turned out we were wrong. One of the suspects had a handgun, a fight broke out, and when one of his accomplices tried to get the gun off him, it accidentally went off. I got in the way of the bullet and by all accounts I'm extremely lucky to be here.'

'Oh, my God ... Well that certainly puts *my* problems into perspective.'

'And like I said, might I be able to help with some of them?'

I doubt that very much, Joanne thought.

'If only you could,' she said. 'I mean … there's the accident for one thing, and all the forms and crap I'm going to have to fill in. Then there's the car recovery and stuff to sort out, not to mention possibly having to stay in this bloody place for the night with Samantha being on her own after what … er … after what happened to *me*, I mean! I know she's worried and I don't like the idea of her being alone and worrying unnecessarily.' Aware that she was having to choose her words extremely carefully, Joanne drew a metaphorical line under matters by pointing to her head: 'So there's a fair bit going on in here that only I can deal with right now.'

Maybe it was just a trick of the unflattering lighting in the waiting area, but Chris thought Joanne's eyes were tearing up a little.

'Oh God,' she sighed, suddenly looking away. 'This is all such a bloody awful mess!'

Chris thought he would try and inject some positivity by suggesting that things could have been a lot worse, and how lucky Joanne had been at escaping pretty-much unscathed.

Bearing in mind what had appeared in her car and made her crash, Joanne considered herself to be anything *but* lucky, but Chris didn't have the faintest idea of what had caused the accident, and that was how it was going to stay.

'Well, it serves me right for taking my eyes off the road,' she said. 'Dogs can be as big a distraction as a mobile phone. I mean, I was dealing with that bloody great hairy lummox of mine because he was playing up in the back and I didn't know how fast I was going. By the time I realised I was running out of road, it was too late to even brake. You know the rest. I suppose the take-off was fine, but I will really have to work on my landings!'

'And that's what you're going to say to your insurance company?'

'Nah … I swerved to avoid a deer as far as they're going to be concerned!'

As much as Joanne's fabrication and glibness had been designed to hide the truth from Chris, it had done little to ease her fears about when the thing from her car might choose to come back and terrorise her again. Just what it was, and what it wanted, remained a terrifying mystery, and Joanne shivered as she recalled looking in her rear-view mirror, straight into those awful black eyes, watching that sickening, maniacal grin stretch across the reflection's face as though its craggy features had been made of rubber.

Joanne needed a moment to be alone, and made an excuse that she needed the toilet, leaving Chris to form his own opinions. From *his* standpoint, Joanne's comment about everything being a 'bloody awful mess' was probably the most honest statement she'd made in those past few minutes. Switching between false bravado and occasional desperation, her changing moods could have been simply down to her suffering a concussion, but they could also have been a pointer towards a much darker reality. Chris remembered her animated state when he'd first begun attending to her following the accident, the scratches on her arms, the twigs in her hair. She'd been absolutely terrified, even asking her dog if they were alone, as though somebody had been pursuing them.

For some reason, Joanne wanted to keep something hidden, and it didn't need the experience Chris had gained from countless interviews during his career in the Met for him to see it. Whatever it was should have been Joanne's business, and Joanne's business alone, but there was something else. Chris may have been born with a naturally inquiring mind, but this was far beyond being a case of just plain and simple curiosity. There was a nagging feeling, gnawing away in the pit of his stomach, that was saying he was missing a piece of a much bigger jigsaw, and it was refusing to go away.

Unaware of Chris's suspicions, Joanne waited for the person behind the drab, grey door of the nearest WC to finish. She felt strangely conspicuous standing in the corridor, as though her plight was on display for everyone to see. After a few moments, the door opened, and a woman emerged, greeting Joanne with a smile that Joanne only just about managed to return.

Grateful for no longer feeling that the eyes of the world were upon her, Joanne entered the secluded dimness of the convenience and leant against the inside of the door, making sure that it was locked. The brave face that she'd been putting on was slipping, and all she really wanted to do was cry. The pain in her shoulder was excruciating, she felt swimmy, nauseous, and the dull throbbing in her head was developing into what she knew was going to be a splitting headache.

Joanne began to fiddle with the tape securing the dressing over her eye so that she could have a look at the cut on her head. On a side wall above a small sink was a small, square mirror, but as she took a step towards it, she was gripped by fear. What if *he* was in there? What if that grinning monstrosity should appear behind her again? A wave of panic triggered an almost overwhelming urge to get away from the mirror and out of the room altogether, but Joanne's sudden dread had stimulated her bladder and she feared she might be about to wet herself.

The toilet was located in the corner of the room, but Joanne still had to alter her position on the seat so as not to risk making any kind of eye contact with the mirror. Just being in a room with it had suddenly become a huge challenge in itself. Joanne buried her face in her hands and silently wept. She even toyed with the idea of not washing her hands if it meant not having to stand in front of her own reflection, but practising a simple act of personal hygiene was at least a part of normality, and she would have a few more moments to compose herself before going back out into the waiting room.

Joanne fixed Chris with a smile as she wandered back over to her seat, hoping that her (probably) bloodshot eyes wouldn't give anything away. She was about to dig into her imagination to spin another far-fetched yarn about having hay fever, but then 'Mrs Joanne Middleton' was called for assessment, and the need to lie was put on hold.

Unfortunately for Joanne, her relief wasn't to last, for her worst fears about being kept in overnight for observation were about to be realised. The examining doctor had been very clear about the risks involved with head injuries and concussion, but she also wasn't ruling out the possibility of a fracture in Joanne's right shoulder joint.

Concussion Joanne could just about cope with, but a fracture hadn't even been on her radar, as she sat pensively, mulling things over alongside Chris in Radiology.

'At least I didn't have to have any stiches,' she said. 'So I suppose being glued up instead is something I've got going in my bloody favour.'

'And your shoulder might not be broken either,' he replied. 'The doctor only said it was a possibility.'

'Are you always this positive?'

'Yep ... glass half-full, that's me all over!'

Joanne chuckled; she was silent for a moment, and then she said: 'Chris, I really can't thank you and your family enough for what you've done for me and Sammy. Just saying it doesn't really seem enough, and I really want to thank you properly. What are your plans over the next few days?'

'None as far as I know, but you don't have to ...'

'Well in that case, I'd like to invite you all over to ours for dinner one evening. Samantha happens to be a marvellous little cook, so I have a very reliable substitute I can bring on if I'm still on the injury list! It really is the very least that we can do.'

'Okay then,' he said, sounding a little surprised. 'I guess you've got yourself a date!'

'Good!'

Nothing about the planning of a dinner party was going to solve Joanne's immediate problems, but at least her mind was going to have something else on which to focus. Smiling, she began delving one-handed inside her handbag and took out one of her business cards.

'That's my mobile number,' she said, passing it over to Chris. 'When the clan gets back, we'll have to sort something out.'

'Definitely,' said Chris, fishing his own card out of his pocket. 'Have you got a pen handy? I'd better write my number on the back, seeing as the one on the front of the card is my work mobile!'

'Detective Chief Inspector Christopher Ryan,' Joanne read aloud when he handed it over. 'Really trips off the tongue.'

The smile stayed on her lips as she put it in her handbag. When *was* the last time she'd willingly exchanged phone numbers with a man she'd known for only a few hours, apart from never? In spite of all that had happened to her, Joanne was becoming increasingly attracted to Chris. He was patient, understanding, *and* entertaining to talk to, and *just* as interesting was that while he'd mentioned living with his son, he hadn't said anything about having a woman in his life.

Unbeknown to Joanne, Chris was feeling the same way about *her*. He couldn't think of any other woman who'd had such a big effect on him in such a short space of time, and the more they interacted, the more beautiful she became.

The break-up of Chris's marriage four years prior had come as a severe blow, the pressure of his career in the Met having finally taken its toll. Chris had thought the marriage had been strong enough to cope, and even though it had been obvious that as a couple they'd been floundering, it had still been a terrible shock when Danielle, his wife of twenty years, had said that enough was enough and decided to leave him.

It didn't take Danielle long to find somebody else after the split, however, and she played Chris a bit like a fiddle, keeping him interested enough in case it all went pear-shaped with her new man. Yet Chris still found filing for divorce extremely difficult, and Danielle went out of her way to make life as difficult as possible for him throughout the whole, sorry, drawn-out legal process.

Andy deeply resented the way his mother had behaved and decided to stay with his father to show his support, but the lengthy and often upsetting episode had left a very bitter taste in Chris's mouth all the same.

The entire affair had left Chris feeling that his life was best lived alone and relationships were something to be avoided like a nest of vipers, and yet, quite suddenly, as Joanne was summoned for her X-ray, he was beginning to hope that the woman he'd been assisting might be as interested in *him* as he was becoming in *her*.

CHAPTER 16

Samantha emerged from Greenoaks carrying a sports bag which she placed thoughtfully in the back of Anne and Andy's car. Wayne had a good view of the red-brick cottage from his vantage point on the opposite side of Preston's small village green, and seeing the holdall suddenly made matters very interesting. All he cared about was finding an opportunity to fulfil his destiny; perhaps Joanne Middleton was having to spend a night or two in hospital, meaning that he might get his chance a lot sooner than he'd originally dared to hope.

Far enough away to be inconspicuous, yet close enough to eavesdrop, Wayne opened his driver's side window hoping that he might get to hear something significant, but instead, the only sounds to greet his ears were that of a tractor rattling along an adjacent road, and the distant whirring of a lawnmower's petrol engine. Wayne's frustration instantly gave way to rage as Samantha and the others disappeared back into the cottage without so much as saying a word to each other. The white wooden door closed behind them, and there was a resounding THUMP as Wayne smashed his fist against the inside of the driver's door. Every ounce of his fury's weight was screaming at him to go into the cottage and close the deal. Beads of sweat glistened on his forehead and the knuckles of his tightening fists whitened as he fought to control that near overwhelming urge, but the risks were too great. The young man with Samantha looked strongly built and more than capable of being able to handle himself, and then there was also that huge dog to contend with. If Wayne included Samantha and the older woman in the mix, he would be well outnumbered. Surprise wouldn't be enough on its own, and the only weapon he had at his disposal wasn't up to scratch yet, either.

Wayne was simply too close to blow it now; he was just yards from his objective, but yet again there was nothing else that he could do other than wait.

*

Anne fell in love with Greenoaks Cottage the moment she saw it, and was astonished to learn that it was only four years old, having been built on the site of a previous dwelling that had been destroyed by fire. Samantha explained that the plans for the cottage had needed to be vetted by the villagers before planning permission could even be sought, because any new build had to blend in with the significantly older period properties surrounding the green. That exterior objective had been achieved seamlessly, but the architect had been given more freedom with Greenoaks' interior.

The front door opened into a large, modern kitchen-diner, graced with natural slate floor tiles and stained oak beams that spanned the width of a pristine, white ceiling. At first glance, the ground floor appeared to be very open plan. Four heavy wooden uprights on the edge of the kitchen separated it from the living room, where an impressive open fireplace containing a log burner and heavy brass companion set was flanked on either side by two sets of French doors. A large Edwardian mirror was a commanding presence hanging on the brick chimneybreast, and there were a few photographs that had been carefully arranged along a rustic, floating shelf. Anne's natural inquisitiveness (or nosiness, as Chris might have put it) urged her to take a closer look, and it was then that she entered a living space where she could look right up into the very roof space of the cottage itself.

Anne had never set foot in a mezzanine house before, and stood looking almost in awe at an entire first floor that appeared to be floating in mid-air above the kitchen. Skylights in the roof bathed the balustraded stairs and landing in bright natural light, as did the French doors with the tastefully furnished lounge. There were two sofas bordering a red Persian-style Tabriz rug, but Anne decided she would wait for the cup of tea she'd been promised by making herself comfortable in the room's solitary armchair.

'Are you sure you don't want a tea or coffee, Andy?' Samantha asked, making good on her vow in the kitchen.

'No, it's fine, thanks,' he replied. 'But I wouldn't say no to a glass of water.'

Samantha took a large glass out of one of the cupboards and filled it from the tap.

'Here you go,' she said. 'Pure Preston Spring, care of the local Water Authority! And on draught, too!'

Andy laughed. Samantha possessed the most inventive wit, as well as the soppiest dog in Harley, who had Andy pinned against the kitchen sink, enjoying every moment of having the top of his head scratched.

'He'll let you do that to him all day,' said Samantha, holding two steaming mugs of tea. 'Come on Harley-Foo-Foo, leave the poor guy alone.' A gesture with her head invited Harley to follow and he obediently trotted on after her.

'He loves dogs, that one,' said Anne, referring to Andy's canine infatuation. 'I think he'd even sell *me* if it meant he could have one!'

It was Andy's dream to own a dog. His mother had been averse to any kind of pet, but even though she no longer lived with them, having a dog was still out of the question because both he and his father were at work all day.

'But if I *could* have one, it would be one like yours,' he said. 'I love German Shepherds and Harley's just brilliant.'

Harley wagged his tail like he could understand what was being said about him, but Samantha could sense regret in Andy's tone and he suddenly looked a little bit dejected. Harley had really taken to Andy, Anne too. There was something about them, their family, to which Samantha was *also* becoming drawn. She remembered Anne talking about Andy's father being involved in an accident and that he was going to be convalescing at her house in Whitwell, another village only a few miles from Preston. Sensing an opportunity to get to know Andy better, Samantha asked: 'So, how long do you think you'll all be staying out here, then?'

'That depends on Dad and his recovery, I suppose,' Andy replied. 'And how long Nan can put up with him, more to the point!'

Anne rolled her eyes.

'Which might not be that long …' she sighed.

'Really?' asked Samantha. 'Chris doesn't strike me as being the difficult type.'

'You don't know half, Samantha, honestly …'

'But seriously,' Andy said, 'I would think we'll probably be here for a while. I've got compassionate leave … I work for a marketing company just outside London, in Elstree. They're being great about everything, and they're cool with me being away for as long as it takes, really.'

'So, you're not a boxer then?' asked Samantha.

Anne snorted into her mug.

'A boxer? Oh, you mean this!' Andy laughed and pointed to his nose which had evidently been broken at some point. 'I'm no boxer! This was an early Christmas present I got last year playing rugby, courtesy of a tighthead prop from Barnet Elizabethans!'

'He looked like a panda all over Christmas!' said Anne. 'Two proper shiners they were!'

'I might have been talking about his physique,' Samantha said with a giggle.

'Yeah, whatever, Sam!' Andy replied. 'Anyway, how about you? What's your line of work?'

Samantha gazed thoughtfully at her tea for a second.

'Well, I'm surprised I didn't tell you this on the way here, bearing in mind I talked about Mum so much … and all of it bad! But anyway, Mum and I actually work together. She's a fashion designer with her own company and label in Covent Garden, but over the past year I've started doing a lot of modelling work. Mum's been brilliant with her advice and finding me a great model agency. That's how she started in the industry herself, but, after she had me, she decided being a model wasn't for her anymore, and she started designing clothes instead. Mum's worked so unbelievably hard and become very successful. She's truly amazing, actually, strong, determined, and *so* driven. Dad left us a few years ago but she just ground it out and now she's a woman seriously on the up. Someday I hope I might be just like her … Oh for God's sake, listen to me going on, praising her to the skies, but I'm just really proud of her.'

'And you've every right to be,' said Anne. 'Your mother's one in a million!'

'One in *thirteen* million actually,' Samantha said, smiling. 'Mum's a blue-eyed redhead. You may have already noticed, but not realised how rare she is. You've got more chance of being struck by lightning than meeting a blue-eyed redhead! And to cap everything she's left-handed too! Anyway, enough about me and Mum. I hope I didn't sound like I was being nosey when I asked how long you were going to be around these parts, it's just that *we're* going to be out here for a good couple of weeks ourselves, and I just thought that seeing as Andy loves dogs so much and gets on so well with Harley, that he could always come over and see him. You'd be more than welcome.'

If there was a more subtle way of getting to know Andy better, then Samantha couldn't see it, but any concerns she might have had about sounding too forward disappeared as his face lit up immediately.

'Really …?' he asked. 'I'd love to! Are you sure it's okay?'

'Absolutely.'

Anne smiled at their interaction, happy to let them chat excitedly, but although *she* was content to stay in the background, Harley apparently wasn't. He had a sudden need, and Samantha seemed a little *too* involved with the strangers for his liking. Anne acknowledged him with a smile as he gently pushed his head under one of her forearms and looked up at her appealingly. Then he padded over to one of the sets of French doors and waited, slowly wagging his tail.

'I don't know much about dogs,' she said, 'but I think somebody might want to go outside?'

Both sets of French doors were securely locked when Samantha went to let him out.

'Mum's got the bloody keys with her!' she said. 'I hate it when she does that! Looks like we'll have to go out on the green if you need to *go* then, won't we boy? Would you like to do the honours for him, Andy?'

Andy jumped at the chance, and Harley began to get excited as he felt his lead being attached.

'It's only little tats though, Harley Farley,' Samantha said to him. 'Not a full-on mega-jobbie.' Chuffing enthusiastically and half barking, Harley bulldozed his way to the front door of the cottage, dragging Andy with him.

'Looks like he might be desperate!' said Samantha. 'So you'll definitely need these.' Andy frowned as he took the nappy sacks from her outstretched hand, but then the door was opened, and he was pulled out onto the drive ...

*

'What the FUCK'S going on in there? What the FUCK'S GOING ON?'

Wayne was ranting to himself inside his car, completely forgetting that the window of his driver's side door was wide open, but luckily for him the village green and the surrounding area remained blissfully unaware of his tirade. He was about to punch the roof for the umpteenth time when he unexpectedly heard a girl's voice call out: 'You'll have to keep Harley on the lead, though, Andy. You can't let him off here.' Like a rambunctious child appeased by a favourite toy, Wayne calmed instantly. To his amazement, the young man from the hospital was on the green with the dog, and Samantha had appeared outside the cottage.

Andy looked towards Greenoaks as Samantha called out to him. She had changed her clothes when she'd gone upstairs to pack her mother's bag, the short skirt and vest-top having been replaced by a more modest attire of blue jeans and a pale pink T-shirt. Perhaps it was just that she was a little concerned about how he was going to handle a very determined Harley, but the self-assured young woman he'd first met didn't seem quite as confident anymore. Andy couldn't help thinking how vulnerable Samantha suddenly looked as she watched from the driveway, and before he knew what he was saying (including even consulting his grandmother), he was asking if Samantha might want to stay with his family in Whitwell.

'I'm sorry Andy, what did you say? I didn't hear you.'

'I said you'd be welcome to stay at ours tonight if you wanted,' he repeated, a little louder. 'Harley would be welcome too!'

'Oh right! Well, it's lovely of you to offer, but I think I've imposed on you enough already ... I'll be fine.'

'Okay then ... But the offer's there if you change your mind.'

The refusal was as polite as it was worrying, and Andy hoped he hadn't sounded too concerned. Keeping Samantha safe was suddenly at the forefront of his mind. Joanne was going to be safely ensconced in the hospital, but Samantha was going to be all alone in Greenoaks, and more than likely at the mercy of The Puppeteer.

Oshina hadn't said exactly who it was that needed Andy's protection, and with nothing else to go on other than the knowledge of having to protect somebody special, he was just going to have to go with his gut instincts about Samantha, and hope that there would be another opportunity of convincing her to stay with his family for the night.

As Andy struggled with his thoughts, Harley chose that very moment to do what he'd needed to do, and instantly the mood changed, Samantha giggling into the palm of her hand as Andy surveyed Harley's substantial deposit on the grass with more than just a hint of trepidation.

She was still laughing when she strode onto the green to assist with the clean-up operation.

'Here,' she said. 'Give me the bag … I'll deal with it.'

The previous conversation between Andy and Samantha; had filtered into Wayne's car like verbal nectar. By the sound of things, he *was* going to have the little bitch all to himself at last! Wayne quickly surveyed his surroundings, working out a plan of attack. The night would be his cover; there were very few streetlights and there was bound to be somewhere secluded enough to park the car. A quick glance at his wristwatch said it was just after four o'clock, enough time to buy a knife sharpener, get prepared and then …

FUCK!

Only a few feet away from Wayne's car was a red bin marked up for dog waste, and both Samantha and the young man that Wayne now knew was called Andy were walking directly towards it. Wayne didn't want to risk being seen by Samantha for fear of being recognised after their encounter on Hampstead Heath, a fear that was in serious danger of becoming a reality.

Harley began to growl and slowed his stride as he picked up Wayne's scent, and at exactly the same time, Andy felt the return of the nausea he'd experienced by Joanne's car. Just ahead, across a narrow strip of road from the waste bin they were approaching, was a silver BMW M3 and the driver's side window was wide open.

Wayne could hear the dog growling, and Samantha was so close he could smell her body spray. Any moment now she could look over and see him! He had to think, and fast! Frantically, he began rummaging around in his jacket for his mobile, and then pressed it against his ear, successfully obscuring the side of his face that would have been visible.

'Oh, there you are!' he said to an imaginary caller. 'No … I'm outside yours … where are *you* then, for fuck's sake? I thought I was meeting you here?'

The intensity of the nausea and the pins and needles between Andy's eyes had increased with every step he'd taken towards the BMW. He knew better than not to trust his instincts after what had happened to him earlier. It *had* to be the man sitting inside the car, and it was obvious that Harley didn't trust him either. If only he could get a clearer view of the driver …

'Andy…? ANDY!'

Anne's commanding tone caused Andy to look back towards the cottage.

'What are you doing?' she called out as the BMW's powerful engine roared into life behind him. 'We haven't got time for you to mess around looking at cars all day! Come on, lad, we need to get back to Joanne!'

'Whoa … that was one stressful conversation in there!' said Samantha, watching the BMW screech away. 'Someone's going to cop it for sure by the sound of things. But Anne's right, Harley Farley, we need to get you back indoors. I have to go and see to Mummy Bear now.'

Wayne berated himself loudly as he drove away from the village green. It was true that the disastrous scenario he'd imagined might not even have come about, but at the same time, it would certainly be in his best interests to ensure against future complacency. Up until then, it had been a case of being an opportunist, of making the most of the chances that had come his way, but that wasn't *really* him. *Scavengers* were opportunists, and Wayne knew he was more than that: he was a Cleanser, a ruthless predator with the purest of instincts for the kill.

With the sound of his M3's exhausts growling throatily through the country lanes, Wayne began to smile as he followed the road signs towards Hitchin. He was going to sort out a knife sharpener, prepare himself and his blade, and lay low in the hotel he'd booked prior to leaving his London apartment.

It would be there where he would wait until it was dark, waiting for the night to open its inky-black curtain upon the theatre of his destiny in which he would play the leading role. The moon would be his spotlight, the village his stage, and the stars in the sky his adoring, heavenly audience.

All Wayne needed to do was learn his lines, and then give the complete performance.

CHAPTER 17

The main hospital building loomed just ahead, a dominating seventies edifice of glass and steel that towered above the trees and neighbouring houses. The return drive from Preston, albeit a relatively short one, had flown by while Andy had been lost in his deliberations, disturbed by the feelings he'd experienced on the village green, and even more frustrated about being unable make any sense of them.

Anne glanced at him in her rear-view mirror.

'Oh, you *are* with us, then!' she said. 'You've been so quiet I thought you were asleep!'

'You're not sulking that you had to get in the back again, are you?' Samantha asked, smiling impishly.

'Like I'd even give you the satisfaction!' he replied.

'Is anybody hungry?' enquired Anne as she pulled into a bus stop close the hospital's Emergency Entrance. 'I don't know about you two, but I'm famished!'

Up until that moment, Samantha hadn't given food a second thought. It had been several hours since she'd last eaten and suddenly she was famished, too.

'Oh God, that was so rude of me!' she said. 'I should've sorted something out when we were at the cottage.'

But Anne didn't consider that Samantha had been rude at all.

'You were a perfect hostess considering all the worry and stress,' she replied. 'And it was hardly the right time, bearing in mind we were in something of a hurry, was it? The tea was a true life-saver in any case! How about you go and take your mum's things in while Andy and I go and grab some bits to eat. What do you think?'

'That's a great idea, but are you sure you don't mind?'

'Of course not!'

Like the grandmother Samantha had always dreamed of, Anne just seemed to have a knack of saying and doing the right thing at the right time. Nothing was too much trouble, she was kind and understanding, and occasionally, whether it was intentional or not, hilariously funny.

She was also very determined.

'And you can put that away, young lady!' she said, as Samantha took her purse out of her handbag. 'We can sort all that out afterwards if needs be.'

'But …'

'No buts!'

Just knowing what Samantha and Joanne may or may not like to eat, was, apparently 'sufficient'.

'You're not going to win, Sam,' said Andy, shrugging his shoulders. 'And anyway, the sooner you get out of the car, the sooner I can sit in the bloody front again!'

Although late in the afternoon, the day was still surprisingly warm and muggy in contrast to the coolness of the airconditioned interior of the Audi estate. Samantha puffed her cheeks out as she stepped into the heat, while Andy joined her with Joanne's overnight bag from the back seat.

'Andy, please let me put something towards the food,' said Samantha, reaching into her handbag again. 'I feel awful.'

But he politely refused.

'Nan's spoken,' he replied. 'Honestly? Once she's got an idea in her head, there's no shifting it, believe me.'

The passenger side window opened unexpectedly.

'I'm watching you!' said Anne. 'Put it away.'

'See?' whispered Andy. 'Just like I told you … look, we've got this, honestly, now go and see your mum. We won't be long.'

He smiled at Samantha as he got back in the car, and then slowly, he and Anne pulled away from the bus stop, leaving Samantha with just her shadow on the pavement for company.

Samantha watched the Audi until it negotiated a roundabout in the distance and disappeared from view. It seemed incredible how such a strong connection had developed between them all so quickly, and yet Samantha knew so little about Andy or his family. Anne hadn't mentioned a husband nor Andy a girlfriend, nothing had been said about Chris having a partner, and Samantha really wanted to know more. Her attraction to Andy was obviously just 'girl meets boy', but the growing affection she felt for Anne could only be due to being estranged from her own grandparents. The solidarity of the Ryan family unit was striking, an admirable togetherness different from Samantha's own which was just her and her mother, and although there could be little doubt that they were everything to each other, Joanne's expression of regret during their emotional exchange in the office spoke volumes about the existential issues between themselves and other members of their family.

With her mother's holdall over one shoulder and her head a mass of thoughts, Samantha headed for the entrance to A&E. The numbers inside had swelled considerably in the time she'd been away, but the same atmosphere of quiet apprehension and boredom prevailed, filling the air as before. A few people were at least *trying* to make polite conversation with each other, passing time as best they could in a sea of otherwise blank and expressionless faces, and it was to those people that Samantha smiled and nodded as she walked towards the reception desk on the opposite side of the waiting area and a head of highlighted blonde hair, the top of which was just visible above a computer screen.

'Hello, how can I help you?' asked the owner of the hair, a pleasant and bubbly, ample-framed woman by the name of Angela McNeil, according to her security badge.

'Hello … erm, I'm Samantha Middleton,' replied Samantha, relieving herself of Joanne's sports bag. 'My mum was brought in earlier this afternoon … Joanne Middleton? I think she's being kept in overnight for observation, and I've got some overnight things in for her.'

'Oh, that's okay, you don't need to check in here again. All you have to do is make yourself known to the staff in the unit before you go in to see her.'

'But what if she's gone into the ward already?'

'Good point! Okay … well, we'd best have a look in that case then, hadn't we? Middleton … Middleton…' Angela muttered Joanne's surname to herself repeatedly as she studied her monitor intently. 'Ah, here we are! No, she's not gone up yet. She's still our prisoner!'

Samantha chuckled.

'And that's *exactly* what she'll be thinking, too!' she said. 'I like it! We could have done with you here earlier when we first came in. The ladies before were a bit … well, let's just say, professional!'

'Try miserable!' Angela suggested, making Samantha laugh again. 'I was in the back. They don't let me out often, you know!'

'Really?'

'No, I'm only kidding. It's just my turn in the hot seat right now, that's all. I just like making people smile if I can. It's the way I am.'

'Well, it's worked with me.'

'Good.'

Angela looked around quickly at the stoical faces of some of the other staff members buzzing around like overly busy bees. The office door behind her hadn't stopped opening and closing in the short time that she and Samantha had been talking. Angela leant forward and lowered her voice.

'Not everyone here agrees with how I am with the public,' she said. 'They believe in cold hard professionalism, just being a face, but I don't think that's always right. I suppose we can get a fair bit of stick in here from time to time … It's not fair, I know, but it's only because of frustration. People moan, but they're complaining about the situation they're in, not us necessarily. But I love people and being a light when it's needed. A laugh or an understanding smile is always welcome, especially in here. What's wrong with a bit of positivity?'

The office door swung open again and a smartly dressed woman appeared. Angela turned and smiled at her, but the woman's austere facial expression didn't change.

'It's being so bloody happy that keeps that one going, I reckon!' said Angela, rolling her eyes.

Samantha directed her laughter into the back of her hand, and Angela's shoulders began to shake as she tried unsuccessfully to supress her own.

'Are you always this happy?' Samantha asked.

'Most of the time, yes. But I will admit that there *have* been times when I've needed a little help.'

There was the hint of a faraway look on Angela's face as she gently touched a simple green alabaster cross that hung on a silver chain around her neck. It appeared as though she were drawing upon a memory, and for a moment, Samantha thought she felt a sense of loss emanating from the jolly receptionist.

'Sometimes we can't find the strength in ourselves when we need to,' said Angela. 'And that's when we need to look elsewhere, which goes back to what I said a minute ago. If I can be a light in just one moment of somebody's life, then perhaps I can give them that little bit of extra they might need … oh for heaven's sake, listen to me getting all deep on you! I'm so sorry …'

'Don't be … And you're not getting too deep at all; I think it's wonderful to be the way you are. I could talk to you all afternoon but I'd better let you get on really.'

'Well, that's very sweet of you to say so,' said a beaming Angela. 'Thank you very much, and yes, I guess I'd better crack on. But before you go, I have to say, young Samantha, that you really do have the most *beautiful* smile. Just make sure you're still wearing it when you see your mum!'

Samantha smiled again, but didn't say anything. She picked up her mother's overnight bag and walked away from the counter, making sure to avoid any eye contact with anybody who'd been kept waiting.

'*A light in just one moment of somebody's life…*' Samantha felt that was exactly what she needed to be as she began searching for her mother's cubicle in the hustle and bustle of the treatment area, having to apologise once or twice for peering in where her eyes weren't welcome. All the staff were busy attending to other patients, and Samantha was loathe to ask where to go, but God above, if she took much longer, she was going to have to make even more apologies to her impatient mother who was bound to be more than just a little fractious over the length of time it had taken her daughter to return!

However, once found, Joanne was far from the crotchety specimen Samantha had expected. She seemed relaxed as she spoke with Chris, although her right arm was being supported in a poly sling and a new dressing was in place over her right eye. Some bruising had come out around the same eye, and there was more on the cheekbone underneath. Although it was pleasing for Samantha so see her mother looking happier than earlier, the bruising hadn't been so evident before, and neither had the swelling on the right side of her top lip.

A lump formed in Samantha's throat and she had to swallow hard just to be able to say 'hello'.

'Hi Sammy!' said Joanne, her face lighting up when she saw her daughter. 'You've got all my stuff, then. You little star!'

Samantha managed to force a smile, but just couldn't bring herself to say anything.

'It's okay, darling,' sighed Joanne. 'I know I must look like absolute crap, but I'm okay; everything's fine ... I had to have an x-ray on my shoulder, but it isn't broken anywhere, so it's just the concussion, that's all and ... oh God, please don't cry ...'

But it was too late, the floodgates had opened.

Chris stood up and immediately offered Samantha his seat, suggesting that it might be best if he left them alone.

'But you don't have to go!' Samantha sobbed. 'Not because of me ... Oh God, I can't *believe* I'm blubbing ... I am such a bloody wuss!'

'Don't be so hard on yourself,' said Chris. 'It's perfectly normal to be upset; it's because everything's just starting to sink in, that's all. Anyway, I'd better go and check in with the others in any case.'

Samantha managed to compose herself, but then her eyes widened.

'Oh yeah,' she said. 'Your mum and Andy have gone to get some sandwiches and stuff. I nearly forgot to tell you!'

'Getting *sandwiches*?' asked Joanne. 'And you *let* them?'

'She wouldn't have had any choice,' said Chris. 'Would I be right in assuming that my dear mother suggested it?'

'She insisted,' Samantha replied. 'And she wouldn't let me give her any money either.'

'Yep, that sounds about right. I'll see you both in a bit, then.'

Chris rolled his eyes and ambled away, shaking his head.

'He's lovely, isn't he?' said Joanne, once he was out of earshot.

'They all are.'

'Are you okay now, Sammy?'

'Yeah, thanks … I am now. I'm sorry I lost it just then, but I think Chris is right about it all sinking in.'

'And also because I look a bit like Frankenstein's monster?'

'Well, that too … when did you say they're they going to tighten the bolts in your neck again?'

Joanne laughed and winced at the same time. The painkillers were starting to wear off, but the sudden mother-daughter banter with Samantha was very welcome.

'I've told Chris that he and his family are all welcome to come to ours for dinner,' she said, wanting to keep things upbeat. 'I think we owe them that at least, don't you?'

'Absolutely! When were you thinking?'

'I don't know, in a couple of days or so maybe? Chris is going to talk to the others and then we can arrange something between us.'

'Cool!'

Although Chris and his family were a welcome positive for Joanne, there was still a looming negative over how and why their paths had crossed. Joanne's mind kept wandering back to her blind panic in the woods, the awful apparition in her car, and suddenly the fact that her daughter was going to be all alone in Greenoaks that night.

'You *are* going to be alright tonight, aren't you, Sammy?' she asked. 'I mean if you want to invite some friends round, that would be fine by me.'

'All my friends are back in London, Mum.'

'But they've got cars, haven't they?'

'And probably other plans!'

'Well, at least you could try calling them, or texting, or Facetiming, whatever it is you kids do these days! You could all get a pizza or something. I'm sure they'll deliver to the village.'

'Mum, will you *please* stop stressing …'

'But I just don't want you to be alone.'

Samantha frowned; what was it, exactly, that was eating her mother all of a sudden?

'Well, I've been left to my own devices on numerous occasions before,' she said. 'And you seemed happy enough about it then, so what's different about now? You weren't even this agitated about leaving me on my own after we got flashed!'

'That's because I had business to attend to that day, remember?'

'Yes, just like nearly every other time …'

Without warning, Joanne swung her legs over the edge of the bed.

'What the hell are you doing, Mum?'

'Leaving.'

'What? But you can't!'

'Watch me.'

'But Mum, you have to stay in. The doctor said you …'

'Sod the what the bloody doctor said!'

But then a sudden, excruciating pain in Joanne's neck and shoulder took her breath away. She screwed her face up and slumped back down onto her pillow in agony.

'See?' said Samantha. 'And what's more, you've got concussion, so you've *got* to stay in here tonight!'

'But Sammy, I can't.'

'Well, you seemed fine about it earlier!'

'I wasn't bloody fine with it at all! I want to come home so we can spend some time together. I mean, it's … it's what we came out here to do!'

'But it's *not* the reason why we came out here, though, *is* it, Mum? I know there's something you're not telling me, so stop treating me like a child! What *really* happened to you today?'

Chris heard Joanne and Samantha's raised voices as he approached Joanne's cubicle with the food his mother had bought. Samantha's frustrated tone and Joanne's defensiveness caused him to slow his stride, uncertain as to what to do next, but then Joanne began giving an account of her accident to Samantha exactly as it had been relayed to him earlier.

'So, it was just an accident, for God's sake!' Joanne said when she'd finished, unaware that Chris was nearby. 'And nothing else … so I'm not treating you like a child!'

'And Harley was on the back seat when all this happened?' Samantha asked.

'Yes …'

'Even though he's *never* been allowed anywhere else in your car other than in the boot space because you're so anal about dog hairs on the seats? And this was even *after* his walk? Muddy paws and stuff?'

'Sammy, for the love of God, please …! I'm not in the bloody mood for any of this … I ended up having an accident because I wasn't looking where I was going, and that's it!'

'Yeah, like hell it is!'

And then Samantha suddenly remembered something. Somehow managing to swallow her revulsion, she took out her mobile, and opened the selfie she'd sent to Abi. Sure enough, The Puppeteer was still in it, lurking menacingly in the background.

'So it was all Harley's fault that you happened to be driving like a lunatic, and nothing at all to do with this!' she said, passing the device to her mother.

Even captured on the screen of a mobile phone, The Puppeteer's empty black eyes had an instant and debilitating effect, and Joanne could only stare hopelessly back at them in horrified silence. The reaction was enough for Samantha to recount the writing appearing in the magazine she'd bought, and how the pages had appeared to take on a life of their own in tandem with the inscriptions.

'I swear that there was nothing there when I took the picture and sent it to Abi,' said Samantha. 'It was only when she told me that there was something weird about it that I saw The Puppeteer, and then I freaked out. I just ran. That's what made me call you, and then I found out that you'd had an accident which I suppose was no coincidence, was it? The Puppeteer hadn't just found *me*, he'd found both of us. He *said* so in writing, didn't he? Today was *just* like back in Hampstead. I don't know why all this is happening to us any more than you do, but it *is* happening, and we're already *way* past you feeling like you have to lie about it to protect me.'

Joanne had been so immersed in her own problems that any potential repeat of the Hampstead experience hadn't even crossed her mind, and she suddenly felt suitably ashamed. Hiding facts and lying to a stranger like Chris for fear of sounding insane was one thing, but lying to her daughter about a situation they clearly needed to be facing together was altogether different. Joanne looked down at the bed, swallowed hard, and opened up about her terrifying experience in Hitch Wood from the beginning, sparing nothing, recalling the intense panic of being hunted and pursued, breaking down as fretful, stinging tears welled up in her eyes.

'And then …' she sobbed, pointing at Samantha's mobile. 'Then that, that bloody *thing* appeared in my car. It appeared in my car and then I crashed …! And that's why I don't want you be alone tonight, Sammy! I have to come home with you, I *have* to!'

And how Samantha would have loved not to have been alone at Greenoaks, but right then, her mother's welfare had to take priority.

'But Mum, you *can't*.' she said, gently clasping Joanne's hand. 'The doctor said it could be a real risk … God, I'd hate myself if you came home and something happened to you!'

'Something happened to me?! What can be worse than what put me in here in the first place? I have to come home! You can't be on your own tonight, you just can't!'

Joanne wiped her eyes with the back of her hand and looked away, and that's when she saw Chris standing just beyond the partially open curtains of her cubicle. He was holding an orange plastic carrier bag and staring right at her. Just how much he'd heard was a mystery, but the likelihood was that it was a lot more than Joanne would have wanted.

But Chris was seeing neither Joanne nor her tears. His surroundings were merging into bright undefined white, and time itself appeared to have frozen completely. Before him stood a tall, serene-looking African man in a white shroud, who looked oddly familiar. The man said nothing, choosing to acknowledge Chris's presence with a bow of his head, a slow, simple nod that said less about politeness or respect and more about reconnection, confirmation that the subliminal familiarity had far more significance than could be understood in that one moment. And then, just as mysteriously as he had appeared, the African vanished, and Chris found himself back in the hospital amongst a hive of activity that seemed shockingly loud as he came out of the trance-like state.

And then his eyes met those of Joanne's, and not for the first time he saw her fearful gaze.

Although the frantic woman Chris first encountered had calmed as the afternoon had worn on, a haunted look had never been far from her otherwise beautiful features, and now it was also apparent on the face of Samantha.

Chris couldn't explain why he felt a sudden and overwhelming sense of duty to protect them both, or why he should just happen to stumble across a memory of a moment of illumination in a dark and desperate corner of his recent past. In that light there'd been an incredible stranger, a noble African man, and Chris realised that he had just encountered him again.

And then Chris remembered his name.

The man's name was Zambaya.

CHAPTER 18

The terracotta walls of Wayne's chosen hotel had stood out when he'd booked it online, and its location on the edge of the town centre made it ideal. Although Wayne wasn't completely averse to the idea of rural life, he was by definition a 'townie', and he'd hoped that the hustle and bustle of the nearby shops and market might make him feel more at home. Another advantage of the large, ex-Georgian townhouse's position was that Hitchin's numerous late bars and clubs would ensure against Wayne's comings and goings raising any suspicions, whatever the hour.

Wayne didn't unpack his bag when he got into his second-floor room, preferring instead to collect his thoughts and test out its fourposter bed for comfort. The dark wood of the room's imitation period furniture complemented its magnolia décor perfectly, creating an atmosphere of welcoming assurance, important for his mental preparation. He was going to have to be at his sharpest in order to bring about a swift conclusion to the mission, and rest would undoubtedly be a vital ingredient in the recipe for its success.

Happily for Wayne, the dark brown, velvet curtains hanging in front of the room's single casement window were thick enough to block out most of the light, and it wasn't long before he drifted off into a deep sleep where The Puppeteer was waiting to offer further encouragement.

It was then that The Puppeteer revealed more of his plan and the significance of Wayne's role within it. Everything The Puppeteer said was thorough and considered, making perfect sense even though it went way beyond anything Wayne could ever have imagined, for the world itself was essential, a jewel in the crown of The Puppeteer's New Order, and harsh changes were going to be necessary.

Humankind was, for the most part, expendable, as the very nature of its billions made it unsustainable. Humanity was toxic, nothing more than an insufferable vat of multitudinous leeches, intent on sucking everything it could out of the Earth. A cull was justified, and how fitting it would be for such a mass cleansing to be brought about by humanity's own hand. Posturing world leaders, arrogant, unyielding and afraid of appearing weak in the eyes of their demanding subordinates, would all together be complicit in committing the ultimate crime, and the war to end all wars would ensue.

But The Puppeteer was quick to point out that the end would usher in the new beginning, when the phoenix of the New Order rose from the ashes of its covetous predecessors, its legions born into the flesh of genetically engineered perfection created for it by human scientists preselected to survive the mass cleansing. The remaining threads of humanity, desperate, destitute and outraged at how their overthrown leaders had failed them, would come to revere their new rulers in the dawning of the new age, and Wayne would be guaranteed a seat at the head of The Puppeteer's table, forever celebrated, recognised for his role in the emancipation of The Puppeteer's Brethren.

Wayne felt energised and full of expectation when he woke enlightened from his slumber. Parting the curtains, he gazed upon the outside world and began to wonder about the changes The Puppeteer had said were to come. It was early evening and the sun was setting slowly and majestically, its lengthening rays surging into Wayne's room, casting his long shadow ominously upon the wall behind. The Puppeteer had advised patience, but Wayne had seen a golden opportunity to close the deal early and he wanted to take it with both hands. The Middleton bitch was right there for the taking, and by the time the sun rose again she would be history, the coming dawn heralding the first of humanity's final days.

It was then that Wayne was struck by the significance of the view of the street below. Looking down upon the people passing by beneath his suite merely underlined his superiority over them, a reminder that the time had come to start work upon the key to the door of a whole new world of endless possibilities.

Sitting innocently inside a humble brown paper bag on Wayne's bed was a knife sharpener he'd managed to obtain from a local hardware shop, and a satisfying scraping sound broke the concentrated silence as he studiously went to work upon the letter knife he'd stolen from Joanne Middleton's office. Just like a craftsman dedicated to perfection, he would stop occasionally to see how the work was progressing, and daylight had turned to dusk by the time he'd finished his lengthy task. A single table lamp illuminated the working area, and its subtle light glinted upon the now deadly razor-sharp edges of the newly honed blade as Wayne turned it slowly to and froe. There was an A4 foolscap pad on the dressing table in front of him and the blade cut through a single sheet as cleanly as a pair of scissors when tested.

Being in possession of such a lethal implement filled Wayne with near overwhelming awe. He pressed the tip of the knife into the palm of his hand and smeared the blood welling up from the wound onto both sides of the blade as a sacrifice to its ruthless efficiency. He would be one with *it*, and *it* would be one with *him*, a oneness for he alone to savour when the weapon cut through the wretched flesh of Samantha Middleton.

Wayne had to unbutton his jeans to relieve the sudden and restricting pressure inflicted upon his manhood. A mental image of Samantha Middleton writhing at his feet, helpless and oozing crimson life served as an instant source of arousal, and he gazed in admiration upon his consequentially potent erection. The stretched skin of the purple tip of his penis was shining in the soft light of the table lamp, and he began to masturbate, climaxing in what could only have been seconds due to the intensity of his burgeoning excitement.

Consumed by the power of his orgasm, Wayne slumped forward until released from its shuddering grip. Some of his semen had mixed with the congealing blood from the wound in his hand and he needed to clean himself up.

Wayne's jeans were still down by his knees when he was finally able to stand. He pulled them up as far as his unsoiled hand would allow as he walked to the bathroom, knowing that his true needs were yet to be satisfied and that *no* amount of imagining was going to match the surely prodigious thrill of taking Samantha Middleton's life from her for real. That moment, of course, was still to come, so in the meantime there was a necessity to complete the mental preparations required to bring about a perfect execution. A good, wholesome meal was also highly important, a requirement that Wayne would be looking to settle as soon as possible.

Wayne washed his hands in the sink, attended to his self-inflicted wound and then turned on the bath taps. He briefly watched the water plunging into the tub and then went to unpack his things while the bath slowly filled. With the sound of cascading water filtering through the bathroom's open doorway, he carefully selected his attire for that evening's jaunt into town, along with some rougher clothes he would be changing into later for his trip into the country. He was also mindful to include some bin liners in which he would be placing any soiled clothing once he'd killed Samantha Middleton.

And yet despite his fervour, Wayne's positivity wasn't to last. Once immersed in what he'd intended to be a calming hot bath, his mind began to wander back to his first encounter with The Puppeteer, and how, without hesitation, he'd entered into a contract to earn eternal sexual favour with Naomi in return for its successful completion. The Puppeteer had mentioned something about a price for his 'kind intervention' in Wayne's life, but hadn't expanded upon it any further, and Wayne had been so swept away by the opportunity to improve his miserable existence that at no time had he considered what price he might have to pay should he happen to *fail* in his quest. The timing of the thought, right when he was preparing for his moment of triumph, was as unwelcome as it was disturbing.

Hurriedly, Wayne finished his bath and towelled himself dry, feeling that it would be more beneficial if he didn't give himself time to dwell upon anything else. It was probably to his advantage that the hotel restaurant had already closed, as it meant that he was going to have to venture out into town in order to get something to eat, and a distraction would keep any negativity from re-entering his mind. Determined to overcome any feelings of self-doubt and vulnerability, he strode naked out of the bathroom, and saw the perfect tonic lying just across the other side of the room in the form of the letter knife he'd so painstakingly turned into an instrument of slaughter. He carefully ran an affectionate finger along the length of its blade and instantly began to feel better, drawing confidence from the bond that he had forged with it in blood. He and his weapon were one. There was nothing that could stop him now. The fleeting lack of belief in himself had passed, and it had, in all probability, been completely understandable. Even the greatest athletes and stage performers felt nerves, so why shouldn't Wayne? And besides, the adrenalin would help to keep his senses sharp and keen.

As Wayne got dressed, he would occasionally glance at the knife. It was like his new 'right arm', but taking it into town with him wasn't an option. His target wasn't in town, it was festering in a stylish country cottage, and, in just a few unimportant hours, that weeping sore was going to be ruthlessly cut out of the face of the Earth.

Hatred duly rekindled, Wayne left his lair, forgetting that the layout of the hotel was like a maze, and his sense of unease and confinement grew as he tried unsuccessfully to find his way to reception. Passageway led to passageway, with old photographs from Hitchin's distant past hung upon their walls. Grainy, ghost-like faces of long-dead local notaries gazed out at him with accusing, sepia stares, and a sense of being judged forced Wayne to quicken his pace until, after what felt like an age, the reception desk and foyer came to his rescue.

Once outside his hotel, Wayne took a deep breath. The air, although warm, was nevertheless fresh and welcoming, and the familiar sound of passing cars created a more comforting feel. Groups of people were milling around, friends and acquaintances too wrapped up with each other to notice the Cleanser hiding in plain sight in their midst. Wayne smirked at how easy it was to blend in and took full advantage by finding a nearby restaurant, but although the food was exceptional, his appetite had completely disappeared. He was like a coiled spring, fidgety, constantly checking the screen of his phone for the time which was passing by unbearably slowly.

Not even a change of surroundings helped when the quiet atmosphere of the restaurant was exchanged for the dynamism of one of the town centre's numerous bars. Wayne hoped that something livelier might occupy his mind a little more and make time pass quicker, but all he saw were people becoming worse for wear from drink. Everywhere he looked, men fawned drunkenly over shrieking, cackling women. It was almost unbearable for him to watch, and the same scene was only going to repeat itself wherever he chose to go.

Stone-cold sober and completely alone, Wayne suddenly felt far too conspicuous amongst the drunken carnage. There were *so many* women, so many eyes that could see into him, and it might only be a matter of time before one of the loathsome bitches got into his head and saw his past. They were like a pack of hyenas, lowlife scavengers, thinking and acting as one, and as soon as one of them knew, so would they *all*.

Wayne knew he had to get out of there. Breathing heavily, he left his untouched fruit juice on the table and began barging his way through the jabbering throng. Stares and tuts of indignation were left in his wake, but Wayne was oblivious, avoiding all eye-contact, the illuminated running man on the green emergency exit sign above the bar's main entrance his only focus as he forced his way through the mass of stinking, unworthy flesh that lay between *it* and the sanctuary beyond.

Once outside, released from the pungent stench of perfumes and hair products that had permeated the confining atmosphere of the bar, Wayne lit a cigarette and took a heavy draw. The calming nicotine immediately began to work its magic, coursing through his veins, massaging his anxiety, and clearing his mind sufficiently to revisit the plans for the coming hours.

A Cleanser … that was what he was truly was, a balance between harmony and chaos, but just for one mad moment, Wayne felt he'd allowed his eyes to be shifted from his glorious prize. The imperfect world such as the one which he was having to endure was not for gifted ones like him, it was a distraction, and he would not be making the same mistake again.

*

It was a little before midnight when Wayne returned to his hotel, and around half-past two in the morning when he slipped back out again through a deserted reception area. The drive up to Preston was quiet and uneventful, and so far everything had gone smoothly, a single streetlight on the opposite side of the village green from the Middleton's cottage illuminated a short stretch of road that ran by a small pond, but everywhere else appeared to be in darkness, providing him with near perfect cover.

Wayne turned into the same narrow road in which he'd waited that afternoon, driving slowly past the cottage, and then further along an adjacent street, sparsely populated by only a few houses on either side. After a short distance, he was able to pull in at the end of a row of parked cars. Ahead of him was an end of terrace cottage, and beyond that all his headlights lit up was a narrow lane that disappeared into open country. He switched off the M3's throbbing engine and waited for the car's interior light to dim before reaching behind him for a small backpack on the back seat that contained a change of clothes, the bin liners he'd readied earlier ... and the knife. Wayne carefully removed it, watching as the blade glinted menacingly in the moonlight creeping into the car through its tinted windows. In just a few moments, that blade was going to be bursting a few vital organs inside Samantha Middleton.

Barely able to contain his excitement, Wayne concealed the knife in an inside pocket of the black bomber jacket he'd chosen to wear for the job and stepped out into the dark, empty street. For a moment, he stood still and listened, his eyes scanning the windows of the dwellings around him for any signs of life, but there wasn't so much as the glow of a lamp behind any one of them. It appeared as though everybody were asleep, but Wayne stopped short of locking the vehicle once he stepped out of it, as engaging the security system caused the indicators to flash, and he didn't want to risk alerting anybody to his presence.

The peaceful village scene was the epitome of everything Wayne had imagined earlier. The moon hung in the sky like a silver bauble, its eerie lunar glow bathing everything in a mysterious half-light, and countless stars flickered in the blue-black canopy of the night; his audience had indeed taken their seats in the theatre of his destiny and now the curtain was about to open.

Walking on a grass verge to dull the sound of his footsteps, Wayne was stealthily making his way back towards the green when he noticed a sign for a public footpath. It was too dark to see where it led, probably into open country, but more importantly, it ran behind the gardens of three detached cottages, one of which appeared to be the Middleton's.

Wayne remembered from his visit that afternoon that there was a side entrance to the cottage, and that was how he'd originally planned to get access to the rear of the property. However, an entrance at the back of the cottage itself would be even better, as the footpath was dark and secluded, hiding him from anybody happening to be coming home late from a night out.

Keeping the roof of Greenoaks in view, Wayne made his way along the footpath to check out his hunch. Tall hedges ran all along one side of the pathway, and cut into them were three randomly spaced gaps that appeared to be entrances. Trembling in anticipation, Wayne crept towards the gap directly opposite the Middleton's cottage and discovered a solidly built six-foot garden gate which turned out to be securely locked when he tried to open it. The tall hornbeam hedge in which it sat was far too thick for Wayne to simply be able to force his way through, so his only option was to climb over the gate itself.

Adrenalin flowing, Wayne pulled himself smoothly up and over the timber obstacle, and dropped noiselessly into a spacious garden on the other side. The rear of Greenoaks was facing him, silent, steadfast, and challenging. White window frames bathed in the moonlight contrasted with the darkness that lay behind their protective panes, and, in that darkness, Wayne imagined his prey in bed, sleeping and unaware.

It was all he could do to supress a sudden surge of glee, his throat aching as the stifled fit of excited laughter threatened to burst out of him, until with renewed focus and intent, he drew the knife from inside his jacket and trained his gaze upon the upstairs windows. This was the exact scenario for which he'd prepared, but first he was going to get the dog out of the way. Dogs always reacted when disturbed, especially protective breeds like German Shepherds, and Wayne's plan involved using those natural instincts to his advantage. It was just a simple case of making the dog bark loud enough to wake the Middleton bitch. Thinking it needed to relieve itself, she would come down and open one of the doors to let it out, and he would rush in, sticking the little tart once or twice right in the guts before slashing the dog's throat as it came back to protect her. After that, Wayne would amuse himself watching the bitch bleed for a while before snuffing her shitty little flame out once and for all.

There was an area of brick wall between the two sets of French doors that would allow him to cover either side, and make an ideal place from which to launch his attack. With his penis hardening in expectation, Wayne slunk onto the patio and took up the position from where he was going to strike. Silence inside the cottage told him that the dog still hadn't sensed him, so the time had come to light its fuse.

Using only enough force to wake a dog and not its owner, Wayne began gently tapping the blade of the knife on a small square pane of glass …

CHAPTER 19

Joanne woke with a start in hospital. The painkillers were doing a decent enough job, but they couldn't stop her from rolling over onto her favourite sleeping side, which was, typically, the same as her injured shoulder, and the pillows weren't the best. She bumped them up with her good arm as best she could and fiddled around with the bed controls to find a more comfortable position, but there was nothing she could do about the blanket which felt scratchy and harsh against her skin through her thin pyjamas. Joanne kicked it off in frustration; it was far too warm to be under the cover in any case; the windows were open as far as their restricted hinges allowed, but the air was still stagnant and uncomfortable.

There was a jug of water by the side of the bed. Joanne poured a little into a plastic beaker and shuddered at its tepid contents.

Why *had* she bothered listening to the doctors and her daughter, only to be treated to this pinnacle of boredom and misery? A quick glance around confirmed to Joanne that she was completely alone. A clock on the wall above the deserted nurses' station said five past three in the morning. Even the *staff* couldn't take it by the look of things; they were probably off having a crafty cigarette somewhere if they were allowed, not that Joanne considered having another living soul to speak to would have made matters any more bearable in any case.

And not even Joanne's mobile phone could be of assistance. The one item Samantha had forgotten to pack was her mother's phone charger, so Joanne couldn't even lift her spirits by reading the amusing WhatsApp conversation she'd had with her daughter before they'd said goodnight to each other.

Six minutes past three!

Tick … tick … tick … Joanne's eyes followed the hypnotic movement of the wall clock's second hand as it continued its inexorable journey around an uninteresting, plain white face, but then her bladder suddenly decided it might be a good time to take a trip to the toilet. With an exasperated sigh, she shuffled across the bed and swung her legs over the edge. Still, it would kill a few more minutes, and there might even be a vending machine around that dispensed bottled water which was actually palatable.

Joanne stepped into her slippers, picked up her handbag and headed towards the unattended nurses' station, a couple of hot drinks steaming in the warm glow of a desk lamp the only clue to it ever having been occupied. There was a door directly opposite marked 'WC' which opened to Joanne's surprise, into a long corridor that stretched uninvitingly towards a distant set of double doors. The passageway's drab, grey walls were more befitting of a prison than a hospital, and the erratic, flickering death throes of a failing strip light added to a sudden and uncomfortable feeling of incarceration.

As there was nothing on the door stating that the entrance was off limits, or Staff Only, Joanne assumed that it was okay for her to carry on. It seemed odd that something as a simple as a public convenience should be so tucked out of the way, but the sign on the door was clear enough, so it had to be down there somewhere.

The corridor was longer than it had first appeared as Joanne began to wander down its depressing length. She had already taken a good number of steps when the double doors at the end opened unexpectedly and a heavily built cleaner wearing grey overalls and a baseball cap backed their way out from behind them. Joanne assumed that the burly figure hunched over a mop was a man, but the flickering light was having a strobe-like effect on her vision and she couldn't be sure.

'Excuse me,' she said, having to shield her eyes from the visual disturbance above. 'Are there any toilets down here?' The cleaner stopped mopping briefly, but didn't reply. Joanne assumed that he hadn't heard her. Perhaps he was wearing earphones under that cap, or maybe he wasn't English and hadn't understood, but then the light above her head abruptly died, leaving an ominous tract of darkness between them.

The darkness had an almost liquid quality to it, and it looked like something was moving just ahead up on the ceiling. Joanne squinted, straining her eyes to see into the blackness, but she couldn't make anything out. It was probably just her eyes playing tricks after the erratic flickering of the dying strip light. She took another step forward and tried her luck again with the cleaner.

'Excuse me?' she asked, raising her voice slightly. 'Are there any …?'

'Do you think that you could ever run again as fast as you did in the forest earlier?' came a dark and unexpected reply.

Joanne felt herself going cold. The cleaner was no longer hunched over his mop; he had drawn himself up to his full height, his full *towering* height. Then he slowly turned to face her, and an all too familiar grin began spreading across his granite-like visage.

'Well, Joanne?' asked The Puppeteer. 'Do you think that you ever could?'

The strip light above Joanne's head chose that moment to flicker back into life, illuminating three of the most hideous creatures, each one bearing a terrifying resemblance to Samantha's description of the Manforms from her

Hampstead night terror.

Two of the monstrosities began stalking Joanne from opposite sides of the corridor, their faces savagely deformed and contorted beyond anything human, their blood red eyes trained intently upon her, hairless, sinewy bodies taut and ready to pounce. A third was up near the ceiling. Considerably larger than its emaciated pack mates, it had a twisted spine and distended belly, a pair of muscular legs straddled the entire width of the corridor, suspending it, almost impossibly, in mid-air. Two specks of fiery orange glowed distantly in a pair of otherwise dark and empty eye sockets that were regarding her from underneath a bulbous, heavy brow, and then its mouth opened into a huge, elongated scream, and a terrifying howl ripped along the passageway.

With near spider-like athleticism, the Manform sprang forwards. Instinctively, Joanne swung her handbag at it in a desperate act of self-defence, but talon-like claws at the end of a swinging, gnarled hand slashed ruthlessly through its strap, proving beyond any doubt the futility of her actions. Joanne kicked off her slippers and ran for her life, urine trickling uncontrollably down the inside of her thighs, the sound of scrabbling claws from the chasing abominations filling the corridor as they came after her.

The Manform on the ceiling let out another deafening howl. Joanne dared to glance back to find that it was almost on top of her, and launched herself full-tilt at the door that led back into the observation ward, swinging it open. A frantic, panicked scream escaped her lips as she skidded through it, slamming it shut behind her, hands pressed against the handle to prevent the pursuing horrors from breaking through.

Two bemused young female nurses were staring at Joanne from the nurse's station.

'HELP ME! FOR GOD'S SAKE, BLOODY HELP ME!' Joanne shouted at them. 'THEY'RE TRYING TO GET THROUGH!'

Sweating from her efforts at resisting the pressure from the other side of the door, she sunk to the floor, forcing the handle up for all she was worth.

'DON'T JUST BLOODY SIT THERE! DO SOMETHING!'

One of the nurses came over and calmly tried to get Joanne to relinquish her grip.

'Mrs Middleton?' she said. 'It's only a toilet …'

'NO! PLEASE!'

'Mrs Middleton … it's fine, now please, let go …'

'BUT YOU DON'T UNDERSTAND!'

'Mrs Middleton!' the second nurse barked. 'If you DON'T calm down, we will HAVE to sedate you!'

The second nurse was also considerably stronger than her more gentle colleague. One by one, Joanne's fingers were prised away from the doorhandle. The Manforms were going to burst through and take her.

'PLEASE ... NO! DON'T OPEN IT! DON'T OPEN IT!' Joanne screamed.

She dived back at the door in a last-ditch attempt to prevent it from being opened, but she was too late.

'You see?' said the gentle nurse. 'It's just a toilet!'

'But ...'

Dumbfounded, Joanne stared into the now harmless, empty cubicle.

'Your confusion is understandable,' the nurse replied. 'You've been involved in a very nasty accident and you've got a concussion. Now, we need to get you back into bed. You're disturbing the other patients.'

'But I thought I was the only ... one ...'

Joanne was shocked to see three other people sitting up in their beds, staring at her, mystified.

'But I don't understand,' she said. 'There was nobody here. Not even *you* were here.'

'We saw you get up and go to the toilet, Mrs Middleton. I think you might even have been sleep-walking ... you did seem rather vacant.'

The gentle nurse helped Joanne back into bed under the accusing glare of her apparently less tolerant counterpart. Joanne instantly knew which one she preferred dealing with.

'I'm afraid I've wet myself,' she whispered to her. 'Have you got anything else I can wear? I've got some spare undies, but other than that all I have is my clothes for tomorrow.'

'I'll get you a gown, Mrs Middleton. Head injuries can be associated with some very unpleasant symptoms. Would you like me to get you something to help you sleep?'

'Thank you, but that won't be necessary.'

The nurse's explanations seemed plausible up to a point. Joanne considered that her experiences of the day may well have manifested themselves into some form of nightmare hallucination. It explained The Puppeteer, but not the Manforms.

Joanne had never seen a Manform ...

And then her eyes fell upon the wall clock, just as it turned seven minutes past three. Her ordeal had felt like it had lasted a lifetime, but barely a minute had ticked by.

A feeling of intense dread began to build inside her. In Hampstead, both she and her daughter had shared experiences on the same night. That afternoon it had been the same. If they were being attacked as a pair, then ...

'You left your slippers and your handbag in the toilet,' said the gentle nurse, having retrieved Joanne's possessions. 'Oh, look, the strap's broken.'

The ruined handbag was all Joanne needed to see.

'I have to get out of here!' she said. 'I have to go home!'

'But you need to rest. You're in no fit state to ...'

'It's an emergency!'

*

The time on Samantha's phone had been six minutes past three when Harley had woken her. All she'd done was go and let him out into the garden, but now she was dragging herself across the living room floor. The front of her top felt warm and wet, and there was an unpleasant metallic taste in her mouth ...

*

'You can't just discharge yourself like that, Mrs Middleton!'

'Try stopping me!'

'There are procedures ...'

'And you know where you can bloody well stick them!'

Joanne felt she could take chances with *this* nurse rather than the Nazi who'd nearly broken her fingers.

'At least let me make a phone call!' she begged. 'My mobile's gone flat. Is there a phone I can use?'

'There's a phone I can *bring* you. All you have to do is plug it into a socket by your bed.'

A breakthrough at last thought Joanne.

'Brilliant!' she said. 'Whereabouts is it?'

'Well, I'll have to find it. You'll have to give me little while depending on where it is.'

'Then I'm going to have to find it myself ... I need to make that call *now*!'

*

Samantha hadn't seen anybody, there'd just been a blow to her stomach, and the wind had been knocked out of her. But then came the pain. A terrible pain deep inside her. All Samantha could hear apart from her sobbing fight for breath was maniacal giggling coming from the man in the doorway behind her, the man without a face who'd stabbed her.

If she could just get to her phone ... it was right there on the coffee table ... then she could call for help.

*

'Mrs Middleton, I can't let you leave the ward!'

Joanne grasped the nurse's hands, made a mental note of the name on her identity badge, and asked: 'Emily ... are you a mother?'

'Yes, I am, but …'

'Then you will know what it's like to love your flesh and blood, and *this* mother needs to call *hers*!'

*

A pair of large, black, Cuban-heeled boots had appeared in front of Samantha's face, and the enormous feet inside them belonged to The Puppeteer.

'You know, Samantha,' he said, crouching down beside her. 'I hope you don't mind me saying, but you don't look at all well.'

He'd almost sounded apologetic.

The insane giggling continued from the doorway, becoming hysterical, excited laughter as Samantha tried to raise herself up in a frantic effort to get to her mobile, but her hand slipped in the crimson pool that was spreading rapidly beneath her, and she slumped back down onto the floor with an anguished cry.

'Oh, that looks really nasty,' said The Puppeteer. 'Does it hurt?'

'Bastard!' Samantha sobbed. 'Why did you do this to me?!'

'Actually, I didn't, but you *do* know that I can close those dreadful wounds, and take away your pain, don't you? Wouldn't you like me to heal you and make it all better again?'

'I don't want anything from you!'

'Hmmm … Still fighting me, then? I really don't understand you, Samantha, when I've given you such a clear and *simple* choice between life and death. So *many* would jump at another chance of life in your position, so why shouldn't you? But I wouldn't take too long to think about it if I were you; I don't think you have much time left.'

Samantha tried to drag herself towards her phone once more, but the pain was too intense. The Puppeteer offered her his hand.

'All you have to do is take it,' he said soothingly. 'And for a small price, I promise that will make *all this* go away …'

A shrill, piercing tone cut through Samantha's desperation just as she was about to reach out and grasp her last chance, and she woke with a gasp. Panic-stricken, terrified and in near darkness, she immediately felt for the horrific, pumping stab wounds to her abdomen only to discover to her indescribable relief that she was lying on a three-seater sofa in the Ryans' living room and not bleeding to death in Greenoaks Cottage.

The tone that had woken her was the incessant ringing of her mobile; it was a ridiculous hour, the caller's number was unfamiliar, and yet Samantha answered, bursting into tears the moment she heard the unexpected, but *oh so comforting* sound of her mother's voice. As they swapped accounts of their mutual terrors, the emotion poured out of them both until the conversation came to a calmer end, and Samantha spoke about how grateful she was that Chris had insisted she stay with his family that night.

But regardless of how safe he made her feel, there was nothing he could do to stop The Puppeteer who could come for her and her mother at will. This time he had even been able to attack them at *exactly* the same time in completely different places. Samantha went cold as she recalled The Puppeteer saying that he was 'everywhere'. Perhaps he'd just wanted to prove the point, but then again, why should he have had to prove anything when the immensity of his power was already evident? It was almost as though he was using her mother for sport, a game, a pleasure rush, the glorification of inflicting fear, but when it came to Samantha herself, his intentions, it seemed, were to convert her, or force her to accept another set of ideals.

As much as The Puppeteer's motivations remained a terrifying enigma, just how close she'd come to giving in and paying the 'small price' of which he'd spoken was enough to make Samantha shudder. It had only been an incredibly well-timed phone call that had prevented it.

'Are you alright, Samantha?'

She looked up, surprised, in the direction of Anne's voice.

'How about we shed a little bit of light on the subject?' Anne suggested, switching on a small table lamp just inside the living room door. She was wearing a white dressing gown, and pink bunny slippers. Anne noticed Samantha looking at the slippers, and wiggled her toes childishly inside them. The movement made their little, black noses move up and down, and Samantha chuckled.

'I'm hope I didn't make you jump,' said Anne. 'I came down because I heard you talking. You sounded upset and I was worried about you.'

Samantha slumped back into the sofa and looked up at the ceiling.

'I'm the one who should be apologising,' she replied. 'Oh God, this is *so* embarrassing! I feel so stupid. I can't *believe* I've woken you up!'

'There's no need to be embarrassed. Was it your mum on the phone?'

'Yes, it was. And I was really trying to be quiet!'

'Is she okay, though? I heard you crying.'

Samantha felt relieved that Anne hadn't heard any details, but then came the sound of more footsteps coming down the stairs, and a very pensive-looking Chris walked into the living room closely followed by Andy.

'Now I've woken *everybody* up!' Samantha groaned.

'What's going on?' asked Andy, making a fuss of Harley who'd begun greeting him enthusiastically. 'Is everything okay?'

'It's fine,' Anne replied. 'But seeing as your dad's down here, the least he can do is make us some of his fantastic hot chocolate! I know I'd *love* one. How about you, Sam?'

Samantha smiled and nodded while Chris headed into the kitchen without saying a word. She felt he might have been annoyed by her behaviour, but Anne was quick to dispel her concerns.

'Don't be silly,' she said, sitting down on the sofa and playfully rubbing one of Samantha's knees. 'Of course he's not. You can't help it if something's upset you.'

'Upset about what?' asked Andy. 'Is Joanne okay?'

'Mum's fine,' said Samantha. 'I'm just a drama queen making a great big fuss about nothing, who's woken you all up for no reason … I just had a stupid nightmare, that's all.'

'So stupid that you felt the need to call your mum at gone three in the morning in hospital?' asked Anne.

'Actually,' Samantha began. 'It was …' But she cut herself short. Going along with Anne's incorrect assumption was going to be far easier.

'Samantha, there's nothing *silly* about having a nightmare,' said Anne. 'They can be really nasty. I used to have recurring nightmares when I was young, right up until I met my late husband, in fact, and then they stopped for some reason. I never really knew what caused them until I started delving into the subject, and I've been interested in dreams and their meanings ever since.'

'Really?' asked Samantha.

Anne nodded.

'Dreams often have a bearing about what is going on around us, or how we feel about situations that are affecting us,' she said. 'Childhood dreams are very vivid in particular, and sometimes I would even get the children to tell me about theirs when I was a headteacher. It was a real insight into any problems they might have been having and always very enlightening … and, I might add, it was often very beneficial for them.'

'And Nan's *still* well into it!' said Andy, before suggesting that Samantha might benefit from speaking about her own nightmare. He seemed genuinely curious for some reason, but Samantha didn't want to make herself look anymore foolish.

'I don't think it's going to help,' she said.

'Is that so?' asked Anne.

'It's … it's just too weird …'

'I prefer the term 'abstract'. How about I tell *you* about my recurring nightmare when I was young, then?'

Samantha nodded. Andy leant forward in his chair, mystified by Samantha's reluctance, but growing ever more certain that it had something to do with his earlier suspicions about The Puppeteer.

'Okay,' said Anne. 'In that case … I used to have a recurring dream about being on a ship in the middle of the ocean and it was surrounded by fog. And in that fog there was something terrible that I could never see. I used to try calling for help, but nobody ever came, and whatever was in that fog was coming after me. Then I would find the captain of the ship asleep in a chair, but there was never anybody else in the dream apart from him and me. He had a hair sticking out of the corner of his mouth and I felt that I had to pull it out but it would just keep coming, getting thicker and thicker and it wouldn't stop. It sounds stupid, doesn't it? But that's what I used to dream and to me it was absolutely horrific. The ship was always the same, the fog was always the same, the captain with the hair sticking out of the corner of his mouth was always there, but I had no control over the nightmare and I could never change anything that happened in it. Sometimes I could have that dream several nights on the spin, particularly when I was away from my parents and under stress at university. I concluded that the nightmare was caused by loneliness, the feeling of being cast away and separated from the people I loved and relied upon the most. The fog suggested I was blinded by my insecurities, the hair in the mouth the pressures I was enduring at the time. So, you see, Samantha, there is nothing stupid about what might or might not scare people in their dreams. Now, how about you try and tell me something about what's been scaring you in yours?'

Chris could hear what was unfolding in the living room while he finished off making the hot chocolate. The African from the hospital had come to him again while he'd been asleep, the one who had called himself Zambaya, and now Chris knew everything all over again. The unexplainable feeling in the pit of his stomach he experienced whenever he was around Joanne and Samantha, and the bizarre nature of their meeting was no longer a mystery, having been replaced in devastating clarity by what was now expected of him.

Even though Samantha didn't reveal the name of the huge, black-eyed, tormentor from her nightmare when she opened up to Anne in the lounge, Chris knew that it was the same evil against which Zambaya had warned. It's gloating delight at Samantha's subconscious suffering made for uncomfortable listening, her unsuspecting innocence and what was yet to come almost too much for Chris to bear.

Anne was also horrified by what Samantha recalled, so much so that she was briefly lost for words, not that she could offer any symbolism for the nightmare once she was able to speak.

'Oh my God, that was truly awful! No wonder you were so upset … ah, lovely, thanks, Chris,' she said, breaking off to take the mug of hot chocolate being offered. 'And you've had this dream before?'

'No ... tonight was the first time, but ...'

'Well, like it or not young lady, you'll be spending the rest of night up in my room with me. I've got a lovely camp bed that I can make up for you. I didn't want you down here sleeping on the sofa in the first place.'

'But ...'

'No 'buts'. I'm sure Andy won't mind staying down here with Harley if needs be.'

'But Anne, what if I have *another* nightmare and wake up blubbing again?'

'Well, I'll just have to pretend to be your mum, then, won't I?'

Anne got up and strode off, her face a picture of determination, one hand securing her dressing gown, the other holding her hot chocolate.

'You're not going to win, Sam ... I thought you'd have learnt that by now,' said Chris, sitting himself down on the sofa in the space that had just been vacated by his mother. They were the first words he'd spoken since coming downstairs and Samantha instantly felt better, especially when he smiled at her and his eyes smiled too.

'You must think that you've invited a complete nutter into your house!' she sighed. 'I feel awful ...'

'Not at all,' Chris replied. 'There's no shame in being terrified about something like that.'

'Especially that big guy with the eyes,' said Andy. 'I mean seriously, like, how does something like that just appear in a dream? That's got to be a total one-off.'

Chris suddenly felt very uneasy. He didn't want to give Samantha any reason to be any more afraid than she already was, and felt a need for them to wrap things up quickly, but Samantha started speaking again before he could act.

'I wish it was,' she said, looking down at the steaming chocolate in her mug. 'I've dreamt about him before ... It was back in Hampstead, but it was totally different.' She stared into space momentarily, before adding: 'You know ... It's almost like there's something going on, a plan or ... God, I wish I could explain it better, but Mum and I got flashed on Hampstead Heath a few days ago when we were out for a run ... And then, literally just after it happened, all these *weird* things started happening to us, stuff going on in the house, then I had the first nightmare. It sounds mad, I know, but that's why we came out here, to get away, thinking that maybe a change of scenery would help, but it hasn't, it's ...'

'Samantha ...' came Anne's voice from the top of the stairs. 'I've made your bed up for you!'

Andy knew that Samantha had described The Puppeteer in her nightmare, and only just managed to hide his frustration at his grandmother's untimely interruption. He managed to crack a joke with a fake warning about his grandmother snoring, but the opportunity to find out *more* about Samantha's experiences had just been figuratively snatched away.

Samantha didn't want to keep Anne waiting. She kissed Harley on top of his head, said her 'goodnights' and then made her way up to Anne's bedroom. Harley's eyes followed every one of her steps as she walked away, his soft whining the only sound to break a strange silence as she went upstairs. Chris thought he might tidy up the living room before going back to bed himself, and took the two dirty mugs that had been left behind into the kitchen with him. Chris expected that Andy would be going to get his duvet, and began to fill up a bowl with water. Lord knows washing up a couple of mugs might even give him a few moments to get his head around what had happened that night!

But Andy *hadn't* gone upstairs to get his duvet.

'What can you tell me about an African guy called Zambaya, Dad?' he asked, having chosen to follow his unsuspecting father into the kitchen instead. 'And maybe you can tell me something about The Puppeteer as well because that's who Samantha was just talking about, wasn't it?'

Chris instantly stopped what he was doing. Andy was reflected in the window behind him, arms folded defiantly across his chest and leaning against one of the worktops.

'Zambaya appeared to me yesterday by Joanne's car and told me you two had a connection,' Andy added. 'I also know that *he's* familiar with The Puppeteer as well, and if you two *do* have a connection, then I guess you must know a lot more than I do. So, what the fuck's going on here then, Dad?'

The expletive made Chris turn round angrily. He expected better from his son and was about to say as much until he saw Samantha standing in the kitchen doorway holding Harley by his collar, having had to bring him back down when he'd gone searching for her upstairs. Her face was a distressing mixture of fear and disbelief.

'You *know* about The Puppeteer?' she asked. 'You know about him?'

Judging by the sudden expression of quiet despair upon his father's face, Andy knew that he was temporarily on his own.

'Yeah,' he sighed, looking down at the floor. 'I've seen him too.'

'By Mum's car? But … but how did you see him when you were *awake*?'

'I just *saw* him, Sam; I didn't have a dream like you did, but loads of weird shit has started happening to me too, just like it has with you, and it all started after Dad's accident … it's … it's like I've got some kind of gift.'

Harley started whining as Samantha began to get upset.

'Is everything alright down there, Sam?' Anne called out from the landing. 'You've been gone a while.'

'It's all good, Mum,' Chris shouted back. 'We're just trying to get Harley to settle.'

Samantha managed to calm herself enough to get Harley to lie down, but she quickly became frantic again.

'What's happening?' she whispered. 'Why's this happening to me? I don't understand! And how come you both know about this too? It's terrifying the life out of me ... and why did I feel like I was *dying* in that nightmare? You're not supposed to feel pain in dreams ...'

'Sam, listen,' said Chris, going over to Samantha so that he could keep his voice down. 'Listen to me ... now's not the time to discuss any of this, okay? But I *swear* that we'll talk as soon as we get the chance; I promise. But we *have* to keep this between the three of us, until we know more ... and we certainly can't let my mother know!'

'I just want to know what The Puppeteer wants with me,' said Samantha. 'I'm even too scared to go to sleep now!'

'He won't be coming for you again tonight,' said Andy.

'He comes for me whenever he likes, so how would *you* know?'

'Because I'm connected to something that's telling me he won't!'

Andy looked up at the ceiling, frustrated that he wasn't going to be able to go into more detail.

'*Fuck* ... I wish there was time to explain it better!' he said. 'But Dad's right, we've got to talk about this when we're properly alone, and we *are* going to talk about it, *aren't* we, Dad, because it's pretty obvious we're all involved, isn't it?'

How was it possible for so much to change in just one day? Chris was only too relieved that the situation had spared him from being asked a plethora of questions he wasn't at liberty to answer, but it was only going to be a temporary reprieve.

Horribly aware of the impossible hand he'd been dealt, Chris accompanied Samantha upstairs, leaving Andy simmering in the living room babysitting Harley.

When they reached the landing, Chris saw that his mother's bedroom door was slightly open, but there was no way he was going to say goodnight to Samantha without trying to give her some more reassurance.

'Everything's going to be fine,' he whispered to her. 'I promise you, Sam. It's like Andy said, you're not alone in this.'

Samantha nodded, her eyes moistened, and then she flung her arms around his neck like a daughter would a doting father. The impromptu act of affection took Chris completely by surprise, and he suddenly felt a terrible surge of guilt, torn between everything he *knew* and what little of it he could disclose to the confused and terrified young woman holding onto him for all she was worth. He even waited until Samantha had closed Anne's bedroom door behind her before retiring to his own room, a show of strength, a sign that he was truly looking out for her.

With the house having finally fallen silent and Samantha's tearful lack of awareness still fresh in his mind, Chris locked his bedroom door and quietly gave in to his own, overwhelming emotions.

CHAPTER 20

Wayne fired up the M3's engine. All he wanted to do was to escape from the scene of his humiliation. He'd been trying to wake the little Middleton slut for over *twenty fucking minutes*, but she hadn't even *been* there, had she? He'd planned everything to the last detail, and she had *no right* to deprive him!

Caring little for the sleeping residents, and showing none of the caution that he had previously, Wayne tore away, enraged, into the night. The throaty roar of his car's tailpipes reverberated among the cottages in the once tranquil side street, and the broad, piercing white beam of his headlights flooded the lane ahead. A multitude of moths and other night fliers plunged into the speeding brightness hurtling towards them through the darkness, but Wayne wasn't paying any attention to the mounting body count.

He suddenly had other things on his mind.

Why did everything look the same out there?

Where the fuck was he?

Wayne turned right, then he turned left, right again, left again. None of the signs made any sense, and none of the names upon them were familiar.

Still wrapped up in the heated conversation that he was having with himself about his misfortune, Wayne failed to notice a sign for an approaching T-junction, and it was too late by the time he'd realised his mistake.

Under normal circumstances, the fact that it was a quarter to four in the morning would have meant no other cars being about on that particularly remote stretch of road, but it hadn't been Wayne's night, and it was about to get worse.

He overshot the junction by about a half a car's length just as a little five-door hatchback happened to be busily making its way along the adjacent lane. The other car swerved violently to avoid him, catching the edge of a high grass verge before coming to a spinning, screeching halt facing the way it had come. Two identically dressed young women immediately got out and began striding towards Wayne's car.

Wearing matching white blouses and short black skirts, they looked like waitresses. The vehicle's dark-haired driver was slightly taller and a little slimmer than her more curvaceous blond passenger.

'Are you *mad* or something?' she shrieked. 'You could've killed us, you fucking *prick*!'

Wayne, too, had stepped out of his car, confronting the fuming woman in the glare of his headlights. *She shouldn't be talking to me like that,* he thought, drawing himself up to his full height. *She's got no idea who she's dealing with!*

Calmly, he looked over to the passenger who was standing back from the altercation. She seemed cautious and unsure about what was unfolding, and a little awkward about her companion's abrasiveness.

'Perhaps you'd like to tell your friend to be more polite?' Wayne said to her. 'I'd tell her myself, but I'm not sure she's worth it.'

The driver's mouth dropped open in astonishment.

'You fucking *what*?' she gasped. 'Just who the *hell* do you think you are? You've got to be on drugs or something; it's either that or you're pissed.' She gestured towards Wayne's idling M3, its four throbbing exhaust pipes growling softly in the background, and added sneeringly: 'Oh how very typical. I see flash little pricks just like you nearly every night, and you *all* think that you can do just what you fucking want. Call the police, Jennie; we'll let *them* deal with this!'

Although Wayne appeared to be letting the torrent of abuse wash over him, inside he was raging. The trappy little bitch couldn't have been any more wrong. *He* was far above *anybody* she had ever encountered, and there would be no need for the police; *he* was the law in this situation, *Natural Law*. Grinning smugly, he reached inside his jacket, a chilling expression that made the young woman baulk slightly, but then she quickly went back on the offensive.

'I tell you what,' she snapped, 'it's a damn good job for you that my boyfriend isn't here, or he'd have …'

With nothing more than a casual flick of his wrist, Wayne buried the heavy blade of the letter opener into her solar plexus, right up to its hilt. His grin widened at the sight of the girl's bulging, fearful eyes, and he gave the knife a little twist for good measure as he quickly withdrew it.

Jennie heard a gasped exclamation come from her friend, and then saw her collapse onto her knees, with the most awful, piercing scream.

'W-what have you done to her?' Jennie asked Wayne, taking an uncertain step towards them. 'Sara? SARA …?'

'Oh, so it *does* have a name, then,' said Wayne, pointing at the stricken woman curled up on the road at his feet. 'But I'm not sure that *Sara* is able to talk to you right now, I'm afraid.'

A pool of blood had quickly begun to form beneath Sara, spreading out steadily on the dirty tarmac. It was on her hands, too, oozing out through her fingers and soaking through her once pristine white blouse.

'He's stabbed me!' she cried out, her eyes wide with panic. 'Oh my God … he's fucking stabbed me!'

Bile instantly began rising in Jennie's throat. They were just on their way home from a lock-in … it had been a wonderful night … this wasn't happening, *how* could this be happening?

'Holy Jesus … SARA!' she sobbed, trying frantically to get to her, but Wayne had stepped in between them. 'L-let me help her' Jennie begged him. 'Sh-she's my best friend … Please, l-let me help her!'

'Oh, I don't think there is much you *can* do for Sara, now,' said Wayne, bringing the bloodied letter knife level with Jennie's eyeline. 'Other than show her your gratitude for making the ultimate sacrifice for you.'

He pressed the lethal blade hard against Jennie's cheek, and all she could do was stare helplessly into his empty, remorseless eyes.

'W-w-*what* sacrifice?' she stammered. 'W-What do you mean?'

'Sara has made her choice and given her life so that y-y-*you* can be p-p-pleasured by m-*me*.'

'JENNIEEEE … It's really bleeding …!' Sara cried.

'PLEASE …' Jennie begged again. 'L-let me call an ambulance. W-w-we won't say anything … *please* …'

'It won't stop COMING OUT!'

Sara's desperate pleas were cutting through Jennie almost as cruelly as Wayne's blade had punctured an artery in her best friend's chest.

'Your compassion and loyalty are touching,' he said, using the very same blade to gently wipe away some tears from Jennie's face. 'You will be justly rewarded.'

For the fleetest of moments, Jennie thought that Wayne was going to relent, but then to her horror, he wrapped an unyielding arm around her neck and hauled her away instead.

'JENNIEEEE!'

'No! *Please* …!' Jennie sobbed. 'Sara … *Please* let me help her … *please!*'

But Wayne was too strong and determined. Jennie couldn't break free of the stranglehold he had on her as she was dragged at knifepoint towards Sara's car and then forced in through the open passenger door onto her hands and knees, across its front seats.

This submissive position Wayne found both arousing and elating. Jennie was trembling and whimpering, begging him not to hurt her, making him feel powerful and in complete control of the moment that he knew was truly going to define him. *This* little prize wasn't going to evade him. *This* was payback for the Middleton bitch, and just reward for all the efforts he'd gone to that night.

Wayne pulled down his jeans and boxer shorts to expose his erection, and raised the back of Jennie's short black skirt. She was wearing a tiny black thong, with which he amused himself for a few moments, slipping a finger under the string of the undergarment and sliding it playfully up and down the cleavage of her fleshy, white buttocks.

Jennie's body went completely rigid at the touch, but then she gasped as Wayne forcibly pushed himself inside her, crying out in pain at the first of his brutal, penetrating thrusts. He was holding his knife just below her stomach, its tip was cutting into her skin, and there was no doubt in Jennie's mind that she would be killed if she tried to resist. Just outside the confines of her ordeal was a horrifying reminder of her attacker's abilities. Trapped in the cramped interior of the little hatchback with one side of her face pressed firmly against the driver's door, Jennie could only look directly out through the windscreen and onto the road where Sara lay on her side in the dazzling beam of Wayne's headlights, blood-soaked and ominously still.

Only minutes before, Sara, her 'Bezzie', had been laughing and joking about the events of that night, but now she lay bleeding to death on the fractured tarmac of a country lane that hardly anybody used. Jennie knew it was extremely unlikely that anybody else would be coming along who could help them and that she too was going to be lying out there as cold and abandoned as Sara before very much longer.

And that moment wasn't too far away. Her attacker's thrusts were becoming even more violent, and then Jennie heard him exhale, and his body tense as he climaxed. She bowed her head in despair at the helplessness and shame of her situation, expecting to feel nothing but the cold, unimaginable agony of the blade at her midriff cutting through her flesh any second, but then she saw a can of body spray lying on the floor of the driver's footwell beside her. The aerosol had obviously tumbled out of one of their handbags when Sara had hit the brakes, and as Wayne withdrew, he inadvertently moved the knife away from her too.

Instinct took over. Jennie seized the only chance she was going to have of escape. Picking up the can, and turning all in one movement, she sprayed its stinging, sickly-sweet contents directly into Wayne's face. The spray struck him squarely in the eyes, and, as he squealed in pain, he also inhaled its choking vapour. Jennie kicked out violently, one of her feet connecting solidly with Wayne's chin. The lucky blow bought herself enough time to open the driver's side door, but as she struggled forwards, he lashed out blindly with his knife and plunged it deep into her right thigh. A terrible shaft of burning pain shot up Jennie's leg and into her hip, and she screamed in agony. Wayne lashed out again, but this time the blade tore harmlessly into the upholstery of the now empty seat.

Once outside, Jennie managed to drag herself to her feet and half-run, half-limp away from the car as Wayne began furiously slashing away at its interior, shrieking at the top of his voice as though gripped by a bizarre childlike tantrum.

As much as Jennie was desperate to get as far away as possible from this vicious lunatic, she couldn't just leave Sara when there was a chance that her friend might still be alive. She struggled as quickly as she could over to Sara's motionless form and knelt down beside her, but Sara's staring, sightless eyes merely confirmed Jennie's worst fears. Overcome by overwhelming grief, she tenderly cradled the head of her dead friend in her hands and sobbed her name, but Wayne had already clambered out of Sara's car and was staggering, knife in hand, coughing and choking towards them.

The pain in Jennie's thigh was excruciating. She could feel the blood from the wound soaking into the material of her skirt, making it warm and sticky, but her survival instincts had kicked in, and they were far stronger than the tidal waves of indescribable guilt and despair over her inability to have fought back sooner.

Adrenalin pumping, Jennie finally turned and ran as fast as her condition would allow, into a field, and away from her attacker.

Throughout the whole sickening and horrific ordeal, Wayne's car engine had been running. Had Jennie's panic not overtaken her so completely, she might even have been able to escape in the silver BMW that had so fatally pulled out in front of she and Sara. As it was, it was Wayne who was escaping, leaving the scene instead of chasing after her. His eyes felt like they were on fire and the back of his throat was stinging from inhaling the heavily scented spray of the aerosol can, but his discomfort was eased knowing he'd caught Jennie with his knife. If the popping sensation of the blade penetrating her flesh had been anything to go by, the injury was probably serious, serious enough to slow her down and make her easier to catch. Wayne toyed briefly with the idea of turning round, finding her and finishing her off. At first the little slut had been respectful and had succumbed to him, but then her mask had slipped and her true colours had been revealed.

Wayne imagined Jennie lying alone somewhere in the fields and woods, bleeding, helpless, surrounded by scavengers waiting for her to die. Having disrespected his talents so crassly, being a meal for rats and other lower life forms would be a fitting end for her, but an even *bigger* positive was knowing that Joanne Middleton's letter opener had made such a formidable weapon. A pleasure to use, sharpened and honed like its new owner, it enabled Wayne to get close enough to look right into the eyes of his prey as he cleansed them.

Not even the magnificent cheetah after the thrill of the chase had the pleasure of looking into the terrified eyes of the antelope at the time of the kill.

But Wayne still felt somewhat unfulfilled at being stood up by his date with destiny. It was obvious that his appetite for the kill was designed to deal with much bigger game than the insignificant prey he'd just encountered, and although he should have been grateful to the two young women for helping him vent at least some of his frustration, it was clear that anything less than his prime target was just a waste of his time and energy. He would just have to stay patient and wait for another opportunity to get to Samantha Middleton.

By the time Wayne found his way back to his hotel, the eastern horizon was illuminated by the newly breaking dawn, and he hurriedly changed his clothes inside his car at the building's rear. He hadn't noticed any blood on him but didn't want to take any risks, a wise precaution given that there happened to be a night porter on duty sitting at the reception desk when Wayne entered. The man acknowledged Wayne with a nod and a knowing grin, and asked politely: 'Was it a lucky night by any chance, sir?'

Evidently, he assumed that Wayne might have had a sexual encounter with some random woman. How typical that one of such low-standing should see things that way. Wayne considered his reply carefully before answering; after all, the night porter's assumptions hadn't actually been that wide of the mark.

'It could have gone better,' he replied. 'Not quite what I was looking for.'

'Better luck next time then, eh, sir?'

Then it was *Wayne's* turn to grin.

'I'm going to make *sure* of it,' he said.

*

Neither Andy, Samantha or Chris had got much sleep following Samantha's nightmare and they agreed that they should start the day early. Chris explained to his mother that Joanne had wanted to be picked from the hospital as early as possible as she and Samantha needed to go back to Hampstead to collect Samantha's car. Joanne's Range Rover was going to be off the road for some time, public transport in the wilds of Hertfordshire was erratic at best, and hiring a car wasn't an option, either, as Joanne was in no condition to drive, and Samantha's young age and limited driving experience would most likely go against her.

Anne was happy to go along with the plan and look after Harley while they were gone, blissfully unaware that another aspect of the arrangement was the others being able to share what they knew about The Puppeteer in her absence.

It was just after six in the morning when Andy, Samantha and Chris left Whitwell. Chris knew of an out-of-the-way café that did a superb breakfast fry-up, an enthusiastically welcomed suggestion even though the little bistro wasn't going to be open for around another hour. It would mean a more roundabout route through the lanes, but it was a beautiful drive out that way, and, as Chris had anticipated, Andy and Samantha soon began to talk, making the most of the extra time.

Clear skies during the night had allowed a patchy light mist to form in some of the fields where it lay in the form of soft, rolling banks in the hollows. The sun was already beginning to disperse it as they made their way, Chris driving and listening intently to what his son and Samantha had to say. The more he knew about the others' experiences, the better, for the moment was surely approaching when he was going to have to contribute something of his own to the conversation, and he was going to have to choose his words with extreme care.

Chris felt like a traitor, maybe not to the overwhelming degree of earlier, but still more than his conscience could comfortably bear. And yet, at the same time, he felt oddly empowered listening to Andy and Samantha. He wasn't consciously aware of having learned anything more from Zambaya, but now that the three of them were pretty much on the same page, he felt as if it might be easier to deal with whatever was coming.

Togetherness was the true power of The Circle, and one of Chris's other concerns *had* been the limits of Joanne's knowledge as its fourth member, but those reservations soon evaporated as Samantha continued to open up from behind him on the back seat.

'Mum saw The Puppeteer on the landing of our house in Hampstead,' she said. 'The same night I had the first nightmare. *He's* the real reason we left. Mum sees him as a reflection; she told me that's what caused her accident yesterday, so you were right, thinking he had something to do with it. He attacked her again last night as well.'

'What …? In the hospital?' asked Andy.

'Yep. Mum and me always get hit together, but in different ways, even though we might be in totally different places. Mum had a really bad time of it last night, though, and that's why she ended up calling me at stupid o'clock this morning because she knew that I would've copped for him, too … Anyway, talking about Mum, I'm really interested to hear more about what happened to *you* now because I remember you saying something about seeing The Puppeteer by her car?'

Andy was thoughtful for a moment as he recalled the extremely unpleasant encounter.

'I just *saw* him like he was a real person,' said Andy. 'Like now, with you and Dad.'

'That's the bit I didn't understand when you spoke about it last night.'

'Yeah, because I need to start from the beginning, like when Dad was in hospital and I went to see him with Nan, and I had this really weird experience while I was waiting. This gypsy woman just came over to me, but it turns out that I was the only person who could see her!'

'That *is* weird!'

'Damn right it was, but it gets even weirder, because she gave me a sort of … of *blessing*, and then warned me about somebody she called 'The Master of Puppets', and then just a few days later I come face to face with him, except that he told me he was 'The Puppeteer', so it's got to be the same guy! Fucked up, yeah?'

'Andy …!' said Chris. 'Is that really necessary?'

'Yeah, Dad … I think it is! I think it sums things up pretty well, don't you? Because I haven't finished yet and because there were others there yesterday, too!'

'Others?' Samantha asked. 'When you saw The Puppeteer, you mean?'

Chris glanced nervously into his rear-view mirror. Samantha's eyes were reflected looking back *directly* into his. The conversation had started to take a very worrying turn for Chris because he'd been caught completely off-guard by the level of his son's apparent involvement.

'The gypsy woman I saw at the hospital?' replied Andy. 'She was there, too, trying to protect me, and so was this big African guy who said he was connected to Dad … That's who I was giving Dad a hard time about last night when you walked in on us, Sam; The Puppeteer and a guy called Zambaya. So, I guess this is as good a time as any to start telling us *your* bit then, isn't it, Dad?'

At least with Zambaya as a starting point, Chris felt he had a harmless enough subject with which to open his account to the others.

As Chris began his story, the road wound on ahead towards some distant woodland in which there hid a terrified, grieving young woman. Jennie was lying in the undergrowth, sobbing quietly, desperate, cold and in terrible pain. She had no idea where she was, but it was becoming clear that she couldn't go on much longer.

Hiding here, hiding there, Jennie was too afraid of staying too long in one place because *he* might still be out there looking for her. And she was *so cold*, shivering so much that her teeth were chattering. God, she felt like she was freezing, but the blouse that had once afforded her a little warmth had long since become a makeshift bandage which she'd tied as tightly as she could around the savage stab wound in her thigh. Although the bleeding had slowed, Jennie hadn't been able to stop it and the cold she was experiencing was due in part to the early stages of shock.

More tears came as another wave of despair swept over her along with another sheet of pain, but then she heard what sounded like a van or a lorry passing by just ahead through the trees and scrub. It took a supreme effort just to stand, but she somehow managed to haul herself towards the source of the sound, each faltering step more excruciating than the last as she grimly struggled forwards through the scrub. The pain in her leg was enough to make her want to sink to the floor and give in, but the ordinary and familiar sound of rubber on tarmac had been like sweet music to her ears, and the thought of passing out just yards from salvation made her dig even deeper into her dwindling reserves.

All of a sudden, Jennie was equally as terrified of succumbing to her injury as she was of being discovered by Sara's killer, but then she caught a glimpse of a narrow road beneath her.

Exhausted, she parted some sparse hedging on top of a steep bank, and tried to lower herself slowly down onto the roadside, but the effort of covering the last few yards had taken its toll and her injured leg didn't want to play the game anymore. Unable to keep hold of the flimsy branches, Jennie lost her balance and slid distressingly down the embankment and onto the road.

*

'…and that's how I found out about Zambaya,' said Chris. 'He said he's an 'Overseer', like a guardian angel or spirit guide.'

'Wow!' Samantha replied. 'A near death experience! That's amazing!'

'And bloody news to me, too!' said Andy.

'So, as you've just heard, neither of us knew anything about each other's experiences,' Chris continued. 'Not until just now, and after Andy dropped the bomb on me that you heard in the kitchen last night!'

'But there's some kind of reason for us all ending up like this,' said Samantha. 'Has Zambaya said anything more?'

Chris looked in his rear-view mirror again. He'd have to be very careful about what he said next.

'Well, he didn't –'

'DAD!' Andy shouted, abruptly. 'LOOK OUT!'

Instinctively, Chris hit the brakes, and mercifully so for the young woman lying in the road directly in front of his car. She tried to get up, but only succeeded in collapsing back onto the tarmac.

'Holy shit!' said a shaken Chris. 'Look at the state of her! Is she drunk or something?'

'No, Dad … she's hurt!' said Andy. '*Badly* hurt …!' and he immediately leapt out of the car with Samantha.

The poor girl was only wearing a bra and a torn, black skirt. There was congealed blood down the entire length of her right leg and a fresh flow was seeping through what looked like a blouse that she'd used as a bandage, forming crimson rivulets across the thigh. It was very evident that the wound was still bleeding badly.

'Oh my God!' whispered Samantha into the palm of her hand.

'Don't leave me … p-please … take me home,' the girl sobbed. 'I w-want to go home. He's … he's killed my friend … he killed my friend and then he raped me … he raped me …'

Samantha looked imploringly over at Chris, visibly shocked and clearly struggling.

'He stabbed my friend … he killed her!' the girl repeated.

'What's your name?' Chris asked, kneeling down and holding her hand. 'Are you from around here?'

'J-Jennie,' she stammered. 'My name's Jennie … I'm from L-Lilley.'

'Oh, Lilley! It's beautiful there. I know it well.'

'I'm c-cold. I'm r-really c-cold.'

'You're doing fine Jennie, just fine, it's going to be okay now.'

Andy suggested he should get the first aid kit from the boot his father's car, but Chris told him to get a blanket instead. 'Let's see if we can warm you up a bit then, first, Jennie' he said, trying his best to keep her calm. 'But we need to get you into the car and off the road, and then we're going to take you to hospital.'

'No! I w-want to go home! I w-want my mum, my d-dad!'

Samantha found it particularly disturbing to see that Jennie couldn't have been much older than herself; probably no more than twenty-one or twenty-two. Leaves and twigs were tangled in her matted, blond hair, and her pretty, round face was pale, and streaked with blood, dirt and tears. She had the most beautiful expressive eyes, but all they could communicate at that moment was a combination of absolute fear and confusion. Samantha remembered her nightmare in the early hours of that morning at the hands of The Puppeteer, and yet, regardless of the terror she'd felt at the time, that was still all it had been. *Jennie's* fear was the consequence of a terrible reality, and suddenly the incident on Hampstead Heath came back into Samantha's mind in a most unwelcome form.

Even though Joanne had tried to put the fear of God into her about what might have happened had Samantha been alone at the time, Samantha had still found being flashed amusing. She'd never even given a second thought to anything bad happening to her: *bad* things always seemed to happen to other people, and a chill shot up her spine knowing that the helpless girl lying on the road in front of her had probably always thought the same.

Suddenly, Hampstead Heath wasn't funny anymore.

'Okay, Jennie,' said Chris. 'We're going to put this blanket around you and then sit you up. Then we're going to get you in the car. Sam, darling, can you open the back door for us?'

Andy and Chris lifted Jennie off the road as best as they could, offering words of encouragement when she cried out in pain at the sudden movement. Then, they carefully carried her to the car and gently laid her on the back seat with her head resting on Samantha's lap.

Just a little way ahead was a turning into what appeared to be a farm track, and Chris took the opportunity to park up so that he and Andy could quickly apply some first aid. Andy moved his passenger seat as far forwards as it would go so that he could assist Samantha in the back and apply pressure to the brutal wound in Jennie's thigh. Occasionally, he and Samantha would exchange glances, appalled as the grieving young woman revealed more of her horrific ordeal. How she'd been raped at knifepoint, forced to look on as her best friend, Sara, lay dying. How she'd had to run away and abandon Sara's body, leaving her dead friend lying in the road.

While Jennie talked, Chris put his foot down. He'd no intention of hanging about, but he still had to take care in the lanes. However, they'd not been travelling long when they came across a POLICE SLOW sign on the side of the road. Chris obeyed the sign and cautiously rounded the next bend. Two police cars were blocking the way ahead by a side turning marked up as a diversion. Without saying a word, he jumped out of the car and hurried towards them.

'What's happening?' asked Jennie. 'Why have we stopped?'

'It's okay,' Samantha told her. 'There are some police in the road and Chris has gone to talk to them.'

'It's Sara, isn't it … they've found Sara.'

'I don't know … there's no way I can tell.'

'I just saw Dad flash his ID,' said Andy, having to twist himself round a little to see. 'He's got us an escort by the look of it!'

One of the squad cars pulled away from the roadblock and came to a halt in the entrance of the turning. Chris climbed back into his car, raised his hand and followed on behind as the officers sped on ahead to keep the way clear.

On the back seat, Samantha was desperately trying to keep Jennie awake as the young woman suddenly began to deteriorate.

CHAPTER 21

'Detective Chief Inspector Mike Devonshire,' said a gruff, stocky man in a tired dark blue suit.

'Joanne Middleton,' Joanne replied, offering him her 'good' hand. 'I'm Samantha's mother, and it'll have to be the left one I'm afraid.'

Judging by his slightly sweaty handshake, DCI Devonshire was finding it a little too warm in the hospital. A thick-set man in his late forties, his broad face was slightly flushed, and tiny beads of perspiration could be seen glistening through his greying, closely cropped hair.

'Been in the wars, have we?' he asked, nodding at Joanne's poly sling.

'Something like that!' she sighed.

Devonshire smiled and introduced his somewhat more fervent and energetic young colleague, Detective Sergeant Ben Willard.

'Pleased to meet you, Mrs Middleton,' said Willard. 'We'll try not to keep you too long, but I'm sure you understand that it's important for us to speak to your daughter and the others.'

Ben Willard was not only a good fifteen years younger than his superior, but also his polar opposite. Fresh-faced, tall, lean and immaculately turned out in a pristine light grey jacket and black chinos, his clipped professional manner was almost as sharp as his keen, steely eyes. A crisp white shirt looked like it had just come out of its packaging and his choice of necktie, dark red and uncomplicated, made Joanne wonder if he might even have been on his way to a job interview.

'Sorry, Mum' said Samantha. 'I know how much you want to get out of here.'

'Take as long as you need,' replied Joanne. 'I think this is far more important.'

'Shall we …?' asked Willard, motioning towards the open door of an adjacent office in which, through its clear glass frontage, Chris and DCI Devonshire could be seen rearranging the seating. Andy waited for Samantha before moving off, and she pointedly leaned into him as he put his arm around her. Their body language suggested a growing mutual affection, and Chris smiled warmly as they approached.

Extreme events often brought strangers together in the most unusual ways, and yet Joanne suspected there had to be more behind such evident bonding. Coming across a seriously injured girl lying in a country lane was certainly extreme, but hardly grounds for such an outward display of closeness, and Samantha looked like she was actually drawing considerable strength from Andy's affection. Joanne's intuition said it had to be somehow connected to the previous night and that something else was playing out which Samantha was yet to mention.

But a hospital was hardly a place for such revelations, and barely an hour had passed since Samantha's grim discovery of poor Jennie Lawrence, so it was hardly the time right for a cosy girly mother-and-daughter chat, was it?

No. As hard as it was going to be for Joanne's curiosity, she was simply going to have to push it to the back of her mind for the time being and be done with it.

There was an array of donated magazines strewn haphazardly around a nearby table through which she began sifting in the hope of finding something of interest, eventually settling upon a glossy that looked like it might contain a bit of gossip. Flicking through its dog-eared pages, Joanne would occasionally peel her eyes away from the rambling editorial and glance over the top of the publication, intrigued at how things were progressing with the others in the office. She could see Willard efficiently making notes while Devonshire slouched in his chair, his necktie appearing a bit looser every time she looked up and heading that little bit further south. The scene may have borne little resemblance to the dramatically enhanced television crime shows to which she was accustomed, but it didn't lessen the brutal reality of what those inside were having to discuss.

Joanne put the magazine back on the table. Who was sleeping with whom in Celebrity Land could wait for another time. All she could suddenly think of was the torment suffered by Jennie's parents and the unimaginable devastation endured by those of Sara, unpleasant, worrying thoughts that persisted until Samantha and Andy came out of the office to join her.

'We've told them everything we can,' said Samantha. 'They're probably talking police matters now.'

'Yeah, Dad told me he wouldn't be too long,' said Andy. 'Mike and Ben were both at the crime scene earlier and they know Dad's in the Met, so they want to bounce a few things off him. I reckon they're probably talking about some really nasty stuff in there right now.'

Joanne looked over to the office. Chris put his hand up as she caught his eye.

'I shudder to think,' she said. 'It must have been an absolutely terrible thing to see.'

And then, for some inexplicable reason, a sickening image of Samantha lying dead in a remote country lane came to the forefront of Joanne's mind. It was so random as to have been put there deliberately by something or somebody just to torment her. Joanne knew the entity that had been hounding them was more than capable of implanting such horrific thoughts and would no doubt be delighting in its latest coup if it were responsible.

'Maybe it might be better to talk about something else?' she said. 'We haven't spoken about anything else since you've been here, really.'

Samantha seemed more than happy to change the subject and started to talk about the earlier plans that had been made prior to leaving Whitwell.

'So,' she began, 'we've decided to go back to Hampstead to pick up my car because we're going to need some wheels out here, aren't we? So I helped to arrange things with Anne until we get back.'

'What sort of 'things', exactly?' asked Joanne, frowning.

'Well, like looking after Harley while Chris and Andy drive us to Hampstead.'

'But don't you think that Anne and her family have put themselves out for us enough already? Anne is *not* a bloody babysitting service for our dog, Samantha! What on *earth* were you thinking?!'

'But Nan was happy to do it,' said Andy, quickly intervening. 'She was the one who *suggested* she looked after Harley. She absolutely adores him.'

'Andy ...' Joanne sighed. 'Andy ... you're an absolute love, you really are ... and your whole *family* is wonderful! But I'm not prepared to keep imposing on you all like this. I totally agree that it's a good idea to pick up Sammy's car, but that's all I agree with. If you want to drop us off at the train station, then that's fine, but I'm not going to have you drive us *all* the way to Hampstead when it's a cinch for us on the train. It's not that I don't appreciate the offer, Andy, because I honestly do, and I really *do* hope that I don't sound ungrateful by putting my foot down on this occasion.'

There was a softness about Joanne's eyes as she spoke, but there had been a marked assertiveness to her tone. Nevertheless, as much as her decisiveness wasn't what Andy wanted to hear, there was little else he could do other than accept her position. He nodded and smiled, yet Joanne thought that he seemed a little ill at ease, but then voices from opposite distracted her. A female doctor had arrived while they'd been talking and had emerged from the office along with Chris and the two detectives. There was a brief conversation and handshakes all round before she left with Willard and Devonshire, and then Chris came back over to join Joanne and the others. He was only too pleased to share some positive news about Jennie, who had been stabilised although still deemed to be in a serious condition.

'Mike and Ben want to see her before she goes into surgery,' he said.

'That's where they're going now.'

'Already?' asked Samantha. 'Wow, they're not hanging about, are they? Is she going to be well enough to answer questions, then?'

Samantha had really connected with Jennie, and Chris was quick to allay any concerns about her being subjected to anything before she was ready.

'Mike and Ben are just going to introduce themselves and try and give Jennie some support. That's all, Sam. The doctor made it very clear that she will need some time before she'll be able to help them with their enquiries, and they'll respect that. I expect they'll be meeting with Jennie's parents, too.'

'I thought Mike Devonshire seemed a bit off,' said Andy. 'He didn't even acknowledge us when he left!'

'He wouldn't have meant anything by it,' Chris replied. 'He was praising you two in there and saying how well you did. It's just that he's just got a lot on his mind right now, son, that's all.'

As far as Chris was concerned, Devonshire had every *right* to appear subdued. Underneath the tough exterior and brusque persona, Mike Devonshire, a father himself, was equally as human as anybody else, and the Lawrences were not the *only* parents with whom he was going to be speaking. There was another grief-stricken set coming to the hospital and they were going to be identifying their only daughter's body. Devonshire had been trying his best to prepare himself for the devastation he was going to witness, but he'd been struggling, and with every passing minute, the moment he'd been dreading had been drawing inexorably closer. As a DCI himself, Chris knew only too well what Devonshire was about to face. He'd had plenty of experience of dealing with tragedies in the Met.

'Anyway ...' he said, clearing his mind of the traumas of policework, and turning his attention back to Joanne and Samantha. 'We've done our bit here; now it's time to get you guys to Hampstead.'

There was an uncomfortable silence as Joanne and Samantha exchanged a brief glance, but Joanne knew that it was all down to *her* to break the news to Chris about making their own way.

'Yes,' she said. 'About that ... Sammy told me what you'd all got planned, but I'd rather we went back under our own steam if you don't mind, Chris. It's a lovely offer, it really is, and so good of you but you've done so much for us and I don't want to inconvenience you any more than we already have. And Sammy and me, well, we've both been through a lot in the past couple of days and I think we could probably both do with spending some time together, really.'

Normally measured and precise in her speech, Joanne's statement had been uncharacteristically rushed. It was clear how awkward she felt about refusing Chris's help, but at the same time it was very noticeable how determined she was to do her own thing with Samantha. All Joanne and Samantha had was each other, they were inseparable, enduring everything together, which put him in a totally impossible position. Obligated to protect Samantha, yet unable to intervene in her life without appearing unnaturally insistent, Chris simply had *no choice* but to let them travel to Hampstead alone.

Joanne could sense that he was disappointed; or was it concern? Either way, the moment was gone as soon as Samantha told Andy that *he* could carry 'Boudicca's bloody overnight bag to the car this time', forgotten in the laughter that followed. Samantha's biting sense of humour had successfully lifted the mood, but it was to be the last of the light-hearted exchanges, as the short drive to the station was a much quieter affair. Joanne thought the atmosphere in the car was tense, awkward even, and Andy and Chris not having anything much to say to each other wasn't helping at all, either.

But the train station was only a couple of miles from the hospital, and it wasn't long before Chris was parking up at and getting Joanne's bag out of the boot space, insisting that he should carry it at least until they got to the ticket office. He appeared to be playing the role of the perfect gentleman, bodyguard, even, and Joanne felt rather protected as he accompanied them up a flight of grey, concrete steps to the ticket hall.

'We'll be alright on the train,' she said as she and Samantha took their places in the queue. 'And thanks again for all you've done for us. Thank you so very much for everything.' Without thinking, she leant forwards and kissed his cheek. 'Tomorrow night then' she added. 'At ours … eight o'clock?'

Chris knew he was blushing when Joanne pulled away, but then Samantha embraced him affectionately and he was able to recover himself.

That mysterious closeness from the hospital waiting room had just shown itself again. Thinking about it made Joanne turn and look back as she headed towards the platform for London-bound trains with Samantha; Chris was still standing there, watching after them.

She smiled at him, and he waved back. A part of her regretted being so insistent about taking the train, but the difficult circumstances at the hospital had meant that she'd hardly spoken to Samantha, and there was a necessity for them to talk about how they were going to combat the darkness invading their lives.

But Samantha had barely said a word in spite of their mutual needs, not even after they'd taken their seats in the carriage. The monotonous sound of the train's wheels upon the tracks was all that disturbed the otherwise unedifying silence, and the others with whom Joanne and Samantha shared their carriage were all consumed by whatever was happening on the screens of their various mobile devices. If it hadn't died already, the art of conversation was drawing its final breaths in a stagnant atmosphere of blatant indifference.

Joanne looked across at Samantha staring glassily out of the window. It was most unlike her to be so subdued and distracted, and Joanne suspected that there was more to her distant demeanour than the distressing encounter with Jennie Lawrence. Believing her best chance of finding anything out might lie in lightening the mood a little, she stretched out one of her long legs and gently began kicking at one of Samantha's ankles. Clearly not in any frame of mind to entertain stupidity, Samantha responded by moving her legs away, but then she smiled and shook her head. Joanne could see that Samantha's eyes were a little bloodshot and heavy-lidded, so she put the idea of striking up a potentially difficult conversation on the backburner and patted the seat next to her instead.

'You look tired, Sammy,' she said. 'Why don't you try and get some sleep until we get to Kings Cross? You've got time. This is a slow train and there are quite a few stops.'

'Is that a polite way of saying I look like absolute crap then, Mum?'

'Well, I didn't want to say anything, but now you come to mention it.'

'You really *can* be a total bitch sometimes!'

'And I can recall you saying that on a few occasions!'

Their gentle banter and laughter slowly subsided, and Samantha promptly fell asleep next to her mother, but as her daughter's breathing got heavier, Joanne's thoughts became darker. The reasons why they were having to return to Hampstead kept coming back into her mind, along with the horrors of the previous day.

Normality, it seemed, had become a thing of the past, a distant oasis of routine, irreconcilable with the present extremes.

Joanne put her good arm around her sleeping daughter. Never before could she remember having felt so desperate. Or so very afraid.

*

But Joanne wasn't alone in searching for answers. Elsewhere, Andy Ryan was determined to get some of his own.

'So, when *are* you thinking of telling me what you know about The Puppeteer and Zambaya then, Dad?' he asked. 'I thought you might have at least wanted to talk about it once we were alone, but you've said sod all since we dropped Sam and Jo off at the station. When you had the chance this morning you only told me and Samantha about how you'd *first* met Zambaya, and I stress *first*, so there must have been other times. And from what I saw yesterday, Zambaya and The Puppeteer have got some serious issues with each other, but I guess that's not news to you, is it? And why were you so worried about Sam going back to Hampstead? *I* could see it, and I'm bloody well sure Joanne could as well.'

Chris had only just begun to scratch the surface about his personal experiences when they'd stumbled across Jennie Lawrence, and then the whole dynamic had changed with the young woman's predicament having overtaken everything else. Up until then, he'd been elaborating upon nothing more than the otherworldly nature of what he'd seen, padding out the account with graphic descriptions without getting into any specifics, but Andy's challenging assessment of his father's lack of disclosure had just put an end to all that. The inquisition that had started in the early hours of that morning had begun again, except this time Andy's tone had been even more hostile. The fact that he even *knew* about Zambaya and the Overseer's ongoing feud with The Puppeteer had taken Chris massively by surprise, but Andy didn't know *everything*, and Chris was determined that it was going to stay that way.

'Well, you seem to know an awful lot about this *yourself* from where I'm sitting, Andy,' he said, trying to fight fire with fire. 'Maybe *you're* the one who should be enlightening *me*!'

'Don't try pulling that one on me, Dad, because this isn't about me, this is about you and Zambaya.'

'Andy, it's like I said! Zambaya just came to me. All I know is that he's an Overseer, the same as that gypsy woman who came to *you*.'

'You mean Oshina.'

'Okay, like Oshina.'

'But Zambaya isn't *just* an Overseer, though, is he?'

'And what gives you that idea?'

'Because The Puppeteer was far too powerful for Oshina when she tried to protect me from him by Joanne's car, but when Zambaya appeared, he protected both me *and* her. He was like … like The Puppeteer's *equal*.'

'So, you're trying to tell me that he's something more than he said he is?'

'Obviously! So, how come Zambaya happens to be so closely connected to *you*?'

'And how the hell am I supposed to know that?'

'Well, he *must* have come to you the way he did for a reason! Zambaya's on a *completely* different level, and somebody like that doesn't come into your life just to say 'hi', does he? And what does The Puppeteer want with us all, anyway, and especially Samantha?'

'I don't know!'

'Because this *is* about Samantha, isn't it?'

'Andy … I don't know! Has Oshina said something to you about her, then?'

'Not directly, no.'

'Well neither has Zambaya!'

'Oh, this is bullshit! We're just going round in circles! There's something going on here *big* time that you're afraid to talk to me about for some reason!'

'I'm not afraid …'

'Like fuck you're not!'

Up ahead was a small grassy area often used by ramblers as a car park. Chris swung the Audi into the convenient layby and slammed on the brakes.

'And you can cut that crap out right NOW!' he snapped. 'Lose the bloody attitude, son! Isn't it clear to you that what's happening is way beyond *either* of us? Look what's happened to *me* as well! Don't you think I'd like some answers too? For God's sake, Andy! What you've had to say has already knocked me for six! All I know is that we're part of something that *neither* of us understands, and we need to talk *responsibly* about what we know, not tear lumps out of each other over it.'

Andy stared out through the windscreen, deliberately avoiding his father's gaze.

'Well, perhaps if you stopped pretending you know sod all we could make a start,' he muttered. 'You didn't go through what happened to me yesterday. One minute I'm looking for Joanne's belongings and the next I'm on my knees, trying not to throw up and staring up at a seven-foot-odd giant that looked like something out of your worst fucking nightmare! If it hadn't had been for Zambaya, God knows what might have happened to me! I take it you haven't seen The Puppeteer yourself then?'

'No,' Chris replied. 'I haven't.'

'Then it can only be because Zambaya is protecting you from him.'

'Oh, come on …!'

'Well, how else can you explain it when the rest of us have? And you didn't see what I did when Zambaya stood his ground and protected me. So, like I said, I know you're hiding something.'

'Andy …'

'Someone like Zambaya comes to you like he does, and then doesn't tell you anything about *any* of this? Give me a break!'

Chris switched off the car's engine and took a deep breath.

'Zambaya warned me about The Puppeteer,' he said. 'He's part of a group or, *faction*, that Zambaya called the Faithless. Zambaya told me that The Puppeteer selects people, recruits them to work for him …'

'Like radicalisation?'

'Something like that, yes.'

'How?'

'In their dreams mainly.'

'Well, he doesn't seem to be trying to radicalise Samantha when he comes to her in her nightmares, so what *does* he want with her?'

'Zambaya didn't *say* anything about Samantha.'

'So, he came to you *just* to talk about The Puppeteer, and nothing else?'

Andy sat quietly for a moment, and shook his head sadly.

'You must think I'm stupid if you expect me to believe anything you've just come out with,', he said. 'Because I *know* there's a lot more to this, and for whatever reason you're not letting on! When Nan and I went back to Preston with Samantha to get her mum's stuff for the hospital yesterday, there was this guy sitting in a silver BMW M3 parked near her house, and when I saw him, I felt similar to how I did with The Puppeteer next to Joanne's car.' He paused to see if there was any reaction, and just for a split second he thought his father looked rattled.

'Go on,' said Chris. 'I'm listening.'

'Well,' Andy continued. 'Remember how I just said I nearly threw up when I saw The Puppeteer? It was part of a really extreme reaction when he appeared. Okay, so maybe the reaction wasn't quite as strong when I saw that guy in the car, but the *sensation* was exactly the same, so I'm guessing ... no ... I'm *saying* that the two of them have to be connected somehow.'

Chris shuffled uncomfortably in his seat, and Andy nodded knowingly to himself.

'It's the gift I told you about,' he said. 'Seeing Oshina at the hospital when I came to visit you with Nan? Oshina *did* something to me that day, Dad, *awakened* me, because then all this weird shit started happening almost straight afterwards. And yesterday, by Joanne's car, Oshina even told The Puppeteer that I'd been 'prepared' for him, so I already know I'm deeply involved. The question is, *how* deep? What exactly *have* I been prepared for, Dad, and why, because after all the bollocks I went through yesterday, I think I've got a bloody right to know?'

'We have to protect Samantha from The Puppeteer,' said Chris. 'That's all I know ...'

'*Just* The Puppeteer, Dad?' Andy began reaching for the passenger side door handle as he spoke. 'I wouldn't be so damned sure about that! And *we're* only going to be able to protect Samantha if you *actually* start telling me everything you know, not that I'm holding out too much hope of that happening any time soon by the look of it ... I'm done with this! I'll walk the rest of the way to Nan's!'

The car door was slammed shut with considerable force, and Chris could only sit in silence, wishing he could revisit those past few disagreeable moments as he watched Andy clamber over a wooden stile and stride away into a field on the other side.

Only *Chris* knew the true purpose of Zambaya's Circle, and yet his son's heightened senses were proving to be just as pivotal to Samantha's safety as those of his own. With Andy being able to detect the presence of both The Puppeteer *and* the assassin, the need for father and son to work together was paramount, but how was that ever going to be possible given the level of secrecy upon which Zambaya was insisting?

Chris suddenly felt an overwhelming sense of panic and anger. Why *had* he been handed such a poisoned chalice without being offered the slightest hint of recourse? If not an already impossible task, the odds against a successful outcome to Zambaya's plans were lengthening with every passing hour because there was a killer on the loose.

Mike Devonshire had been adamant that the brutality he'd witnessed first thing that morning was totally out of character for North Hertfordshire, which made the DCI suspect that the perpetrator was far less likely to be a local. Those words alone made it terrifyingly apparent to Chris that Jennie Lawrence and Sarah Murrell had, tragically, been in the wrong place at the wrong time and that their attacker might only have been out in those parts because he'd been intending to kill Samantha. Maybe Samantha had only survived due to her being persuaded to stay with his family, and that pure fluke alone had prevented her meeting the same unspeakable fate as Sarah Murrell.

But luck had a terrible habit of running out. Andy's account of the mysterious car he'd seen parked so close to Joanne's cottage, and his strange physical reaction to its driver had been truly chilling for Chris, for there could be little doubt that Andy had encountered The Puppeteer's chosen assassin. Even worse was that the assassin knew how to find Samantha, and that man could be anywhere, including being onboard a London-bound train.

With his heart racing in tandem with his thoughts, Chris continued driving towards his mother's house in Whitwell.

If *only* he'd been able to talk Joanne into letting him drive Samantha and her back to London.

CHAPTER 22

Wayne lay on his bed, staring at the ceiling of his hotel room, fighting tiredness for fear of falling asleep, dreading the rebuke that was bound to be coming from The Puppeteer.

Perhaps watching Samantha Middleton for another day or so to familiarise himself with her movements would have given him a better opportunity, and he wouldn't have come up so miserably short. She had a dog, for fuck's sake! All he'd needed to do was watch her for a while, find out where and when she walked it, and wait until she was out in the open. His original thinking had lacked sufficient clarity, impatience had taken over, and he'd totally blown it. He'd even left himself exposed during his steak-out the previous afternoon, almost having his cover blown by a stinking bag of dog shit!

Wayne screwed up the duvet cover in frustration as he thought about his quarry, safe and sound in the cosseting surroundings of its herd, an innocent doe-eyed calf unaware of his burgeoning threat. Maybe the dog *was* actually an unwitting key to any future success. Like a lioness waiting for a young and inexperienced zebra to get detached from their number, Wayne was going to make sure that any naivety on Samantha Middleton's part would cost her just as dear.

But thinking about that hungry lioness only reminded Wayne that he was absolutely starving as well as shattered. It was well past ten in the morning, the hotel had long since stopped serving breakfast, and yet he didn't dare take so much as a single step out of his lair to get anything to eat for fear of what might be awaiting him in the outside world. In the cold, unforgiving light of day, he would be vulnerable to every set of prying, judgemental eyes that could look into his mind, a world of metaphorical vultures circling, ready to feast upon his every weakness.

Wayne covered his face despairingly. Regardless of the risks, he simply *had* to get himself together and face his fears. He only had to look at The Puppeteer as an example of courage and tenacity, for The Puppeteer had spent hundreds, *thousands* of years resolutely picking away at the web of lies and deceit spun by his enemies, and stood on the verge of a glorious victory over them. Wayne's master was a beacon; The Puppeteer had never given up in the pursuit of his precious vision, and Wayne needed to be a far better man in order to do that vision justice.

Slowly, he allowed his hands to slide back down his face until he was staring at the ceiling once again. He would venture out and show his face all in good time, but first he needed to get some rest.

*

A taxi pulled away in Hampstead, leaving Joanne standing and regarding her house in Winnington Road as though momentarily bewitched. On the outside, nothing seemed to have changed at all, and yet there was no reassurance to be had in that familiar façade. The last time Joanne had *entered* the house, she'd been returning home from a night of celebration. The last time she had closed its heavy wooden door behind her, she'd been running away.

Originally, Samantha and Joanne had only planned to collect Samantha's car and then drive straight back to Hertfordshire. There hadn't been any intention of going into the house, but Joanne had been unwilling to use the toilets on the train, and Samantha's needs were just as pressing, judging by the way she'd marched purposefully up the driveway and hurried inside.

With considerable trepidation, Joanne followed on a little while after. For all the property's outer aesthetic beauty, the inside of Winnington Road would be forever tainted. The entrance hall may have been just as light and airy as ever, and the personable scent of its recently polished hardwood floorboards calmingly intimate, but just knowing that The Puppeteer and his Manforms had been in the house was enough to make Joanne want to turn round and walk straight back out again. It was only her uncomfortably full bladder making her stay, but like a fearful, over-imaginative child, she just couldn't bring herself to go upstairs alone to use her ensuite.

Joanne called out her daughter's name, but a muffled response from behind the door of the downstairs cloakroom said that the only other option available was off-limits. For one desperate moment, she even considered going in the back garden, but then Samantha miraculously appeared in the entrance hall.

'God, you took your time!' said a very relieved Joanne. 'I'm absolutely bursting!'

'Well, you could have gone upstairs!' Samantha retorted, as her mother strode towards the cloakroom. 'Actually, I rather wish you would … it won't be great in there … please don't judge me!'

But the appeals went unheeded. Embarrassed, Samantha wandered into the kitchen to get herself a drink of water, letting the tap run at full strength into the sink for a few moments to drown out the sound of her mother's laughter. On the draining board were a few items that had been washed on the morning they'd left for Preston. There hadn't been enough washing up to warrant loading the dishwasher, so what little there'd been had been done by hand. It was very uncharacteristic for any cutlery, cups and bowls to just be left out like that, so Samantha decided she would put what little there was away.

The simple task only took a few seconds, but the crockery reminded Samantha about the forthcoming dinner at Greenoaks, and that she could do with finding something suitable to wear from her wardrobe. She went upstairs with a head full of ideas, but it was as she headed along the landing to her bedroom that her pace began to slow.

That was where it had all begun.

The bedroom door was wide open, and Samantha peered cautiously inside, wary of leaving the relative security of the landing. Her room was a total mess, the duvet cover of her once relaxing double bed kicked almost completely off, a crumpled reminder of having been woken from that first nightmare by her mother.

And then two crimson orbs began to glow menacingly in the darkness of a terrifying memory, staring out from the twisted, hideous face of a lantern-jawed Manform. The creeping grin of The Puppeteer followed, his black, empty, hypnotic gaze sucking her in.

It was as if it were happening all over again.

Samantha backed away into her mother's bedroom where two discarded towels lay strewn across another unmade bed, yet another appalling reminder of just how desperate they'd been to get out of the house.

Heart pounding, her breathing unbearably loud in the overpowering silence, Samantha began to ask herself why she'd even *felt* like going upstairs. Had it been the need to search for an outfit, or had it been *him* luring her up there so that he could terrorise her again? Suddenly it felt like The Puppeteer was right there with her, and his unspeakable Manforms, too.

Panic set in and Samantha rushed out of the bedroom, hurtling with a shriek into a tall figure that had appeared out on the landing.

'Ow ...!' cried the figure. 'Mind my bloody shoulder!'

'Mum ... *Jeez*!' said Samantha. 'You scared the *crap* out of me! What the hell are you doing sneaking around like that?'

'I heard you walking about upstairs, so I thought I'd come up to see what you were up to. What were you doing in my room anyway?'

At first Samantha claimed she'd been looking for an outfit that had been put in the wash, but then she admitted how her mind had started playing tricks on her.

'I suppose I just freaked myself out,' she said. 'But it really doesn't feel right here anymore, does it, Mum?'

'No, Sammy, it doesn't.'

'I really wish you'd have let Andy and Chris come back with us. We'd have felt safer having them here.'

That may well have been the case, but Joanne also knew that they were going to have to return home at some point, and what would they do then? It was a lengthy in-depth discussion that they were going to have to have another time, and definitely *away* from Winnington Road.

Enough was enough as far as Joanne was concerned. They'd more than finished at the house and it was time to head back to Anne's and collect Harley. If Samantha needed something to wear for the dinner party, they would just have to go out clothes shopping and look for something new. It would undoubtedly be a welcome tonic for them both, and *anything* would be better than thoughts of returning to Hampstead.

*

Having found himself languishing in what appeared to be a dungeon, Wayne would have swapped his problems for Joanne's in a heartbeat. Chained to a thick wooden post, manacled in such a way that he could only raise himself up onto his hands and knees, the rough stone floor beneath his naked body was harsh and cold, the only light afforded him from ghostly flickering flames dancing in a circle of tall candelabras.

Wayne had been dreading The Puppeteer's retribution, and the malignant atmosphere of his surroundings grew heavier as the entity himself emerged from the gathering gloom.

'I thought that as you were feeling a bit down, Wayne, I should offer you something by way of a little encouragement,' said The Puppeteer. 'I sense that you need some motivation … redirection, and we are glad to be of service.'

The crafted form of Naomi appeared next to The Puppeteer, the perfect skin of her immaculate curves shining seductively in the candlelight. Wayne smiled in anticipation of a new game, but his elation was to be short lived, for lumbering beside her, attached to a lead like an obedient dog, was a creature only fit for a nightmare. The chains that held Wayne captive began to clink and rattle as he tried unsuccessfully to back away from the monster and the inquisitive gaze of its glowing red eyes.

'W-w-what's that?' he asked. 'What the hell is *that* …?'

'You mean *this* little thing of beauty?' asked The Puppeteer, gesturing towards the object of Wayne's terror. 'Well, if you think it's that important, I suppose there's no harm in telling you … It's called a Manform, Wayne, a failure made good by a simple choice to serve me another way. Perfection attained by the hand of my mercy. Am I not merciful, and is my creation not magnificent?'

The Manform's nauseatingly disfigured face contorted into a jagged grin at the compliment, and its gaping mouth began to salivate uncontrollably, sensing Wayne's sudden desperation.

'I *know* I screwed up!' said Wayne. 'I *know* I need punishing, but I won't fail you again ... please!'

'Oh, my!' said The Puppeteer. 'Punishment? Is that what you think this special moment is all about? Yes, you made a mistake, but you're not being punished, my boy, you're about to be enlightened!' Then, he turned to Naomi and commanded: 'Release him.'

Wayne heaved a huge sigh of relief, but The Puppeteer hadn't been talking about *him*. With an audible *click*, the clip of the Manform's lead was detached, and the demonic creature moved forwards, sniffing the air which was heavy with the scent of Wayne's fear.

Naomi began to masturbate, aroused by the futility of his frantic struggles and the Manform's growing interest in their helpless prisoner. Her gasps and moans of pleasure filled the darkness of the dungeon as she embraced Wayne's suffering, while the Manform moved around to Wayne's vulnerable, raised behind. A heavy steel collar around Wayne's neck only allowed him to move his head so far, but the chains that bound him were shortening, becoming ever more restricting. Panic-stricken, unable to keep the alert and curious monstrosity in sight, Wayne began thrashing around even more violently in a final desperate act to escape, but then the Manform leapt onto his back, forcing him to submit.

Most of the back of Wayne's head and neck were grasped in the Manform's enormous mouth from which sticky, rancid saliva had once again started to ooze. Wayne looked up beseechingly at The Puppeteer, but the only advice on offer was that moving probably wasn't in Wayne's best interests.

'It might be best to let it play,' The Puppeteer said. 'It's a power thing with Manforms. But that's domination for you!'

Wayne began to sob and whimper as the Manform began to fidget and adjust the angle of its haunches at his rear while Naomi sounded as if she might be about to explode.

'Wayne,' said The Puppeteer over her squeals of sexual delight. 'Prepare to be ... *inspired*!'

Naomi cried out as she climaxed, and Wayne screamed in pain as the aroused Manform viciously rammed its huge deformed erection into him.

'NOOOO! GOD ... PLEEEASE, NOOOO!' he shrieked, but the Manform's powerful jaws only tightened their grip on his neck.

'One has to insure against moments of weakness, Wayne,' The Puppeteer continued. 'Or in your case, moments of weakness and *arrogance*. They can be so *very* costly ...'

'I WON'T SCREW UP AGAIN … I PROMISE … OH GOD … I PROMISE!'

The penetration was agonising and deep. Wayne felt like he was being split in half, such was the ferocity of the Manform's brutal thrusts.

'MAKE IT STOP! PLEEEASE … MAKE IT STOP!'

'Suffering has to be *personalised*, Wayne! Otherwise, it isn't *pure*. Everybody has a personal hell … and this is yours.'

'JEEEEEEESUS CHRIIIIIIIST!'

'You see, it's *my* way, or it's … *this* way …'

'I'LL DO IT YOUR WAY! I PROMISE I WILL … I WON'T FAIL YOU! PLE-EE-ASE … MAKE IT STOP!'

And then abruptly, everything changed. The hideous creature vanished, and the harsh stone floor of the dungeon was replaced by a luxurious red carpet in a stately looking lounge. Wayne noticed that his manacles had also mysteriously disappeared. It had all happened quicker than the blink of an eye, and the only similarities to Wayne's previous situation was the presence of Naomi and The Puppeteer.

'Which do you think is worse, Wayne?' asked The Puppeteer. 'Failure, or knowing what failure will bring? I understand that you might have been wanting to know, so it was a pleasure for me to enlighten you.'

The question of being indebted to The Puppeteer had been brutally answered. Humiliated, ashamed and utterly degraded, Wayne could only look down at the floor while Naomi sidled across the carpet to be at his side.

'I won't fail you,' he said as she gently stroked his face. 'Believe me, I won't.'

'Of *course* you won't,' The Puppeteer replied. 'I have every confidence now that we have been able to give you a little piece of encouragement. But I would advise you against trying to plan anything again, Wayne. Let *me* create the opportunity you crave, and then you can look forward to enjoying the sweet trappings of a successful outcome.'

Naomi looked up at The Puppeteer over Wayne's shoulder and smiled.

CHAPTER 23

Anne Ryan went to attend an impromptu coffee date with some friends soon after Chris returned home. She'd taken Harley for his walk and kept him suitably entertained, but the baton of responsibility was to be passed to Chris until Joanne and Samantha came by to pick him up.

A very calm and satisfied Harley lay stretched out on the floor at Chris's feet, and Chris couldn't resist reaching down and rubbing the dog's belly. Like his mother's coffee date, petting Harley was a very simple pleasure, something ordinary in an increasingly extraordinary world. Regardless of the grim circumstances under which he'd met Devonshire and Willard that morning, being among fellow detectives had served to remind Chris of the camaraderie he enjoyed with his own colleagues in the Met, and right then was as good a time as any to check in with them.

A quick scroll through the contacts on his mobile uncovered Chris's perfect tonic, his department's resident joker, Detective Constable Connor Stevens, who turned out to be just as happy to hear from his superior.

'Hey, Chris! Great to hear from you! How are you doing out there in the sticks?' he asked.

'Not bad at all thanks, Connor, even if I *am* living with my mum right now! How's young Laura? I can't believe she had to see things go tits up like that! Is she okay?'

It was the first opportunity that Chris had had to ask after the young detective's welfare since his accident.

'What ... Horrible Harris?' asked Stevens. 'She coped pretty well, all things being equal, so don't worry she's fine, just as horrible as ever!'

There was the sound of a female voice protesting in the background which quickly turned into a shriek of approval when Chris's name was mentioned.

'Actually, we're working together on a new case,' Stevens continued. 'Things have got a bit messy round here lately. Two women have been murdered; one in Mill Hill and the other one just around the corner from here in the industrial estate ... a dancer from *Electrix*!'

The sound of the front door opening made Chris look up, and Harley immediately went to greet whoever had just come in. Andy made a big fuss of the dog as he passed by the living room door, but pointedly blanked his father. Completely.

Chris glared after him as Andy made his way upstairs, not that Andy noticed or would have even cared. He was more intent on finding out what was going on in his other world, the world in which the people he cared about most shared everything that mattered without any hesitation, and the privacy of his bedroom was beckoning to that end. Lured by the appeal of social media, Andy closed his bedroom door behind him, grabbed his laptop and flopped onto the room's single bed, grateful that his grandmother had fully embraced the computer age and had Wi-Fi.

Although Andy's was the smallest of the three bedrooms in his grandmother's house, it was in no way cramped, the bed was comfortable, there was a small lamp on a bedside table that glowed warmly at the flick of a switch and a tallboy wardrobe spacious enough to store enough clothes for an indefinite stay in the country. The room's single window, although small, provided plenty of daylight, and Andy had always felt at ease in there whenever he'd stayed in the past. He was still troubled by the regrettable confrontation with his father, however, whose baritone voice could be clearly heard filtering up from the living room directly beneath him. Andy guessed the conversation was with one of his colleagues in the Met, and the only surprise was that it had taken as long as it had for his father to get involved with matters back in Colindale.

Andy shook his head. He'd had more than enough of police business for one day. He was checking his Facebook account and was about to comment on a friend's recent post, when the screen in front of him suddenly took on a mind of its own.

Hello Andy! said an unexpected message.

Andy stared blankly at the text, mystified, as none of his contacts appeared to be 'active'.

How are we today? the screen asked. *Saved any more damsels in distress?*

A feeling of uneasiness started to grow in the pit of Andy's stomach. He was about to ask who the mystery messenger was, but the machine responded before he could even start typing.

You don't know? Maybe you're tired ... had a bit of a sleepless night last night, didn't you?

The comment made Andy pull his fingers sharply away from the keyboard as if it were made of hot metal, and every one of the hairs on his forearms were standing to attention. His breath began to condense in the air as the temperature in the room fell sharply.

Has the penny dropped yet? And there was Oshina wanting me to believe that you were perceptive.

'I *know* who you are!' Andy replied out loud.

The acidic demeanour of The Puppeteer was unmistakeable, even in print, and yet Andy was experiencing none of the physical symptoms he associated with being in the entity's presence. More to the point, just how *had* The Puppeteer managed to evade his senses so easily?

Because I am everywhere, Andy, The Puppeteer replied. *And I can appear in any form of my choosing. I even know what you are thinking, as you can tell. Oh, by the way, how is young Samantha today? We got so close last night she even bled for me. I'm sure she must be looking forward to meeting me again …*

'Leave her alone!'

And why should I do that when we are getting on so famously? I am merely interested to find out if she is as worthy a vessel as it is claimed, and if not, once I have finished with her, you will be welcome to whatever is left.

'What the fuck?'

Oh, of course, they haven't told you yet, have they? I mean, not even your own father will tell you anything. But that's the thing about being involved with The Truth, Andy, it hides in dark corners and only tells you a part of the story. 'Seek and ye shall find', and all that guff! It might help if it gave you a starting point, like telling you the dangers of being the open channel that it has made you. You're like a poorly tuned in radio and anything can tap into your frequency. Cold for the time of year, isn't it?

The bedroom had become so cold that Andy felt like he was sitting in a freezer, and he began to shiver violently. There seemed to be movement all around him, and out of the corners of his eye impenetrable shadows began to flow, black and liquid-like, meandering down the walls, spreading across the ceiling, oozing out of the room's corners.

*There are all sorts of undesirables lurking in between the walls that separate our worlds … * The Puppeteer taunted. *Can't you just relate to their feelings?*

Andy's surroundings darkened further as he desperately tried to block out the hatred being whispered into his mind.

Brrrrrrr … it's cold enough to be Christmas, isn't it! 'Hark the Herald Angels sing!' Can you hear the angels, Andy? Are they not singing to you?

The whispers had turned into the glorification of appalling savagery. Andy's mind burned with horrific thoughts and images of the most barbaric acts, and there was nothing he could do to close the floodgates.

All this, because you are an open channel, Andy, wrote The Puppeteer. *A door through which the angels are coming in numbers. You are drawing them in, but you are doing nothing and they're blaming you. It's your fault they're here. What are you going to do for these poor lost souls? Are you simply going to judge them for what they have done?*

In a bid to escape his living hell, Andy struggled off the bed, only to collapse in a heap under the weight of his inhuman ordeal.

'Hark the herald angels sing, glory to the new-born king!'

Chris had just finished talking to Connor Stevens when a resounding THUMP caused him to look up. The impact had been severe enough to wobble the light fitting of the living room ceiling, and, outside in the hallway, Harley was growling and staring up towards the landing, hackles raised.

Without a second thought, Chris jumped up and rushed up the stairs. He burst into Andy's room to find it as cold as the middle of winter, and his son curled up on the floor with his hands over his ears, his eyes screwed up so tightly that there were white crow's feet in their corners. A strange collection of messages was streaming across the screen of Andy's laptop as it lay on the bed, a screen totally black apart from the bold white letters forming the texts, and then, incredibly, it addressed Chris personally as if were a living, sentient being: *Hello Chrissssssstopher ...* it said. *How good of you to drop in. I don't believe we have spoken yet, have we?*

Chris was so stunned that he was unable to move. How could a piece of machinery do that?

Not much of a conversationalist, are you? the screen taunted. *Never mind ... I'm just giving young Andy here a humility lesson. After the way he addressed you earlier, I'm sure you won't mind!*

As Chris remained rooted to the spot, a beacon of light appeared in Andy's darkness. Amongst all the carnage to which he was being subjected, he could miraculously see his father.

'TURN IT OFF, DAD!' he yelled at the top of his voice. 'THE FUCKING LAPTOP ... TURN IT OFF!'

Andy's desperate pleas startled Chris from his jaw-dropping focus upon the computer, and he leapt forwards and did as his son had implored, severing The Puppeteer's link with the human dimension.

For a few moments, Andy felt detached and confused, the contrasting silence of his welcome release almost overwhelming. Only seconds before, his bedroom had played host to a dark and alien world of disembodied corruptions, an onslaught of human suffering. Now, all the horror and near endless butchery had gone, and the familiarity of his surroundings was coming back into focus.

Andy shakily propped himself up against his bed. It was about as much as he could do to pull himself up.

'I couldn't get up ...' he whispered. 'The laptop ... I couldn't get to it ... I didn't have any control.'

The all-consuming battle against The Puppeteer's rabid brethren had left him feeling weak and nauseous. Fearing he was about to be physically sick, Andy reached out with a trembling hand towards a nearby wastebin.

'Jesus, Andy,' said Chris, crouching down to Andy's eye-level. 'What the hell was going on?'

Andy lifted the front of his T-shirt and wiped away at his sweat-soaked face.

'It was *him*,' he replied. 'In the laptop … The Puppeteer … he came *through* the fucking laptop to get to me!'

'But that's impossible!'

'Do I *normally* look like this after I've been on Facebook? You must have seen what was coming up on that thing! The Puppeteer used it like a portal, just like he did with Joanne's car yesterday. He used the connection as a point of focus … they came, though, hundreds of them … I couldn't stop them.'

'*Who* came through?'

'The fucking Faithless, Dad, that's who! But like you said, The Puppeteer hasn't come for *you*, and you'd better pray that it stays that way because you've got no idea what it's like, what he makes you see …'

Chris listened in horror as Andy recalled everything he'd witnessed, having looked through the eyes of every perpetrator, and felt exactly what *they* had felt when committing their terrible crimes. Andy's voice cracked with emotion as he relived what it had been like to be in the mind of a suicide bomber, about being one with such cold calculating lucidity, and a warped justification for what was about to unfold. The terrified faces of the bomber's innocent victims, trapped in the confines of the bus would be forever etched upon Andy's mind as the terrorist championed a god that would never have condoned such a brutal act of human destruction, and then detonated the hellish creation.

Then came the moment Andy had been forced to gaze along the barrel of an assault rifle into the wide, tearful eyes of a terrified little girl before the sickening, deranged killer who'd shared the experience so joyfully with him squeezed the trigger and slaughtered her in front of her helpless classmates. As the little girl dropped to the floor, the chuckling murderer switched the weapon to automatic, and riddled the classroom with hellfire. Screaming, bloodied children fell before him, but the gunman wouldn't stop, revelling in his barbarity as he continued his murderous rampage throughout the school.

Eventually he would turn the weapon upon himself, but the bullets that were to splash the killer's brains to the four winds would still not be enough to release Andy who had, by then, become an arsonist, watching and giggling insanely as the fire he'd started burned families young and old alive. Andy could still hear the terrified screams coming from inside the blazing apartment block, and the lunatic's laughter became hysterical whoops of delight as one of the victims jumped to their death from an upper-storey window. Andy couldn't tell if it had been a man or a woman making a last desperate bid to escape the inferno. They had been on fire when they'd leapt.

As 'the angels had sung' they had revered The Puppeteer. *He* was going to bring them their freedom, they'd said. *They* were going to live again and the physical sacrificing of their bodies was just a temporary measure. Every act of cruelty and brutality had been committed willingly, and it was The Puppeteer that had planted and nurtured every hate-filled seed. Some of the 'angels' had been bitter, angry people who'd felt that they'd been sold short by their own kind, while others just had an axe to grind against their respective societies. Disturbingly, all of them had been ordinary people before that dark malevolence had entered their lives.

'But the worse part, Dad,' said Andy. 'Is that they made me enjoy it, *all* of it … no matter what it was, no matter what I was seeing, it made perfect sense to me. I enjoyed *everything* … I know what it feels like to enjoy killing, to destroy innocent people … I know, Dad, because I was *made* to!'

The account became too much for Andy who finally gave in to the swell of emotions that had been building up inside him.

Chris did the only thing he could in the circumstances, and something his sudden guilt said he hadn't done nearly enough as a father. He put his arms around his sobbing son and held him.

Andy's experience had served as a terrifying reminder of the limitless capabilities of the Faithless as described by Zambaya, and now he was a target for that same unspeakable evil. As Andy wept in his father's arms, Chris searched his mind for something supportive to say, but there wasn't a single crumb of comfort to be found there, for the harder he tried to reconcile his thoughts, the more something else was becoming frighteningly obvious. There was an undeniable bond developing between Andy and Samantha, and it suggested that Andy's place in The Circle wasn't *just* about his ability to sense danger. It was becoming uncomfortably clear to Chris that his son's role was even *more* pivotal, that he'd been chosen to be the father of The Truth's envoy.

A sudden surge of anger made Chris hold Andy tighter. Zambaya had said *nothing* about *that*, so where was the justification in keeping so much from his own son when The Truth had withheld that most important of facts from Chris himself?

Despite his anger, Chris knew he still had to respect that part of his vow of secrecy to The Truth, but he *could* reveal much of the rest without compromising that trust. Andy deserved *that* much, at least.

'There are a few beers in the fridge,' said Chris as Andy slowly began to calm. 'I think now's a good time to open a couple and do some talking, don't you?'

Harley became very animated as soon as he saw them coming down the stairs and didn't stop being a noisy pest until Andy was able to calm him down and reassure him. Chris got two cold beers out of the fridge while Andy was occupied and quietly placed one of the cans in front of his son where he was sitting at the kitchen table. Then, he changed the water in Harley's water bowl even though it didn't need changing and wiped down an already spotlessly clean worktop. Andy looked up and frowned as his father stood staring out of the kitchen window for what seemed like an age. It was very clear that there was something playing deeply on his mind. Silences, and his father making himself unnecessarily busy were generally pointers to the beginning of a difficult conversation, but the silence on this occasion seemed particularly tense and protracted.

Andy went to reach out to for his promised beer, but stopped as his father took an unexpectedly deep breath, and said abruptly: 'Samantha is in the way of something The Puppeteer wants. That's why all this is happening to us.' He stopped staring out of the window and turned to look at Andy whose hand was stuck halfway to his still unopened can.

'I'm sorry that you're so involved in all of this, son,' he said, 'and *truly* sorry that you've just had to go through what you did upstairs. I'm sorry about *everything*. I'm sorry that I'm not in control of anything, and you've got every right to be angry, every right to say all the things you've said, and you were right about only being able to protect Samantha if we share what we know.'

'What's she in the way of, Dad?'

'To tell you about that, I'm going to have to go right back to the beginning. It means repeating a few bits, but you wanted to know everything.'

Shocked and terrified in equal amounts as his father opened up, Andy listened as all the knowledge gleaned from Zambaya about the Faithless and The Puppeteer, and The Truth and the Supreme Collective, was revealed. Chris didn't spare any details, apart from those for which he was sworn to secrecy over Samantha's direct role in The Circle and the part that Andy himself was likely to play. He didn't hold back from admitting his own doubts and fears about Samantha's safety, he didn't paint any other picture other than the one which showed the true scale of the task they all faced.

'And the thing is, Andy,' he said, 'is that none of us has got any choice; we've all been chosen for this and whatever we do, it all ends the same if we don't protect Samantha.'

'Jesus, Dad!' said Andy. 'I've just seen what the Faithless are capable of, and what if the guy I saw by the village green *is* one of them? What if he *is* connected to The Puppeteer? This is seriously deep shit! Does Sam know anything about this?'

'No,' replied Chris. 'She doesn't, and that's where your awareness will be a really big help.'

'Well, it wasn't a few minutes ago!'

'But the thing you need to remember, Andy, apart from staying calm, is that the man you saw can't do what The Puppeteer can, and if he *is* something to do with this, then he's already shown his hand!'

'I wish I'd got a better look at him.'

'But that needn't matter because when he's around, we'll know, thanks to you. It's why Oshina awakened you at the hospital. But somehow, you, me, or both of us, need to stay as close to Samantha whenever possible without raising any alarm bells. It's what The Circle is asking us to do; we've all got our own roles and I'm no different.'

Andy nodded slowly.

'Do you know what *your* role is, then?' he asked.

'The same as yours,' Chris replied. 'Protecting Samantha.'

'But I think there's more to come from you. You still haven't seen The Puppeteer. I'm not going to throw my toys out of the pram like I did before, Dad, but you need to ask yourself why The Puppeteer hasn't attacked you like he has me, Samantha and Jo.'

'Well, I'm sure it's only going to be a matter of time …'

'But that's what I'm saying! He *would* have done so by now if he was able to! It's obvious he can't get to you because of Zambaya, Dad, well, obvious to me after what I saw yesterday. The Puppeteer gave me the impression that Zambaya being involved with us was like a massive come-down for him, like he was a part of something much bigger like that Supreme Collective you just spoke about.'

Andy looked across at his father and took a thoughtful swallow of his beer.

'Look, Dad' he said. 'When I was going through all that upstairs, I was completely helpless, like some fucking … *plaything*, and then all of a sudden, there was this light. But it was *Zambaya's* light, the same light that protected me and Oshina at Joanne's car, but this time it was coming through *you*. You were right there with me in the thick of everything that was happening but you had *no idea* what was going on, like you were in some kind of *bubble*. Dad … there's something very different about you. I know I've accused you of holding out on me before, but now I *believe* that there's more to you than you can possibly know … I could sense you were different when I came to the hospital to see you, like you'd been changed in some way, but I couldn't explain it … I still can't, but I'm also beginning to think that The Truth was probably behind you getting shot. I've seen too much to believe in coincidence anymore, and don't they say that God's supposed to 'work in mysterious ways', or something like that?'

'Oh, come on Andy! That's ridiculous ...'

'Is it? The Truth had to get its message to you somehow even if it meant killing you for a few minutes. It had to get the message through because Samantha's obviously so important to its plans and you were a part of the cycle of events to bring us all together. If the way Zambaya came into your life isn't enough to convince you, then how do you explain your miraculous recovery? You should still be in hospital. People spend *weeks* in hospital recovering from injuries like yours, Dad. It just isn't natural ... *none* of this is.'

Harley chose that precise moment to come to Chris for a bit of attention, providing a bit of welcome respite. Andy had worked out so much for himself and had added some very compelling points that shouldn't be ignored. The level of Zambaya's personal standing had never entered Chris's mind any more than he'd considered getting shot as being anything less than a freak accident, but as Andy's words slowly began to sink in, so the mystery deepened. Deliberately or not, the finer details of the constantly changing situation were being withheld from all of them, the threat to Samantha being the only constant. Her safety was more important than anything else, and being aware of the danger meant that Andy would no doubt be looking to spend more time with her. There was every chance that their bond would continue to grow, and the more time they spent together, the greater the chances of conception.

And there, in a nutshell, was a tragic irony. An unwanted pregnancy was a common fear for most parents when it came to their own flesh and blood; Joanne wouldn't feel any different, and yet Chris was yearning for that very eventuality between Andy and Samantha; and sooner, rather than later.

At that moment, Harley began to fidget. He pricked up his ears and stared through the open kitchen doorway, wagging his tail. Barely a second later the doorbell rang, and he made a beeline for the front door where two female voices had started offering words of encouragement as he began to whine excitedly in the hallway.

Andy seemed as relieved as Chris to hear Joanne and Samantha's voices at the door, but Chris made him wait before letting them in.

'Andy, as hard as it's going to be, we've got to act as if nothing is wrong,' he said. 'They might want to talk about The Puppeteer, maybe they won't; who knows? But they haven't got a clue about any risk to Samantha and that's how it's got to stay. I know it doesn't sound right, like it never felt right for me to keep so much from you, but you've got to keep it all under wraps, regardless of anything they might ask. Whatever is truly going on, it's bigger than we know, and we've got to stand together and see it through.'

Andy nodded, and father and son embraced.

CHAPTER 24

Joanne wasn't used to small cars, preferring bigger, more rugged vehicles like her Range Rover, and she wasn't the best passenger in the world, either. The motorway had been relaxing to the point that she'd even briefly nodded off, but country lanes in a very nippy Mini Cooper with Samantha behind the wheel was making Joanne nervous. The car had originally belonged to Leanne, who had intended to trade it in for a new model before Joanne had intervened and bought it for Samantha as a reward for negotiating her first year of motoring without incident. Pepper white with black alloys and a classy black and white chequered-flag roof, the unexpected gift had been love-at-first-sight for Samantha, and since then, she and 'Madge' had done many happy, accident-free miles together. Joanne felt that she ought to feel a little more at ease considering her daughter's unblemished driving record, but it wasn't until the roads widened and they approached Hitchin that she finally felt more comfortable.

Samantha wasn't used to driving with her mother as a passenger and had been totally oblivious of Joanne's trepidation. Her mind was more focused on Harley's needs as she entered the outskirts of the town.

'Do you think Harley's going to be okay on his own?' she asked.

'Well, of course he is. We're only going to be a couple of hours. Honestly, Sam, you and that bloody dog!'

'It's just that he was so pleased to see us when we picked him up. I hated leaving him behind at the cottage all on his own.'

'Well, we could hardly bring him shopping with us, could we?'

'But Andy and Chris were happy to come with us and look after him.'

'Like they'd really want to get roped into a shopping trip with us two! Andy and Chris have done more than enough for us already. I've told you how I feel about that. Anyway, you shouldn't let Harley guilt-trip you so much. He gets away with far too much sometimes.'

Samantha muttered an unsatisfied 'guess not' as she kept her eyes peeled for a parking space, which presented itself on her second circuit of the car park. She nipped into it eagerly and came to a halt expertly within the white lines that marked the rectangular bay.

'Wow! That *was* impressive!' said Joanne. 'I couldn't have swung mine in there like that.'

'That's because it's a tank.'

'It is *not* a tank!'

The drive back from London had certainly improved Samantha's mood. She seemed much sharper, and the jovial exchanges continued as they walked along a thoroughfare that brought them out into the bustling rural vibrancy of Hitchin's town centre. Refreshingly different to the often insular coldness to which they'd become accustomed in London, the town centre was full of warmth and character. A few large retail outlets were present, but numerous smaller shops selling anything from antiques to fine arts and crafts were nestled amongst them, their mysterious yet ornately dressed windows inviting all to venture into temptation, including Joanne.

Joanne had distinct preferences when it came to fine art, and an original piece by a local artist that just happened to be on display in a side street art shop had truly appealed. She had a perfect place in mind at Greenoaks for the stunning female study, and the shopkeeper, a lady who conveniently lived near the village of Preston, kindly offered to deliver the painting on her way home later that afternoon, after Samantha raised concerns about the portrait being too big to fit in her car.

Buoyed up by her unintentional purchase and the extremely helpful shopkeeper, Joanne continued browsing among various independent shops away from the busy high street, and, having snapped up a pair of killer heels in one of them, found herself being drawn by an inviting window display into another. The clothes shop was surprisingly bigger inside than it had appeared from the street. Modern LED lighting from a suspended ceiling reflected off shining chrome rails and bounced off painted white brick walls, but if the general feel of the shop lent itself to minimalistic modesty, the clothing on display was anything but.

Strangely, for one so successful in the fashion trade, Joanne cared little about where she bought her clothes, and took even less interest in the labels inside them. All that mattered was the type of look she wanted to achieve and that same rule applied when it came to dressing for a dinner party.

'Formal or casual?' Joanne asked Samantha as she began looking along a rail of rather exclusive-looking black evening dresses. 'What do you think?'

But Samantha didn't answer. She was looking at something a little more daring.

'Come on, Sam, help me out here, will you?' Joanne asked again.

'Help you out with what?'

'Oh, for God's sake … formal or casual, what do you reckon?'

'Neither …'

'Oh, that's *very* bloody helpful!'

Samantha removed a dark, almost midnight blue dress from another rail and thrust it out in her mother's direction.

'How about something completely different?' she suggested, grinning. 'How about *sexy*?'

The material was soft and luxurious, and the cut subtly revealing and figure-hugging. Samantha held it up against her mother and cocked her head to one side, admiringly.

'I think this is absolutely perfect,' she said. 'I reckon you'll look amazing in it!'

'Nah,' said Joanne, shaking her head. 'It's not me.'

'*Not* you? Well, that's rather odd.'

'Odd ... Why?'

'Because it's one of *yours*!'

Samantha gloatingly waved the label BY MIDDLETON in front of her mother.

'Ooh, you little wretch!' said Joanne.

'Well, why *not* underline how you feel about Chris by making a proper statement? And that look of denial won't wash with me, either. I saw the way you looked at him when we picked Harley up, and as for all the chat between you ...'

'I was only being friendly.'

'Tell me you're not interested in him.'

Joanne could feel herself blushing.

'Oh God,' she sighed. 'Did I make it that obvious, then?'

'I think inviting him to dinner was a pretty big statement of intent in the first place,' replied Samantha. 'Even if you *did* try and disguise it by inviting the rest of his family ... and it's not like he refused, is it?'

A cautious smile began to form on Joanne's lips.

'So, you think he likes me then?' she asked.

'I don't think there can be much doubt about that, Mum, so let's make sure you'll be looking your best.' Samantha turned Joanne in the direction of the fitting rooms only a few feet away. 'Let's see you how *he's* going to see you,' she said.

But Joanne hadn't heard her.

The cream curtain of the nearest available cubicle was pulled back completely, and that's when the fitted mirror inside froze Joanne to the very depths of her soul. To Samantha, who couldn't understand why her mother had suddenly gone completely rigid, the mirror was just a mirror, but to Joanne it was about as welcoming a sight as a swimming pool to a hydrophobic.

In Joanne's mind the mirror glass was darkening, giving way to a cold all-consuming blackness, the same blackness that had stared into her before, in her car, her home and in the hospital.

'Joanna ... Joanna ...'

The mirror was challenging her to gaze into its stark and loveless soul. 'Joanna' had been her father's pet name for her when she was a child, and Joanne was a child again at that moment, terrified about facing a tormentor.

'Joanna ... Joanna...'

How Joanne wanted to run away but she was rooted to the spot, panic swelling inside. If she looked directly at the glass, she just knew she'd see *that* sinister face grinning sickeningly back at her.

A little girl stopping in front of the fitting room broke the spell. She was pulling a funny face at herself in the mirror before being joined in the fun by what appeared to be her slightly older brother. The pair giggled at their reflections for a moment before being ushered away by their apologetic mother.

Joanne had been released; she felt stupid and ashamed of herself for being so afraid, but, somehow, a simple piece of reflective glass had suddenly become a doorway to hell itself.

'Mum ...? Mum, are you okay?'

Samantha's voice seemed to be coming from miles away, but then Joanne came back to her senses.

'Yes, yes, I'm fine,' she said. 'Absolutely fine ... I was just looking at those two kids playing in the mirror. My mind must have wandered off somewhere.'

'Well?' Samantha asked.

'Well, what?'

'Are you going to try the dress on or what?'

'No, sod it!'

Joanne turned and went to walk away.

'Where are you going?' asked Samantha.

'I'm going to pay for the dress, that's where I'm going!' Joanne retorted.

'But ... you haven't even tried it on.'

'So?'

'But you always ...'

'Shut up, Sammy! Please, just shut up ... I'm going to pay for this dress, I'm going to get out of here and then I'm going to get some air, *and* a coffee ... alright?'

Considering that the dress was the right size and she'd designed the darned thing anyway, Joanne felt that buying without trying was worth the risk. She could try it on in the more comforting surroundings of her cottage, and if the worst came to the worst and she wasn't happy with how she felt in it, she still had the next day to exchange it or find something else to wear for the evening.

But Samantha had been left fuming about bearing the brunt of her mother's irrational behaviour. An atmosphere thick enough to be cut with a knife prevailed as the two of them walked in strained silence to a small discreet café in a quiet side street. The café wasn't far from where Joanne had bought her dress and she glanced across ruefully at Samantha as they sat down at a small wooden table outside in the sun.

'I'm really sorry, Sam; I shouldn't have snapped at you like that,' she said.

'What the bloody hell *was* all that about?' Samantha asked.

'Please don't start on me again.'

'I'm not starting, Mum, I just don't know what got into you.'

Joanne looked away. The last thing she needed was having her ear bent by her daughter again, and her eyes noticeably moistened before she could reply.

'Mirrors,' Joanne sighed. 'I just can't *bear* being near mirrors. Not after what's been happening to me. All I could see was a bloody great mirror in that shop's fitting room and I just couldn't go in there. Even toilet mirrors freak me out. I had to sit back to front on the loo seats in the hospital to avoid looking at them!'

'I bet that was an interesting sight!' said Samantha, trying to make amends for her impatience.

Although Joanne managed a chuckle, it was only a fleeting moment of fun.

'Christ, Sammy,' she said. 'You're right … I'm so sorry; I'm an absolute bloody mess! I just wish I knew what the hell's been happening to us.'

As Samantha sat and regarded her frightened mother trying to process the chaos and terrifying uncertainty surrounding them, there was one undoubted positive that Samantha felt she should air. Quite how her mother was going to react, knowing that Andy and Chris were both aware of The Puppeteer was anybody's guess, but something had brought the four of them together, and it didn't seem fair for her to remain unaware of the fact. It was a risk that Samantha knew she just was just going to have to take.

'We're not alone, Mum,' she said. 'Andy and Chris know all about The Puppeteer as well.'

Joanne almost choked on her coffee.

'You've *told* them?' she gasped.

'No, they already knew … I overheard them talking about it last night after I had my nightmare. We talked more about it on the way to the hospital this morning.'

'But how do they know?'

'Andy saw The Puppeteer when he was by your car yesterday. He's got some kind of psychic gift, and I have to believe him because he was able to describe The Puppeteer, perfectly. It's like we're all connected somehow although Andy doesn't know why.'

All Joanne could do was listen through something of a haze, but it clearly explained the bond between Andy and Samantha at the hospital, and also shed some light upon their close interactions with Chris. No wonder they'd all seemed so reticent.

'And what about Chris?' Joanne asked. 'And Anne? Does she know anything about this?'

Samantha took a sip of her own coffee and shook her head.

'Chris hasn't had the chance to share much,' she replied. 'So I don't know, to be honest. He didn't get to say anything much last night, and then when we came upon Jennie this morning, everything else went out of the window. Chris was very clear that he didn't want Anne to know about anything, though, so I'm pretty certain that she hasn't got a clue about any of it.'

What Samantha had hoped should be a comfort to her mother seemed to have only instilled more fear. Joanne seemed unwilling to make eye contact; she was distracted, clasping her coffee cup with both hands as if she didn't want to let it go, like a child with a security blanket.

Samantha reached out and cupped Joanne's hands in her own.

'Mum, I think Chris and Andy are here to help us face The Puppeteer,' she said. 'I'm sure of it ... I feel *safe* when I'm around them.'

'And how are they going to help us? We barely know them for one thing!'

'But they're facing it and we have to face it too, Mum! Wherever we go and whatever we do, The Puppeteer will follow us. I've got no idea what he wants, but he can come for me whenever he likes, just like he said. His eyes are everywhere; those creatures you saw last night ... the Manforms? They're everywhere, too, he sees *us* through *them*. That's how he was able to find us so easily after we left Hampstead. There's a reason why we met Andy and Chris, and Chris *told* me we're not alone in this anymore. There's something about them, and after what I heard last night and this morning, I believe him. You should as well because I don't think that it's a coincidence how they just suddenly came into our lives!'

Joanne began to panic at the thought of the horrific Manforms in the hospital corridor and the memory of her flight through Hitch Wood. For all she knew, Manforms were watching her right then and her eyes began searching anxiously for any sign of their presence.

But the only place from which their tell-tale, oily black shadows were oozing was from the darkest recesses of her own mind. Instead, all Joanne could see around her were scenes of normalcy that she so desperately craved, people talking, laughing, joking and enjoying life, and she was on the outside, looking *in* to the life she once knew.

And if Samantha was right, what *was* the purpose of their uncanny connection with the Ryans, and how had it even come about? Would this be it for the rest of their lives, and if so, what would be the purpose of anything if, as Joanne felt right then, she could no longer be part of the normal world?

Joanne stood up suddenly.

'I want to go home!' she said. 'I don't want to be out here anymore …'

*

Wayne saw Samantha sitting outside the coffee shop as he passed the corner of the same street. She was with her mother who seemed to be getting rather animated about something.

Having woken from The Puppeteer's 'inspiration', Wayne had been held captive by such overwhelming fears that his hotel room had become nothing short of a prison for the damned. Escape was escape, even if it *did* mean venturing outside where he was most vulnerable. But something had given him the courage to set foot into the open, and as much as he was shocked at coming across Samantha Middleton so unexpectedly, it was clear that it had been completely by design.

'It really is *such* a small world, isn't it?' said the voice of The Puppeteer in Wayne's mind. 'Do you see how easy it is when you let me guide you?'

But Wayne was too fixated on Samantha to answer and clenched his fists as Joanne stood up suddenly and began to march off, with Samantha close behind. The little bitch was *still* out of reach even though she'd almost been close enough for him to spit on.

'Patience, Wayne,' came the reassuring voice of The Puppeteer once more. 'Trust in me. The next time you feast your eyes upon her, she will be gift-wrapped.'

CHAPTER 25

Samantha's concerns over the effects of her revelations had been well-founded. A tense journey back to Greenoaks had ensued, and she had to act as though nothing was out of the ordinary when her mother, having asked for the antique mirror hanging over the fireplace to be taken down, had then insisted upon its immediate disposal.

As valuable as it was, the mirror was languishing on the living room floor with its reflective surface facing the wall. Two other much smaller mirrors, one from the bathroom windowsill and another that had always hung on a wall on the landing, had also been removed, ready to be donated to any local charity shop prepared to take them.

But Samantha was totally against the treasured family heirloom from the living room suffering a similar fate by going to auction.

'It was your Great Auntie Vivienne's,' she protested. 'You told me once that she left it to you when you were a child! You can't just get rid of it like that, Mum ... I won't let you do that to her.'

Suddenly, Joanne hated The Puppeteer as much as she feared him. How could he just cause her to disregard one of her most precious mementos like that? It would have been an absolutely unspeakable crime.

'No, you're right!' Joanne said. 'Just protect it as best you can and store it in the utility room. Maybe I'll be able to hang it up again someday, assuming I haven't been sectioned in the meantime!'

Samantha lovingly stored the old mirror as instructed, and the female study that Joanne had purchased earlier in the day was delivered not long after. Every bit as large as the mirror it had replaced (but thankfully much lighter as far as Samantha was concerned), the portrait made the room feel slightly smaller once it was hung above the fireplace, but Joanne couldn't have cared less. With its burnished reds, oranges, creams and browns, the portrait was not only a perfect fit with the room's décor, but also a new and uplifting focal point. Feeling calmer as a result of the change, Joanne decided that it was time to start thinking about the following night's entertainment. Greenoaks felt like a fortress to her because nothing untoward had happened there, and planning something ordinary that *normal* people did was extremely welcome.

A pleasant phone call to Chris regarding his family's culinary preferences led Joanne to settle on baked lamb with rosemary as a main course, along with a redcurrant and mint sauce. A good Caesar salad would serve as a starter and decadence itself would be offered as dessert: a choice of strawberry cheesecake or chocolate gateaux. Throw all the farm-fresh vegetables into the mix and Joanne knew she would end up buying enough food to feed an army, but Chris and Andy both looked the types to have large appetites, so too much would certainly be better than not enough. Such planning deserved the mug of coffee that appeared on the table in front of her courtesy of Samantha, and, after a few sips, Joanne decided to finally go and try the dress on that she'd bought in town.

Samantha was busying herself entertaining Harley in the garden until he decided that quenching his thirst was more important, and it was as Samantha followed him into the cottage that she noticed the barely touched coffee on the table where she'd left it. Samantha shook her head. On the landing above, she could see her mother standing in the doorway of the master bedroom.

'Mum,' she called out. 'You've left your coffee downstairs.'

But Joanne couldn't answer. The small wave of euphoria she'd been riding upon while climbing the stairs had fizzled out as soon as she got to her bedroom. Not only could she see the beautiful dress lying on the bed where Samantha had left it, but also the full-length mirror lurking menacingly in the room's corner.

'The Cheval mirror,' said Joanne as Samantha came to join her in the doorway. 'I'd completely forgotten about the Cheval mirror ... I came up to try on that dress, but I can't, not with *that* bloody thing in there.'

'Do you think The Puppeteer's in there, then?' asked Samantha.

'I don't know, Sammy. Back home I was standing right in front of the window when I saw him, and yesterday in the car he was right in my eye-line. Apart from the hospital, he's only appeared as a reflection *behind* me so I can't tell if he's going to be in there or not.'

Samantha passed Joanne the coffee she was holding and strolled into the bedroom. At first even *she* felt a little trepidation at the thought of what might lie in wait for her when she went to look at the glass, but she stared at her reflection regardless. Adjusting her position so that she could see her mother reflected in the doorway, she said: 'He isn't here, everything's fine.'

But Joanne stayed put.

'Fine until *I* look into it, probably,' she muttered.

And then Samantha had an idea. Without leaving the room, she called out to Harley, who came bounding enthusiastically up the stairs. He hesitated once he was on the landing but Samantha beckoned for him to come to her in the bedroom.

'What are you doing, Sam?' asked Joanne, grabbing Harley's collar as he approached. 'You know he's not allowed in the bedrooms.'

'Mitigating circumstances, Mum. I'm exploiting his sixth sense.'

'*What* …?'

'Well, you know how miners used to use caged canaries to check for gas down the pits before they went down themselves?'

'Yeeesss …?'

'Well, Harley's going to be *your* canary to check for The Puppeteer.'

'Isn't Harley a little bit too big to be a canary?'

'Mum, for God's sake, I'm trying to help! Listen, if The Puppeteer's around, Harley will sense him and react. Don't you remember what he was like that day at Hampstead when he went nuts at something we couldn't see? And then there was yesterday when you were in the car together? Didn't you tell me that he started crying out *before* you saw The Puppeteer in the mirror?'

Samantha's reasoning sounded convincing enough for Joanne to relinquish her grip of Harley's collar. She was half expecting him to start growling as soon as he entered the bedroom, but instead he padded obediently over to Samantha and rolled over at her feet for a belly-rub.

'I guess that means the coast has to be clear, then,' said Samantha. 'Come on, Mum … you can do this!'

Like a terrified patient making their way to the infamous dentist's chair, Joanne stepped tentatively into her bedroom, her eyes never leaving Harley for an instant as she moved forwards. Samantha could see the effort her mother was having to make just to enter her own room, and yet it was pleasing to be a part of it, all the same.

'Here, Mum, let me help you with that,' she said as Joanne began fiddling in vain with the catch of her poly sling.

A sudden sense of freedom invited Joanne to roll her injured shoulder to relieve some of the stiffness, which she regretted instantly.

'Sore?' asked Samantha.

'Very …'

'When's your next dose of painkillers due?'

Joanne glanced at her wristwatch.

'Round about now, I think, but sod the tablets! I've managed to get *this* far, and I want to try on this dress!'

Following a little more assistance from Samantha, Joanne discovered that the dress was a perfect fit, and just as (if not more) importantly, she was happy with how she looked in it. Having Samantha and Harley by her side for security gave her the confidence to study her reflection at length, which pleased her even more, but being *alone* with the mirror was always going to be a step too far. Once Joanne had finished with the try-on, she asked for the

Cheval mirror to be moved into Samantha's bedroom, which she did without hesitation.

Phobias can be unbearable for those who have to endure them, and as much as Joanne was grateful for Samantha's help and understanding, it was very clear that Samantha was battling some of her own. As the late afternoon gave way to early evening, and night's curtain began spreading like a shroud across the surrounding fields and woodlands, Joanne could feel her daughter's anxiety growing in intensity with every darkening hour.

Even though Samantha had to have been completely exhausted by the events of the past twenty-four hours, she seemed unwilling to give in to her obvious fatigue. There were programs to catch up with on TV, and friends who needed to be contacted. Samantha assured Joanne that she would 'turn in when she was ready', but 'ready' didn't seem as if it were ever going to happen. Joanne felt totally useless, she could reduce her own risk of encountering The Puppeteer by choosing not to look at her own reflection in a mirror, but Samantha had no such luxury. Simply being human meant that she'd be forced to go to sleep eventually, and when she did, The Puppeteer and his Manforms would probably be lying in wait for her...

*

Chris wasn't just tired, he was angry, and had fallen asleep that way as a result. The sense of outrage he'd been feeling had drawn Zambaya into his dream-state and now the pair of them were sitting together upon their familiar rocky outcrop. Zambaya regarded Chris quizzically, waiting for him to look up, but Chris chose to avoid the big African's gaze.

'Anger taints the soul,' Zambaya said. 'It is hollow and useless, and should not be a part of you. I am here to talk, Christopher, as your thoughts have summoned me.'

The soft rumble of Zambaya's voice drew a little of Chris's sting. His resentment began to fade, although what lay behind it remained.

'That's easy for you to say,' he said. 'But I've got every reason in the world to be angry. It's not easy having to hide what I know from the people closest to me.'

'You are speaking of Andrew?'

'Who else! He's going to be the father to your envoy by the look of it and you didn't even tell me! He's one of the most important parts of your plan and now he's become a target for something I don't have the power to stop, so how else am I supposed to feel?'

Zambaya sat in a moment of calm and contemplative silence as he considered his answer, and when he spoke again, his tone carried an unexpected yet gentle air of forcefulness.

'Your concerns as a father are natural and understandable,' he said. 'But I must also remind you, Christopher, that our responsibilities are to others, also. It is not The Puppeteer that should concern you, but the person he has selected to end the life of the chosen mother. No amount of teaching can make ready even the *strongest* warrior to stand against The Puppeteer, but against the flesh and blood of his choosing you will have every chance. In you, Christopher John Edward Ryan, The Truth has seen enough to have chosen you as a protector, and a *protector* you will remain for as long as The Truth needs it to be so. But remember that I *too* walk in your shoes, I *too* have been chosen, for this is *our* journey and *our* fight, more than it is yours alone.'

What was left of Chris's personal sense of injustice disappeared like air escaping from a deflating balloon. He couldn't remember ever feeling as humble, but Zambaya was quick to reassure him that merely being human did not require forgiveness.

Yet in spite of Zambaya's unquestioned knowledge, the identity of The Puppeteer's assassin remained a dangerous unknown. Since Andy had spoken about a suspicious car and driver so close to Joanne and Samantha's cottage, Chris had been like a cat on hot bricks, and even Joanne and Samantha embarking on an innocent shopping in broad daylight had been of nagging concern.

'I am afraid I cannot help you,' said Zambaya, much to Chris's disappointment.

'But surely The Truth must know *something* about him,' Chris protested.

'I wish it could be different, Christopher, but no.'

Zambaya explained what making a deal with The Puppeteer meant to the individual who struck it. They immediately became a part of The Faithless and, as a consequence, the light of their soul was lost to it.

'So, the light of the chosen assassin will no longer be visible to The Truth, and that is how The Faithless hide among you with such great success,' he said.

'But they can see what *you* do,' said Chris. 'See what *your* plans are. How can they do that and it not be the other way round?'

'Because The Truth speaks openly, Christopher, but not with the spoken word with which you are familiar. Its message is carried in the wind, the water, in everything that is. Through The Truth's omnipresence, the world is preparing for its miracle, and speaks of it as such. The Faithless would have heard it too.'

The longer that Chris spent in Zambaya's presence, the more he became aware of the incredible accuracy of Andy's appraisal of the mystical African, who simply *had* to be of a far higher standing than that of an Overseer.

Perhaps there and then was the right time to broach that subject.

'Who *are* you, Zambaya?' Chris asked. 'I know you are *far* more important than you say. Andy told me how you protected him and Oshina yesterday, and he is convinced that's why The Puppeteer hasn't come for *me*. That's it, isn't it? The Puppeteer can't get to me because of *you*.'

'I am just a man on a hill,' Zambaya replied. 'I can see farther, that is all.'

'A hill that just happens to be the Supreme Collective?'

This time Zambaya would only smile.

CHAPTER 26

It was a little after half-past eight in the morning when Joanne woke, somewhat later than usual. To her surprise, she'd managed to sleep very well, no doubt a testament to the last dose of painkillers she'd taken before going to bed.

Joanne searched her mobile for something vaguely interesting in the news, but it was as she scrolled through the headlines that it occurred to her that it was rather quiet in the cottage. Both she and Samantha were usually early risers, so it was distinctly possible that Samantha would already be out walking Harley. Joanne lost interest in her phone and got out of bed to make herself a coffee, her mouth dry and morning-like, so a fresh taste in it would be more than welcome.

Venturing out of her bedroom onto the landing, she peered over the balustrade into the living room below and was surprised to see Samantha fast asleep on one of the sofas. She was lying half underneath the duvet from her bedroom, and was wearing a red and white flower-print onesie. Staying downstairs with Harley for company must have made Samantha feel more secure than being alone in her own bedroom, and, thankfully, it appeared that there had been no terrors for her to endure while she'd slept.

Stretched out on the floor alongside Samantha's makeshift bed like a hairy black walrus, Harley also seemed completely at ease. He lazily opened his eyes and lifted his head as Joanne came downstairs, only to stretch out again with a deep, satisfied sigh.

Joanne crept into the kitchen as quietly as she could and put a couple of scoops of fresh ground coffee into a cafetière, then a slightly groggy voice from the lounge saying 'good morning' made her add a couple more.

'Morning, Sammy,' she said. 'I'm sorry if I woke you.'

'It's cool,' Samantha replied. 'I was only dozing.'

'You managed to sleep well down here, then?'

'Like a log by the look of it. I got a bit cold watching telly, so I went up and got my duvet. I don't remember anything after that so I must have gone out like a light. What's the time?'

'About quarter-to-nine, and I've got some coffee on the go, too.'

'Ooh you hero …! I'll go and have a shower while it's doing its thing, and then I'll take Harley out.'

'But what about breakfast?'

'You can chuck a couple of bits of bread in the toaster for me if you like!'

Apart from finding Samantha asleep on a sofa, the morning was no different to any other they'd enjoyed as a family before all the terrifying experiences had begun. It wasn't something Joanne wanted to think about right then, for fear of spoiling a good moment, and while she was waiting for Samantha's toast, she thought she might as well draw the curtains over the French doors in the living room. The *swish* of the parting curtains was a cue for Harley to get to his feet, and Joanne dutifully let him out into the garden.

Joanne chuckled to herself as she watched Harley roll over and over on the lush, green lawn, snuffling and snorting. It was easy to envy his simple life when she considered the complexities of her own, and that's when she realised that it had been a few days since she'd called the office. Joanne knew that Samantha would only object if she were to find out, and the usual accusations about her mother being unable to switch off would undoubtedly follow. But the reality for Joanne calling in had less to do with her inability to switch off and more to do with having a girly chat with Leanne, to talk about the things that Joanne felt she was genuinely missing, ordinary run-of-the-mill stuff, the mundane, and not the unexplained.

By the time Samantha was ready to go out with Harley, Joanne was busting to make that phone call. She was already reaching for her mobile when Samantha stopped suddenly by the back gate.

'Mum?' she called out. 'Have you unbolted the gate this morning?' Joanne was a stickler for making sure that things were secure, so the back gate being left unbolted was highly irregular.

'Maybe it was Mr Dawson?' Joanne replied, referring to the gardener who tended to Greenoaks on a regular basis. 'I'll have to have a word with him and tell him to be more careful in future.'

'But Mr Dawson's not been here since we arrived, and he's got a key for the garage. He always comes through that way because the mower and stuff are in there.'

Harley began sniffing around where Samantha was standing, seemingly picking up a strange scent. All Joanne wanted to do was call Leanne and she began to wonder if Samantha were ever going to leave.

'Oh, I don't know ...' she said, sounding a little impatient. 'Maybe you forgot to lock it the last time you took Harley out?'

It seemed plausible. Samantha shrugged her shoulders.

'Yeah, maybe ... okay,' she said. 'See you in a bit.' Then she closed the gate behind her and went to walk down the path that ran along the back of the garden, but she had to wait for Harley, who'd hesitated. He was giving the grass on *that* side of the gate a thorough investigation, too.

Joanne waited a few moments to make sure the coast was well and truly clear before calling her office, mentally preparing what she was going to say to Leanne about having to stay away from the office longer than originally planned. Leanne was a good friend as well as a PA, so she *would* understand about the length of time it might take to repair a damaged Range Rover, wouldn't she?

'Good morning, Middleton Designs …' came Leanne's chirpy, positive tones.

'Hi Leanne,' said Joanne, smiling. 'It's only me. How's things?'

'Hey there, boss! All under control here! How are you guys doing in Costa-del-Preston, then? The weather's beautiful, so it must be *lovely* out there!'

'It certainly is, yeah, *gorgeous* … Ow, *bugger*!'

Having her arm supported hadn't been Joanne's idea of fun, and she hadn't replaced the poly sling after trying her evening dress on, not that it would have prevented her shoulder objecting to a mobile phone being wedged between itself and her neck in any case. The pain was briefly excruciating and enough to take her breath away for a moment.

'Well, they are and they're not, actually,' Joanne admitted. 'I've had bit of an accident and I stacked my bloody car!'

'Oh shit! How bad? Were you hurt?'

'I got a bit banged up but nothing major … got a cut eye and some bruises, and my shoulder is bloody caning me, but it could have been a lot worse. But it looks like I'm going to have to be out here for a little while longer, Leanne … while the car gets repaired. The insurance insisted on having it done locally so I didn't have any choice. Is everything really alright there? Are you guys going to be okay to hold the fort for a few more days if I'm not about?'

There was an audible sigh from the other end of the line followed by a 'Leanne Lecture' about work being of lesser importance than health and that Joanne should be spending more time relaxing. For a moment, Joanne thought she was listening to Samantha.

'We're on top of everything here, Jo, honestly,' said Leanne. 'Everything's running as smoothly as the skin on my bottom, in fact … well, apart from that offensive weapon you call a letter opener going missing and me having to open the post with my fingernails, I suppose.'

Joanne laughed loudly.

'The letter knife was on my desk the last time I saw it,' she said. 'It's probably under a pile of paperwork and I'm sure it'll turn up sooner or later. I can't speak for your bottom, though; I've never seen it in the flesh so I can't really pass judgement on that one!'

According to Leanne, she was all about 'relearning to love herself' following the hit she'd taken after splitting from her boyfriend. It was something that Joanne could relate to when she remembered how inadequate *The Bastard's* affair with his young and energetic secretary had once made her feel about herself. But Leanne ensured the conversation didn't turn maudlin and another outburst of laughter followed after she announced: 'So it's official … I'm a totally hot bitch and my boobs aren't half-bad either! Ah … yes, that reminds me! While we're on the subject of boobs and bums, I've been through that new photographer's portfolio, you know … the one that Leonard put you in touch with?'

'Oh wow, I'd completely forgotten about that! What was his name again? Oh God, I'm absolutely crap with names!'

'Joshua Gains,' said Leanne. 'Just before you swanned off to your country retreat, you told me he was going to be dropping his portfolio into us, remember?'

'Isn't he the one you thought was a bit odd?'

'Yeah, a bit, but I've got to tell you, Jo, he's absolutely brilliant! What he does isn't my thing or yours, but he's phenomenally talented, a real artist. His use of lighting and angles are superb, and I reckon he could easily cope with a fashion shoot.'

Leanne's enthusiasm took Joanne by surprise. Like the rest of Joanne's team (with the notable exception of Leonard Slater), Leanne didn't consider Harvey Davies anything less than a presumptuous, egotistical pig, but had always maintained that he should be tolerated because he was so good at what he did. Yet here she was, the 'Gatekeeper' who'd reduced so many other hopefuls to rubble, recommending somebody completely untried.

'Joshua Gains is *that* good?' asked Joanne.

'Absolutely,' Leanne replied. 'I think he'll be ideal for us. Leonard is looking to organise an on-location shoot for the new swimwear. I've got to go through some ideas with Leonard this morning, funnily enough. He's set up a conference call with an agent whose interested in that part of the new line. We could try Joshua out on that if anything comes off. I didn't think I'd be hearing myself saying that somebody else could equal Harvey, but I think our Mr Gains could even surpass him.'

'Okay,' said Joanne. 'You've convinced me. He must have left some contact details, so if you can text them to me, I'll get in touch with him to set up a meeting as soon as possible.'

Dealing with photographers was usually Leonard's remit, but Joanne had reservations about his 'interest' in Harvey Davies and insisted that she should be involved in the conference call. After protesting to begin with, Leanne eventually relented. Joanne was very laid back and amenable for the most part, but there was a latent steeliness to her nature that wasn't wise to cross, and Leanne considered it best not to argue.

But the same couldn't be said for Samantha, who, on returning from her walk with Harley, was interested to know why her mother was still downstairs in her pyjamas. Joanne confessed she'd called the office to speak to Leanne and had ended up wanting to be involved in a conference call a little later.

'Why the hell did you do that for, Mum? Why can't you just leave them to it and relax? What is it with you and work? It's not normal!'

Joanne might have been prepared to take a lecture from her PA, but she wasn't in the mood to take another one from her daughter. Joanne's expression turned to one of thunder, and Samantha realised she'd just lit the shortest of her mother's fuses.

'You know,' Joanne retorted. 'I'm getting pretty bloody *bored* with being told what I can and cannot do by everybody, especially *you*, young lady! Just who the bloody hell do you think you are? If I choose to ring Leanne and see how things are, it's my prerogative. It's my company, and perhaps you need reminding just how much we've benefitted from it.' Joanne made a sweeping movement with her hand, gesturing at the beautiful interior of the cottage. 'All this, for example,' she said. 'Do you think we'd have this if it weren't for the company? Do you think I just pulled it all out of thin air?'

'Well, of course I don't ...'

'That we'd have the lifestyle we have now?'

Five words were about as much as Samantha could get out as Joanne continued to unload, fuming: 'Well perhaps you'd better think twice next time before you put the boot in then, hadn't you? One day you may well even be running things. And the reason I'm going to be involved in the conference call is because it *happens* to also involve the latest project, the one in which *you* had more than just a little input!'

A very confused Harley appeared in the kitchen area with his head held low. He wasn't used to hearing raised voices, and his doleful brown eyes were peering uncertainly up at Joanne from under his worry-wrinkled brow. The forlorn stare was enough to stop Joanne's rant temporarily, and Samantha seized the only opportunity she was going to get to speak before her mother could build up another head of steam.

'I'm sorry, Mum,' she sighed. 'I know I shouldn't have gone off on one like that. I just wish you'd take a step back that's all, especially since the accident and stuff ...'

Samantha's apologetic tone paid off, and Joanne offered her own apologies for flying off the handle, and for laying it on a bit thicker than maybe she should. Calling Leanne had been nothing other than a need to call a friend at first, but then the conversation had taken on a completely different complexion once she'd learned about the potential new photographer.

'And I suppose that's probably the only reason I'm getting involved in the meeting at all,' she said. 'You know how I hate having to work with Harvey, Sam. Just the thought of him makes my skin crawl. I know he was very complimentary after the last shoot, but it was probably just a blip. He couldn't remain sincere if his shitty little tattooed life depended on it; it won't last … Anyway, I said I'd be giving this new photographer a call afterwards. I know Leonard normally organises that kind of thing, but for some reason I don't trust him on this one. Something's making me feel I need to deal with this myself, just to make sure.'

'Well, if it's going to make you feel better, why not?' said Samantha. 'And it'll teach Harvey a lesson for sure if it all goes well!'

'Thanks, Sammy. And I *will* try and switch off after this, I promise. It may please you to know that Leanne gave me a bit of a talking to as well when I rang, and not everybody can be wrong I suppose!'

'An admission from your own lips, Boudicca, your *own* lips!'

Joanne pulled her disapproving face, and Samantha was 'persuaded' to make breakfast as a way of making amends.

But Samantha's retribution didn't end there. *After* breakfast, she was sent packing and instructed to pick up a leg of lamb from a local butcher, and get all the vegetables and desserts for the evening meal. With Samantha out running errands for a couple of hours, Joanne would have time to concentrate on her conference call, and then she would be able to contact the photographer who had so impressed Leanne.

*

Wayne was once again staring at the ceiling of his hotel room, absorbed in his thoughts, astounded at happening upon Samantha Middleton when he'd least expected, but frustrated by how luck continually seemed to enjoy conspiring against him. Yet, there *was* a crumb of comfort to be had, and it was in the certainty that The Puppeteer would have Samantha Middleton delivered exactly as he'd assured. Wayne couldn't quite imagine the scenario, but what he *had* been able to imagine had brought him immense pleasure, and he was about to pleasure himself again when his mobile unexpectedly burst into life.

The derailing of Wayne's lurid train of thought was enough to make him jump up from his bed. He swung a disgruntled hand over towards the source of the digital intrusion, but only succeeded in sweeping the phone off the bedside table, sending it skidding across the carpet and under the dressing table on the other side of the room. Cursing under his breath, Wayne dropped down onto his hands and knees. The device was still ringing, vibrating noisily against the skirting board, and he had to crawl right underneath the dressing table in order to retrieve it. Without looking at the screen, he put the mobile to his ear and answered.

'Hello?' said a woman's voice. 'Is that Joshua Gains?'

'Speaking.'

'Oh, hi Joshua, it's Joanne Middleton from Middleton Designs? We spoke recently and my PA has told me about your portfolio.'

Wayne shot up in amazement, smashing the back of his head painfully on what turned out to be a very solidly built dressing table. Joanne heard a distinct THUMP followed by a stifled 'FFFFFFFUCK!'

'Are you okay, Joshua?'

Wayne looked around for something to punch but thought better of it.

'I'm fine,' he replied, rubbing away frantically at the stinging pain. 'Just fine ... yes, I remember calling you a few days ago.'

'You sound a bit distracted. I could always call back when its more convenient.'

But Wayne's discomfort was beginning to ease, and there was every chance that this was the opportunity The Puppeteer had promised. Keenly interested in how things might develop, Wayne did his best to sound professional.

'I wasn't doing anything that can't wait,' he said. 'Did your PA like the portfolio?'

'Yes, she did! She was very impressed and that's why I called, because I was wondering if we could arrange a meeting and discuss things further?'

All the pieces of the puzzle were falling into place, just as The Puppeteer had promised. Wayne's palms were clammy and he was sweating with excitement.

'When did you have in mind?' he asked, swapping the phone briefly over to his other ear in order to wipe his face.

'Sooner rather than later if that's okay with you,' Joanne replied.

'Sounds good to me! I'll, erm ... I'll just go and check my diary to see when I'm free.'

Wayne put his mobile down on the bed and strode into the bathroom to give himself a few moments to think, and there, staring back at him in the mirror, was a cause for immediate concern. Short of surgical reconstruction, his face might be a problem. There was no way that Wayne could look much different to the day he'd shown the Middleton bitches his need on Hampstead Heath, and the moment they clapped eyes on him, their mental alarm bells might ring and ruin everything. Mind you, he *was* unusually dishevelled for one who's usual preference was being cleanshaven, so maybe the thickening stubble on his face could be developed into something sharper, more fashionable and … and what a *difference* a new hairstyle could make!

New image, new Wayne, a change was long overdue, and maybe he might even have been worrying himself unnecessarily. The whole thing on Hampstead Heath had happened so quickly that it was debatable if Joanne or her whore-born daughter would have even be able to recognise him, and besides, he hadn't done anything wrong, he'd just been expressing his feelings.

Swallowing his hatred, Wayne hurried out of the bathroom and returned to his conversation with an unsuspecting Joanne.

'I'm sorry about that,' he said. 'I'm a bit disorganised. The pitfalls of living out of a suitcase! I know my diary is around somewhere, but rather than keep you holding on, why don't I get back to you either later today or sometime tomorrow?'

'I guess tomorrow's just as good,' Joanne replied. 'I'm still away from the office in any case, so I daresay we can't do anything much until I get back.'

A devious smile began to spread across Wayne's face at the uniqueness of his position, but even though he knew he was gaining Joanne's trust, it wasn't necessarily going to be enough to guarantee him a shot at the title. It would be wise to wait an extra day, and see what The Puppeteer's next masterstroke might be.

'Whatever … I'm easy,' he said. 'But if I remember rightly, the last time we spoke, you said something about going to Hertfordshire for a few days? If you're still going to be out that way, I don't mind meeting you *there* if needs be. Business is business, Joanne. It doesn't matter to me how far I have to travel to take care of it …'

CHAPTER 27

As late afternoon became early evening, the air of expectancy in Greenoaks continued to grow, but despite Joanne's best efforts she hadn't been much help with the dinner preparations for the coming evening. Having a daughter so adept in the kitchen was a godsend for Joanne, who, having finally been told by Samantha to 'either do something useful or bugger off and go chill somewhere!' had opted for the latter and was now lying up to her neck in a bath full of soft, tingling bubbles. She had even been able to wash her hair with one arm, something of a moral victory considering the wound had only been glued, not stitched, and needed to be kept dry.

As a temporary hinderance to all things culinary, Joanne was making the most of being allowed to fully relax while listening to how things were progressing downstairs. The bathroom door was slightly open, the tantalisingly delicate fragrance of slowly roasting, herb-scented lamb drifting through the gap, and Samantha was singing tunelessly along to the playlist on her mobile phone. Occasionally, she could be heard telling Harley what a good boy he was, and it wasn't difficult for Joanne to imagine him sitting motionless like a hairy bookend, hoping for a scrap of anything edible to be thrown in his direction.

Everything seemed to be going exactly to plan, and Samantha sounded like she was happy and buzzing. Joanne herself was looking forward to having a very desirable man round for dinner and she wanted to look her best; one didn't get a second chance at a first impression, and although it wouldn't be the first time they'd met, it *would* be the first time Chris had seen her in full 'Battle Dress'.

But looking her best wasn't going to happen all by itself, and Joanne was definitely going to need some assistance with her hair. Washing it had been the easy part and that had been difficult enough, but drying it ....? She carefully manoeuvred her lengthy frame out of the tub, slipped on her bath robe, towelled her hair as best she could, and then wandered downstairs to see if Samantha could be prized away from the kitchen.

'Wow!' said Joanne as she walked into the dining area. 'It looks absolutely amazing in here!'

Samantha had even found time to go out into the back garden and cut some flowers to make an eye-catching floral centrepiece of rich blue delphiniums and red and yellow lupins. Either side of the stunning arrangement, two open bottles of red wine were standing to attention, overseeing the rest of the immaculately set table.

'Thanks Mum,' she said. 'I'm really glad you like it.'

'Like it? It's incredible, Sam. You've done yourself proud; you really have. Anybody would think we're expecting royalty!'

Samantha's face lit up.

'All the starters are done,' she said, 'and the desserts have pretty-much thawed out. There are two more bottles of red wine open on the side, the lamb is taking care of itself, and the veg will be a doddle. Oh, and I made sure I used the best cutlery like you asked. I think we're pretty much all set, Mum!'

'So, it's just *us* to sort out now,' said Joanne. 'Actually, Sammy, I know you've had to do all this, but you wouldn't mind being an absolute love again and …'

'Help you do your hair? Of course I will! I was going to offer anyway.'

It was just like the best times they'd enjoyed as a family were back. Samantha happily went about drying and styling her mother's hair, but didn't have enough time to help with her make up. Using any kind of mirror, even a compact, was totally out of the question for Joanne, but Samantha's genius suggestion about her mother using the front camera of her mobile saved the day. After that, it was down to 'Boudicca to do the bloody rest herself!' and Samantha was finally free to concentrate upon getting *herself* ready.

Joanne managed to struggle into her underwear and evening dress, and was putting the finishing touches to her make-up when Samantha strode into the room to see how her mother was getting on.

'Oh my God, Mum!' she gasped. 'You look absolutely stunning. Give me a twirl, then!'

'Are you sure this isn't a little too over the top?' asked Joanne. 'I mean, it's just a dinner party … are you sure I'm not showing a bit too much leg?'

'No way, you look *incredible*! Nothing wrong with showing a bit of thigh with legs like yours!'

Mother and daughter giggled as Joanne donned her high heels and performed a pirouette, looking like catwalk royalty in her revealing evening dress. Samantha's black, skinny-leg jeans and dark red, low-cut fitted top was a far more relaxed image in comparison, a casual-cum-sexy look that may have suited her down to the ground, but still made Joanne feel guilty about her misdemeanours of the previous day that had caused Samantha to miss out on a new outfit.

'Don't be silly,' Samantha said. 'Tonight isn't about me, it's about *you* shining, and you really *do* look beautiful, Mum!'

'Thanks, Sammy.'

'Chris won't be able to take his eyes off you …'

A chiming doorbell and the sound of Harley's huge bark ended the conversation. Joanne looked at her watch which said it was a little before a quarter-to-eight.

'Bugger!' she said. 'They're early!'

'Better than being late,' replied Samantha before briskly descending the stairs to welcome their guests.

Joanne followed at a more sedate pace in her heels, and her excited daughter had already opened the front door before Joanne even reached the living room. Harley seemed just as eager to get involved in the reunion, enthusiastically dividing his affections between each of the visitors as they entered, but mostly his affection was directed towards Andy, and he chuffed excitedly as Andy leant over him and energetically ruffled his coat.

'Oh my God, *Jo* … look at you!' said Anne when she saw Joanne. 'And just look at this table! And what *beautiful* flowers!'

Anne's praise made Joanne smile, but she was quick to give all the credit to Samantha. The smile became a broad grin when she saw Chris.

'How are you feeling?' he asked. 'Any better?'

'My shoulder's still painful,' Joanne replied, 'but much better than yesterday, thank God!'

There was a moment of hesitation. The casual form of Chris that Joanne had first met had been replaced by a much smarter version wearing a dark grey suit and crisp, white open-necked shirt. He was also wearing a scent that was doing wonders for her, and she felt that her lips might have lingered a little too long upon his cheek when they'd politely exchanged kisses.

'How about some drinks?' she asked, having to pull herself away to speak to Anne. 'We've got some of those beers for Chris and Andy that you told me about, there's gin and vodka, and probably far too much red wine!'

'Ooh lovely,' replied Anne. 'I think I'll make a start on the wine in that case!'

Joanne laughed and went into hostess mode, while Anne watched Chris's eyes following every one of Joanne's steps as she walked away across the kitchen.

'Doesn't she look *beautiful?*' Anne whispered. 'She's made *such* an effort, and look at that fabulous dress! Aren't you glad I made you go out and buy a new suit now?'

But Chris didn't answer. He was too enthralled by Joanne and the incredible dress that was sweeping over her sculpted figure, hugging her like a second skin. Joanne's poise and sophistication spoke volumes about her previous life as a model, and what little make-up she'd used had been immaculately applied, the deep red lipstick on her appealing lips matching her auburn hair to perfection. The day before, that hair had hung over her shoulders like a long, wild, shaggy mane, but right then it was worn up in a loose chignon, exposing the soft, fair skin of her graceful neck. For all Chris knew, he could have been staring at Aphrodite.

'Are we going to stand here all night like pieces of furniture?' Anne asked, blowing into his ear. 'Or are we going to sit down and join in?'

Chris smiled weakly and went to join the others while Anne grinned knowingly to herself. Her intuition said that Joanne was every bit as interested in Chris as *he* was in her, but his 'she-bitch' of an ex-wife had hurt him so badly it was debateable if he would act upon anything even if he sensed it. Chris had been alone for too long, but as far as Anne was concerned, it was about time he moved on with his life.

As the Ryan family's designated driver, Chris would only allow himself to have one drink, but it didn't stop him relaxing and getting involved as the dinner progressed. Unlike some dinner parties and social get-togethers he had attended before, Joanne's little soirée didn't have the stilted edge that had to be overcome at the beginning. Here were two families keen to get to know each other, and the level of interest that kept the conversation flowing was genuine rather than cringingly polite. As captivated as he was by Joanne, however, Chris kept finding himself looking over towards Andy and Samantha, and it pleased him to see that they appeared to be getting noticeably closer.

Eventually, the three-course meal was successfully negotiated, and all that remained were empty plates, dishes, bowls and discarded serviettes. It was then that Anne decided she needed to make her excuses and go outside and get some air.

As is often the way with social occasions, the wine tends to flow, and with Anne it had done so in torrents. Since the passing of her late husband, John Ryan, Anne had been reluctant about joining in with social gatherings and was somewhat out of practice in the art of having a good time. Joanne and Samantha with their infectious personalities, however, had managed to bring the old devil out of her once again, something that had become apparent when Anne found herself having to concentrate on pronouncing her *Ss* to avoid sounding slurred.

It hadn't been difficult for Anne to become very fond of Joanne and Samantha, and she especially wanted to see Chris happy again. Joanne was undoubtedly the perfect foil for him, and the way the two of them seemed to hit it off reminded her of how John and she were when they'd first met.

Losing John had left a gap in Anne's life impossible to fill, but the same sense of loss needn't be the same with Chris, regardless of how hard his marriage break-up had hit him. Anne sighed as she sat down at a garden table. She missed her late husband so much it was almost unbearable sometimes. The midsummer night was warm and welcoming, its sky perfectly clear and bejewelled with countless stars. How John with his wit and joviality would have loved being a part of that wonderful evening!

'Are you alright out here on your own, Anne?'

The sound of Joanne's voice caused Anne to come back to her senses rather abruptly.

'Oh God, I'm so sorry!' said Joanne. 'I didn't mean to make you jump.'

'Don't worry, Jo, you didn't,' Anne replied. 'I was just in a world of my own.'

'I know that feeling only too well! You're okay though, aren't you?'

'Yes, yes, I'm fine, I just felt like a bit of fresh air, that's all.'

'Can I get you anything else? Another glass of wine perhaps?'

'Pfffft … I think you've poured enough wine down me already! Another one and I'll be *under* this table, not just sitting at it!'

Joanne laughed out loud.

'Am I a bad influence on you, then?' she asked.

'Oh, most *definitely*! But tonight was just what the doctor ordered. And can I just say what a *wonderful* evening it's been, and how well Samantha did with everything. That daughter of yours is an *exceptional* cook, you know! I'm guessing she learnt from you?'

Although Joanne took full responsibility for Samantha's culinary skills, it wasn't in quite the way she would have liked. Joanne explained that the fashion industry could be hard and relentless, which meant working long hours, and it wasn't unusual for her to leave the house early in the morning and return well into the evening. The result was that Joanne felt less inclined to make herself anything worthwhile for dinner after a long day, so Samantha had taken it upon herself to learn to cook, making sure that her mother had a decent meal to come home to whenever she was detained at the office.

'It makes me feel guilty sometimes,' said Joanne. 'Samantha should never have felt the need to do all that for me, and there are times when I can't help thinking that I haven't been there enough for her.'

The admission made Anne frown.

'I don't know how you can say that,' she said. 'Don't forget that I was once a headteacher. I've encountered all sorts of parents and I can see that you're a fantastic mother. Just look at the wonderful relationship you two have; that young lady's an absolute credit to you, Jo, she really is.'

'Thanks Anne ... I really appreciate that, and I'll tell Sammy that you said she's an exceptional cook, too. She'll take that as a *real* compliment knowing it came from you.'

'Good God! Am I *that* matriarchal?'

'No, of course you're not! Samantha just thinks a lot of you, we both do. I think she sees how close you are to Andy and it's something that she doesn't have with her *own* grandmother. I'm afraid that I haven't seen eye-to-eye with my mum for a number of years now. In fact, our whole family isn't what you'd call close, so it's really just Sammy and me I suppose.'

'That's very sad.'

'Yes, it is rather. But we don't want to talk about that and bring the vibe down now, do we?'

A sudden outburst of laughter made them look towards the cottage where Andy and Samantha, themselves a little worse for wear with drink, were making their way out into the garden. Behind them through the open French doors, Joanne could see Chris clearing the dining table.

'Oh, bless him,' said Anne with a chuckle. 'He's being *such* a good boy. Looks like I raised *him* well too!'

'I'm sorry, Anne,' said Joanne. 'But I can't sit here and let him do that. If you'll excuse me, I won't be a minute.'

Joanne strode into the cottage just as Chris was about to remove half an empty bottle of red wine from the table.

'You don't have to do that,' she said. 'You're a guest!'

'Well, Mum would only give me a hard time if I didn't' Chris replied. 'Even if she *is* a bit tipsy.'

It was very obvious to Joanne that Anne was three sheets to the wind, but she gave the impression that she hadn't noticed.

'Well, I hope she's going to be okay,' she said.

'Ah, don't worry, Mum will be fine. It's great to see her enjoying herself again actually.'

Chris carefully took a stack of crockery over to the kitchen sink and began to roll up the sleeves of his shirt.

'What *are* you doing?' asked Joanne.

'I'm going to help you wash up, especially as you only have one arm!'

Joanne opened a door in a nearby unit to reveal a dishwasher.

'We don't *wash up* here,' she said. 'We use one of these, a woman's best friend, but I guess I'm not going to stop you filling it up for me; I hate doing that at the best of times!'

Entertaining and funny, Joanne had been the perfect hostess, and Chris had to laugh when, with an air of total authority, she lifted the door of the dishwasher with the heel of one of her shoes, and then closed it sharply with a shove of her rear end.

'Right!' said Joanne, switching on the machine. 'Tea or coffee?'

'A coffee would be lovely, thanks.'

Joanne went outside to see if anybody else was interested, which turned out to be a complete waste of time.

'Well, it seems that the uncultured rabble out there don't want an after dinner coffee,' she said as she came back into the kitchen. 'So I guess it's just you and me, then.'

It was as she began struggling to open a fresh pack of ground coffee that it occurred to Chris how he and Joanne were as alone as they were going to be that night. Throughout the evening, he'd felt himself becoming ever more attracted to her, and really wanted to know if she felt the same way about *him*. The sense of disappointment he would undoubtedly feel if it wasn't the case was very unsettling, and he might even run the risk of making himself look completely stupid, but he was never going to find out if he didn't pluck up the courage and at least *test* the water.

Oblivious of Chris's misgivings, Joanne put the stubborn packet of coffee back down on the worktop and began searching through a cutlery drawer for a pair of scissors.

'Do you want me to have a go at it?' Chris asked.

'Be my guest!' she replied. 'I don't seem to have any grip for some reason.'

'Well, instant's just as good, Jo. You don't have to go to all the trouble of making fresh if it's just us two.'

'Ooh ... how very considerate, but how very *dare* you! We don't do *instant* in this house any more than we wash up!'

An odd, semi-expectant kind of silence followed their laughter as they looked at each other, as though either one might be waiting for the other to say, or instigate, something more. Songwriters penned classics about such situations, and Chris, uncertain and daunted by the effect Joanne was having upon him, could only continue to wonder what he should do or say next.

'I've really enjoyed tonight,' he said, wishing he could be more imaginative.

'Good ... I rather hoped you would.'

Another pause followed. The conversation felt like it was becoming a little stilted. Somehow, Chris had to dig deep and find out where he stood.

'Jo...' he began.

'Hmmm?'

'Oh God ... I'm not very good at this sort of thing.'

'Not very good at what?'

Joanne had enjoyed the numerous smiles and glances they'd exchanged during dinner, aware that something was building up between them, and Chris's hesitancy was only adding to the tension.

Chris looked down at his feet and shuffled them nervously.

'Well,' he said. 'I was just wondering if I could take you out one night? Dinner, perhaps ... or a drink ... a film maybe? I mean, I know you're very busy ... But I just thought ... you know, while you're out this way?'

'Or we could do all three!' Joanne replied, glad to put him out of his misery. 'I'd be happy to, whenever you like.'

'You would?'

'Absolutely!'

Was that relief or surprise on Chris's face? Either way, his expression was a picture, but it didn't matter as Joanne had seen more than enough to be convinced about his sincerity. After her accident, when many others would have left the scene having done their bit, Chris had stayed. He had kept her upbeat, made her laugh during some dark moments, and he'd charmed her again that evening during dinner. At one point, she nearly asked him where he'd hung up his armour and parked his white horse!

Joanne made a point of standing right next to him at the sink as she went to fill the kettle. Chris could smell her perfume and the delicate scent of coconut from the hair conditioner she'd used. She was so close that he could feel the warmth radiating from the bare skin of her arm.

No words were being exchanged, but the silence was far from awkward. Joanne reinforced her acceptance of Chris's invitation in a way that surprised even herself. She kissed him. At first Chris seemed shocked, but then he responded, pressing his lips against hers. Joanne dropped the kettle noisily into the sink, and wrapped her arms around him, ignoring the pain from her shoulder. Was that *his* heart she could feel pounding in her chest, or was it her own? Consumed by the moment, she found herself wishing that they were *completely* alone, scarcely believing the intensity of what was passing between them, and Chris, too, was being swept along in the same passionate tide. For once in his life, it was neither a time to analyse nor to question, it was all about him and Joanne right then, and nothing, and nobody else, seemed to exist.

But Chris and Joanne were not the only people lost in a world of their own. Anne strolled casually back into the cottage looking for the bathroom, and her eyes widened when she saw Chris and Joanne together at the kitchen sink. She *had* been just about to ask Joanne for directions to the nearest convenience, and was rather relieved that she hadn't just launched into it as per her usual style, but then to her alarm she heard Andy and Samantha. Immediately, Anne turned and put a finger to her lips, hastily gesturing for them to go back, their frowning, baffled faces amusing her as she continued to quietly usher them away until they were all outside in the garden.

'What's wrong?' asked Andy.

'Oh, nothing,' Anne replied. 'Nothing at all, I just think that, er … I just think that we should give Jo and your dad a bit of privacy.'

She bit her lip and glanced at Samantha, who immediately grabbed Andy's hand, and hurried with him towards the side of the cottage where some shrubs were illuminated by the light from one of the kitchen windows. Anne tried her best to dissuade them, but her objections fell upon deaf ears. Everything about that coded look had filled Samantha with delight, and she stood with Andy in their garden vantage point, watching their respective parents continuing their embrace at the kitchen sink.

'Wow!' said Andy. 'Your mum and my dad?'

'I know,' whispered Samantha. 'Isn't it brilliant?'

'I thought they were supposed to be making coffee!'

Samantha stifled an excited giggle and shared a celebratory high five with Andy before throwing her arms around him.

And it was Samantha who thought it might be a great idea to suggest putting Andy and his family up for the night. Joanne certainly didn't have objections, and Chris, totally unaware that anybody else other than he and Joanne knew about their little after-dinner dalliance, took full advantage by having another couple of drinks.

Anne was offered the spare room and retired shortly after midnight, and around an hour or so later, Joanne and Samantha were offering their apologies for needing to turn in themselves. Joanne brought some blankets and pillows down from the airing cupboard upstairs, leaving Andy and Chris to decide which one of them was going to have the largest of the two sofas in the living room.

Father and inebriated son decided that the fairest way to decide was the toss of a coin, something Chris regretted immediately when Andy drunkenly called correctly.

But Chris resigned himself to his fate without complaint and made himself as comfortable as possible. After all, he wasn't going to be sleeping next to Harley, who was happily taking up precious sofa room alongside an already comatose Andy. Grinning to himself, Chris turned out the living room lights, and for a few minutes in the tranquil gloom of Greenoaks Cottage, all he could think about was Joanne. Then his mind moved on to Andy's developing relationship with Samantha, and how they were going to be able to keep her protected without drawing attention to the fact.

As strong as the growing bonds *were* that were bringing The Circle closer together, one careless mistake was all it might take to blow it all apart.

CHAPTER 28

Andy's senses were somewhat blunted when he awoke to the sound of singing from the kitchen. The copious amounts of beer and wine he'd consumed the night before meant he'd slept far heavier than usual, and for a few moments he was rather confused as to why he'd woken up in strange surroundings on a three-seater-sofa. He remembered why when Samantha came strolling into the living room in a bath robe, a steaming mug of coffee in one hand and a couple of slices of toast on a small plate in the other.

'Well, good morning,' she said with a smile. 'How are you feeling? A little thick-headed perhaps?'

'Yeah, you could say that …'

'Can I get you anything? Paracetamol? Ibuprofen?'

Andy sat up slowly and rubbed his eyes.

'Nobody likes a smartarse,' he retorted. 'God above … I feel like I'm hanging out of my arse!'

'Hmmm. You can always rely on my mum to come up trumps on the wine front. She knows her stuff, you know!'

'Tell me about it. I've got a mouth that feels like the bottom of a birdcage, all shit and feathers! Anyway, how come *you're* so bloody lively this morning?'

'I'm an early riser *and*, unlike *some*, I didn't mix my drinks!'

'Yeah, yeah, whatever!'

Andy and Samantha had taken every opportunity at the dinner party to get to know each other better, and inevitably, in more private moments, that had meant sharing what they knew about The Puppeteer. It was hardly party conversation, but Samantha was grateful for the chance to speak freely, and judging by the way she was goading Andy about his hangover, it was clear that she had enjoyed another peaceful night following her last brutal encounter with the entity in Whitwell.

Eventually Andy's mind began to clear and he ceased being so much of an object of ridicule, but it still came as something of a surprise for him to learn that it was just the two of them in the cottage.

'Bloody hell!' he said. 'Dad's gone out already? Shit, *he's* keen!'

'Mum and Chris left with Anne at least an hour ago,' said Samantha, looking at the clock. 'Just after nine, I'd say. Harley went as well. They're taking Anne home first and I think your dad is going to pick up a change of clothes for you, and then he and Mum are going for a walk with Harley. I think your dad's got some stuff to do with Anne later, but he's coming back with a change of clothes for you first.'

'And they planned all this while I was still asleep?'

'Yep, while you were out like a light, stinking on the sofa. They'll be gone ages ... Which means we've got the place *all* to ourselves for a while.'

'I'd better get myself freshened up in that case! Is it okay if I use the bathroom?'

There had been something distinctly odd about Samantha's tone, and her expression had even bordered on being suggestive. Andy knew he could be slow on the uptake occasionally, but he couldn't believe that Samantha would be so forward as to give him a come-on so soon.

'Of course you can!' Samantha replied. 'Feel free to have a shower if you want.'

'Really?'

'Well, everybody else has! Come with me; there are loads of towels in the airing cupboard.'

Andy followed Samantha upstairs.

'There *was* a new toothbrush in the cabinet as well,' she said. 'But I think your dad might have used it. You can use mine if you like, it's the red one. There isn't any manly shower gel, though, so you'll have to use mine or Mummy Bear's body wash. Your dad smelled like Mum when he left this morning, so I wouldn't worry too much about it. I think he'd even used her deodorant, too!'

'Just as long as you don't tell anyone at the rugby club,' said Andy. 'My hard-tackling reputation would be in the sewer and I'd never live it down!'

The sound of a mobile phone ringing in Joanne's bedroom put an abrupt end to the exchange. Samantha realised that her mother had forgotten to take it with her, and apologised to Andy about needing to see who it was in case it was important. Andy understood and made his way into the bathroom while Samantha went to answer the phone.

'Hello?' she said.

'Hi, is that Joanne Middleton?'

Wayne guessed that the soft, well-spoken voice that had answered might belong to somebody else. Although it wasn't *dissimilar*, he remembered Joanne's as being a little deeper.

'No,' said the mystery voice. 'She's not here at the moment, this is her daughter, Samantha. Can I help or take a message for her?'

In his shock, Wayne almost dropped his mobile. Until that moment Samantha Middleton had only been a target, something he had to destroy and not a real person. It had never entered his mind for an instant that he would be having any kind of interaction with her, and he was briefly lost for words.

'Hello …? Are you still there?' Samantha asked.

'Oh, yes … yes! I'm sorry, I got a little bit distracted then … it's Joshua Gains.'

'Oh, the photographer chap! Mum's spoken to me about you, and says you're really rather good! I don't normally get to speak to you guys because Mum or Leonard normally deal with it. Do you know Leonard?'

Samantha was bright and bubbly, and her confidence was making Wayne feel slightly uncomfortable.

'No,' he replied. 'I haven't spoken to him directly.'

'He's great; you'll love him! He always deals with Mum's fashion shoots, so I guess that's what you do?'

'Well, Joanne *does* want to discuss a fashion shoot,' Wayne replied, trying to hold himself together, 'but I'm actually a figure photographer. I mainly study nudes, the female form.'

'Really? That's quite a bit different to fashion though, isn't it?'

'No, I don't think so; the female form is art with or without clothes, so to me it's just another form of expression. It's still about capturing a moment on camera and conveying something, or sending a message.'

'Wow … I've never thought of it that way! You're very passionate about this, aren't you? Have you been doing it long?'

Samantha didn't sound put off at all, and her interest had put Wayne more at ease. A door previously closed to him was beginning to open.

'About ten years,' he replied. 'I was lucky enough to get a few breaks early and then managed to establish myself more as I went on.'

'Have you always studied nudes, then?'

'*Mainly* nudes … but I also study individual parts of the body like hands, eyes, mouths. Once I even had to photograph somebody's toes for a pharmaceutical company that was marketing a new cream for athlete's foot!'

Samantha laughed, but Wayne wasn't bothered; the happier she was to engage him, the better.

'So, your line of work's rather varied then?' she said.

'The toes were a bit extreme, I guess, but I'm also known for my facial studies. I've always been drawn to women's faces, and *your* facial features are particularly striking if you don't mind me saying so.'

There was a short silence as Wayne's slip sunk in on both sides of the conversation.

'My face?' Samantha asked. 'But we haven't met …'

Thankfully for Wayne, help was at hand in the most unlikely form of the letter knife he'd taken from Joanne's office.

'There's a photograph of you on your mother's desk,' he said. 'I saw it when I dropped my portfolio off. Her personal assistant told me who you were when I asked.' Wayne closed his eyes and shook his head, scarcely able to believe how close he'd come to screwing things up. Again.

'Oh yes, of course, I know the one,' said Samantha. 'And thank you for the compliment, although I always find it strange seeing me as the camera sees me.'

'Well, the camera definitely seems to like you! Have you ever considered being a model?'

'Actually, that's what I do!'

'And why doesn't that surprise me? You'd make an *ideal* subject for a facial study. You've got *great* bone-structure and very expressive eyes.'

'Do you really think so?'

Flatter the bitches and see where it leads! thought Wayne. *She's just as susceptible as the rest of her vile, shit-stinking kind.*

'Absolutely!' he said, grinning to himself. 'How would you feel about doing some modelling for *me* …?'

Along the landing from Joanne's bedroom was the bathroom where a reinvigorated Andy had finished showering. As he pulled up his jeans and fastened his belt, he heard Samantha's footsteps padding across the carpet on the landing outside, followed by the sound of music.

He left the bathroom and peered over the balcony, assuming that the music was coming up from the living room below but it was deserted. Then, his eyes followed his ears and he turned his head towards Samantha's bedroom, instead, where she could be seen standing, still in her bathrobe, and scrolling intently through her phone's playlist. He knocked gently on the already open door, and she invited him in with a smile.

'That was a delicate knock,' she said, cancelling the song she'd been about to play. 'I know a lot of the wood in the house is reclaimed, but the doors aren't *that* fragile.'

The tell-tale tracks of historical woodworm were clearly visible in the old door as Andy entered a bedroom considerably larger than he'd expected, easily accommodating a king size double bed, double wardrobe, a solid chest of drawers and dressing table. A full-length Cheval mirror was angled out into the room's centre where a thick cream rug partially covered an expanse of polished oak floorboards. A distinct aroma of recently treated timber hung in the air, its pungent edge smoothed by the inviting sweetness of Samantha's body spray. The combination added to an already semi-expectant atmosphere, but Andy didn't want to get ahead of himself as he might easily have misread

Samantha's expression in the living toom. There hadn't been a mirror in the bathroom, so this was as good a time as any to check his hair in the Cheval to take his mind of things and avoid making himself look like an idiot.

'I don't suppose you've got a hairdryer I could borrow, have you?' he asked. 'I've got the same kind of hair as Dad, and if I leave it to dry on its own, I'll just end up looking like a bloody loo brush!'

'Well, hark at you, Mr Vain!' Samantha replied, opening the top drawer of her dresser. 'There you go! I'm going to enjoy messing it all up again when you're done …'

Samantha had no intention of passing Andy the hairdryer. She closed the drawer back up and, before his astonished eyes, moved towards him.

'We're alone,' she said, but then she froze.

Instead of the surge of passion that Andy might have expected, he was engulfed by an awful feeling of nausea and a griping pain in his stomach that doubled him up. The Cheval mirror was just behind Samantha and, framed within it, was an equally horrifying reflection.

'I must apologise for my recent absences, Samantha!' said The Puppeteer, bowing theatrically. 'I wouldn't want you to start thinking that I was no longer interested in you now, would I?

Samantha wanted to scream, but she was unable to make a sound. No longer a vison in a nightmare, The Puppeteer had just *materialised* in the room, an overpowering, physical manifestation whose presence seemed to be turning the air around her into a heavy, suffocating mass. Immediately she felt drained of everything she was, and tears of desperation began to stream down her face.

'Is this an inopportune moment, then?' asked The Puppeteer. 'I just thought I might drop in, but it looks like I've interrupted something. Perhaps I should have called first …'

'Leave her alone!' said Andy, having finally managed to force himself upright and found a way to breathe. 'Leave her the *fuck* alone! She's done *nothing* to you!'

The Puppeteer immediately shifted his unblinking focus away from Samantha, the reflection of the bedroom window in his obsidian eyes the only clue for Andy that he wasn't staring into empty black holes. Andy wanted to swing a punch at the gloating countenance towering above him, but didn't have the strength to even clench a fist.

The Puppeteer's unearthly grin widened impossibly.

'Some protector,' he said. 'So it's down to *me* to look after Samantha's virtue, then, seeing as you cannot be trusted. I shall not stand by and allow my *divine* Samantha to be sullied by the likes of *you* or any other, as there are none among you worthy of such a precious jewel. You are no protector; *I* will be her chaperone. Wherever Samantha's innocent feet shall tread, mine shall surely follow.'

Samantha's legs buckled and an anguished cry escaped her lips. Andy managed to catch her before she fell but his own strength was ebbing just as quickly, and for a moment he feared he might drop her. He glared at The Puppeteer in a further act of defiance, but The Puppeteer's attention lay elsewhere, upon a silver pocket watch that he'd apparently just produced from out of thin air. There were no hands and no numbers upon its face, and yet he studied it, intently.

'Oh my, how weak the flesh,' he said. 'Time has conspired against us once again, Samantha, and I am not one who believes in outstaying his welcome. My work here is done, and you can now take comfort knowing I will always be on hand to defend your ripe young innocence.'

The Puppeteer melted away as quickly and mysteriously as he'd appeared, but Samantha kept her face pressed against Andy's shoulder.

'It's okay, Sam,' he said. 'He's gone now. I can't sense him anymore.'

Andy's legs felt like they were made of rubber and he knew that they wouldn't be able to support the two of them much longer. He staggered with Samantha to her bed, and they collapsed onto it together.

'Why *is* he doing this to me?' Samantha whispered. 'Just when I thought it might be all over, he comes back like that … And what did he mean by all that weird stuff? It's just like everything else he's ever said to me, just stupid riddles and nothing makes sense. I just want to get out of the house and keep running, but I can't even stand up. I've never felt as drained as this in my life.'

All the hope Samantha had gained from a few days of peace had just been completely sucked out of her, and the dejection in her voice was painful. All Andy could do was hold her in his arms as she began to sob quietly.

'I wouldn't blame you if you didn't want anything to do with me,' she said. 'I wouldn't blame you at all.'

'I'm not going anywhere, Sam! This hasn't changed anything …'

'But it has! You heard what he said, he's never going to leave me alone!'

'Which just makes me even more determined! All that 'protection' stuff was just bullshit; it's more like we're a threat to him if you ask me.'

'But how can we be any threat to *him*? Look what he's just done!'

Andy had to be careful with his choice of words. He suspected a massive positive could be drawn from their latest encounter, but he couldn't let anything slip about The Circle.

'But look how he went so seriously *big* this time, Sam! Something is telling me that he doesn't want us to be together, and that's why he had to make such a huge statement.'

'But surely he could just do the same thing anytime he wants!'

'Could he? Listen, we're both wasted because The Puppeteer had to draw upon *our* energy to sustain *himself*. When I saw him before, it was like we did just now, but he was between our world and his, so he could hold his form because he was in the flux. But in *this* world, he's limited; I saw the face of the pocket watch he was holding and it was blank, and yet he said that time was against him. Time doesn't exist in his world, but it does in this one, and he was only here for a few moments which means he can't hold a *physical* form for long. In *our* world he's weak, Sam, he *really is*! He doesn't belong here, and if he doesn't belong here then it must be possible to shut him out somehow!'

Samantha was too tired to answer, let alone labour the point. She wished that she could draw comfort from Andy's words, wished that he could be right, but regardless of his fight and determination, there was nowhere to hide from The Puppeteer, and at any given moment he could just come to her in any form of his choosing.

Emotionally crushed, her spirit broken, Samantha had no choice but to resign herself to an unknown fate. Her only certainty was that the flame of resistance that had once galvanised her against The Puppeteer had been well and truly extinguished.

CHAPTER 29

Almost as soon as she had closed her eyes, Samantha found herself naked and alone in a bleak and empty wasteland of fine grey ash, being mysteriously drawn to a solitary arched wooden door, latticed with blackened strips of iron. It had no frame, nor did it sit in the wall of a castle for which its ancient, weighty and weather-beaten appearance seemed suited, and yet it stood proudly in its isolation, an almost monolithic memorial to grander times.

Samantha saw a large, ornate doorknob and felt obliged to turn it. The sound of a heavy catch being disengaged greeted her ears, and the door opened inwards into a charmingly simplistic room, bathed in the soft, heartening glow of a crackling log fire. It was a far cry from the dereliction through which she had just passed, and her previously naked body had also suddenly been dressed in a fine red velvet evening dress.

In front of the fireplace, a rustic candlelit table had been discretely set for two, and the host was about to make himself known.

'My door is always open to waifs and strays, Samantha', said The Puppeteer. 'For me, entertaining is always a pleasure, and I must say that *this* little pleasure is *most* unexpected.'

For some reason, The Puppeteer didn't hold as much fear for Samantha on this occasion.

'No more games!' she said. 'What were you talking about in my room and why do you keep coming to me?'

An open hand gestured for Samantha to be seated at the table, while The Puppeteer eased his imposing frame into the chair opposite.

'Drink with me, Samantha,' he said. 'Let us talk … you *are* my guest after all. Once we have drunk from the same cup, there will be no more secrets between us.'

A carafe of red wine appeared on the table in front of him, along with a single fishbowl wine glass. Samantha took a step forward, but then hesitated.

The Puppeteer tutted in self-admonishment.

'Ah, yes, how rude of me,' he said. 'Please, allow *me*.'

The empty chair in front of Samantha eased itself away from the table as though moved by an unseen hand, leaving just enough room for her to sit down upon it. Reluctantly, she accepted, and with an unerringly steady hand,

The Puppeteer smoothly poured a quantity of wine out of the carafe before sliding the half-full glass invitingly towards her.

All it needed was a simple sip and Samantha could have her answers, but something was holding her back. An inner voice was telling her not to trust the sincerity of the moment as there was bound to be a price.

'No,' she said, sliding it back. 'I want to know what you want with me first.'

The Puppeteer pursed his prominent lips, but he didn't respond. His cold black eyes studied Samantha intently in the crushing silence, while a thoughtful thick finger toyed with the slender stem of the wineglass. Samantha waited for what seemed like an age, teetering on an emotional and expectant knife-edge, hoping he would relent, but The Puppeteer just calmly pushed the glass back in her direction.

'Forgive me,' he said. 'But I do not believe that you are in any position to start making any rules.'

The weight of the unrelenting gaze and the fruitless search for answers became too much. Samantha shot up from her chair.

'Just tell me WHAT YOU WANT!' she shouted, slamming her hands down on the table. 'I said no more GAMES!'

A backhand of which any tennis player would have been justly proud was directed at the wineglass. Samantha was surprised at the strength of her fury in the presence of her nemesis, but no sooner had the fragile goblet been sent spiralling across the room than another had immediately taken its place. Above it, suspended bizarrely in mid-air, hung the glistening, ruby-red contents of its predecessor.

The Puppeteer made sure every drop was invisibly funnelled into the replacement wineglass before speaking again.

'Oh, such *passion*', he said. 'But come now, Samantha, you come to me demanding answers and just *expect* me to enlighten you? I mean, what would be in it for me? Now, perhaps if you have something to *offer* me, we might be able to come to an agreement?'

While she was standing up, Samantha could look down at her giant tormentor. It gave rise to an unexpected feeling of superiority, especially as Andy had worked out The Puppeteer's inability to sustain a physical form. If they could find a way to shut him out as Andy had suggested, she could yet learn to protect herself. For a moment, she felt like she had the upper hand.

'I'm not going to offer you anything!' she said.

'How unfortunate. And by the way, I am not as 'limited' in your world as you would like to think; far from it. The limited one is you, restricted by the arrogance of The Truth. Things could be *so* different if you allowed them to be. Haven't I said how you could be so much more if you joined *me*? How much we could do together? You have already taken a big step coming to me so freely, so why stop there?'

There was a disturbing aura of self-congratulation about The Puppeteer, and Samantha suspected it had little to do with her going to him of her own free will. It was obvious that her remaining unenlightened was to his advantage, and not just a stick with which to beat her.

'You talk about The Truth like it's a *person*!' she said 'What is this *Truth* because I don't know anything about it? I've got no idea what it is or what you want with me!'

The Puppeteer slowly began to grin. As gentle as he'd been throughout their meeting, the return of the vile expression proved he had no intention of revealing anything. The willingness with which Samantha had entered his realm had shown her to be weak and susceptible, and the sense of futility and desolation she suddenly felt was overwhelming.

'Why *did* I come here?' she whispered, grimly aware of the mistake she'd made. 'You're nothing but a sick *bastard*!'

'But you do me a disservice, Samantha. You judge me harshly without having any idea of what we could become.' He began running another long, thick finger temptingly around the rim of the new wine glass. 'Perhaps we might be able to start again. Are you *absolutely sure* you don't want to be more forthcoming?'

'Why don't you just leave me alone!'

'Well, if you would rather my interest in you remain purely out of *necessity* rather than choice, then so be it. I was willing to make a pact with you, but alas …'

The remark was left hanging, menacingly, and the door through which Samantha had entered The Puppeteer's realm began to open. Through the widening gap she could see her bedroom, and she and Andy passed out upon her bed.

'Your knight awaits you,' said The Puppeteer. 'Not that he can ever become your prince, as I have already found you a suitor.'

Samantha froze.

'That surprises you, Samantha?'

'But you said …'

'Well, it goes without saying that it would still have to be in accordance with my terms and conditions, of course, and, just as obvious would be how you might wish to fulfil his needs and desires. So, it's not *all* bad then, is it? I mean there might be hope for you after all.'

'*What* suitor? … *What* needs and desires?'

'Now that would be telling! Goodbye, Samantha. Your presence has once again been *most* amusing.'

Grinning again, The Puppeteer nonchalantly rocked back in his chair, and in the blink of an eye, Samantha was naked and back outside in the desert. With The Puppeteer's puzzling words weighing heavily upon her mind, she turned and tried the doorknob of the door that had slammed shut behind her, but it refused to admit her the way it had before. The Puppeteer had had the last laugh once again. Frustrated, Samantha began pounding her fists angrily on the ancient doorway, but the wooden obstacle stood firm against the desperate onslaught. Finally, tearfully, Samantha sunk to her knees in the endless decay of her surroundings, abandoned, afraid, and terribly alone.

*

Joanne returned to Greenoaks, invigorated by her walk with Chris and Harley, to find it unexpectedly quiet. She called out in the silence but there was no reply. 'Ooh, no kids,' she said. 'We can …'

The sound of Harley whining at the foot of the stairs cut her off in mid-flow. Under normal circumstances following a long walk, he would make a beeline straight for his water bowl, but on this occasion his only concern was the top of the staircase. He began to growl as he tentatively mounted a few steps, never shifting his gaze from the silent landing above.

'Sammy …?' Joanne called out again. 'Sammy, are you up there?'

The nervousness in Joanne's voice was palpable. Chris tried to get a response from Andy, but to no avail. The only other time he'd seen Harley behaving as cautiously was when The Puppeteer had come for Andy in Whitwell.

'Wait here,' he said, trying hard to conceal his own anxiety. 'I'll go and check upstairs.'

A change of clothes and a can of deodorant had been hastily stuffed into a carrier bag for Andy's benefit. Chris was still carrying it without thinking as he reached the landing where Samantha's bedroom door was wide open, and Harley was standing motionless in its threshold.

To most people in the modern, camera-phone age, discovering two youngsters lying asleep in the middle of the day would have been an irresistible photographic opportunity, something to be shared as a source of amusement for a later date, but not for Chris on this occasion. Although he couldn't speak for Andy, who'd still been out cold when he and Joanne had left earlier, Samantha in comparison had been a bundle of teenage energy. Right then, however, she appeared to be flat out from complete exhaustion, stretched out *across* the bed with Andy, as though they'd both just fallen on to it.

'Something's terribly wrong; I know it,' said Joanne from behind him, having crept quietly upstairs. 'I only have to look at Harley to know.' She placed an uncertain hand on Chris's arm. 'Samantha's told me that you and Andy both know about what's been happening to us recently; we've *got* to wake Samantha right now.'

Chris and Joanne strode as one into the room just as Samantha's previously motionless form began to jerk spasmodically, until she woke with a sudden jump, violent enough to lift her momentarily off the bed.

To begin with she seemed unaware of anything going on around her until Harley began to nuzzle her incessantly, but waking Andy was Samantha's priority, nobody else seemed to exist and her efforts noticeably gained more urgency when he at first appeared unresponsive. When Andy finally *did* wake up, he too seemed extremely vague, and his first conscious act was to reach out to Samantha.

Andy's embrace expressed reassurance and affection in equal amounts, and the way Samantha responded showed how much she needed both. For two young people to share such an intimate moment in front of their parents was highly unusual, and it only reinforced Joanne's fears.

'He's back again, isn't he, Sam?' she asked.

Everybody in the room knew who *he* was in the question. Samantha was a picture of despair as she pulled herself slightly away from Andy and looked down at the floor.

'He just appeared,' she mumbled. 'Out of nowhere …'

'In a dream like before?' asked Chris.

'No,' Samantha replied. 'I mean he was right *here*!'

'He materialised,' said Andy. 'That's what Sam's trying to say, it's like he was flesh and blood just like us. He wasn't here long but he really drained us. I've got no idea how long we've been out …'

The sudden sound of Samantha bursting into tears cut him short. From the moment Andy had held her in his arms, the remorse about consciously seeking out The Puppeteer had been building, and now her river of guilt had burst its banks. Both Andy and Joanne did their best, but Samantha was inconsolable.

'Andy, I'm *really* sorry!' she sobbed. 'I know you said there might be a way we could fight him, but I can't take any more and I went to him while I was asleep. I just wanted to know why he said all those things … I wanted to know what he *meant*. I'm *so* sorry.'

The unthinkable consequences of Samantha finding solace with The Puppeteer made Chris go cold. Had she made a deal? Was she still an Innocent and able to bear the child? Approaching The Puppeteer voluntarily was the last thing Chris had expected from Samantha, and God only knew what else she might have found out!

'But nothing he says to me *ever* makes any sense,' Samantha continued, much to Chris's relief. 'He never tells me anything, but it's *so* obvious he's hiding something from me, and he gets a real kick out of me not knowing.'

'But we *can* fight him,' said Andy. 'You haven't done anything wrong and nothing has changed.'

'Damned right it hasn't! My life is totally over!'

'No, it isn't, Sam; don't talk like that!'

'I might just as well be dead, and I wish I bloody well was!'

That was *it* as far as Joanne was concerned. Chilled to the bone, she asked for a few moments to be alone with her daughter, but Samantha insisted that everybody should stay.

Samantha looked and sounded totally broken, and although it had been made in the heat of the moment, the force of her outburst suggested an element of intent. The possibility of Samantha becoming her *own* assassin had never even entered Chris's mind, and yet The Puppeteer could well have already looked at it as a viable option. The way he was just eroding her piece by piece seemed as if it was all just part of another plan, because if his chosen assassin should fail, then Samantha could always come up with the solution herself. All The Puppeteer wanted was Samantha dead, and by whatever means possible.

Not for the first time, Chris found himself consumed with guilt. However inadvertently, he'd left Samantha exposed. The Puppeteer had appeared purely to nip the chance of anything happening between the two young lovers firmly in the bud, and if Chris had been present in the cottage instead of galivanting around with Samantha's mother, the situation would never have come about. Passing Andy the change of clothes he'd collected from Whitwell, Chris suggested that it might be a good idea to make some tea and coffee. He was struggling to come to terms with his mistake and needed to be alone.

The previously calm atmosphere of the cottage had changed, poisoned by fear and uncertainty, but at least Harley seemed to be more like his usual self, having followed Chris faithfully into the kitchen. Harley had a strong reaction when he sensed the presence of The Puppeteer, and Chris found himself occasionally watching the dog closely, looking for any sign that the ultimate uninvited guest might be about make another unwelcome visit. The idea of that malevolence coming for Chris *himself* had moved disturbingly to the forefront of his mind. Surely it was only going to be a matter of time, or was the protection offered by Zambaya that much stronger as Andy had previously suggested? Chris tried to erase it from his mind until the sharp click of the kettle switching itself off startled him. He cursed himself under his breath for his edginess and then went about preparing the coffee, but then some distant strains of music began to filter down from Samantha's bedroom, the sound of something familiar to lighten the heaviness of the air at last.

Chris had just found out where the mugs were kept when Joanne walked into the kitchen, her confused and troubled expression unnerving him instantly.

'How's Samantha doing?' he asked. It seemed like a ridiculous question under the circumstances, but it was the only thing he could think of to say.

'Like she's somebody else if I'm being honest,' Joanne replied, flopping down dejectedly onto a chair at the kitchen table. She was silent for a moment, but then she took a deep breath and leant forwards with more authority.

'Listen, Chris,' she said. 'I need to know *everything* you know about this. Samantha's in bits, and Andy says that you're the best person to talk to about it. What the hell's happening to my daughter? If you really *do* know what's going on, then as Samantha's mother I think I've got a right to know!'

Despite her suddenly assertive tone, there was no lack of warmth in Joanne's eyes as she gazed inquiringly at Chris, but they demanded a truth that he couldn't possibly reveal. Joanne had quickly begun to mean everything, and yet he could tell her nothing.

Chris sat down opposite Joanne and clasped her hands in his.

'I hope you've got an open mind,' he said.

'Right now I think that I could believe just about anything,' she replied.

Just as he had before with Andy and Samantha, Chris started from the very beginning. Joanne was horrified and yet enthralled by his terrifying account of what it was like to die, about another side of life, and learning about a mystical African called Zambaya.

All the time Chris was speaking, he seemed perfectly at ease with what he'd experienced even though it was way beyond the familiar condition of human physicality and consciousness. At times, Joanne felt like she was listening to somebody elaborating upon a series of surreal dreams, but yet such detailed awareness was far more than could be easily imagined or invented.

When Chris began speaking about The Puppeteer, Joanne understood that Samantha's tormentor was the antithesis of what Chris had referred to as The Truth, but it was very noticeable how he suddenly became inexplicably vague when it came to The Puppeteer's direct involvement with her daughter. Considering the knowledge that Chris clearly possessed about everything else, the sudden ambiguity regarding what Joanne wanted to learn about most was extremely disappointing, and more than a little suspicious.

'So, are you telling me this is something that we've just got to put up with?' she asked. 'Because that's what it sounds like. Andy and Samantha are certain that we've all been brought together for a reason, but you didn't say anything about that.'

'But I've told you all I can,' replied Chris.

'Have you? The Puppeteer isn't random; he's a planner, Andy told me that too, so is Sammy a part of a plan as well?'

'It's a possibility …'

'A possibility? I think it's a lot more than that, Chris! I never used to believe in the Devil, but it's like he's taken over our bloody lives! Nothing you've just said explains why Sammy's become a target for something like The Puppeteer, and from what I've just heard upstairs, the lengths he's going to are extraordinary. If you're avoiding the issue for whatever reason, then stop because I need you to be honest with me. She's just an ordinary girl, for God's sake, so why *is* he doing this to her? God Almighty, it's enough to make you think she's going to be giving birth to the second-bloody-coming!'

It was just an off-the-cuff remark laden with bitter irony, and yet the result was like an incendiary bomb being dropped in the room. Chris's expression of total dismay spoke all the words he was unable to say, and Joanne realised that she'd just unintentionally hit the most unbelievable of nails squarely on the head. Immediately she tried to dismiss it; the very notion was ridiculous, but Chris's noticeable alarm and The Puppeteer's ceaseless obsession with Samantha all pointed to a terrifying reality.

'But that's *impossible*,' she whispered, shaking her head. 'It *has* to be!'

All Chris could do was look down at the table and avoid looking Joanne in the eye. Living a lie to protect Zambaya's secret had simply proved too much, and suddenly he couldn't have felt any less inclined to deny what she'd just uncovered despite her devastation.

'I'm so sorry, Jo,' he said. 'Truly I am.'

'So it's *true*?' she asked. 'That's what all this is really *about*?'

'The Puppeteer, *your* family, *my* family,' Chris replied. 'All of us meeting the way we have? We've all been brought together because The Truth has chosen Samantha to bear its child.'

'But why? Why choose *my* little girl … *my* baby? I don't understand!'

'Why any of us? I don't understand it either, Jo. I'm so sorry.'

Instead of being targeted by a malignant evil like The Puppeteer, Samantha should have been enjoying every moment of life's big adventure. It was bad enough in itself that Zambaya and the Supreme Collective had expected Joanne to remain unenlightened in the face of her daughter's misery, and when she learned that Samantha was going to have to remain completely unaware of what was being planned for her, she snapped completely.

'You seriously expect me to just … just … *keep* this from her?' she asked, snatching her hands away from Chris's grasp. 'Like you were intending to carry on keeping it from *me*, no doubt?'

'But I've been sworn to secrecy, Jo … by Zambaya. Apart from me, you're the *only other* living person that knows, and it's got to stay that way. None of us asked for this, none of us has had any choice, and believe me it's not exactly been easy for me living with what I know about this either!'

Without thinking, Chris had just made the most inappropriate comment imaginable. To a desperate mother, frantic about the welfare of a child, nothing else mattered, and in Joanne's case, that child happened to be her only daughter.

Whatever Chris may or may not have been going through wasn't even on Joanne's radar, and it seemed like he was just making a case for himself. Was it her imagination, or were most men just *born* selfish?

'I think I should take Samantha out somewhere,' she said. 'I need to get out of the house.'

'Sounds like a good idea to me. Where shall we go?'

'Not *we*, Chris, *I*.'

Joanne shrugged her shoulders at his evident hurt.

'Well, *you* being around isn't exactly going to change anything, is it?' she added. 'I mean it's like you just said, it's 'not exactly been easy' for you either, has it?'

And then she began to lash out at him, making it clear that she thought Chris was only interested in protecting his and Zambaya's interests rather than Samantha's.

'I mean, why *else* would you have wanted to keep it all from us?' she asked.

'Jesus, Jo! It's nothing like that! How can you even *think* that?'

'Well, what else am I supposed to think, other than keeping your secret meaning more to you than us? Just think about what Sammy and I have been through, then ask yourself how *you'd* feel if it was the other way around … you know, everything all hunky-dory, all singing and dancing, and then BANG! something comes into your life that's so evil, even the *air* crushes you when it's near. Something that casts a shadow over *everything* you do … sits there, like a cancer, just waiting to spread into another part of your life! And to top it all, just when you think that things can't get any worse, you find out, purely by accident I might add, that the most precious thing in your life has been chosen to give birth to God!'

An awfully heavy silence descended upon the kitchen once Joanne's onslaught had abated, and the sudden absence of music filtering down from

Samantha's bedroom only added to its weight. Chris thought he might try a different approach.

'I know how difficult it must be,' he said. 'Believe me, I *do*, but ...'

'And how the hell could you *possibly* know, Chris? Huh? Tell me! You have no *bloody idea* what it's like to endure what *we've* had to! Anyway, I seem to remember you saying something about helping your mother this afternoon.'

'What?'

'Well, it's important to her, isn't it?'

'Come on Jo, *nothing* is as important as this!'

'And you think I don't know that? That's why I need time to be *alone* with my daughter! I've known her face for nearly twenty years, Chris, and it's killing me to see her like this. I've never seen her looking so desperate and fragile; she needs me now more than ever!'

'What's going on?' came Samantha's questioning tone, cutting through the tension. Joanne and Chris had been so involved with each other that neither of them had been aware of Andy and Samantha coming downstairs.

At first Chris was afraid of what Samantha might have heard, but neither she nor Andy seemed perturbed about anything other than seeing their respective parents having a very obvious disagreement. Despite Chris's relief, however, their untimely appearance had destroyed any hope of an immediate resolution to matters between him and Joanne. Chris knew he'd lost Joanne's trust, and there seemed little hope of him ever getting it back.

The Puppeteer was winning.

What should have been keeping The Circle together was tearing it apart.

CHAPTER 30

'And how would you like it, sir?'

Momentarily side-tracked, Wayne stared blankly into the mirror at the hirsute barber's reflection, and then at his own. Having a haircut on this occasion should be more than just a trim. Wayne wanted the Middleton's respect when he cleansed them and felt his appearance should matter, but he couldn't imagine anything markedly different from what was gazing cluelessly back at him.

'How about I let *you* decide?' he suggested.

'Hmmm,' mused the barber. 'Do you have anything particular in mind?'

'Not really.'

'Are we talking job interview, business meeting, or hot date?'

'Let's just say that I intend to create an impression!'

Wayne smiled knowingly, and a toothy grin appeared through the barber's dark and well-groomed beard.

'Well in that case, my friend,' the barber said. 'We'd better make sure you're going to be sharp enough then!'

"Sharp enough ..." Wayne chuckled to himself at the irony and the thought of the lethal blade in his hotel room awaiting him like a hungry lover. In time that hunger would be satisfied, but in the meantime, Wayne was happy enough to get prepared for the bloodletting.

Relaxed in a dark green leather chair that was far more comfortable than its slightly worn appearance might have suggested, Wayne felt completely at ease with himself. As a natural loner, he couldn't have picked a better time to get his hair cut. Not only was the barber's shop pleasingly empty of customers, but all the other stylists were at lunch, so there was nobody around that might be able to see into his head. The barber was also an unsuspecting and uncomplicated man with simple views on life, and someone to whom Wayne could oddly relate. Before long, through the sounds of buzzing clippers and clicking scissors, a conversation had begun to develop in tandem with Wayne's new look. It transpired that the barber was having trouble with a particularly demanding girlfriend, and Wayne found it something of a struggle not to offer his services. Sometimes it was difficult to bear the cross of his incredible talent and hide such a unique gift from others less fortunate than himself, and as much as Wayne wanted to help the poor downtrodden barber, there was other, far more important business that needed his attention.

Wayne found himself having to concentrate upon his reflection to contain his overwhelming lust for the kill, and was quickly surprised by his developing new image. He'd never really been bothered about his appearance before, and if it hadn't had been for the unique opportunities that had presented themselves leading up to that point, that would have undoubtedly remained the case. But, as the barber continued to work into the blank canvas of Wayne's once unruly thatch, Wayne was struck by how different he'd suddenly begun to look. The boyish, rather angular face that he'd become accustomed to now seemed fuller somehow, broadened by the short crop above and around his ears. His jawline seemed more masculine, and the stubble he'd been unintentionally cultivating had been neatened, sharpened into something neater and more clearly defined. The transformation was so extraordinary that Wayne began to wonder if he might be looking at somebody else.

A few minutes and a little sculpting wax later, the quirky, haphazard and dishevelled Wayne Terry was gone, the pathetic creature once scared of its own shadow dead and buried, and like a phoenix, Joshua Gains had risen gloriously from its miserable ashes. Where Wayne had failed in his chaotic efforts, Joshua Gains was fated to succeed, and Joanne and Samantha Middleton wouldn't know what had hit them.

But such positivity was hardly evident in Chris's car where all Andy could feel was his father's absolute, silent dejection.

Whereas Chris and Andy had both been given a warm send off by Samantha, Joanne and Chris hadn't exchanged so much as a word, and the atmosphere between them had almost been toxic. Andy could only guess at what might have happened to bring about such a dramatic change in their relationship, but if the discomfiting mood in the Audi estate was anything to go by, the topic wasn't open for discussion.

Andy felt that he was entirely to blame for what he was seeing: Joanne, scared out of her wits over what was happening to Samantha, had been looking for her own answers, and it might have been the worst decision he'd ever made in his life to suggest that she should approach his father in pursuit of them. It might have made Andy feel even worse knowing that Joanne and Samantha weren't speaking to each other, either, for just like the tense, silent interior of Chris's car, all conversation between them too had become a complete nonentity. Joanne had insisted on leaving the house and going into Hitchin town for a bite to eat, but neither she or her daughter had any appetite to speak of, and Samantha was clearly sulking about having her time with Andy cut so inexplicably short.

Joanne felt hurt and guilty at the same time, finding Samantha's frosty attitude about as easy to swallow as Chris's devastating revelations. Their whole world lay in ruins, and as they wandered aimlessly through Hitchin town centre's narrow, cobbled streets, she could see no end to the nightmare.

It was then that Joanne's eyes fell upon a fluorescent green poster, brazenly mounted upon a billboard outside an old public house. Under normal circumstances, the words 'Psychic Fair' wouldn't have held any interest for either her or Samantha, but something other than just mere curiosity seemed to be drawing them in.

Via a freshly painted glossy black door, Joanne and Samantha entered a quaint and relaxing bar. White walls and contrasting black beams proudly showed off the pub's Tudor heritage, and the acrid smell of fresh paint and creosote hanging in the air suggested the premises had only recently been refurbished. A smiling bartender directed Joanne and Samantha to a narrow flight of stairs that led to a function room called The Hayloft, an intimate, low-ceilinged room in which several stalls displaying a variety of spiritual and oriental artifacts had been comfortably arranged. A row of small, leaded windows along one side of the room only permitted entry to a small amount of light, but The Hayloft still retained a warm and welcoming feel in spite of its dimness, and whispered conversations from a handful of visitors competed with strains of calming meditation music, flowing freely from an unseen sound system.

Samantha's eyes were drawn to some Celtic art, but Joanne felt herself attracted to a simple stall displaying a collection of glittering crystals, polished gems, and numerous colourful tarot card decks. Fascinated, Joanne picked up a book on the subject of the tarot, and began to flick randomly through its pages.

'Interesting, isn't it?'

The bubbly voice made Joanne look across at the round and friendly face of the woman running the stall.

'The tarot,' the woman said. 'A very interesting subject.'

Joanne placed the book back on the table.

'Oh, I'm sorry,' she replied. 'I hope you didn't mind me touching anything.'

'There's nothing wrong with curiosity or taking an interest,' said the stallholder with a smile. 'Are you thinking of learning how to read the cards yourself?'

Joanne shook her head.

'No … I've always been a bit wary about that sort of thing for some reason.'

'Wary? Why?'

'Well, it's all bit weird, isn't it?'

'And yet you find yourself at a psychic fair?'

Joanne had absolutely no idea what had drawn her in, and found herself unable to come up with any kind of an answer.

'Well, right there might be the root of your problem,' said the stallholder. 'Because it's all about perceptions. The tarot is very misunderstood and misrepresented, pretty much like *everything* on a spiritual level ... I suppose that's because of how we are, as people, I mean. If we don't understand something, we either mock it or fear it. There's never an in-between.'

The woman's enthusiasm was captivating, and she seemed happy to speak openly, but for all the evident sincerity on display, Joanne had her doubts.

'So, how do tarot cards work, then?' she asked. 'Can they really predict the future?'

'If I had a fiver from everyone who'd asked me that, I wouldn't have to do this in my spare time!' the stallholder replied. 'And that's another misconception that a lot of people have. The tarot is more about guidance and enlightenment. Sometimes we all need a little help with our personal journeys. By showing us our past and how it has brought us to the present, the cards can indicate where we are going, or, how a certain situation is likely to unfold. In my experience, not *everything* is set. It all depends on the influences around us in the here and now.'

The stallholder glanced across at Joanne and sensed that she was looking at a deeply troubled woman.

'I take it you've never had a reading done, then?' she said.

Joanne shook her head.

'Well, in that case, how about we change that right now? It'll only take a few minutes.'

After a moment's deliberation, Joanne's curiosity finally got the better of her and she reluctantly agreed. The stallholder smiled, reached into her handbag and took out a white silk scarf which she carefully began to unfold, revealing a colourful, beautifully illustrated tarot deck. Then, she passed the cards over to Joanne and advised her to shuffle the pack, split it into three separate stacks, and then place each one face down upon the table.

At first, Joanne was all fingers and thumbs. The cards were considerably larger than the standard playing variety, and numbered seventy-eight, significantly more than the fifty-two with which she was familiar. It didn't help that she was beginning to feel nervous, either, but eventually she stopped fumbling, and once she was satisfied the cards had been shuffled enough, split the deck into three as instructed and waited.

'Your influence is now on the cards,' said the stallholder. 'Each stack represents a part of your life, your recent past, your current situation, and what is to come. Now, take one stack and spread it out, pick one card and turn it over so that it's face up.'

Joanne chose a stack to signify her recent past and selected a card. All the cards were face down, and yet she felt oddly drawn to the back of one in particular, which revealed itself as The Hermit when turned over. A sombre, solitary male figure clad in a drab brown robe and carrying a lantern, the card suggested loneliness until its symbolism was briefly outlined as being a break from the complexities of life and a need for more emotional balance, calmness and guidance. It was all relative and easy to listen to, but then the stallholder began to go into even more depth.

'In this past position,' she said, 'The Hermit can signify that there has been a refusal to face up to the truth and that this is something that needs to change.' She looked over at a visibly unsettled Joanne. 'Shall we see how The Hermit links with your current circumstances?'

Just as before, the back of one card seemed to stand out more than any of its neighbours once Joanne had spread out the second stack. This time, she turned over The Empress, but any sense of joy suggested by the pictorial beauty of a woman seated in a flourishing garden was to be destroyed by its meaning. A symbol of fertility, nurturing and motherhood, the card of The Empress was often symbolic of a coming pregnancy.

Everything Chris had said was being confirmed before Joanne's disbelieving eyes. Her heart was pounding so hard in her chest that her ears were throbbing. With trembling hands, she somehow managed to turn over a card from the third and final stack that represented her future, a card framing the regal image of a powerful-looking king holding a golden chalice.

Unlike its predecessors, the third card was both untitled and unnumbered, but that didn't lessen its importance.

'The King of Cups,' the stallholder said. 'A man who has the quality of being able to keep his head when all around are losing theirs. He stands for strength and protection; a stabilising force.' Then, she placed the king, precisely and respectfully, sideways across the other two. 'Although the king of cups is a future influence, I sense that this influence is also in your present,' she added. 'There is no ring on your finger, but this suggests to me that there is a man in your life, and according to this card he has a role to play in what needs to be resolved. This is made clear when we link him to the other cards of The Hermit and The Empress, and we are able to read all three influences together.'

Joanne stood in complete silence, struck dumb by all she'd seen and heard.

Despite his otherwise enduring expression, the King of Cups stared out at her accusingly, almost like he was demanding an explanation as to why she'd so badly hurt the good man his card represented. Chris was utterly blameless, just another part of The Circle along with the rest of them, and God only knew what it must have been like for him having to bear such an impossible truth alone. Joanne knew she'd made a terrible mistake turning on him the way that she had, and suddenly she hated herself.

'Angela?'

The stallholder looked up and saw Samantha.

'Oh my God, it *is* you!' Samantha added. 'I wasn't sure at first!'

Fortunately for Joanne, Samantha had chosen a very opportune moment to recognise the receptionist from the A&E Department from the day of her mother's accident, and Joanne used the perfectly timed distraction to blink away a couple of tears, unnoticed.

'Well, if it isn't the girl with the beautiful smile!' said Angela. 'Samantha, isn't it? And judging by the uncanny resemblance, I'd say that this lady here has *got* to be your mother!'

A more collected Joanne managed to introduce herself, and then Samantha noticed the upturned tarot cards on the table in front of her.

'Wow!' she said. 'I'd no idea you did this! Do you do readings as well, then?'

'Most of the people I work with think I'm a witch!' Angela replied. 'I was just giving your mum a quick demonstration.'

Samantha was surprised by her mother's sudden curiosity in the tarot, but according to Joanne, the 'interesting' reading had been 'mainly about work stuff'.

'That bugger there is probably Harvey Davies!' she said, pointing to the King of Cups. 'He thinks far too much of himself!'

'I think your mum's been working too hard, Samantha, but I daresay she's heard all that before from you!'

The laughter that followed seemed slightly forced. Angela didn't need all of her psychic ability to see that Joanne was trying to keep something hidden, and there was something else making her feel very uneasy. The longer she spent in Samantha's company, the more she became aware of a disturbing presence and a mysterious darkness. The beautiful smile Angela remembered from their previous encounter just didn't seem the same, but perhaps the cards would shed some light on the matter.

'Well then, young Samantha,' said Angela. 'Seeing as you seem rather interested yourself, would you like to see what the cards might have to say to *you*?'

Samantha agreed without so much as a second thought, and Joanne suddenly felt extremely anxious. Angela had been so incredibly accurate before, and it was possible that she could reveal the secret that Chris had been struggling so valiantly to keep.

Almost unable to watch, Joanne held her breath as Samantha turned over her first card, which was The Eight of Swords. Angela described the unnerving image of a bound and blindfolded woman surrounded by eight lethal-looking blades as being something of a paradox when read on its own, so Samantha was invited to turn over the second card from her 'present circumstances' to get a better idea of how the two would work together.

But if the first card hadn't been disturbing enough, the second, an image of a man and a woman plunging to the ground from a blazing lightning-stuck tower was seriously alarming. The illustration was like something straight out of a seventies disaster movie, and not for the first time since she'd been in Angela's company Joanne's heart began to beat faster.

'Well,' said Angela. 'Swords are a suit that deal with matters of the mind, our mental perceptions, and the eight suggests that recently you have felt restricted, lacking freedom, that you are feeling powerless. The card of The Shattered Tower not only speaks of unexpected events and great shock, it can also point to a breaking down or breaking away from an outworn sense of values. Next to The Eight of Swords, The Shattered Tower suggest a need to break free of something that has a strong, mental hold over you. Would you understand what that means?'

A whispered 'yes' from Samantha sounded almost unbearably loud in the intense silence. Joanne hoped that it was her imagination, but Angela had started to look concerned.

And then Samantha turned over her last card, depicting a horned, grinning black-eyed abomination that stared chillingly out at her. Held in each of his two gnarled hands were a set of heavy chains, at the ends of which a manacled man and woman stood captive, prisoners of the creature's vile intent. Samantha instantly put her hand to her mouth and Joanne's heart nearly leapt out of her chest.

'The Devil,' said Angela. 'His card sits across the others, and combined with The Eight of Swords and The Shattered Tower it says that you are bound to something from which you feel you mentally and spiritually cannot escape, an obstacle that seems immovable.'

Samantha's distress confirmed to Angela why a part of her had decided to attend the fair when most of her couldn't have cared less. Angela had definitely got out of the wrong side of bed that morning, her mood had been suitably foul, and the idea of standing and smiling at curious patrons who couldn't really have given a damn about what she had to sell had hardly filled her with enthusiasm. But something inside her had said that her presence at the fair was going to be a necessity for somebody, and the necessity was standing right in front of her in the form of a terrified young woman who looked like her world had just been turned completely upside down.

The darkness Angela had sensed was a scar on Samantha's being, a sore to be opened at will by the unspeakable evil that had left it. Mother and daughter had both had readings, and there would undoubtedly be a connection between them, but Angela's primary concern right then was Samantha. Angela asked another stallholder to watch over her display for a few moments while she took both Samantha and Joanne into a side room. Once in private, she held Samantha's hands in hers and said: 'I can see that you're frightened, Samantha, and I don't believe it was just the reading. I can see that there is something near that has a very nasty hold over you.'

'Yes,' Samantha whispered.

'I really want to help you, and I think I can.'

'I wish you could.'

But Joanne was in no mood for anything resembling false hope. It wasn't so much Angela's authenticity that was the issue, it was Samantha's sudden fragility.

'Come on, Sammy,' she said. 'We ought to go.'

'But Mum …'

'*I'm* not the one you need to protect Samantha from,' said Angela. 'I'm trying to help her. I *know* I can help her.'

'And just how do you think you can do that?' asked Joanne. 'You have no idea what my daughter's been going through, and a few tarot cards wouldn't have been able to tell you!'

'Mum, *please!*' Samantha sighed. 'At least let's listen to what Angela's got to say!'

Joanne went to grab Samantha's hand and lead her away, but Angela had other ideas, subtly positioning her large frame to prevent it.

'I can understand how all this must seem to you right now, Joanne,' she said. 'Some random woman that you've never met thinking that she suddenly knows best? But I can see *much more* than you know, and I can tell that your daughter is under what we call Psychic Attack. She's being haunted or attacked by a bad spirit, and I didn't need the cards to tell me that because I can *see* it, I can see that Samantha's been marked by an entity, and it comes to her frequently.'

Angela saw the colour drain from Joanne's face. Samantha saw it too.

'Mum?' she asked again. 'Please … I really think we ought to listen.'

'Bad spirits leave these marks,' Angela continued. 'Scars on our souls and upon our being. It's how they seem to find us at will, no matter how hard we might try and hide from them. Now, Samantha, tell me what's been happening to you.'

Joanne listened intently as Samantha told Angela everything from the very beginning. She had to admit to herself that she had been astonished by Angela's abilities, but just couldn't find it within herself to trust the mystical stallholder as much as her daughter.

'It's like The Puppeteer took a part of me that first time,' said Samantha, having finished her account. 'And I can't get it back.'

'That's because he *did* take something from you,' said Angela. 'And he's replaced it with a part of himself.'

'Oh my God! Is that what he did?'

Angela thought for a moment.

'The only way I can explain it is that it's a bit like when we visit a website and the site leaves a tracking cookie on our computer. It makes it easier for us to find that website again. What this entity has done to you is the same, but in reverse. What we need to do is either delete that cookie or make it invisible, so that the spirit can no longer 'see' you.'

'Or maybe we could just alter my cookie settings?'

Angela laughed, heartily.

'Just keep that attitude going, Sam, and you're going to do just fine!'

And then she reached out towards something resembling a small black briefcase and opened it up, carefully removing a number of clear plastic bags. Each bag contained a different type of crystal or highly polished stone.

'These gems are pure,' said Angela. 'Nobody else has touched them. Now, Samantha, just like you did with the tarot cards, I want you to select three bags.'

'Any three?'

'Any ... and then out of each bag you've chosen, remove just one random stone.'

Samantha did exactly as she'd been told, and then waited.

'Why did you pick these stones in particular?' asked Angela.

'They just drew me to them. I felt them pull me ... I can't explain it any other way.'

'It's because you allowed the stones to speak to you. They chose *you* equally as much as you chose *them*.'

Joanne had never heard of anything so stupid. Forgetting how she herself had been so curiously drawn to the cards she'd chosen for her tarot reading, it was all she could do just to remain silent. Angela could sense Joanne's hostility, but she was too busy explaining the benefits of Samantha's choices to bother with such narrowmindedness.

'The stones you have chosen, Samantha, are Fire Agate, Black Tourmaline and Dalmatian Jasper,' she said. 'It's an *extremely* potent combination. Each stone has strong protective or healing qualities, particularly the Tourmaline, which is a powerful protector even on its own. Some of the energy from the spirit that comes to you is trapped *inside* you, that's the part of him he has left behind. The Fire Agate will draw it out, the Dalmatian Jasper will heal the wound, and the Tourmaline will deflect the entity and those dreadful creatures you spoke about if they try to come for you again. These stones have been forged either *in*, or *by*, the fires of the Earth herself; they come to you by divine grace, and divine grace only. Not even the entity that attacks you can match *that* power. Now, put them in this and keep them with you at all times.'

Angela passed Samantha a small black velvet pouch which was attached to a braided cord necklace. Then, she hung the simple combination around Samantha's neck.

'There,' she said with a smile. 'All yours!'

Samantha held the pouch briefly in her hand.

'Thank you *so* much,' she whispered and gave Angela a hug. 'I don't know what else to say. How much do I owe you?'

'Nothing.'

'But ...'

Angela made a gesture towards her rotund build.

'This is a gift from somewhere even bigger than me!' she said. 'The stones are rightfully yours.'

The more Joanne listened, the more far-fetched everything became, and it was particularly disturbing for her to see how easily Samantha had been taken in. Despite Angela's sincerity and conviction, all that mattered to Joanne was Samantha's wellbeing, and no amount of hocus-pocus was going to help in that respect. The Puppeteer wasn't going to go away, and when he decided to brutalise her again, the consequences would doubtlessly be even *more* devastating. What use would these stupid little stones be then?

Joanne made out as though she was going to follow on behind Samantha once her daughter had left, but stopped and closed the door instead.

'You seem very sure about this,' she said. 'I *do* believe you have a gift, Angela, and I really do appreciate that you have your beliefs, but I doubt you've ever experienced anything *like* what comes for my daughter, and what really worries me is that you seemed to have convinced her that there's a chance of this working.'

'If she's allowed to *believe*, there's *every* chance that it will!' Angela replied.

The swipe had hardly been veiled, and Angela immediately regretted her frankness when she saw the shock on Joanne's face.

'Listen … Joanne,' she sighed. 'I'm a mother too, and I know how I would feel in your position.'

'But you're not *in* my position, *are* you?' Joanne replied.

'But that doesn't mean that I can't see it from *your* perspective, does it? Look, sometimes it helps when somebody else is looking in from the outside. It's like when you're standing too close to a large painting and you can't see as much as somebody who's standing further back, right? I can't explain how or why I see things that others can't, but there was a reason why you and Samantha came here today, and now Samantha's been given something to hold on to.'

'You think that three stupid little stones that aren't going to change anything is something to hold on to?'

'Was there anything 'stupid' about your readings earlier, then?'

The swift rebuttal stunned Joanne into silence. As if she needed reminding!

'I don't blame you for being protective,' Angela added, taking full advantage. 'But I'm not trying to be a cuckoo in the nest here, Joanne. It isn't as though Samantha has suddenly stopped listening to you, is it? I can sense that there is a lot of guilt around you, that you have judged somebody unfairly at a time when you cannot afford to be judgemental, and I'm not talking about me, either. It's a gift to see what others can't and my gift is genuine, but I don't need psychic powers to see how much Samantha looks up to you and how much you mean to each other, and that makes it even *more* important that she feels she has your *support* in this, Joanne, and not your *doubts*.'

Tears instantly welled up in Joanne's eyes. Once again, Angela had been spot on. She had no idea of the true scale of the problem because otherwise her gift would have allowed her to 'see'. It was further evidence for Joanne that the secrets of The Circle were meant to remain intact, and that she was going to have to be stronger for Samantha than she'd ever been before.

'I'm sorry,' said Angela. 'I didn't mean to upset you. Being a medium means that I say what comes into my mind at times like these because the truth is often the hardest thing to accept. But *something* brought you here today to hear all of this, something that wanted to make you strong by facing some facts. Faith is a shield for many; I'm living proof, but faith is only a *weapon* when we learn to truly believe. Your daughter is a born fighter, Joanne, just like you are. I can see how much the two of you have been through together in the past and, in some ways, this is no different, but you *both* need to believe she can win in order for her to come through.'

Joanne wanted to offer her thanks as well as apologise for her prickly attitude, but the lump in her throat wouldn't let her speak. Instead, all she could do was smile weakly and walk away with her thoughts rather than crumble in front of a complete stranger.

With the sound of Joanne's footsteps quietly fading away, Angela closed the door of the side room and reached for the alabaster cross around her neck that she'd shown Samantha at the hospital. There was clearly something extremely special about Samantha and her mother that had attracted the purest evil into their lives, but whatever it was had been mysteriously hidden from Angela's eyes. Angela had to admit to herself that Joanne was right about her never having experienced what had been coming for her daughter, for it was more than just a 'bad spirit'. Whatever had left the horrific mark that she had seen upon Samantha's being had power beyond anything she would ever wish to encounter.

Angela kissed the alabaster cross and clutched it to her chest.

And then she prayed for Joanne and Samantha.

She prayed so hard, her whole body began to shake.

CHAPTER 31

Anne frowned. Although helping to fine-tune the organisation of a village fete wasn't Chris's usual remit, it seemed reasonable enough for her to expect more from him than just plain, disinterested silence. His lack of involvement wasn't going unnoticed by the rest of the Whitwell Village Council, either, as they all sat awkwardly contemplating their various beverages in Anne's living room.

The atmosphere was uncomfortable and sterile, but Chris couldn't have cared less about a village fete or it's noble, charitable cause. The only cause that mattered to him was Joanne and Samantha, and they could have been anywhere right then, out of sight and unprotected.

And just as bad all of a sudden was that he had no idea where he stood with Joanne, either. Did she still want him in her life? Was there going to be any chance of a future for Andy and Samantha? Everything was floating in the air, scattered like helpless dandelion seeds drifting randomly upon the whim of a summer breeze.

Chris's mobile decided to burst into life from a worksurface in the kitchen. Without so much as an apology, he leapt up from his seat, thinking it might be Joanne, but his enthusiasm dissolved immediately when he saw the name of Connor Stevens on the screen instead. Disappointment must have been all too obvious in Chris's voice when he answered, judging by the apparent concern in his colleague's tone.

'Are you okay, Chris?' the young detective asked. 'You sound a bit pissed off. Have I picked a bad time?'

Chris thought about the vultures waiting to pick his bones clean in the living room, and realised that his colleague had actually timed his call to perfection.

'No, it's fine,' he replied. 'You're okay, Connor, I wasn't quite with it, that's all.'

'I could call back?'

'No, please … carry on.'

Previously, Chris had said he was happy to be kept up to speed on the two ongoing murder cases back at his Colindale base, and Stevens had decided to get in touch as there had been some significant developments. Chris looked for somewhere more private so as not to be interrupted. The garden would be ideal, and the back door was conveniently located in the kitchen so he could sneak out without being noticed. The meeting was getting up to speed judging by the murmuring coming from the living room, and after a furtive check to make sure no one was looking, Chris took his opportunity to escape, and stepped outside.

'Sorry about that, Connor,' he said. 'Mum's got some stuff going on ... what have you got?'

'Well,' Stevens began. 'We're now certain that the Mill Hill and Colindale killings are connected, and we've got a very strong suspect, a guy called Wayne Terry.'

Stevens went into a little more detail, revealing Wayne's connection with Monique and the part she'd played in the breakdown of Wayne's relationship with his mother.

'There was no forced entry at Mill Hill, so we think that Miss Dacourt must have known her killer,' he said. 'Wayne Terry's name also came up from our enquiries at the strip club in Colindale. Terry knew the victim there as well. He was seen with her and we've got matching DNA profiles from both murder scenes, and matching fingerprints.'

'Sounds like a really solid start,' said Chris. 'So very well done there! You've obviously got enough to bring Terry in. Are there any more developments on that score?'

'Yeah, we've got enough to bring him in alright, but Terry's disappeared. His neighbours say he left suddenly and hasn't been seen since. We got a search warrant and forced our way in; I'm at his flat now with the team ...'

'Christ! That was quick!'

'Thankfully, yes, because there's been some more going on since we obtained it. Two young women were attacked a few days ago out where you are, and Stevenage nick has been in touch with us today. I believe you know DCI Mike Devonshire there? Anyway, the thing is, Chris, they just got the DNA results from the samples their team obtained and they match the profiles of the ones we have here. We've got three dead women now, and the finger's pointing straight at Terry.'

Chris shuddered as a chilling veil of coldness unfurled itself around him. Wayne Terry could be far more significant than Stevens knew! There was every chance he was The Puppeteer's chosen assassin.

The whole dynamic had changed dramatically all of a sudden. Somehow, Chris *had* to smooth things over with Joanne in order for him to keep Samantha in sight, and it was vital he knew as much as he could about Wayne Terry. If Terry *was* the assassin, he might be less of a planner and more of an opportunist, which would make him even *more* dangerous.

'Is anybody building up a picture of the suspect?' he asked. 'What about his movements, habits ... Does he drive? Are there any photographs of him, or any CCTV footage, and what about the other attacks in Mill Hill and Colindale ... do they appear random or premeditated?'

'Bloody hell, Chris ... I thought you were supposed to be resting! We're working on it. Relax; you make it sound like you want be involved!'

'What exactly did Mike Devonshire say to you today, Connor?'

'That he wanted it known how bloody good you were at your job!'

'That's nice to know but it wouldn't have been everything!'

'... and that it was you who found the girl who survived the attack on his ground.'

'So now can you understand why I might want to know something, then! I know what the killer's capable of, and now that DNA has eliminated any reasonable doubt about a connection, I want to lend my expertise. If I can help Mike Devonshire, I will, and if between all of us we can catch this bastard before he kills again and it means I have to get involved, then so be it. If Wayne Terry killed the two women in your area, and then he killed Sarah Murrell, there's a strong possibility he might still be out this way ... and if he *is* still out in these parts, then I'm out here too!'

'But you're off-duty, on the sick!' Stevens protested. 'And you're the DCI!'

'Come on, Connor, you arrested a bloke when you were on holiday once, so don't give me that! I know I'm on the sick and that I'm a DCI, but that doesn't change anything. I'll always be a bloody copper no matter what!'

Eventually, Chris's younger colleague gave in and began to share everything he knew, which turned out to be disappointingly little. There was nothing on any database. No previous convictions, not even juvenile, although there was evidence of some past mental health problems. Stevens revealed they'd found an exercise book with some odd quotes, and there were some old appointment cards for a local drop-in centre, but while it would require further investigation, there was nothing to immediately suggest that Wayne Terry could be dangerous. In fact, he appeared to be totally clean. His neighbours all said how Wayne kept himself to himself and that he was always alone, but when they did see him, he was always well-mannered and polite. He seemed to be the perfect neighbour.

'That's what they said about Ted Bundy,' said Chris, referring to the notorious American serial killer. 'Anyway, go on.'

'We found some clothing in an outside bin,' said Stevens. 'It looks like there's blood on some of it, but we don't know who it belongs to yet. We've bagged it for tests, and we've got some good fingerprints from the flat. It seems like Terry just upped and left though, which is suspicious, but otherwise there's nothing unusual, well, apart from owning the weirdest candle I've ever seen …'

The final part of Wayne Terry's radicalisation was sitting on the dining table in the living room, and while Stevens had been speaking, his eyes had unintentionally met those of The Puppeteer's as they stared out at him from the waxwork. Stevens had previously considered the oddity nothing more than a distasteful sculpture, but this time there was something altogether more sinister about it. The gaze was holding him transfixed, and no matter how hard he tried, he couldn't seem to tear his eyes away. There was something about the inhuman expression, the unblinking stare that was reaching out to him, inviting him to reciprocate.

'How would you like to play a game with me, Connor?'

All of a sudden, Stevens' thoughts sounded like somebody else.

'Connor?' asked Chris, wondering if his phone had lost its signal, but the screen said he was still connected. 'Connor?'

It felt like everything Stevens was, was being tested. Unable to resist the lure of the effigy, he took an uncertain step forward, and then another, until he was standing right in front of the candle itself.

'There's a good boy,' said the strange voice inside his head.

All Chris could hear was his colleague's heavy breathing. He knew Stevens was right there. Why wasn't he answering?

But Stevens wasn't with Chris at all. Everything seemed to be fading into grey apart from the nightmare features of the face before him.

'It's playtime, Connor,' the voice continued. *'Why don't you have a seat at my table?'*

Was it his imagination, or had the already manic grin just widened a little further? The thought made Stevens shudder violently enough to bring him partly back to his senses. His superior's exasperation did the rest.

'COME ON, CONNOR!' Chris yelled down the phone.

Stevens came to, astounded to find himself sitting at the dining table. He felt uncomfortable and edgy, and strangely unable to recall the gist of the conversation he'd been having.

'Oh shit … sorry, Chris, I got a bit distracted. There's a fair bit going on here right now to be honest. Perhaps I should call you back later?'

The young detective sounded different, distant and uncertain, but Chris thought it best to leave things where they were. It was very possible that Stevens had just disclosed everything he could in any case, and Chris's phone had started bleeping a low battery warning.

'Okay Connor,' he said. 'Perhaps I'd better let you get on. But make sure you keep me in the loop with any more developments, you hear?'

'Yeah, will do Chris … catch you later.'

As he cut the call, Stevens could feel himself being drawn to the candle once more, and he hurriedly spun it round to avoid making eye-contact.

'What did you do that for?' asked a sharp, female voice.

Stevens turned to see a curious colleague in the form of Detective Constable Harris.

'It was giving me the fucking creeps, Laura!' he replied.

'But you're not wearing any gloves!'

Stevens had completely forgotten he'd removed them before making his call to Chris.

'Well, it's not as if the fucking thing's got any bearing on anything, is it?' he argued. 'And anyway … do *you* want to keep looking at it, then?'

'No,' Harris admitted with a frown. 'No, I don't …'

'Well neither do I!'

*

Joanne's footsteps sounded every bit as hollow as she felt as she descended the wooden staircase from The Hayloft. She'd tried to call Chris a couple of times but all she'd got was his voicemail. Perhaps he'd switched his phone off because he didn't want to talk to her; it was nothing less than she deserved, in any case.

Still in turmoil over what she'd seen and heard, the few moments it took to cover the short distance back into the bar were never going to be enough for Joanne to gather herself completely. Through one of the bar's two bay windows, a rather impatient-looking Samantha could be seen waiting outside, and Joanne's already overstretched emotions had to ride another wave of terrible guilt. Samantha wasn't just her flesh and blood; she was her entire reason for living, and yet Joanne had no choice but to continue living a lie just like Chris.

The emotional pendulum swung once more. The bright sunshine outside was a perfect reason to wear a pair of dark sunglasses, and wearing sunglasses was a perfect way for Joanne to hide her reddening eyes. Making sure that the sunglasses were in place before she left the pub, Joanne greeted Samantha with what she thought was a confident smile, but the harder she tried to be brave, the faster she fell apart. And then to make matters even worse her mobile started ringing, and it *wasn't* Chris.

'Can you take this for me?' Joanne whispered, handing the phone to Samantha. 'I can't do this right now …'

Samantha did as she was asked.

'Hi Joshua,' she said, having seen the name on the screen. 'It's Samantha again, Mum's a bit tied up right now. Can I help or would you rather call her back?'

In his hotel room, Wayne caught a glimpse of his reflection in the dressing table mirror. He took a longer look and had to stop himself from giggling in excitement. He'd gained all the trust he needed. Joanne not only had his details stored on her phone, but Samantha was *also* totally at ease with him. Wayne quickly went into friendly mode.

'No need,' he said. 'You'll do just fine! I was just looking to confirm a date for our meeting; I mean, meeting with your mum!'

Wayne rolled his eyes and shook his head. *No more fuckups*, he thought, but Samantha seemed unconcerned.

'That's okay, I know what you meant,' she said. 'When did you have in mind? I can run it by her and get back to you? Oh, hang on a second, she's waving at me.'

Joanne wasn't one to listen in on one side of a conversation that involved her directly, and despite her desperate state of mind, decided that she *would* take the call after all.

Samantha handed the mobile back and apologised for failing to mention how Joshua had called earlier. The day had completely got away from them and it was hardly surprising. Joanne shook her head and mouthed 'don't worry'. Joshua wasn't fazed by it either; the only thing that seemed to interest him was making an appointment.

'Well, I'll probably be back in London at the end of next week,' said Joanne, 'so perhaps it might be best for us to meet then?'

Wait until the end of next week? Wayne had come out to Hertfordshire to settle a score and complete The Puppeteer's task. There was no way he was going to be made to wait that long, and he had to think quickly, but then something else just seemed to take over his thoughts, and he began to speak words that were not his own.

'Well, I'm away on business myself,' Wayne heard himself say as though listening in from the outside. 'I'm up in Birmingham all weekend, but I'll be heading back down again on Monday. I remember you saying that you were going to be staying in Hertfordshire for a while, not far from St. Albans ... Preston wasn't it? Somewhere far more relaxing than London, anyway! If you're still going to be there on Monday, why don't I stop by and meet you there on my way back, say … late afternoon or early evening?'

On Joanne's side of the conversation, the idea had been so smoothly communicated that there seemed no way that she could refuse. Joshua sounded like such an easy-going guy. What a refreshing change from the egoistical, self-obsessed monster that was Harvey Davies, and what a *fantastic idea* to have an informal business meeting in the comfort of Greenoaks.

'Well, if you're happy to do that, then why not?' she replied. 'The cottage is very easy to find, and I'm sure you've got Satnav.'

Wayne made sure he made all the right noises in all the appropriate places as Joanne gave him her address in Preston, totally unaware that he'd been there before.

'Gift-wrapped,' whispered The Puppeteer into Wayne's mind as the call ended. 'Exactly as I promised.'

*

Joanne's thoughts immediately returned to contacting Chris the moment she'd finished speaking, but just as before, her efforts proved fruitless. Samantha could see the distress on her mother's face, and suddenly felt terribly responsible.

'Is it Chris?' she asked.

'I've got to speak to him!' Joanne replied. 'I was a total bitch earlier, and I know I've really hurt him … I just want to tell him I'm sorry!'

'Oh God … Please don't tell me you two have fallen out because of me!'

'No, Sammy, it isn't like that.'

'When me and Andy suggested you should ask him if …'

'Sammy, it's *not* your fault.'

'But if I hadn't had …'

'*None* of this is your fault … okay? I'm the one who wanted to ask all the questions.'

'And you didn't get any? Is that why you two were arguing?'

But nothing could have been further from the truth. A vitriolic mixture of heartbroken, angry and afraid, all Joanne could say was that everything was totally messed up before completely unravelling.

Despite her mounting concern and curiosity, Samantha decided that there were more important matters to attend to first. Passers-by were beginning to stare, and the last thing she wanted was for her distraught mother to be the centre of any unwanted attention. All Joanne wanted to do was speak to Chris, but Samantha was adamant that they needed to be somewhere more private. Eventually Joanne agreed, and as they headed back to the carpark, Samantha tried to call Andy in an attempt to get hold of Chris another way. All she was able to raise, however, was Andy's messaging service, but then she had a brainwave. She had Anne's number stored in her phone, too.

'How about I give Chris's mum a call, instead?' Samantha suggested. 'Perhaps we can get hold of him that way? I'm sure he must just as desperate to talk to *you*. There must be a reason why you can't get hold of him, Mum, because there's no way he would be deliberately ignoring you. Shall I give it a go?'

All Joanne could do was snivel and nod in agreement.

So much for being strong for her daughter as per Angela's instructions. Right then, it was the other way around!

CHAPTER 32

Chris's mobile told him he'd had four missed calls at exactly the same time as its battery chose to go flat, and a tsunami of frustration swept over him as he stared at its lifeless black screen. His phone charger was probably somewhere upstairs, but Andy often used it, and seeing as his son wasn't the tidiest of people, it could have been left lying anywhere. Chris burst into the house and through the kitchen, completely forgetting about the still ongoing meeting. The chattering throng fell silent as he stood self-consciously in the living room doorway. A couple of the guests offered him an embarrassed smile, but the others ignored him completely. Anne glared at him with a face like thunder before taking a deep breath to compose herself, and then she politely addressed the gathering.

'Well,' she said. 'It looks like we're set for a fortnight's time, then. If anyone can think of anything else, feel free to call me, and thank you everybody for your time today.' Another reproachful look was cast in Chris's direction. Evidently the word 'everybody' didn't include *him*.

The guests rose as one as the meeting concluded and gathered in the hallway. Chris thought it best to hang back and wait until it was clear, but as soon as the opportunity presented itself for him to go upstairs and look for his charger, his way was barred by his mother.

'And just what the bloody hell was all *that* about?' she asked. 'I've never been so embarrassed in all my life! I know seven old fogies and a village fete might not be important to you, Christopher, but it's bloody well important to me and the village. I can't believe you … I really can't!'

Chris went to walk away; he really wasn't in the mood for any kind of confrontation with his irate mother, but Anne had other ideas.

'I haven't finished with you yet!' she snapped. 'And as for Andy … well, he barely said a *word* to me and then he went straight back out again! What is it with you two? Have you upset him, too? What's going on?'

There was nothing that Chris could say. He knew he'd behaved appallingly, and needed somebody to blame. Both Joanne and his son had their reasons for bailing out on him, but Zambaya had no such excuses. Where *was* his all-seeing Overseer when he was needed most?

'I'm sorry, Mum,' said Chris. 'I really am. I've just got a lot on my mind, that's all.'

All Chris wanted to do was find out who'd been calling him. He so much wanted to believe it was Joanne, but she'd been so angry when he'd left Greenoaks that he couldn't see how it was going to be possible. He looked every bit as deflated as he felt. The last time Anne had seen anything like it was during his marriage break-up, and the sight of him looking so crestfallen suddenly struck a very unhappy chord with her.

'But you were so enthusiastic about everything this morning,' she said. 'What's happened to my number one son?'

Anne was trying her best to lighten the mood, but Chris's response was to look down at the floor and just shake his head.

'I'd better go and charge my phone,' he muttered.

'*Sod* the bloody phone, Chris, *talk* to me! You've always been able to talk to me about *anything*! Oh, for God's sake who the hell's that?' Anne glared at her own mobile that had just started to ring. 'Bloody typical!' she said.

Chris saw his chance to make a getaway and made for the hallway, but then he stopped.

'Hi Samantha!' he heard Anne say. 'Oh sorry, Jo! You two sound so much alike ... no it's fine, we've finished ... well, of course it's alright! Yes, yes, he's here, I'll pass you over to him.'

Anne turned to Chris and handed him the phone.

'It's Joanne,' she said. 'She sounds rather upset. It seems you're making a bit of a habit of it today, aren't you?'

Joanne began to apologise profusely the moment she heard Chris's voice.

'Oh my God!' she said. 'I've been trying to reach you for ages! How could I have been such a bitch to you after everything you've done? I can't believe I was such a cow ... what would your mother think? Oh God, you haven't said anything about me, have you?'

'Of course not! You were just upset; it doesn't matter now.'

'I'd hate it if she were to think badly of me ...'

'Jo, it's fine!'

'And how can you be so understanding?'

'Because that's the way I am.'

'Well, can't you at least *try* and drop a Feel Bad Bomb on me? Why don't you start going into one about how hurt you are, like I would if it were the other way round? I'd feel better about that! Now I feel even shittier! You absolute pig! How can you be so bloody selfish?'

As the conversation unfolded, Joanne began to sound less comedic and relieved, and more like her usual assured self. Totally different from the firebrand of earlier, Chris could only wonder at what might have brought about such a dramatic change, and assumed that the general chit-chat was a sign that Samantha might be close by.

'Yes, we're sitting her car,' Joanne replied, 'and I'm on her phone because you wouldn't answer mine!' She suspected that Chris wanted to talk, and replied in code about Samantha's welfare so as not to raise her daughter's suspicions.

'She's okay, Chris, bearing up well considering. Thanks for asking and being such a sweetie, and I'd really like to make things up to you. Have you got any plans for later? The weather's going to be a beautiful all day, great for a barbeque, so, if you guys are free, how would you feel about coming over and joining us?'

The clever façade was impressive, and Chris accepted Joanne's invitation wholeheartedly. In a few short minutes everything had been arranged and all that he had to do was turn up 'sometime around seven!'

Having had his spirits massively raised, Chris thought that the very least he owed his mother was a cup of tea and another apology, something she was happy to accept. He explained that his mood had been down to a bit of a misunderstanding with Joanne, and that he'd also become involved with some police issues back at his base in Colindale. It was something that had been weighing heavily upon him because he wasn't there to supervise the ongoing investigation, and a more experienced hand had been required.

There was an element of truth to both stories, and Anne seemed reasonably happy with the explanations.

'Well at least you seem a lot happier which is good to see!' she said. 'But I was worried about you because I haven't seen you look like that for a good while. Joanne seems so easy going, so what was the misunderstanding?'

'Oh, it was nothing really … it was just something silly, that's all, and it's all been resolved now. Anyway, Joanne's invited us all over to hers for a barbeque this evening.'

Anne gazed at Chris thoughtfully as she took a sip of her tea.

'Okay,' she said, smiling. 'I can already see how much Joanne means to you, so whatever this 'misunderstanding' was, I'm sure that it was anything but 'silly'. And I can *also* see that it's none of my business, so I think this evening is more about you two and whatever it is that you need to sort out, so I'm going to pass if that's okay with you. All I want is to see you happy again, Chris, that's all, even if it *does* mean that you don't want to talk to me about things like you used to! And you'd better get your finger out and start tracking Andy down, otherwise you'll have Samantha to answer to, and I'm not so sure that she's as understanding as her mum!'

Neither Anne nor Chris were to know that Andy wasn't very far from the house. He'd taken himself off to a nearby tract of woodland that had been a favourite haunt of his whenever he'd come to visit his grandmother as a young boy, but right then, his chosen surroundings had less to do with recalling happier times, and more to do with hiding himself away. Childhood memories couldn't have been further from Andy's mind as he sat dejectedly on the trunk of a fallen tree, tossing pebbles into the crystal-clear water of a babbling stream at his feet. The sound of flowing water coursing serenely between moss-covered banks should have been calming, and yet he could find no comfort sitting there other than it meant he was out of harm's way and couldn't destroy anyone else's life.

A slightly bigger pebble was thrown with a little more force into the gurgling water. Andy could blame himself all he wanted for putting his father in a difficult position, but no amount of self-admonishment was going to change anything. Joanne's anger had to have been down to something else, a hidden detail revealed either by accident or design that was way beyond anything already out in the open.

But the constant quest for answers was also putting The Circle at risk. Given Zambaya's presence, Andy knew his father's role in it was far more significant than that of his own, and maybe he would to do well to remember his place.

Andy sprung up from his decaying seat and began striding towards the edge of the wood and the footpath that led back to his grandmother's. If the time he had spent alone had done nothing else, it had brought about something of an epiphany, and a sudden urgent need to try and make amends. All he could hope was that the realisation hadn't dawned upon him too late, and he broke into a run as he left the treeline, but no sooner was he out in the open than the ping of a text alert made him stop and check his mobile that had been silently languishing in the back pocket of his jeans. Having been unable to get any phone signal among the trees, Andy had only just received the message his father had sent, and a notification of two missed calls from Samantha. But he didn't have time to return them. Not unless he wanted to run the risk of making him and his father late for that barbeque!

It only took around ten minutes for Andy to get back to the house, and apart from a couple of wisecracks about how easily (and how *fast*) Samantha could make him run, nothing else was mentioned about his impromptu disappearance. In fact, none of the tension Andy might have reasonably expected existed at all. All he could feel was his father's sense of relief at how divisions had been either healed or avoided.

And that feeling was equally apparent at Greenoaks, where Joanne was just happy to be getting what she saw as a second chance. Suitably dressed down for a barbeque in a simple white T-shirt and black slim-fit jeans, she was so keen to make things up to Chris that when he got out of his car, the polite, simple embrace she'd intended as a welcome developed into a full-on hug.

And then Harley came rushing out of the cottage to greet the visitors too.

'I thought I told you to keep an eye on that dog!' said Joanne as Samantha came out in hot pursuit.

'I was turning the burgers and he snuck out!' Samantha protested. 'You know what an escapologist he can be, and I haven't got eyes in the back of my head!'

Samantha's white denim mini skirt just about covered the tops of her thighs, but the rest of her long, slender legs were on jaw-dropping display. Andy studied them in astonished silence, failing to notice the long-handled spatula she was holding in one of her hands.

'Anyway, working the barbeque should be a man's job,' she said, 'so now you're here, which one of you two is going to volunteer for the job?'

Andy was still focused on Samantha's legs, and Chris took full advantage.

'I nominate *him*,' he said, pointing to his son. 'Andy always helps out at the rugby club's barbeques and he's great behind a grill!'

'What?'

'You're on barbeque duty, son.'

'I am?'

'Too right!' said Samantha, thrusting the spatula firmly into his hand. 'I'm not wearing a bloody apron for anybody, and I don't want to be getting fat all over my new top, either; I only bought it this afternoon. What do you think, Andy? Do you think it works on me?'

Andy hadn't even noticed Samantha's brand new orange vest top, having been hypnotised by the sheer amount of leg that she had on display, but he still managed to make all the right noises about how fabulous she looked.

Joanne chuckled as Samantha took him by the hand and strode back into the cottage.

'I promise you I never raised that daughter of mine to be such an exhibitionist,' she said. 'But I think she's definitely worked out Andy's weaknesses, not that *you* were much help, roping the poor guy into doing the cooking like that ... I never knew you had it in you, Mr Ryan, you devious git!'

'I think Andy might have put it a bit stronger than that!'

'As I can well imagine!'

A man passing by smiled at Chris and Joanne as they laughed on the driveway, and it was as Chris acknowledged the stranger that he was struck by the most profound thought. Although their little gathering would have appeared nothing out of the ordinary on the outside, nothing could have been further from the truth, and all of a sudden it seemed incredible how relaxed everything appeared to be. Much, if not all of it, could be put down to how they'd overcome the biggest challenge to their group so far, but far bigger challenges lay ahead. They were all a part of The Circle, but Samantha was its beating heart and the light around which everything else revolved.

Without her there was nothing.

No hope.

No future.

Samantha was at the centre of everything, and yet she was the one from which *everything* was having to be kept. Only he and Joanne knew the true purpose of The Circle, and not even *Joanne* was aware of The Puppeteer's dark intentions of ending her daughter's life.

Chris tried to put the thoughts to the back of his mind but they kept resurfacing, especially during the course of the evening when Samantha began to talk about her experiences with a remarkable woman called Angela, and how Angela had given her the tools to shut out The Puppeteer.

It was noticeable how bubbly Samantha sounded, how full of life she was. All she wanted was to live without fear, but Chris knew that there was still so much to be afraid of. He hoped that he didn't look as daunted as he felt, and listening to Samantha's compelling account made him wonder just how close The Circle had come to suffering irreparable damage. What might have happened without Angela's timely intervention? Or had it been less to do with uncanny timing, and more to do with other influences working in their favour? Just who or *what* had guided an unwitting Joanne and Samantha into a simple hayloft holding a Psychic Fair?

Joanne herself had said very little on the subject until Andy and Samantha began to amuse Harley, leaving her sitting alone with Chris on the patio. While they were out of earshot, Joanne took the opportunity to speak quietly about her first-hand experiences of Angela's abilities, admitting that while she still had her reservations, the change in Samantha had still been nothing short of miraculous. 'I can't believe the difference in her,' said Joanne. 'Sammy's just like she used to be. It's wonderful to see her relaxed and happy again, so I suppose I shouldn't be questioning it really.'

'It's only human to question,' Chris replied. 'And I can assure you I've asked my own fair share of bloody questions!'

Joanne chuckled quietly.

'Yes, I guess you probably have. But I think being around Andy's made a huge difference with Sammy too. Look at them, don't you think they look great together?' She squeezed Chris's hand and gestured with her head towards the cottage. Once they were safely inside, she asked: 'Andy's going to be the father of this child, Chris, isn't he?'

Chris looked down and swallowed hard.

'I've been thinking about that too,' he replied. 'And yes, I think he is. But he doesn't know anything about it. And I didn't know either, Jo; Zambaya didn't tell me, I had to work it out for myself, just like you.'

'Chris, it's okay, I'm not angry with you … how *can* I be after today?'

'But I know you must be worried …'

'Well, of course I am! Samantha falling pregnant so young worries me full-stop, even if we *are* talking about her conceiving something as special as this. But it's not just Sammy, is it? It's both of them, but you seem more concerned about Samantha for some reason.'

The last thing Chris wanted was to arouse any suspicions in Joanne because in his bitter experience, she had an uncanny knack of stumbling upon the truth.

'I'm just concerned about her because she hasn't got any choice,' he said.

'But neither has *Andy*,' Joanne replied. '*None* of us has for that matter by the look of it. My accident, the way our two families were thrown together; everything's following a pattern. I'm even beginning to wonder if me being a total bitch and stropping off with Samantha this morning was supposed to happen too! Angela's reading gave me a right kick up the backside, so maybe it *had* to happen that way because I'm such a headstrong cow! I'm so sorry for the things I said, Chris, really I am.'

He reached out and drew Joanne gently into his arms.

'Jo, we've already done this, and it's fine,' he said. 'Stop being so hard on yourself. How else were you supposed to react? I'd have probably been exactly the same if I'd been in your shoes.'

For a moment Joanne was silent, but then she said: 'You know, it's funny, but I just can't seem to imagine you in a pair of heels, somehow!'

At least Joanne still had her sense of humour.

'It's the only thing keeping me sane,' she added, as their laughter died down. 'How I'm managing to get my head round it all, but I still don't know how I'm to cope with Samantha having to be kept in the dark about everything, and that I'm part of the lie. It just seems so damned cruel with all she's had to go through, but then I've also thought about what this will mean in the end, and that helps in a strange sort of way. That's the light at the end of my tunnel, Chris, the only way that I can accept it … well, that and knowing that she won't be facing it alone, I suppose.'

They stood in the quietness of their embrace. Chris allowed his hands to caress the subtle curve of Joanne's waist and she in turn found her fingertips exploring the broadness of his shoulders and back. It was a touch that brought him out in goose bumps, and he could feel himself getting aroused, in spite of having just been privy to her deepest fears.

Joanne stopped stroking Chris's back and leant back to look at him. He smiled back at her, weakly, scarcely able to hide his embarrassment at his ill-timed erection.

'Would you guys like to stay again tonight?' she asked, totally unperturbed.

'Well ... yes, that would be great,' Chris replied, relieved at not getting slapped. 'That's if you're sure you don't mind.' He almost cringed at how stupid that must have sounded. *Why else would she have bloody well asked?* he thought.

'Well, in that case, perhaps it might be a good idea to give Anne a ring and let her know you're staying?'

Chris seemed to be at a loss as to what to do next. Joanne's mouth curved into a delicate smile, but she thought it best to continue as though nothing had happened. He would only have crumbled completely if she'd told him how impressed she was!

'You left it on the coffee table,' she said.

'Huh?'

'Your mobile ...? It's on the coffee table?'

'Oh yes, yes, of course it is ... thanks.'

Thank God for the dishwasher! Loading it up with dirty plates and crockery was all that kept Joanne from exploding into a fit of the giggles. Chris's line of work demanded a high level of self-control, but he certainly hadn't been able to exercise any during those last few moments. She bit her lip and continued to make herself busy in the kitchen, while Chris obediently walked into the lounge to phone his mother.

*

In contrast to the pleasant warmth of the day, a distinct chill accompanied the later hours. Consequently, the party continued indoors, where more drinks and a good film seemed an ideal way to wind things down, but it wasn't long before the excesses of the evening began to catch up with them all. Unsurprisingly, Samantha was the first to doze off, closely followed by Andy, and the pair of them had fallen asleep cuddled up together on the larger of the two sofas in the living room. Harley lay stretched out on the rug beneath them. Occasionally, he would snort and snuffle in his slumber, but otherwise, all was peaceful inside Greenoaks Cottage.

As Andy and Samantha were taking no further part in matters, Joanne found some relaxing music to suit the tranquil mood, and put her head on Chris's shoulder as she sat back down beside him. Chris had one arm around Joanne, one ear on the stereo, and a tiring eye on Samantha, who he kept half-expecting to jump awake from another Puppeteer-induced nightmare at any moment.

And yet, despite his fears, she continued to sleep soundly in Andy's arms, undisturbed by anything from this world or the next. Had she really been able to blind The Puppeteer and his Manforms the way Angela had suggested, or was The Puppeteer just biding his time, adapting, formulating and engineering another way to enter their lives? Zambaya had once compared The Puppeteer's ingenuity to that of a supreme strategist, a calculating chess master without equal, so how could it be this easy?

'Look at them,' whispered Joanne, unaware of how far Chris's thoughts had taken him. 'They look so peaceful.'

'Who?'

'Andy and Sam, who do you think? Come on, Chris, try and keep up!'

'Sorry …'

She smiled and snuggled up closer to him.

'I think they look lovely together, and yet they've got no idea how important they are. They look just like a normal girlfriend and boyfriend, but they're anything but.'

'Normal'. There was Joanne's favourite word again, and something for which she'd been yearning in some more recent, anxious times. But what *sort* of 'normal' was is it that she wanted, exactly? Joanne's definition of 'normal' had changed completely since she'd met Chris, a man who'd quite unknowingly bypassed all of her defences and caused her wall of self-denial to start crumbling brick by imprisoning brick. With edifying clarity, everything Joanne had been missing in life had begun to reveal itself, candidly. 'Normal' suddenly meant nothing but living to work, or having to battle feelings of guilt. 'Normal' meant being unfulfilled, and having to lie to herself that the feeling of emptiness to which she'd become accustomed didn't exist. 'Normal' was all about a sense of having to prove herself when the need to do so had long since passed.

As the music she'd selected played soulfully in the background, Joanne continued to explore her innermost thoughts. The more she saw Andy and Samantha together, the more she had to accept the inevitability of their future, but what of her own? Unlike Andy and Samantha, Joanne's future was, as yet, unwritten. Her past was a legacy of selflessness, her present a foundation for all that was yet to happen. The pressures Joanne placed upon herself were both enormous and unreasonable, and however strong its appeal, striving for continued success had come at a price. Wise beyond her teenage years, Samantha had often accused her mother of ignoring her own needs, and there was no denying that she had been right all along. Perhaps it *was* Joanne's time to take more of a back seat when it came to her business, and having supressed her desires for fear of the pain they might cause her should she fall for another man, maybe it *was* time to finally free herself and jump, unrestrained, into the flow.

'You're very quiet,' said Chris. 'Are you okay there?'

'I'm just enjoying the moment,' Joanne replied. 'And thinking about what a lovely time we've all had tonight.'

Chris began stroking Joanne's hair, an involuntary act of affection that provoked an immediate response.

'Hmmm ... that's nice,' she said. 'I like my hair being stroked. I find it very relaxing. I reckon I must have been a pampered pussycat in a past life, maybe in Egypt, you know ... a Pharaoh's favourite feline.' She heard Chris chuckle quietly. 'Sometimes Sammy spends ages just brushing my hair,' she continued. 'If I've had a stressful day at the office, she runs me a bath and then sorts her moody old cow of a mother right out. She just seems to know how to handle me, so I suppose it shouldn't really amaze me when I see how well she can handle *herself*. I know I can be overprotective; as if I need reminding! But when I see Samantha and Andy together, I can start to see that I shouldn't worry so much.'

Joanne peered up at Chris, and he stopped stroking her hair.

'I feel different all of a sudden,' she said, 'but I can't explain why ... it's like a part of me that I didn't know I had knows something that the rest of me doesn't. God, I wish I could explain it better, but that's just how it feels.'

'Maybe it's because you've accepted?'

'Maybe. If letting everything in and accepting means that I'm not so afraid anymore, then I probably have.'

But Chris still had his own fears to contend with. The Truth's envoy was yet to be conceived, and there was still a clear and present danger to Samantha. Unwelcome thoughts of his earlier conversation with Connor Stevens came back hauntingly into his mind, but Samantha was safe as long as she stayed among them, and in spite of his troubles, his eyelids started to feel heavy all of a sudden.

'Now look who's gone quiet!' said Joanne, giving him a gentle prod. 'You're nodding off!'

'It's these damned sofas ...'

'Nothing to do with all the beer, then?'

'I haven't had *that* much!'

Joanne laughed in the back of her hand.

'Well, I suppose it has been rather a long day' she said. 'I don't mind if you want to turn in. I think I might go up myself actually, otherwise it won't be long before we're *all* flat out down here!'

She sat up so that Chris could get to his feet, but stopped him waking

Andy and Samantha.

'No, don't,' she said. 'They're well away and Samantha looks like she's set for the duration. She slept down here the other night with Harley for company, and she's got Andy here with her as well this time.'

Chris took it upon himself to go and fetch some pillows and blankets from the airing cupboard on the landing, while Joanne quietly busied herself with what little was of left of the tidying up, and she literally stumbled into him as he came back down into the living room with his burden.

'Where are you going with all that?' she whispered.

'Well, there's going to be three of us down here.'

'And there *is* a spare room, you know?'

'Oh yeah, I forgot about that!'

Most of the bedding Chris was carrying had been for Andy and Samantha, and he set about making them as comfortable as possible, grateful that he wasn't going to be spending another uncomfortable night on the smaller of the two sofas like he'd had to before. Joanne watched him as she stood on the landing. She saw him cover the pair with the blankets and then place one of the pillows ever so carefully under Samantha's head so as not to wake her. Then he stood motionless for a few moments, watching over her, almost like he was standing guard.

Chris's apparent sense of duty towards Samantha was as mysterious as it was wonderful, and yet Joanne felt no reason to question it. He was like the father she'd always dreamed of for her daughter, and every bit as loyal and protective as Angela's tarot reading had suggested. Joanne had so much admiration for Chris, and she'd realised that afternoon just how much having him around truly meant. His modesty only allowed him to see himself as an ordinary man, but Joanne saw him as so much more.

It was time to let go of all the heartache in her past. She smiled warmly at Chris as he walked quietly back up the staircase towards her, her eyes never leaving his as she gently took him by the hand, and led him into her bedroom.

CHAPTER 33

Housekeepers have often stumbled upon examples of extreme untidiness when going about servicing vacated hotel rooms. In the case of a certain hotel in Hitchin, however, the housekeeper had discovered the polar opposite, a suite that had been meticulously cleaned throughout by its previous guest. The bed had been completely stripped, and all the bed linen, including the duvet cover, had been placed in the bath with the used towels. Even the waste bins had been emptied, the tops of every bag neatly tied and carefully placed upon the bathroom floor.

Nobody had seen the resident all weekend; all meals had been delivered by room service, and any offers to clean and service the room during that time had been politely declined. Rumours had begun to circulate among the staff about the recluse staying in their hotel, tales of strange comings and goings at peculiar hours, and apparently he'd been like a coiled spring when he'd checked out that morning. The receptionist claimed he'd barely made eye contact with her, let alone spoken.

The eccentric and quirky often attracted unfair attention, but it was each to their own as far as the housekeeper was concerned. She shook her head sadly about those who had nothing better to do than cast unfounded aspersions, and then went back to her duties. For all she knew, the same rumourmongers among the hotel staff probably had plenty to say about *her* behind her back, too.

But the staff members who *had* seen Wayne in reception that morning hadn't been exaggerating his tension. Reports of Sara Murrell's murder were all over the local news, and regardless of how much satisfaction he'd gained from the public airing of his exploits, Wayne knew that the police would be going over everything with a fine-toothed comb. Of course, it was possibly far too soon for them to have any idea of the perpetrator's identity, let alone be able to connect anything to that hotel, but regardless, Wayne had considered it unwise to rely on the alias he'd cunningly used at check-in. The legitimacy of 'Joshua Gains' aside, his only other insurance lay in the precautions taken to cover his tracks. He had painstakingly cleaned every surface of his room, every doorknob, handle and switch. Nothing had been left to chance, yet it was impossible not to keep going over things in his mind in case he might have overlooked something. But perhaps the worst part was knowing how much time he was going to have to kill before the arrival of his golden moment with Samantha Middleton. The day was going to feel like an eternity, but if there was any consolation to be had, it was imagining the release of his ferocity when that moment finally came.

Wayne smiled to himself.

He was going to make sure the little bitch got everything that was due to her.

*

While an uptight and strung-out Wayne Terry feverishly counted down the hours, minutes and seconds, Samantha Middleton, his target, was relaxing in the spacious beer garden of Preston's only village pub, enjoying the early afternoon sunshine along with her mother, Andy and Chris.

There was another family sharing the garden with them. They had a little girl who Joanne estimated to be around three or four-years-old, and Harley, who was chilling out in the shade of a large nearby beech tree, had become the centre of the excited child's squealing attention. He seemed to be just as fond of the little newcomer as she was of him, rolling onto his back and inviting the occasional belly-rub, but Andy and Samantha had taken on a supervisory role just to be on the safe side. Harley, as usual, was being an absolute gem, but he was still a very big, powerful dog, and it would have been extremely unwise to have taken his playful demeanour for granted in the presence of an infant for too long.

Even so, the whole scene had a very natural look and feel to it. Both Andy and Samantha were happy to play along with a very young and exuberant child, and for a fleeting moment, it was like Joanne was getting a glimpse of a possible future.

Chris was also looking on, but his mind was elsewhere, like wondering why he should be feeling even more on edge about Samantha's safety. It was Monday, nothing had changed from how things had been over the weekend, they were out all together as a group, so what *was* it about being outside in a pub's beer garden that had turned him into a cat on hot bricks? Chris had even selected a table that gave him a clear view of the car park and village green, and he was giving the area yet another visual sweep when Joanne playfully bumped him with her shoulder.

'You're very serious,' she said, adding a semi-comical frown. 'And that's your second bottle of tonic water … *just* tonic water, I might add! Are you sure you don't want something a bit stronger?'

'I'm sorry,' he replied. 'I suppose it's because I'm not used to drinking during the day … and certainly not on a Monday!'

'Oh, how *very* disciplined of you, Detective Chief Inspector Ryan! Are you always this disciplined, or are you just worried about me taking advantage of you again?'

No doubt loosened up by a couple of glasses of red wine, Joanne seemed to be totally at ease with everything, so Chris decided that seeing as the gauntlet had just been thrown down, then the very least he could do was accept the challenge of having a pint. It was just as he was getting up from the table that his mobile chose to scupper his plans. It was on the table right in front of him, and DCI Mike Devonshire's name was clearly displayed, illuminated on its screen. Joanne recognised the name immediately as one of the detectives she'd met at the hospital, and she nodded reassuringly as Chris apologised for it being a call he needed to take.

'Hi Mike,' he said, walking a short distance so Joanne couldn't hear what was being said.

'Hi Chris. Are you okay to talk for a few minutes?'

'Yeah sure. What can I do for you?'

'Just keeping you in the loop like I said I would. We've detained somebody this morning in connection with the Sara Murrell killing. A bloke called Wayne Terry.'

Chris's heart missed a beat.

'Christ!' he said. 'My people have been looking for him in connection with two killings in *our* area!'

'I know they have. I've already called them. I spoke to a young chap, Stevens I think it was, anyway, he told me he'd been working on the case.'

The unexpected news had numbed Chris at first, but then an incredible sense of relief began to grow.

'That's really great news!' he said. 'Jesus … your lads don't hang about! How did you manage to track him down?'

Devonshire revealed that it was more a huge stroke of luck than brilliant policework.

'Just a Public Order offence to be honest. Terry was looking at somebody's girlfriend outside a pub and happened to make a few lurid comments. Then it all kicked off.'

'Did he have a weapon on him?'

'No, nothing. He didn't have any identification on him either; not even a driving licence, but he's a really smug bastard with a bit too much to say, which is how he managed to get himself nicked! Things escalated when a foot patrol got involved, and Terry ended up making threats against one of the officers because he didn't consider her 'worthy enough' to talk to, among some other weird stuff he came out with. Anyway, the long and the short of it was that he was brought in and when his name lit up the system, we called your people in Colindale. They're going to be picking him up from here for questioning tomorrow morning. Terry's not asked for a brief yet and we want to ask him a few questions ourselves, but that'll be a bit later this afternoon. It's DS Willard's job, but bollocks to protocol because I might even do it myself! I know it's not the norm, but that's just me. And how would you feel about sitting in as an observer? I'm sure you'd like to be there too, given what you already know about him.'

Try keeping me away! thought Chris.

A huge weight felt like it had been lifted from his shoulders, and the thought of witnessing Wayne Terry being skewered by Mike Devonshire made his sudden elation difficult to control.

'Sounds great to me,' he said. 'I'd be more than happy to as long as Colindale are happy.'

'Can't see it being a problem,' said Devonshire. 'I've already suggested it to them!'

The Puppeteer's assassin was sitting impotent in a police cell, and with a considerable body of evidence already mounting, Chris was confident Wayne Terry would be remaining in custody.

'You're looking rather pleased with yourself,' said Joanne as Chris joined her back at the table. 'How was Mike?'

'Yeah … he's fine.'

'And …?'

Chris looked around to see if anybody was listening.

'Well, *strictly* between you and me,' he whispered, 'they've detained somebody in connection with Sara Murrell's murder, but they can't go public with it yet.'

'Wow, that's brilliant!'

'It sounds like they've got a real breakthrough. But he's also in the frame for something in *my* neck of the woods, which means it kind of involves me directly. I hope you don't mind, Jo, but I've been given clearance to sit in on an interview with the suspect later this afternoon.'

'Well, that's good isn't it?'

'Well, yes …'

'So why are you sounding so apologetic?'

'Because I don't know how long it's going to take.'

Joanne reminded Chris that she'd heard him offer his assistance to Mike Devonshire if the need arose, and fully understood the importance of what could be about to unfold.

'So, you go and do what you have to and don't worry about it', she said. 'I'll make sure I've got dinner ready for early evening and you can always reheat it if you get back later than that. Is there anything you fancy in particular? After all, Mr Ryan, we *do* need to keep your energy levels up now, don't we?'

Life was suddenly about living again and everything seemed to be falling into place, the way ahead seemed altogether brighter, and the possibilities once again endless. The icing on the cake would come when Chris looked into the eyes of the man chosen by The Puppeteer to kill Samantha, and know that that man had failed. But three women had been brutally murdered and there could be no sense of victory or celebration, for, ultimately, it was going to be down to Chris and his colleagues to bring some closure and some semblance of justice for their grieving families.

As the afternoon wore on, Chris called into headquarters, making it appear that he was familiarising himself with the progress of the investigation. Despite his earlier confidence, he needed to be sure in his own mind that there was sufficient evidence to keep Wayne Terry behind bars where he belonged.

Throughout those painstaking hours, Chris had been mentally preparing himself to share an interview room with a monster, but when the moment arrived, it turned out that Wayne Terry wasn't anything at all like Chris had expected. Far from being a rabid animal one might have felt metaphorically obliged to euthanise, Terry was sharp and well turned out. A surprisingly slight frame belied the brutality of which he was allegedly capable, and his innocent, clear blue eyes expressed a near child-like interest in Chris and Devonshire as they took their places opposite him at the interview room's solitary, black plastic-coated table.

Devonshire checked that the interview was being recorded.

'Interview commenced at eighteen thirty-six,' he announced. 'DCI Mike Devonshire of Stevenage Police speaking; other officer present, DCI Christopher Ryan of Metropolitan Police, Colindale.' He then addressed the suspect directly, asking him to provide his full name and date of birth.

Chris sat back in his seat, watching and listening closely as Devonshire continued with the procedure.

'Why have you waived your right to a solicitor, Mr Terry?' Devonshire asked.

The question was answered with a disinterested shrug of the shoulders.

'A verbal answer for the benefit of the recording please, Mr Terry.'

'Because I don't need one, that's why.'

'Well in that case, I need to remind you that you do not have to say anything, but it may harm your defence if you do not mention when questioned something which you later rely on in court. Anything you do say will be given in evidence. Do you understand the caution, Mr Terry?'

'Yep.'

'So I suppose you won't mind me reminding you that the reason why you are here is partly about your behaviour this morning, especially as to why you found it necessary to violently threaten a police officer who was just doing her job.'

'I didn't threaten anyone.'

'And you consider that addressing a police officer by saying 'it's a good job you're wearing a fucking stab vest' isn't threatening?'

'Not particularly, I was just making an observation.'

'An 'observation'?'

Devonshire glanced down at his notes. 'So can you clarify what you meant when you said to her that 'your lousy, stinking flesh isn't worthy', then?' he asked. 'And that given the chance you would 'drop her in an instant'. Don't either of those quotes convey anything threatening to you either?'

'Nope.'

'I'm quoting what you said, Mr Terry.'

'If you say so.'

'How about I ask where you were in the early hours of last Tuesday, and what you know about the death of a Miss Sara Murrell?'

'Asleep, probably, and erm ... nothing.'

'Only probably asleep? Well, what about Miss Jennie Lawrence? Does she mean anything to you?'

'Nope.'

'What sort of car do you drive, Mr Terry? Probably something flash like you, I suppose?'

'No comment.'

'Something to throw around a few bends out in the lanes because you probably thought there was nothing else about out there at that time of the morning? But then you ran into a couple of young women and it got out of hand, didn't it?'

'No comment.'

'They had a bit of a go at you, didn't they? Got your back up a bit, didn't it? Like the police officer this morning. Was she a bit out of order too, Mr Terry? Was she walking a bit of a tightrope like the others? I bet you'd have loved to have stuck a knife in her like you did to young Sara Murrell, wouldn't you?'

'No comment.'

The interview had taken a completely different course from what Chris had expected. Questioning Terry about the earlier Public Order Offence was one thing, but moving onto a murder enquiry which was supposed to be handed over to the Met was quite another. Even though Chris had no choice but to remain silent as an observer, he was nevertheless astounded by Devonshire's sudden hostility and the suspect's almost unnatural coolness, but then there was a discrete knock on the interview room door. A uniformed officer entered with a message for an extremely disgruntled Devonshire that he was urgently needed on the phone.

'Interview paused at eighteen-forty-five,' said Devonshire. 'DCI Devonshire has been called away from the interview room.'

'Elvis has *left* the building!' said the suspect after Devonshire had stopped the tape and closed the door of the interview room behind him.

The sarcasm from opposite went over Chris's head. Almost. With Devonshire absent and the tape paused, Chris almost felt tempted to get in a few blows of his own, but he wasn't there in that capacity.

'Is something funny, Mr Terry?' he asked instead.

'Only that you think you're so very smart, Mr Ryan. Such arrogance I find extremely entertaining, especially now that we are alone. I may not be who you think I am.'

Chris frowned. The response to the question had been as unexpected as it was menacing, and unless his mind was playing tricks, the atmosphere in the room had become noticeably heavier. The suspect had also developed a discernible accent that hadn't been present at the start of the interview.

'I'm not sure you're in any position to start playing any games, Mr Terry,' Chris replied, but he was starting to feel apprehensive at how quickly the dynamics of their encounter had changed.

'Ooh, games,' said the suspect, grinning insanely. 'I like to play games. Why don't we play a guessing game and see how smart you *really* are?'

The unidentifiable accent was getting stronger, wrapped in a husky voice of dark and threatening intonation that was oozing effortlessly through the thickening air.

'Oh, come on, Mr Ryan, let's play … Where's your sense of adventure? I know a good one that might suit your powers of deduction. How about Hangman? Who do you think I am …?'

*

Devonshire flopped breathlessly into his office chair to take the phone call. As far as *he* was concerned, forensics had better have a good reason for making him rush around when he had much better things to do.

'Devonshire,' he growled. '…Well, that's where I was, you dragged me out of the interview with him! What …? Well, they *have* to bloody well match! They're whose? You're absolutely sure about that …? Okay, thanks …'

Disbelievingly, Devonshire replaced the receiver.

*

Harley sat in the kitchen of Greenoaks Cottage wearing a forlorn expression. His late afternoon walk had been curtailed by a combination of Joanne losing all track of time, and a sudden consequential rush to prepare dinner.

'Oh Harley, I'm so sorry about your walk,' she said. 'I'll make it up to you tomorrow, I promise.'

But Joanne's contrition wasn't anywhere near good enough for Harley who remained suitably unimpressed.

'Well, how about a bowl of your favourite biscuits then?' she asked.

Bribery wasn't working either. Harley lowered his head and peered up at her dolefully. The guilt trip had begun in earnest, and Joanne began to wonder if he could lay it on any thicker. 'Come on dog,' she groaned, 'I'm doing my sodding best!'

*

In the interview room, Chris watched helplessly as the suspect's once crystal-clear blue eyes turned completely black and his right forefinger traced the first of three invisible dashes upon the surface of the table.

'Let's begin then, Mr Ryan,' the suspect said. 'Give me a letter.'

The first three dashes were followed immediately by nine more, but Chris was totally unable to speak.

'No idea where to start, Mr Ryan? How about I give you a clue? The trick with hangman is to start with a vowel. I believe 'e' is the most commonly used vowel in the English language? Would you like to try that one? Oh come, come … I'm surprised at you!'

The relentless taunting continued, unchallenged.

*

'What's up with Harley?' asked Samantha who'd just arrived in the kitchen.

'He's got the hump with me, that's what,' sighed Joanne. 'He hasn't really been out properly today, and now he's making me suffer for it.'

Harley increased the intensity of his silent protest for Samantha's benefit. Joanne narrowed her eyes at him, but then she had an idea.

'I suppose Andy could always take him out,' she said. 'If they go now, they'll still have plenty of daylight left.'

Harley's ears pricked up immediately, and Joanne felt herself scowl at the sudden change in his demeanour.

'Where *is* Andy by the way?' she asked.

'He's out in the garden,' Samantha replied. 'I'll just go and get him and then we can take Harley out over the fields.'

'Who's *we*?'

'Me and Andy.'

'Uh-uh, no way José, you said you'd help me do dinner!'

*

There seemed nothing that Chris could do to escape from his sudden mental captivity.

'Perhaps a consonant or two?' the suspect suggested, strengthening his mesmerising grip on the situation. 'Maybe a 'p' for example … that might work; you never know. But, if you're still at a loss …'

Leaving his unfinished statement hanging ominously in the air, the suspect leaned across the table and fixed Chris with a lifeless, unblinking stare.

'Mr Ryan,' he sighed. 'I am truly shocked, and, if I'm to be brutally honest, more than a little disappointed! There really isn't any substance to you, *is* there? Not one *significant* little *fibre*. I feel rather cheated, actually. I would have expected far more from one so *dedicated* to protecting the Innocent. Time's up then, Chrisssssssstopher. Game over. You now dangle upon a string just like the others. I hear the tolling of a distant bell …'

CHAPTER 34

Joanne looked up from the recipe on the screen of her mobile phone in the direction of the chiming doorbell. For a moment she found herself staring blankly at the casually dressed and slightly built man standing in front of her on the door step. He was wearing a lightweight leather bomber jacket, blue jeans, and trainers; there was a silver laptop tucked underneath his arm and an interested smile fixed upon his face.

'Hello,' said the stranger. 'I'm Joshua Gains. I *do* hope I've got the right house; I'm looking for Joanne Middleton?'

*

In the interview room, the suspect suddenly seemed frightened and confused.

'Who are you?' he asked when he saw Chris. 'What's going on?'

Chris started at the questions, as if he'd been woken unexpectedly from a deep slumber.

'Is something wrong, Mr Terry?' he asked.

'What are you talking about?' the suspect replied, looking around wildly at his surroundings. 'My name's Gary Brewer!'

'I believe you've already said your name is Wayne Terry.'

'No ... that's *bollocks* that is; I couldn't have! I just *told* you my name's Gary Brewer, and ... and you're a ... you're a fucking *copper*! What the fuck's going on? You're fitting me up with something, aren't you? Trying to pin some shit on me!'

'Why would I be doing that? You've made a pretty good job of that yourself by the sound of it, threatening a police officer.'

'What the *fuck* are you talking about?'

'Well, that's why you're here isn't it?'

'But I haven't threatened anyone! I haven't got a *clue* what you're talking about!'

Disoriented and clearly distracted, the panicked man seemed to be on the verge of tears.

'Calm down, Mr Terry. Perhaps you might want to exercise your right to a solicitor now?'

'Why do you keep *calling* me that? I told you my name's Gary Brewer! And why should I need a fucking brief when I haven't FUCKING DONE

ANYTHING!'

Devonshire strode back into the interview room, accompanied by a uniformed office.

'Mr Terry now says he's called Gary Brewer,' said Chris.

'Well, that's probably because that's who he is!' muttered Devonshire. 'We're terminating the interview ... Constable, can you please take Mr Brewer back to the custody suite ...?'

'But I haven't done anything,' Brewer sobbed, as he was escorted away. 'I haven't!'

Chris couldn't believe what he was hearing.

'But you heard what he said! He gave his name, date of birth, *everything* ... how could he have known? And I know we haven't got any clear-cut CCTV footage of Terry, but he was a very good match for the description Jennie Lawrence gave us.'

'I can't explain it either, Chris. But for some reason the results of the fingerprints took a lot longer than usual to come back and they don't match any of the others from the crime scenes, *or* Terry's flat. I'm sorry, Chris. I've been wasting your time here.'

Since Devonshire's return, the vagueness from which Chris had been suffering had begun to clear. He could remember being sucked into a mind game in which he had become completely powerless, a prisoner to unbreakable and hypnotic vocal bonds.

And then he remembered the voice Samantha had once described ...

And the empty black eyes about which *all* the others had spoken ...

Chris's stomach began to tighten ...

The Puppeteer ...

'BASTARD!' he yelled, jumping up and sending his seat skittering, clattering across the interview room. 'THE *BASTARD!*'

'What the fuck?' asked Devonshire, but Chris had already burst out of the interview room and into the corridor. He'd been tricked. They *all* had. Even poor Gary Brewer had been calculatingly used.

Checkmate ...

The Puppeteer had moved another piece on the chessboard, using an innocent man as a mouthpiece, but the gambit had been devastatingly effective in luring Chris away and handing The Puppeteer's assassin a clear run at Samantha!

Chris grabbed the nearest available phone in the operations room, but he couldn't remember Joanne's number.

He needed his mobile ... his jacket ... it was in his jacket ... but *where was* his *bloody* jacket? Files and papers flew in all directions as he lashed out in frustration while other officers could only look on in astonishment, Devonshire included.

'Jesus, Chris!' he said, having only just managed to catch up. 'What the hell's got into you?'

'I've got to warn Jo …'

'Warn her about what?'

'There isn't time, Mike!'

'What the fuck's going on, Chris?'

Chris saw his jacket hanging over the back of a chair in Devonshire's office and bolted towards it.

'Wayne Terry is after Joanne's daughter,' he said. 'That's all I can tell you!'

'But …'

'Mike, there isn't time to explain!'

'Come on, Chris!'

'I SAID THERE ISN'T TIME!'

Chris wrenched his mobile out of his jacket, and began to scroll frantically through its stored numbers.

*

Samantha smiled as Joanne introduced her to Joshua, and apologised to him for being in the middle of preparing dinner.

'It's all Mum's fault,' she said. 'She forgot you were coming.'

'So did you!' Joanne retorted.

'Never mind, it's nice to meet you anyway,' said Wayne, almost a little *too* smoothly for his own liking. Inside his jacket was the blade with Samantha Middleton's name on it and she was close enough to be stuck with it there and then, but before he could react, she moved away and began staring out of the kitchen window at his car.

'*Very* nice,' she said. 'It's an M3, isn't it? One of my dream cars.'

Samantha sounded so impressed that Wayne thought she might be up for going for a drive if he suggested it. What a perfect way to get her alone!

'Along with Leonard's Aston Martin and your dad's Bentley!' said Joanne, instantly quelling Wayne's ardour. 'Now, Samantha Middleton, how about you just make yourself useful by buggering off upstairs? I'm supposed to be having a business meeting with Joshua!'

'Suits *me*,' Samantha replied. 'Beats peeling bloody spuds!'

There'd been no dog barking when Wayne rang the doorbell, and the cottage was completely devoid of any other voices. With Joanne out of the way he was going to have Samantha all to himself.

'Would you like a drink, Joshua?' asked Joanne.

Wayne had really liked the way Samantha had looked at him when they were introduced. She was even more beautiful close up than he remembered, and she was probably in her bedroom waiting for him to satisfy her lust …

'Joshua …?'

His need was so strong, and only Samantha could sooth it. In Wayne's mind the fantasy had begun in earnest, with Samantha's moans of pleasure merely the forerunner to her ultimate sacrifice at the altar of his ecstasy …

'Joshua? A drink?'

'Huh?'

'Can I get you something to drink?'

'Oh God, I'm sorry! Long drive and all that. A glass of water would be great, thank you.'

Wayne began staring out of the kitchen window, relieved at being released from his imagination. The Puppeteer had engineered everything, and there could be no distractions if he were to fully repay the debt owed to his tenacious mentor.

As Joanne filled a glass with cold filtered water from a filter jug in the refrigerator, Wayne slowly began slipping his hand inside his jacket, comforted by the reassuring, unforgiving rigidity of the concealed knife at the ends of his fingertips.

No more bullshit.

It was time.

Wayne was an ambush predator in the presence of an unsuspecting quarry and the kill would be suitably simple and efficient. As soon as Joanne was close enough, he would strike out with the speed of a cobra, a rapid little flick of his wrist that would take care of everything, just like it had taken care of the abusive little bitch in the country lane a few nights earlier.

Joanne closed the fridge door and began to walk across the kitchen, and saw that Wayne was still standing up, staring out of the window.

'You *can* sit down,' she said, but then she noticed that there were beads of sweat on his forehead. 'And you can take your jacket off, too, if you're feeling a bit hot.'

Out of Joanne's view, Wayne's fingers closed around the handle of the lethal blade in his pocket.

'No, it's fine,' he said. 'I'll keep it on for now.'

He half turned to face her, but then a loud ringtone burst out unexpectedly, filling the kitchen with the sound of digital chaos. Wayne nearly jumped out of his skin, but Joanne was too intent on checking the phone she'd left by the cooker to notice. She smiled when she saw Chris's name on the screen and offered her apologies for the intrusion, leaving Wayne's glass of water on the dining table as she headed for the back garden to take the call.

Behind her, unseen, Wayne slumped onto one of the dining chairs as though he'd been kicked in the stomach. The phone call had broken his concentration and completely drawn his sting. If he were to follow her, she could suspect something was amiss and he might lose the upper hand. Unwilling to take any unnecessary risks, Wayne knew he would just have to wait for another opportunity.

Unaware of Wayne's frustrations, Joanne was only too thrilled to be hearing from Chris.

'Hello darling,' she said. 'How's it …?'

'Jo, oh thank God! Thank God you're okay!'

'Well, of *course* I'm okay …'

'Listen, Jo, please listen. You've *all* got to get out of the house.'

'But …'

'Just get over here to the police station.'

'But why? What's wrong?'

'There's no time to explain Jo. Please … please just do as I say!'

'But I've got a guest. I'd completely forgotten about a meeting with a new photographer, and he's here!'

'Can he hear you?'

'No, he's in the kitchen and I'm outside …'

'Is his name Joshua Gains?'

'Christ, yes! But …'

'Try and keep your voice down, Jo.'

'Chris, you're scaring the shit out of me now; what's going on?'

Chris took a deep breath.

'Jo, I have to tell you that Joshua is a very dangerous man and it's not his real name. Mike Devonshire is listening in to this and he's getting you some help. Police officers are on their way and they'll be there in minutes; just do as I say and you'll be fine.'

Joanne was barely holding herself together.

'Oh my God,' she sobbed. 'Oh my God, oh my God ….'

'Jo, just try and stay calm. Are Samantha and Andy there with you?'

'Sammy's in her room and Andy's out walking Harley.'

'And is Joshua still in the kitchen?'

Joanne dared to glance over her shoulder. The dining table was partially obscured by a protruding wall, fortuitously shielding her from view.

'I think so,' she whispered, 'and I don't think he can see me either.'

'Okay, Jo, that's good, really good; you're doing just great. Now, if you don't think you and Samantha can get out of the house without being noticed, then go to Samantha's room and barricade yourselves in. I promise you that help is coming, and I'm not going to be far behind. Everything will be okay if you do what I've told you. Just do what you have to do to keep yourselves safe. I'm on my way to the car *right now*. Remember, do what you have to do.'

Abruptly, Chris rang off.

Slumped against the frame of the open French doors, Joanne cautiously checked behind her again and saw that she was still hidden from whoever it really was in her kitchen. Chris had rung off so quickly that the sudden absence of his calming tones had left behind a silent and terrifying unfillable void, but there was no time to lose.

'Do what you have to do.'

Joanne uttered a barely audible sob as she carefully removed a heavy brass poker from the companion set in the living room fireplace, hoping upon hope that she wasn't going to have to use it as a weapon. Then, with tears of shear panic clouding her vision, she made her way as quickly and as quietly as possible, upstairs to Samantha.

*

Chris had done all he could to influence matters at Greenoaks Cottage apart from pray. Wayne Terry had gone there with the sole intention of killing, and the fact that he hadn't already done so might have meant he'd become uncertain of himself. But as Chris rushed with Devonshire and Willard into the police station's car park, the precariousness of the situation struck home once more.

'Four units are heading to Preston right now,' said Devonshire as Chris's hope evaporated. 'And I've also got ambulances and paramedics on their way just in case. The paramedics are just a precaution, Chris, they might not even be needed.'

But Devonshire hadn't even been able to fool *himself* with his attempted reassurance, let alone Chris. Devonshire had already had first-hand experience of Wayne Terry's capabilities, but as appalling as the brutal murder of Sara Murrell had been, even *that* motiveless attack paled into insignificance compared to the horrific images he'd received earlier from Chris's colleagues in the Met.

Devonshire was trying his utmost to stop recalling one in particular, but it was useless. A dancer's death mask was indelibly imprinted upon his mind, frozen upon her once pretty face as the tragic girl lay butchered and degraded behind an abandoned warehouse in Colindale.

What might be awaiting them in Preston didn't even bear thinking about.

CHAPTER 35

Samantha was lying on her bed, studying her phone intently, when her mother came into the room. Her face was flushed and tearful, and she instantly put her finger to her lips as she locked the door behind her.

'What are you doing with that?' Samantha whispered when she saw the poker in her mother's hand.

'We need to stay in here,' Joanne replied.

'What?'

Joanne quickly looked round the room until her eyes fell upon a nearby chest of drawers. It was made of solid oak and looked like it would make a good barricade. 'Come and give me a hand with this,' she asked.

'Why? What's wrong?'

'Keep your bloody voice down! It's Joshua. He's not who we think he is and he's very dangerous! Chris just called in the nick of time to warn me, if you're wondering. Now, come and help me move this bloody thing in front of the door ... *quickly*!'

Wayne had taken a position behind the wall giving him cover from Joanne, repeatedly going over a new scenario in his head. Unaware and unsuspecting, she was going to walk back into the kitchen, and with one thrust Wayne was going to drop her. Having been able to refocus his thoughts, the only thing that could stop him was if he started to overthink such a simple plan instead of acting it out. All he had to do was keep his concentration, keep visualising Joanne walking back into the kitchen, and the rest would just fall into place.

But the wait, just like the silence, was becoming unbearable.

What was taking her so fucking long?

Unable to contain himself any longer, Wayne peered carefully round the edge of the wall and into an empty living room, but then his eyes were drawn upwards to the ceiling by the sound of footsteps ... and something heavy being dragged across the floor of the room above him.

Something snapped inside ...

That fucking phone call ...

Thinking time was over. Wayne had all the anger he needed to fuel him.

Joanne and Samantha heard him come thundering up the stairs as they continued their struggles with the heavy chest of drawers, and he'd already covered the narrow landing before they could finish pushing it in front of the door. The doorknob rattled noisily as its old lock managed to keep Wayne at bay before the whole door shuddered violently in its frame as he began savagely kicking it.

*

'MOVE OVER, GET OUT OF THE WAY!' Devonshire yelled as Willard had to brake for what felt like the umpteenth time to avoid rear-ending another car that had taken too long to pull over and let them through.

'I hope I don't have to brake like that again or Chris will be in our backseat,' said Willard, peering anxiously in his rear-view mirror.

Devonshire glanced behind him. Chris was so close that only a part of his Audi's bonnet was visible above Willard's parcel shelf.

'Never mind that, Willard; just keep going,' said Devonshire. 'I'm sure he's been involved in more high-speed pursuits than you've had hot dinners.'

'Maybe I should I try and get off this road …'

'No, stick to this one. There'll be less traffic across country.'

Willard hit the accelerator and switched his siren on once again as another car appeared ahead of them in the distance.

*

Joanne cried out as the bedroom door vibrated under Wayne's repeated attempts to break through. Like all the others in the cottage, it had been reclaimed to be aesthetically pleasing and considerate of the cottage's original character. How Joanne regretted that decision when she saw the fragility of the wood. The top hinge of the bedroom door was loosening and looked like it might give way at any moment. Instinctively, she pressed her back against it.

'Keep dragging it over, keep dragging it!' she shouted at Samantha as her daughter struggled on her own with the chest of drawers. 'Just a couple more feet!'

Wayne could hear Joanne's voice clearly and he plunged the heavy-bladed letter knife into the wood, hoping to hit something fleshy on the other side. Joanne screamed when the blade tore through, missing her face by millimetres, and she leapt away fractionally before another blow pierced the wood right where she'd been standing. Dragging Samantha with her, Joanne raced to the bedroom window to see if they might be able to leap to safety, but the door finally gave way under the weight of another sustained assault, and the room was showered with wood dust and splinters as Wayne came raging in behind her.

The strength Wayne possessed was far greater than Joanne would have thought possible for one so slightly built. For a moment, he stood staring at them, but then with a face contorted by a fury Joanne could almost feel, he sprang towards Samantha. Without thinking, Joanne swung the poker with everything she had. There was a sickening THWACK as it caught Wayne on top of his forehead, and he recoiled from the blow instantly, sinking to his knees.

'BITCH!' he shrieked. 'YOU FUCKING BITCH!'

Joanne's lucky strike had bought them some time, but it was never going to be enough. It was like being in a nightmare as she and Samantha did their best to scramble away. Samantha felt like a heavy weight in her arms as Joanne swept her out of the bedroom and onto the landing, but then one of Samantha's ankles gave way painfully beneath her and she collapsed to the floor, pulling her mother down with her. Desperately, Joanne tried to get Samantha back on her feet because Wayne was already back on his behind them.

'YOU'LL PAY FOR THAT, YOU FUCKING BITCH!' he screamed.

Half-blinded by pain, driven by uncontrollable rage, Wayne bore down on Joanne and Samantha once more. Joanne heard him coming and instinctively threw herself over Samantha, crying out in anguish and terror as the blade of Wayne's knife slashed through the flesh of the arm she'd raised in self-protection.

*

It was calm and quiet in the meadow where Andy had been walking with Harley. The air was warm and still, and full of the scent of lush grass and wild flowers. At the top of a small incline was a hedgerow and a road they needed to cross to get back onto the path leading to the rear of Joanne's cottage. Although regularly used by cars, it never got to a level that one might consider busy, but Andy thought it best to err on the side of caution and was in the throes of attaching Harley's lead when Harley suddenly went rigid and then bolted off unexpectedly. Andy immediately gave chase, frantically shouting out Harley's name, but he was no match for the athletic black shadow streaking away from him towards edge of the field whose finely-tuned, canine hearing was full of the distant, desperate screams of its owners.

*

Wayne's momentum had carried him past the two women. He'd overbalanced and was now on his hands and knees between *them* and the top of the stairs, between *them* and their only means of escape. Blood was pouring down his face from the pumping split in his forehead and the whites of his wide and staring eyes were clearly visible through the glistening crimson mask. Grinning triumphantly, Wayne dragged himself upright, and Joanne's heart sank at the strength of his apparent resolve. The searing pain in her arm was unlike anything she'd ever experienced as it hung limp and useless by her side, and the heavily bleeding gash made for a sickening sight. She felt like she was fit for nothing other than death, but Samantha had taken up the fight on their behalf, determined that this *evil bastard* wasn't going to hurt her mother again.

With her ears full of her mother's screams telling her to run, Samantha wrenched the poker from Joanne's grasp by its shaft, raised it above her head, and braced herself. She wanted to close her eyes, to pretend the bloodied lunatic lunging towards her along the landing was just another nightmare, and that when she opened them again, he'd be gone.

But then the reality hit home, only *this* time it wasn't her mother's screams filling the confines of the upstairs of the cottage, they were Wayne's. Harley had his entire weight behind his perfectly timed leap, propelling Wayne sideways into a wall. Wayne raised a frantic arm to protect himself, but Harley was all over him, tearing at his face and throat with his teeth and claws. Wayne lashed out in desperation and caught Harley in the belly with his knife. The valiant dog yelped in pain, but bravely fought on, driven by his instinct to protect as Wayne struggled to stand, plunging the knife into Harley twice more, into his back and his flank.

Harley's courage brought Samantha to her senses and she lashed out with the poker, wincing as its heavy brass handle crunched against Wayne's undefended temple. Dazed, disoriented and unable to keep his balance, Wayne staggered backwards against the wooden balustrade of the landing. Samantha unleashed another blow. Another followed, and another, each strike accompanied by an unrestrained shriek of triumph. She couldn't stop herself from swinging, it was either *him* or *her*, but then came the sound of cracking, splintering wood as the balustrade gave way, and a helpless, unconscious Wayne plunged head first onto the floorboards of the living room below.

The desperate battle for survival was followed by a tense, forbidding silence. Samantha limped to what remained of the shattered balustrade to see Wayne lying in an untidy, crumpled heap directly beneath her. His mouth gaped open, his eyes, fixed and staring, gazed up at the ceiling, and his bloodied, battered head seemed to be set at an impossible angle compared to the rest of him. For one mad moment, Samantha half expected him to rise up and come after them again, but then she realised that he was dead.

The blood-spattered poker fell from her hand onto the landing with a heavy, resounding THUMP and a surge of bile burned in her throat at the sight of Wayne's cruelly twisted neck. It took everything she had to stop herself from throwing up, and only the sound of her mother's sobbing broke the gruesome spell.

Samantha rushed to the airing cupboard and hurriedly found some towels which she immediately pressed against the awful wound in her mother's arm, but Joanne seemed totally unaware of her own predicament.

'Harley's dying,' she sobbed, lovingly stroking his neck. 'My beautiful boy

… There's nothing I can do for him.'

Harley lay panting with his head in Joanne's lap while her body shook with uncontrollable grief. Choking back her own tears, Samantha knew she had to stay calm and rational. Harley's intervention had been selfless, brave and decisive, but her overriding priority was attending to her mother.

Everything had happened so quickly. One moment Samantha had been relaxing and making a mental wish-list from a clothing website, and the next she'd been involved in a desperate fight for life. Had it been courage, or just raw instinct that had given her such extraordinary strength in the face of Wayne's savage attack? Or had she been inspired by Harley's bravery, and the way her mother had been prepared to make the ultimate sacrifice by acting as a human shield?

A feeling of panic began to build inside her as she continued her attempts to staunch the persistent flow of blood oozing from her mother's arm, but then she heard shouting coming from downstairs. Help had arrived!

Chris, Devonshire and Willard had come bursting into the cottage through the front door at the same time that Andy arrived through the back. For a moment, Andy could only stare with revulsion at Wayne sprawled out on the living room floor, but Samantha's frantic cries quickly snapped him out of it.

'Andy, we're up here!' she called down. 'It's Mum. She's hurt and we need an ambulance!'

'Paramedics are already on their way!' said Devonshire against a sudden backdrop of sirens and flashing blue lights. 'We'll take things from here, son, you go with your dad and help your girlfriend.'

'Oh Christ!' said Willard when he saw Wayne's twisted, lifeless body. 'I guess that's him, then!'

'It looks like it. Start sealing things off with uniform, Willard, and I'll get this mess covered over. Those people up there don't need to see any more.'

But Wayne Terry was the least of Chris's worries, and Joanne was too weak to care about the sudden commotion and too preoccupied with keeping Harley as comfortable as possible.

'Jo, Sam, thank God!' said Chris as he sprinted onto the landing with Andy. 'Thank God …!' but he stopped abruptly when he saw Joanne's blood-soaked clothes.

'It's her arm,' said Samantha. 'He caught her with the knife. I've done my best but I can't stop the bleeding.'

Andy looked away as his father carefully peeled back the bloodstained towel.

'You've done a great job, Sam,' said Chris. 'Just great. Your mum's going to be fine and an ambulance has just pulled up, but we could probably use a couple more towels.'

Samantha managed a smile between Andy's squeamishness and Chris's encouragement. She went to the airing cupboard, and more towels spilled out on top of her as she reached up to the top shelf. Under normal circumstances, she would have found the towelling avalanche hilarious, but grief and desperation had finally got the better of her and she finally fell apart, flinging towels and bed linen in all directions. The outburst forced Andy to put a comforting arm around her shoulders and gently lead her away downstairs and out into the garden.

'She was so incredibly brave,' said Joanne. 'But I think it's all beginning to sink in with her, and we're about to lose Harley, too.'

Chris had been so focused on Joanne that he hadn't even noticed Harley lying motionless in front of him.

'Oh shit, no! Not Harley … let me have a look at him.'

But Joanne shook her head, sadly.

'It's too late,' she said. 'There's nothing anyone can do. I only wish there were because we owe him our lives, me and Sammy. If it hadn't been for Harley, God knows what might have happened. He was very brave, too, weren't you, boy?'

She stroked Harley's neck but he barely responded.

It was right about then that Joanne felt the strangest sensation of butterflies in her stomach, and the very nature of her hands began to change. At first it was just a pleasant, tingling warmth in their palms, but before she knew it, adrenalin had begun to flow, coursing through her, unhindered. With slow, deliberate movements, her hands took on minds of their own and started moving over Harley's stricken form, but Chris's guilt had caught up with him, and he hadn't noticed.

'This is all my fault,' he said. 'None of this would have happened if I'd been here. I'm so sorry, Jo. I should never have left you all exposed like this.'

But Joanne seemed too engrossed with comforting Harley to answer. Chris bowed his head and decided to check on her arm, although, mysteriously, there seemed to be less wound to treat when he peeled back the towel. Before his astonished gaze, the once savage gash was beginning to close, until within a few seconds nothing more than a superficial cut remained. With trembling fingers, he reached out as the incredible healing ran its course, and then Harley lifted his head and looked up, once again keen and alert. Bright-eyed and apparently back to his normal exuberant self, he began licking Joanne's face enthusiastically.

Joanne could only stare at Harley in amazement, but then the butterflies came again along with a spark of familiarity from a beautiful, distant memory.

A radiant smile of recognition made its way across her face as she took Chris's hand in hers.

'Chris, it's *here*!' she said.

Chris was still trying to process everything he'd just witnessed, and his puzzled expression made Joanne laugh, quietly.

'The *child*!' she whispered into his ear, placing his hand gently on her abdomen. 'The Puppeteer got it wrong …'

Two rather confused paramedics chose that very inopportune moment to join them on the landing, only to find that they wouldn't be required. A lot of the blood on her clothes was from her assailant, Joanne said, and her dog, who'd been cut on one of his paw pads, but he was going to be fine.

'And I'm fine too,' she added, gesturing toward her arm. 'It's not as bad as it looks. I'm just a bit shaken, that's all, and things are just a bit raw and emotional right now as you can see. I'll be down in a minute if you want to check me over, but can you just give us some time together first, please? Thank you.'

The paramedics went back downstairs and told Chris and Joanne to take all the time they needed, a request of which they took full advantage, embracing in shared, uninhibited joy and relief.

'You?' Chris asked, unsure whether to laugh or cry. '*Us* …? But how? It was Samantha. It was supposed to be Samantha!'

'Was it?' Joanne replied, gently wiping away a stray tear from his face. 'I'm not so sure that it ever was. I'll tell you all about it when things have calmed down …'

※

Wayne was confused. The cottage had disappeared, and so had the sun. The clear blue of the early evening sky had been replaced by a swirling mass of slowly rotating cloud, and he was being mysteriously drawn through a desert of fine grey ash to a distant and curiously inviting medieval door.

From horizon to gloomy horizon, the desert stretched, apparently endless and daunting. It had to be a dream. The surreal and otherworldly surroundings certainly suggested as much, but the dream was going on and on, remaining constant as if time no longer existed; only the distance between Wayne and the ancient wooden door had altered, narrowing to such an extent that he could suddenly reach out and touch its splintered, weathered exterior.

Hoping an escape route might lie behind it, Wayne reached out to an ornate doorknob he couldn't resist turning and stepped over the threshold into a small, candlelit room. There was somebody lying upon the grey flagstones of the floor who appeared to be asleep. They were encircled with tall candelabras, and, curious to find out who it might be, Wayne stepped forwards to discover it was his own corpse.

Wayne buried his face in his hands in despair. Had he failed?

'Yes, I'm afraid you have,' said The Puppeteer from the shadows. 'You may as well make yourself at home, Wayne. Everything you are is mine now.'

'But the girl ...'

'A valiant try I must say, and no matter how glorious, a failure nonetheless.'

The surroundings began to close in, and a low guttural growl rumbled menacingly in the encroaching darkness.

Wayne pleaded for a second chance.

'But you can send me back!' he begged. 'Please send me back ... let me prove myself!'

But his frenzied appeals were greeted with nothing but unfeeling silence. Naked and terrified, Wayne knew what was coming next. The ring of candelabras burst into life once more, illuminating the dungeon from his nightmare, only this time he wouldn't be waking up in the safety of a comfortable hotel room. Heavy chains and manacles, clanking links of bondage, ensnared him in an instant by the neck, wrists, and ankles, and he was brutally dragged, sobbing and helpless, across the cold and unforgiving dungeon floor towards a now familiar black wooden pillar.

As Wayne wrestled with his tightening bonds, Naomi appeared with a slavering Manform by her side.

'Naomi, please,' he begged her. 'Please don't do this to me.'

But Naomi's eyes were colder and blacker than he remembered them being before, and her previously beautiful expression was nothing but a mask of pure indifference.

'Why should she take pity upon you, Wayne?' asked The Puppeteer. 'What is it that you can offer her now, exactly? This is your personal hell, where debts are paid for the fulfilment of others. Naomi has invested so much of herself in our vision, and is entitled to a right of pleasure in watching you reflect upon your abject failure.'

Wayne bowed his head in the silent aftermath of The Puppeteer's jibe, and closed his eyes to avoid the keenly interested blood-red gaze of Naomi's new pet. Suitably condemned, nothing could truly prepare him for the eternal, inescapable retribution that was to come, but the silence went on without incident. Was his naked vulnerability a part of The Puppeteer's entertainment for the potential viewing hoards, or was it something else? Wayne dared to open his eyes, and discovered to his amazement that the dungeon had disappeared along with his manacles. The Manform had also vanished inexplicably. Only The Puppeteer and Naomi were still present, standing motionless in the desert of ash through which Wayne had walked subserviently to his sentence.

They were both looking in the same direction ... up.

Wayne began to wonder what might be behind his apparent reprieve, but then his thoughts were disturbed by tiny slivers of light beginning to dance upon the powdery surface ahead of him. Wherever the beams touched, the ash began to stir as though awakening, and yet it was only to be a minor prelude. Without warning, the rotating maelstrom overhead was split in two like it had been bisected by the flashing blade of a warrior's broadsword. Through the turmoil poured a cascading curtain of light, and where it struck, the ground itself burst into life. Faces were formed everywhere in the ash, suffering, agonised faces. Wherever Wayne's astonished eyes would cast their gaze it was the same, life erupting from what had appeared lifeless, the birth of unlikely flowers from seeds sown in total desolation. The light was offering sanctuary, deliverance, a flight towards the loving arms of salvation, and that light was coming to Wayne himself. He stared into the flickering white and gold, and for a moment its captivating brilliance bewitched him. He felt a yearning to belong in such sublime beauty, but something was preventing his escape. The light told Wayne that it was only who he truly *was* that could be accepted.

The Puppeteer had radicalised Wayne's alter ego, and it was that second, opportunistic personality from which Wayne's true essence had to break free. *That* kind of freedom was going to come at a price as salvation was a gift that had to be earned. Wayne had to repay another debt, and one far bigger than that of The Puppeteer. He had to redress the horrific cruelty administered through his physical being.

Slowly, agonisingly, Wayne was torn from himself, and in that separation he was forced to relive and experience the horror of his second side's brutality. The parasitic beast within fought tooth and claw, frantically trying to remain a part of its abused and victimised host, but Wayne had willingly given himself up for atonement and was finally free to fly.

The melee of redemption continued until eventually all was calm. The Truth had reclaimed many, and yet its light stayed focused on two old adversaries as they stood facing each other.

'The Truth is here for you, too,' said Zambaya to The Puppeteer. 'See how its light awaits you?'

'Here for *me?*' The Puppeteer asked with a shrug of his huge shoulders. 'Really, Zambaya? Well, perhaps you can answer me this ... why, when I am presented with a chance of such alleged *salvation*, is it offered to me *not* by The Supreme Collective, but as lip service by one its minions? How typically insulting. Evidently I am not *that* important to them, am I old friend, and *unlike* The Truth, I do not choose to abandon my own?'

The Puppeteer reinforced his point with a bold gesture towards the surrounding horizons, where a significant number of The Faithless' hoards were massing in the shadows having chosen to remain at his side. Among their depleted yet defiant ranks, a multitude of Manforms was shifting menacingly, red eyes glowing in the darkness. No doubt keen to show loyalty to their master in a bid for favour and elevation in status, they, like the rest of The Faithless, would continue to pose a considerable threat in the future.

'I believe that you might be outstaying your welcome,' said The Puppeteer as the numbers continued to swell. 'But there *is* another observation I would like to make before we go our separate ways once more, and it is this: humanity, Zambaya … why is it so sacrosanct to you when it is nothing but wasteful and avaricious? I fail to see why you go to such lengths to save it. I mean, how many times is it now? And where it has got you? It never seems to learn, and here you go again, having to send another one of your own to salvage *your own creation's* wreckage. Granted, humanity amuses me greatly, but I am not to blame for *all* of its failings. Such a *vile* species has the means to destroy *itself* without me; it seems all too willing to turn against its makers at the slightest amount of provocation, and the patience of The Truth must be wearing thin. The Truth is *all* things, including nature, and our *mother* has always had her own way of balancing the books, hasn't she? The Supreme Collective cannot keep looking the other way while its precious creation continues to desecrate and destroy, can it? One way or another, Zambaya, humanity will eventually pay for the freedoms bestowed upon it.'

As The Puppeteer began to fade, his questioning black eyes remained fixed upon Zambaya's. They were the last part of the entity to disappear, but it was more than just an act of defiance. It was The Puppeteer reminding The Truth and Zambaya that his eyes would always be upon them, and that in the centuries to come, the hatred would be restored to humankind, and the cycle of destruction would begin again.

CHAPTER 36

Chris lay with Joanne in his arms, absorbing the calm of Winnington Road, and listening to the familiar sounds of a peaceful Hampstead night daring to trespass through their open bedroom window.

The odd car passing smoothly by, the evening breeze gently disturbing the leaves among the branches of the tree-lined thoroughfare, and occasionally, from out in the leafy green acres of the nearby golf course, the distant haunting cry of a lone tawny owl.

Joanne's head rested upon Chris's chest. She was thinking about how many big decisions they'd made together and how much had changed since the nightmare had ended. Yet even though their metaphorical ship was sailing upon much calmer waters, its destination was still unknown, and one decision Chris had made for himself was stuck in the forefront of her mind.

'Are you sure you're doing the right thing, leaving the Met?' she asked suddenly. 'I really *don't* want you to end up regretting it.'

'Wow!' he replied. 'Where did *that* come from?'

'Oh, you know me, Miss Spontaneity! It's just that I know how much the Met means to you.'

Although Chris would always look back on his police career with justifiable pride, there was also a big part of him that wondered how he'd ever managed to do it in the first place.

'*Meant* to me, more like,' he said. 'I'm not going to regret leaving all those long hours behind me, and as for that sodding paperwork … why would I be missing any of that?'

'Ooh … I bet you're really good with paperwork. I'm total crap with that kind of thing! How about you come and work for me, and help me deal with mine?'

Chris chuckled and said he'd think about it.

'But going back to my time in the Met?' he added. 'Maybe it was less about dedication and more about filling my life with work because there was nothing for me to go home to, apart from Andy who'd rather have been out with his rugby mates anyway. So, I had nothing else apart from the Met, or the gym, but everything's so much different now.'

'And I know all about living to bloody work, too,' said Joanne. 'But we still haven't discussed what you're going to be doing instead of chasing bad guys, have we? Are you *sure* you don't want to come and work for me and solve my paperwork issues? I'd give you a very competitive package, and you'd get bed, breakfast and evening meals ... plus, you know, some *other* benefits?'

'What ... like a telly in my room with all the sports channels?'

'Oh my God, that is *unbelievable* ...!'

'Okay, maybe not the sports channels!'

An explosion of laughter followed, like that of children on a sleepover, which they quickly got under control so as not to wake Andy and Samantha who were sleeping in the room directly opposite.

'If it means you're always going to be able to make me laugh like that, then you can have what you like!' said Joanne. 'That's such a special gift.'

'But nowhere near as special as yours,' Chris replied. 'What does it feel like, knowing you're carrying a miracle?'

In Joanne's opinion *every* pregnancy was a miracle, but Chris argued that a spark of life capable of healing its own mother and a beloved family pet made matters entirely different.

'Which reminds me,' he said. 'I know we don't talk about what happened that night at Greenoaks, but you never *have* told me how you knew you'd conceived.'

'You mean instead of peeing on a stick like *normal* women? It's just a blur now, really, Chris. I wish I could describe the feeling that I had inside me at that moment, but I instantly recognised it when it happened.'

Chris frowned.

'So you'd felt it before?' he asked. 'Was it the same when you conceived Samantha, then?'

'No,' Joanne replied. 'That was all about missed periods, and I *did* pee on a stick that time!'

And then she told Chris about her dream in the garden at Greenoaks, the myriad of tiny orbs in The Nursery of The Truth, and The Shepherdess watching over them.

'It was the most beautiful dream,' Joanne recalled. 'And in it I saw the spirit lights of all these children that were going to be born, but I didn't know that one of them was going to come to *me*. The Shepherdess was holding one of the lights in her hands and offered it to me. It was different to all the others and when I touched it, it was magical, and now I know that it was the spirit of what was going to be *our* child. Isn't that incredible, Chris? I actually *touched* the spirit of our *own child*, and that's how I knew I'd conceived that night because I remembered how that connection had felt!'

From the moment Joanne had reached out in her dream and touched the tiny orb, the process had begun. From then on, *she* was going to be the way

The Truth's envoy was to come into the physical world, although whether the child had chosen Joanne or Joanne had chosen the child would always remain a mystery.

But the *mystery* for Chris was why he'd been protecting Samantha as the envoy's chosen mother when it was clearly destined to be somebody else.

'Were you told that it was going to be Samantha, then?' asked Joanne.

'No, I wasn't,' Chris replied.

'So, you must have just assumed it when you met us, then.'

'Well …'

'Oh, come on, Chris! There's no harm in assuming that it had to be some young hottie and not somebody staring down the barrel of middle-age like me!'

'Ooh, *that's* harsh!'

'But true! Even *I* thought Angela was talking about Samantha when she gave me that tarot reading. I wasn't thinking about my dream, or The Shepherdess, or that it had ever had any meaning for me at all for that matter.'

Joanne broke off momentarily, and when she spoke again, both her tone and the subject matter had changed. Only days earlier, Samantha had learned that she wasn't going to have to stand trial for the manslaughter of Wayne Terry, but despite everybody's enormous relief at the news, Joanne was having far more trouble than any of the others overcoming a huge sense of injustice.

'I just know that Sammy didn't deserve any of that,' she said. 'She'd been through enough as it was. I'll never forget her bravery, how hard she fought. She was relentless. I was completely useless, and if she hadn't defended us the way that she did, Wayne may well have succeeded in killing us both and The Puppeteer would have won.'

Chris's eyes widened. It was an expression of shock Joanne had seen once before at Greenoaks, only this time she felt no anger. Instead, she smiled and gave him a reassuring kiss.

'It's okay,' she said. 'I understand why you had to keep that bit from me.'

'But … but how long have you *known*?'

'Pretty much since I conceived. Wayne was being used as an assassin.'

'But you never said anything!'

'Because it doesn't matter, and anyway, it's not as if you knew *everything* is it? You protected me as the chosen mother without knowing it, and it was you who completed The Circle by being the child's father. Zambaya made sure he kept *all* of that from you. Samantha was a very convenient decoy, keeping The Puppeteer interested in her long enough to enable *us* to conceive The Truth's envoy. The Puppeteer knew that the child could only be conceived by an uncorrupted Innocent, and Samantha would have surrendered that light if she'd succumbed to him. That's why he kept trying to corrupt her, and why The Truth gave her the strength to resist. Wayne was there to make absolutely certain the conception couldn't happen, and he nearly succeeded.'

As much as Chris wanted to contribute to the conversation, all he could do was listen, staggered by how much Joanne actually knew.

'All the answers are inside me,' she said. 'But it's more like a *feeling* than a voice, and the more I bond with this little life the more I learn and understand. But the strangest thing of all is that I feel honoured about having this responsibility when I would never have volunteered for it in a million years! I'll always have a problem with how The Truth used Samantha, though, but then I think about how we were all being used in the end because it wasn't just Wayne Terry who was a puppet, we were *all* puppets one way or another. Anyway, enough for now, and no more bloody secrets from now on, okay?'

'Apart from the whopper we've been keeping from Andy and Samantha,' said Chris. 'How about that one?'

Not many things annoyed Joanne as much as hypocrisy, especially when she could be just as guilty of the sin as anybody else.

'I guess we can't keep it from them anymore, can we?' she sighed. 'And I won't be able to hide the fact that I'm pregnant for much longer, either! But if we're going to tell them, then I think we have to tell them everything.'

'*Everything*?'

'Don't you think it's best? The Puppeteer hasn't reappeared since I conceived, thank God, and nobody's even questioned it, but as far as I'm concerned, Andy and Samantha have every right to know why they went through what they did. And I'm not carrying an ordinary child, either, and they need to be prepared for what's coming. We'll tell them tomorrow.'

'As soon as that?'

'Absolutely. I'll do us all something special for dinner, and then we'll open up to them. Everything will be fine, Chris. Trust me, I know.'

Revealing all was the biggest decision of them all, but the need for secrecy had long since passed. It was all about preparation now, and Joanne soon drifted off to sleep in the reflective silence that followed.

Chris listened to Joanne's steady breathing, wishing *he* could be just as far away instead of analysing a sudden and uncomfortable thought: what *had* happened to Zambaya since the conception? It wasn't until Joanne had dropped Zambaya's name into the conversation that Chris realised he hadn't heard anything from his inspirer for weeks. So much had changed and Chris had been swept along with all of it, never once sparing a thought for his dependable spiritual guide and ally.

The likelihood was that he was never going to see Zambaya again. The conception would have completed The Circle, and Zambaya's work had effectively been done. What other reason could there be for the lack of contact other than the understated Overseer having returned quietly and inconspicuously home to The Supreme Collective?

A sense of loss continued to nag away at Chris like a form of guilty, emotional toothache, until his eyes finally closed and he found himself drifting, unrestrained, and gazing down upon a vast sweeping valley of shimmering grassland. Everything was bathed in the most glorious light, and a broad meandering river flowed effortlessly through the splendour, reflecting the twilight blue of the sky above.

'Welcome again, Christopher!' said a deep, rich and familiar voice.

To Chris's amazement, he'd suddenly stopped flying, and Zambaya was right there beside him. They were sitting upon the same high plateau which had been their vantage point in previous meetings, and yet despite the unexpected pleasure of being in Zambaya's company once more, it was sad for Chris to think it was going to be for the last time.

Zambaya studied Chris intently for a moment.

'I sense that there is deep regret in you,' he said. 'Why would your heart be heavy when it should be as light as a cloud?'

'Because our work together is done,' Chris replied. 'And now you'll be returning to The Supreme Collective.'

'So, you think that you are here to say goodbye?'

Chris looked down and nodded.

'Hmmm,' said Zambaya. 'Then perhaps, Christopher, I should remind you of our first encounter. Did I not tell you *then* how I have watched over you since your birth? That when your time in your world is finished, how I shall be here to receive you into mine? Until that time comes, I will be walking every step of your pathway with you, for this is *our* journey. The Supreme Collective expects more from us, so our 'work together' is *far* from 'done'.'

The heavy sadness in Chris lifted immediately, and Zambaya went on to share more of his enthralling knowledge. He spoke at length about shared joy and responsibilities, and that the 'the man on the hill' was going nowhere! But as always with Zambaya's teachings, there was much for Chris to absorb, and on this occasion much of what Zambaya had to say didn't matter. The most important question surrounding Zambaya's continued presence had been answered, but something else had entered Chris's mind as he waited patiently for his loquacious teacher to finish speaking.

'Just one more thing if I may, Zambaya,' he said with a grin. 'Are Joanne and I going to have a boy or a girl?'

Zambaya shook his head, sadly.

'Questions, Christopher John Edward Ryan,' he sighed. 'You *still* ask far too many …'

<THE END>

ABOUT THE AUTHOR

Stephen David Curtis is an English author, who now resides in Cambridgeshire in the United Kingdom.

Originally from Mountnessing in Essex, Stephen spent most of his life living in North Hertfordshire, having moved there with his family in 1968 at the age of four.

He grew up on a council estate, and had a state education, where he discovered creative writing at secondary school in the form of poetry, with the occasional short story thrown in for good measure.

Rather than stay on and study for his A-levels, however, Stephen left school at the age of sixteen to expand his horizons in full-time employment, a decision that would lead him to develop a new circle of friends, some of whom were musicians.

And it was music that became an all-consuming passion, with a career that was to span four decades, both professionally and semi-professionally, as a guitarist, vocalist, songwriter and lyricist.

Somehow during this time, Stephen still found time to became a family man, and is a proud father of a son and daughter, both of whom have seemingly inherited Stephen's Rock'n'roll genes! His daughter, Emily, is a songwriter, lyricist and singer, and his son, Ashley, is both a guitarist and graphic artist.

But circumstances and priorities often change. Stephen's passion for music is a flame that will never truly go out, but his focus these days is less on writing songs, and more upon creative writing of another kind. And this brings us nicely onto his debut novel, *Circle of Innocents*, a story that only came about because of an idea he floated during a deep, 'what if' conversation amongst friends. Perhaps those closest to him should choose their words more carefully in future, instead of replying with things like: "That sounds like a bloody good idea for a book!"

And the rest…is history!

Circle of Innocents is just the beginning of what Stephen intends to be a new and rewarding journey, and there are many more ideas in his vivid imagination that he hopes will also end up in print.

In the meantime, however, all Stephen really wants is for you to enjoy reading *Circle of Innocents* every bit as much as he enjoyed writing it.